Praise for [...]
superlative sp[...]

COLD SHOT

"Before it's in the news, it's in Mark Henshaw's novels. *Cold Shot* has all the hallmarks of a masterful espionage thriller—killer action scenes, heroes and villains on every side, suspense to spare, a timely plot, and above all else chilling insight into the secret world of intelligence. You will be entertained and amazed."

—Stephen Hunter, *New York Times* bestselling author of *I, Ripper*

"Well-rounded and fascinating characters with enough personal foibles to give them depth. . . . Henshaw has a firm grasp of how the intelligence community operates, and uses that knowledge to deliver another winner. Readers seeking a revealing portrait of the covert world need look no further."

—*Booklist*

"Combines inspired data analysis, corrupt geopolitical maneuvering, and searing action."

—*Publishers Weekly*

"Tense, suspenseful, and loaded with immersive detail. . . . Henshaw provides a Clancy-esque level of detail but without dragging the story down."

—*Kirkus Reviews*

RED CELL

"A lean and efficient effort fueled by an infrequent quality: believability. In this deft novel of intelligence, the CIA actually shines."

—*Kirkus Reviews*

"An intriguing debut. . . . The narrative's authentic details about spycraft will be irresistible to hard-core spy fiction aficionados, who will eagerly seek Henshaw's next dip into the CIA pool."

—*Library Journal*

"Henshaw has written a story that is as powerfully relevant as *The Hunt for Red October* was during the Cold War; it's a very good read and an impressive debut that will appeal to fans of political thrillers that pack a punch with verisimilitude."

—*Fredericksburg Free Lance-Star*

"*Red Cell* is as smart as it is exciting, a thriller that makes you think from the edge of your seat. Mark Henshaw's unique perspective from the inside makes it all feel terrifyingly real."

—Howard Gordon, co-creator of *Homeland* and author of *Hard Target*

"Mark Henshaw is the real deal and he delivers big-time in his debut novel. Only a decorated CIA analyst like Henshaw could take you this deep into the psyche of CIA operatives—and even deeper into one of the most dangerous and imminent geopolitical flashpoints of our times. If the events Henshaw plays out on the pages of his novel have not already taken place in secret, they may well play out in public sooner rather than later. Mr. President, this intelligence briefing is worth your special attention."

—Thomas Greanias, *New York Times* bestselling author of *The Promised War*

Also by Mark Henshaw

Red Cell

COLD
SHOT

A Novel

MARK HENSHAW

POCKET BOOKS

New York London Toronto Sydney New Delhi

Pocket Books
A Division of Simon & Schuster, Inc.
1230 Avenue of the Americas
New York, NY 10020

This book is a work of fiction. Any references to historical events, real people, or real places are used fictitiously. Other names, characters, places, and events are products of the author's imagination, and any resemblance to actual events or places or persons, living or dead, is entirely coincidental.

First Pocket Books paperback edition December 2015

POCKET and colophon are registered trademarks of Simon & Schuster, Inc.

For information about special discounts for bulk purchases, please contact Simon & Schuster Special Sales at 1-866-506-1949 or business@simonandschuster.com.

The Simon & Schuster Speakers Bureau can bring authors to your live event. For more information or to book an event, contact the Simon & Schuster Speakers Bureau at 1-866-248-3049 or visit our website at www.simonspeakers.com.

Manufactured in the United States of America

10 9 8 7 6 5 4 3 2 1

ISBN 978-1-4767-9933-9
ISBN 978-1-4767-4565-7 (ebook)

For my father,
First Sergeant Carl M. Henshaw, USMC,
who held *Red Cell* in his hands but never got to
read it. I miss you, Dad, every day.

Who sows fear, reaps weapons.

—Friedrich Dürrenmatt

COLD SHOT

The house seemed out of place for this town, larger and more ornate than the others Marisa Mills could see from the rooftop. She guessed that there were only a hundred buildings scattered across the settlement, all bricks and dirty cement, mostly shops on the ground floors with apartments above. This particular home was one of the largest structures of any kind within sight, smaller only than the three mosques she could identify. It was two stories, white with columns in front and a small dome on top. A mud-colored concrete wall enclosed the villa's courtyard, head-high with iron gates on opposing sides. The owner was clearly Sunni. No such home would have survived unscathed in this town had the owner followed any other religious path. The Sunnis here had little tolerance for the Shiites, less for the Americans, and the butchery of recent months had left Marisa wondering whether the residents weren't killing just for sport now.

That the owner had money wasn't even in question. Whether the man supported the insurgency was a question that the Army Rangers moving to surround the building intended to settle.

"They're moving a bit fast on this one," Marisa observed.

"You know the Rangers," the man to her left said. "They're not really happy unless they're engaged in a little property damage." Jonathan Burke held his own field glasses to his eyes and swept them over the soldiers moving toward the house.

"Patience is a virtue."

"And not actually part of the Ranger Creed," Jon noted. "I thought you were going to miss this one."

"My flight was late."

"I keep telling Congress I wasn't even at Abu Ghraib. But you know congressmen. They lie so much that they can't believe anyone else tells the truth. But it helped that there are no traffic laws around here. I made up for lost time after we landed."

"I thought patience was a virtue."

"No sense rushing into a firefight if you can take your time and shut the enemy down before things begin," she replied. The two CIA officers were lying on a rooftop a hundred meters from the raid site. The woman was, in fact, lying closer to Jon than was strictly necessary but he seemed oblivious to Mari's frustration. A pair of Rangers were prone near the edge of the rooftop forty feet to their right. One half of the sniper team there had his hands wrapped around a Barrett M82 rifle. The other was staring at the house through a Leupold Mark 4 spotting scope.

"You sound like a Sun Tzu disciple," Jon said.

"Nope. More like Stalin." She stared down at the compound through a pair of Leica Viper binoculars and envied the courtyard roof inside. Any shade in this country dropped the temperature twenty degrees, but she and Jonathan were in the open, exposed to the Iraqi sun for which boonie hats and sunglasses helped little even at this early-morning hour. Although the sun still sat low on the horizon, it was well over a hundred degrees, and would be twenty degrees hotter by noon. "Who was the first guy who thought settling down *here* would be a good idea?"

"The Sumerians," Jonathan replied. "First settled at Eridu in the Ubaid period, about 5300 BC."

"Did the Good Lord not give you a sense of humor or did you get it shot off?" She could see Rangers moving to the outside corners of the compound wall, ready to catch any of the "squirters" who might manage to slip out once the raid began. Humvees and an MRAP sat on the four roads surrounding the building, turning the intersections into kill zones covered by mounted M240B machine guns should the enemy bring reinforcements armed with anything heavier than light arms. The Army had assigned a helicopter to the operation, some model she couldn't identify, which was circling at a distance. Marisa would have preferred an AC-130, but she supposed that an airborne howitzer was overkill for this sort of thing.

"My talents don't lie in comedy."

"No, they lie in puzzles," she told him. "That's why I'm surprised you're still here. The big riddle's been solved—there's no WMD in this country. The only thing left is a big manhunt and that's not a puzzle. It's just prisoner interviews and tedious grunt work. I've been watching you long enough to know that you don't do tedious."

"You've been watching me?"

"Langley would recall me if I didn't watch people," she said. "But there's a new unit in the Directorate of Intelligence I think you should consider. It's called the 'Red Cell.' George Tenet stood it up right after 9/11. Sounds like they're a bunch of contrary thinkers who don't have to tie every little comment back to some piece of intelligence like the rest of the analysts. I think you'd be happy there."

"I thought you wanted me around."

Marisa looked at Jon sideways, subtle, hoping he would catch her gaze. *Was that one professional or personal?* There were very few women assigned to Task Force North, most of them were from CIA's Special Activities Center, and Marisa Mills was far and away the one who drew the most attention from the men. The soldiers watched her for reasons not remotely professional and usually came on to her like the D-Day invasion. Jon was different, always subtle, maneuvering around her. He was a puzzle all his own. She didn't know where she stood with him—but she liked a man who could put her off balance. It didn't happen often. "If you're going to stay, I've got some uses for you," she said, choosing her words with care. "But I have to think about what's best for my people and not just for me. This is boring stuff, it's going to go on for years, and 'Sherlock' isn't a term of endearment in the DoD." It was one of the more polite names she knew had been aimed at the man lying to her left.

Jonathan looked at her sideways but didn't answer further. "I'm surprised you found this one," she said, changing the subject. "We've had Mr. Farzat under the hot lights for three weeks trying to crack him."

"The guy had saved fifty copies of the same Microsoft Word file on his laptop and they were all thirty megabytes in size. I thought that was worth a look."

"But you don't read Arabic."

"Not a word. Total chicken scratch," he agreed. "I do Farsi."

"And you're not a cyber-analyst," Marisa observed.

"Nope."

"And you still managed to get enough intel from it to pin this place as an insurgents' weapons cache," she finished.

"That last bit has yet to be proven," Jon said.

"Humility doesn't become you, Jon. But that was some nice work," she told him.

"I aim to please."

"What made you think you'd find something?" she asked.

"Everyone makes mistakes. You just have to find them."

"That's a happy thought. But you weren't the first one to look at that laptop. Why didn't any of the other guys find it?" Marisa asked.

Jon shrugged. "The hard drive was stuffed with porn, and not the pretty kind. They were probably too busy with those particular folders."

"So why were the Word files so large?"

"They all had embedded graphics. That's when I called one of your boys who does read Arabic. Far-zat was counterfeiting bills of lading for cargo boxes transiting the Syrian border at al-Qaim. They had everything listed as 'medical supplies.' My guess is that he was trying to make sure the forms didn't look fuzzy when printed. So some of the Deltas took a day trip and grabbed some of those 'supplies.' Artillery shells, every one of them, all made in Iran. Probably meant for IEDs." Jonathan reached up and adjusted the focus on his field glasses a hair.

Marisa cursed. "I'd love to grab a few of those Iranian Quds Force officers who're teaching the insurgents how to build them. Send them back to Tehran minus a few choice body parts."

"No argument here."

"And all of the crates were addressed to this place?" Marisa guessed.

"Yeah, but we can't figure out who owns the house. There was no addressee on the bills and half the property records in this country went up in smoke when the Army invaded."

"Whoever does hold the deed probably has an arsenal in the basement. Maybe we'll get lucky and this'll be the one that leads us to Zarqawi."

"Hope springs eternal," Jon said. He pointed, then looked back through his binoculars. "Curtain's going up."

At the compound wall, a Delta Force operator cut the chain by a side gate with bolt cutters and eight more moved past. The Deltas were all unshaven, scruffy hair, dressed in tactical pants and boots, with body armor over their T-shirts. They split into four-man stacks, half taking a position by either side of the door. The second man in the stack left of the door began fixing a frame charge to the front while his team scanned the area for threats.

"I hope nobody's on the other side when that goes off," she said.

"Nobody important, anyway."

The frame charge ripped the door from the hinges, shredding it to kindling in an instant. The left stack of Deltas were through the hole before the sound faded, M4 carbines raised to eye level. Marisa watched the right stack follow through her Leica.

"Always love that bit—" Jonathan started.

A muffled *thump* erupted from the far street north of the compound, smoke and fire rising. He twisted his head and watched as the Humvee flipped in slow motion onto its side, the Ranger inside already dead and starting to burn. Silence on the comm, then yelling, and Marisa swearing off to his right, but his brain refused to process the jabber. Gunshots started to sound . . . somewhere, the cracks of M4s firing off rounds. He tried to scan the rooftops through the scope, but the time passed by so slow. Rangers on the street were yelling at him and each other and he couldn't move fast enough—

Then the world snapped into focus.

"Contact! Mortar, half klik north!" somebody yelled over the radio.

The mortar shell hit the rooftop seventy feet to the right. The shock wave knocked Jon prone and he felt it push him toward the edge. The wall of air, compressed hard, hit Marisa like a punch across her entire back and the woman pitched forward over the edge. Jon grabbed for her and managed to get his hand on her leg. Her weight dragged him forward. He pushed hard against the low wall with his one free hand, stopping his slide, then pulled against her, spinning himself until he could get his feet in front of him. He put his boots against the low concrete rise, grabbed Marisa with his other hand and pulled and lifted her back legs first with a grunt. He grabbed her belt and hauled, and finally she came up far enough to help, grabbing the roof wall with her hands.

She rolled over onto her back, chest heaving, eyes wide. Mortars went off below, more yelling in two languages. Jon looked right—

The snipers were dead, their bodies contorted and burning.

The Rangers below had no overwatch. The mortar crew had the high ground.

Jon scrambled to his feet and ran to the sniper post. The Barrett M82 was still there, lying by the parapet a few dozen feet away from its former owners. He lifted the gun, checked it for damage, then swung it to his right. The world seemed to be moving far slower than his mind was going.

"Contact! Small-arms fire at northwest corner!" Another call from the other side of the compound.

He could count the number of buildings with more than five stories on his two hands. The town was only a mile square and they were near the center, so any shot he had to take would be ridiculously close by sniper standards—

Near the center. He didn't like that thought.

"Contact! Small-arms fire and RPG, south side!" People were yelling over each other on the radio now, contacts in every direction.

"I suggest you D-Boys find a basement," somebody called out over the radio to the men in the house.

"Screw that," one of the Deltas in the house replied. "Nobody's home and the party's outside. Coming out."

Another explosion tore up the dirt inside the compound's northwest corner. The masonry soaked up the blast, protecting the Rangers on the street outside but they still ran for cover inside a covered porch just across the street. A third mortar round landed in the courtyard, this one ripping a hole out of the eastern wall.

Finally Jon found them. There, on the mosque, by the dome, two men standing by a tube pointed at the sky. *Dumb,* he thought. *Up on a roof, exposed. Can't hit and run.*

One of them reached up to the barrel, dropped

a round. Jon put the crosshairs on the man but he moved out of the way, reaching down for his next shell. Jon held the crosshairs on the empty space where the man would have to return. His heart was hammering at his ribs, hard enough to shake the rifle a bit, but the distance to the target was less than two hundred yards, close enough that it wouldn't matter. He took a deep breath, let it go and stopped the urge to breathe again, then took up the slack on the Barrett's trigger. The man stood. Jon drew his finger back.

The rifle finally roared and the .50 round punched through the insurgent's chest cavity. The bullet ripped his heart out . . . and Jon, with the scope to his eye, saw sunlight through the hole at a hundred fifty yards.

The moment stretched out for eternity, the insurgent hanging in the air, the Iraq sun shining through his chest cavity, the look of shock just starting to form on his face—

Then the world sped up and the insurgent collapsed, falling out of sight. His partner froze and Jon shifted the scope onto the second target. The insurgent was panicked, not thinking, and started to fire his AK-47 wildly, desperately trying to hit whoever had taken down his friend. Jonathan didn't think. He pulled the trigger again. The bullet entered the man's face at his nose and severed his brain stem as it went out the back. His head came apart in a red spray and that moment also slowed down, burning the image into Jon's mind with a clarity and definition that he'd never known before.

He stared at the space where the man had stood, trying to process what he'd just done. He closed his eyes tight. The image of the man's head going to pieces was frozen there against the black void—

"Jon?" Marisa said, panic rising in her voice.

Jonathan opened his eyes again. Marisa had risen to a knee, her HK416 at her shoulder, shooting at someone he couldn't spot immediately. Two more blasts ripped up bricks and rocks inside the compound within a second, dirt and cement flying in chunks, then a third. He scanned across the rooftops, couldn't find the crews. *At least two more mortar crews . . . ground level, behind some buildings,* he realized. *Not stupid like the first one.* He wouldn't be stopping those with the Barrett. "Super Three-One," he yelled into the radio, calling out to the orbiting helicopter. "Multiple mortars. Don't see them on the rooftops. They're all yours."

"Roger that," the pilot radioed back. The AH-6 Little Bird dove toward the town's edge.

"Contact!" someone called out over the radio. "Vehicle approaching northwest—"

Jon heard the screeching of tires. A pickup roared around the northwest corner. "Down!" he yelled to Marisa. The woman fell prone next to him on the roof and covered her head with her hands.

The Ranger standing in the back of the Humvee swung his M240 and fired, bullets ripping into the approaching bomb. The truck driver was torn apart by the stream of lead, blood and brains flying inside the vehicle, his body slumping forward, but the truck kept coming. It slammed into the Hummer, knocking it sideways, then disappearing into a fireball that rose far above the rooftop where Jon and Marisa sat. The entire building shook under them and Jonathan thought for a moment it might cave in and drop them onto the street.

Sixty seconds, four dead. Jon was surprised to find his brain tracking the numbers.

More gunfire from below, the Rangers firing down

alleyways at targets Jonathan couldn't see. Dirt was kicking up in columns large and small from mortars and bullets, soldiers moving to shelter, firing back in every direction. Muzzle flashes erupted from the windows of the nearby houses. All of the shooters were inside the buildings, firing out, none exposed on the roofs where Jon or the Little Bird could get open shots.

Kill box. We're in a kill box.

Marisa emptied her rifle at some window. She pulled another magazine out of Jonathan's vest, ejected the empty and replaced it, racked the slide, and went back to business. "Jon, nine o'clock, two uglies tossing grenades down on the guys," Marisa said. "Hunkered down on the roof. I can't get 'em and I'm wasting your ammo trying."

Jonathan shifted his weapon, saw no one. A concrete porch jutted out from a second-story door above a butcher's shop, with a cinder-block wall three feet high for a rail. A hand reached over and tossed a grenade into the street. It went off, hurting no one. It would be another shot less than a hundred yards. Jon watched the spot, waiting for them to stick a head up, but they refused him the courtesy. Another hand reached over, blindly tossing a grenade, this one landing on the other side of the car sheltering a pair of Rangers taking cover from the mortars. The grenade went off, blowing out windows and tires.

One of the Rangers in the street raised up from behind a parked car, raised his rifle to his shoulder to fire at some target Jon didn't see, then jerked, spun, and fell on his face. One of his fellows reached out, took him by the grab handle on his vest, and pulled him out of the open.

"Man down! Medic! MEDIC!"

Jon cursed, aimed the Barrett at the porch, judged the target by memory, and pulled the trigger. The .50 round covered the distance and smashed through the cinder block. He saw no impact, but blood sprayed against the porch door. The dead man's partner figured out that the wall was no shield, jumped up, and began firing an AK-47 wildly. Marisa raised up onto one knee, hosed down the porch with her HK, three of her shots hitting the man in the stomach, and he fell over the wall into the street.

Another mortar shell hit the roof, this time eighty feet left, and the shock wave knocked them flat again. "Time to be going," Jon told her. "They've got our number." He pushed himself up to a crouch. He shouldered his pack, grabbed both the Barrett and Marisa's hand, and dragged her toward the side stairwell.

Bullets were hitting the parapets now. Someone hadn't liked his work with the Barrett.

"Get off the roof, Mari," someone called out on the radio. "We're bugging out."

"We have two dead up here—" she answered.

"Not your problem," the radio told her. "Four Black-hawks inbound, they'll clean this place out and the Rangers will recover them. We need you to fall back."

"Roger that," Marisa said, her response automatic. "See you at the MRAP."

"If you're late, you're humping it out on foot."

Jon reached the stairwell and stuck his head over. Insurgents were turkey-peeking around the far corner of the alley. He pulled his head back as one of the Iraqis jumped out and opened up, lead smacking off the stone stairs. "Can't go down that way," he told Marisa.

"Five stories up," she noted. "Can't jump over the side."

Jon pointed to a mortar hole in the ceiling. They ran over, looked down, and saw no one. Jon drew his sidearm and went down into the hole, his Glock 17 in his gloved hands.

The room was empty. "Clear," he called out. Marisa sat on the hole's edge and let Jon help her lower herself down from the roof, her khaki boots kicking up dust on the floor as she landed. Jon moved to a nearby doorway, pistol raised. Marisa put her HK to her shoulder, following behind.

He kicked the door open, leaned out far enough to scan the hall, then stepped out of the room. He turned left, the Glock at eye level. Marisa came out behind him, sweeping the hallway behind. A stairwell was visible at the hallway's far end. Smoke was starting to fill the corridor now, coming from whatever room the first mortar round had taken out. *Gotta get downstairs before we can't see.*

They were almost to the stairs when someone yelled in Arabic behind them. Marisa's HK went off, a three-round burst, then another. Someone screamed in agony and the yelling turned to constant shouts. Jon pulled Marisa around the corner at the hallway's end a half second before someone sent their own burst of gunfire toward them from the other end.

"Go!" Jon yelled. He moved to the stairs, covered the hall, Glock up and firing, while Marisa took the stairs down by threes.

No one met her at the bottom. "Clear!" she yelled. Jon followed her down and circled around to the next flight downward, Marisa covering the hallway on that floor. They moved through the hallways and down the staircases, covering each other as they moved for the building lobby that opened halfway down.

The entrance was wrecked, glass in chunks everywhere that their boots crushed into smaller shards as they moved for the door.

"Cover the hall," he ordered. Marisa took position by the entryway to the corridor, her rifle pointed at the black-and-white-tiled floor. Jon reached the front door. Windows framed the wooden entrance on each side, the glass smashed out. Jon tried to scan their position but the small spaces restricted his vision too much. He turned to the door, stood to the side and opened it, checking the street.

Another mortar shell took out a storefront up the street; the crack of guns was almost constant now, and yells and screams could still be heard from a distance he could judge over the other sounds. He'd fired enough AK-47s in training and knew the sound. There were far more of those going off than the M4s his unit carried.

"MRAP, this is Mills, holding position inside the front door, down five stories under the sniper nest," Marisa called out on the radio. "Any chance we can get a pickup?"

"Roger that."

The next minute took a quick eternity to pass before Jon heard an engine roar and the massive armored carrier rumbled around the corner, drawing fire. The turret gunner riding on the back swung his weapon and poured lead into a nearby house. The vehicle stopped in front of Jon's position, parked on the dirty sidewalk angled against the direction of the hostile fire, and the rear door opened almost into the building.

"Mari!" Jon yelled. "You coming or staying?"

The woman cursed and ran for the door. He covered the rear hallway with his pistol as she raced past him and leaped inside the armored vehicle. Arms reached out to grab her and they pulled her into the dark confines of the truck. Jon followed behind, unslinging his Barrett and handing it to the first set of hands he saw. He holstered his Glock, then pulled himself inside and jumped into the cramped space. Rangers were everywhere, almost no room to breathe. Another Ranger inside slammed the rear door and threw the handle, locking it shut. Bullets snapped against the metal door and the top gunner returned fire round for round.

"Go! Go! Go!"

The driver shifted gears and stomped the pedal. The MRAP moved with a jerk, tossing everyone toward the back. Jon caught Marisa, saving her from cracking her head on the rear door. "Watch the hands, boy," she muttered.

Jon's answer was cut off by the sound of the machine gunner above yelling something no one could hear over the sound of the big weapon firing. The driver was cursing Iraqis in ways that suggested he should've joined the Navy instead. The MRAP picked up speed, then pitched off axis as something exploded nearby. The driver straightened it out, shifted a gear, and let the monster truck have all the gas it wanted.

"You okay?" Jon asked. Marisa was still pushed up against him. She made no effort to extricate herself.

"Still here," she replied. "Everything's attached."

"That's something." Jon slumped back against the rear metal door, his hands trembling hard, and he closed his eyes.

"Jon? Are you okay?" Marisa knelt down beside him. The man was pressing his hands hard against his eyes and his whole body was shaking. "Are you shot?" she asked, panic creeping into her voice.

"No."

"Then what is it?"

Behind closed eyes, Jon saw an insurgent's head come apart, Iraqi sunlight shining through the hole in another man's chest. "I see it . . . I can't stop seeing it."

He knew that he would be seeing it for a very long time.

TWELVE YEARS LATER

Rappelling onto the ship was a terrible risk.

The enemy surely was carrying rocket-propelled grenades that could knock a helicopter from the sky and the entire team would die either in a fireball or in the water. But there is no good way to board a hostile ship on the open sea save to come alongside with grapnels or caving ladders and climb aboard. It was night and a rare squall cut the visibility across the waves, but the enemy might hear an outboard motor and the operation would then become an assault on an elevated, fortified position. The enemy would be crouched behind metal rails, shooting AK-47s down at men trying to climb wet ropes with no cover.

Rappelling was the only option.

The enemy was not completely foolish. Lookouts stood fore and aft, but the man keeping watch on the foredeck was half asleep, smoking cigarettes to stay awake, and couldn't see more than fifty feet out into the ocean. There was no moon and the *Markarid*'s own deck lights didn't illuminate far in the rain. The rush of the bow through the water muffled the sound of the Bell 214 helicopter until it was close enough.

A single round from an Austrian Steyr .50 rifle punched through the lookout's chest and buried itself in the deck, and the pirate went down without a sound.

The first four men dropped their rope bags out the door, pushed out of the cabin, and fast-roped to the deck. There was movement on the deck aft of their landing zone. The enemy had spotted them now and panicked Somalis were rushing around the bridge. A hostile rushed out from the ship's island carrying a long tube and lifted it to his shoulder. The Bell's door gunner saw him, swiveled his GAU-16 toward the man and opened fire. Ten .50 rounds hit the target and spun him sideways, spraying blood. The pirate's dying reflex was to press the RPG-7's trigger. The warhead fired down at the deck, then ricocheted off at a flat angle. It flew wildly in a crazy arc until it struck a cargo container and exploded, blowing bits of other men into the sea and onto the bulkheads.

The sniper saw it through his Steyr's scope and cursed. The fireball left a burning hole in the deck with smoke rolling off into the wet air. There were no other ships within visual range in this storm and the rain would quickly snuff the fire, but satellites could see such things and this mission was covert.

The second four-man stick slid down to join their brothers and the sniper followed. He unhooked his harness, pulled the Steyr over his shoulder, then waved. The door gunner released the ropes, then yelled to the pilot, who made the helicopter a moving target again, flying slowly along the starboard side toward the cargo ship's stern.

The sniper knelt on the roof of a cargo container and extended the bipod under his rifle. The other men raised their carbines and moved aft.

One of the braver pirates stood from behind the rail, shouldered his rifle and fired, hitting nothing, then yelled and waved at other men, trying to direct them forward. The sniper put the crosshairs on the man's chest. It wasn't a long shot—the *Markarid* was only 199 meters long. The Steyr's barrel erupted and the .50 round took out much of the target's chest when it passed through his center mass.

The pirates were in a panic now. They'd seen men go down in one gory spray after another, which left most of them afraid to stick their heads up. One raised his AK above the metal rail and pulled the trigger, firing blind and waving the gun in the general direction where he thought the soldiers were. The gun kicked high and most of the bullets landed somewhere in the Gulf.

The sniper reached for another bullet tucked into his vest, an armor-piercing round. The Steyr was a single-shot, bolt-action rifle, which forced the sniper to reload each round by hand. He slid the black-tipped slug into the ejection port and pushed the bolt forward. He stared through the Leupold Ultra M3A scope mounted on the Picatinny rail above the Steyr barrel.

The pirate hiding behind the rail raised his AK again and began waving it over the railing as he fired. The Steyr roared, the bullet punched through the metal barrier, and the sniper saw the pirate's blood paint the bulkhead behind in a red spray.

The assault teams reached the superstructure. Now they would have to shift to urban warfare tactics. The ship was the length of a skyscraper and full of narrow passageways, metal doors, and hatchways—countless places to hide and barricade and ambush. They would control the bridge in a few minutes, but clearing the ship would take much longer.

Time to abandon the Steyr. The sniper had his own MPT-9. He checked the carbine and started to move forward. It took him more than a minute to reach the strike teams waiting for him at the superstructure.

Sargord (Major) Heidar Elham of Iran's Army of the Guardians of the Islamic Revolution took the lead position, raised his rifle to eye level, nudged open the hatch, and stepped inside.

Elham stomped up rusting metal stairs that swayed slightly under his feet. The vessel struck a hard wave and the soldier's stomach twinged a bit. Drugs alone were keeping his dinner down and he wondered why Allah would leave it to the Great Satan to invent something so useful as Dramamine.

Elham loosened the strap on his carbine, which hung vertically in front, his right hand resting on the pistol grip. He pulled his balaclava off his head and stuffed it into one of the pockets on his vest, which was already heavy with his radio and other kit. The humidity in the Gulf of Aden held the heat like a sponge and he thought about pulling his gloves off, but decided against it. It was dark; pitching ships had an infinite number of exposed metal surfaces, corrosion was everywhere on this one, and he had no desire to risk tetanus.

The sound of gunfire ripped the air behind him, echoing up from belowdecks through some open hatch closer to the ship's bow. Elham didn't flinch. He knew the sound of his own men's weapons.

Pirates were vicious people, but they had no training, no coordination, no organized tactics. Like all bullies, the pirates had been terrified to face someone more capable than themselves. It had been the slaughter he'd expected and Elham was fine with that. Now his men were clearing compartments, looking for cowards hiding under some bunk or inside some locker or cargo container. His own team had taken no casualties beyond a sprained ankle when one of his men had lost his footing on a ladder trying to reach cover.

Elham reached the top of the ladder and found three of his men smoking Russian cigarettes. It was a foul habit for a soldier, Elham thought. A man who tried to stay in shape for ten-kilometer forced marches and then smoked to relax was a fool, though he kept such thoughts to himself. He kept his disapproval to a short look and a grunt.

"Is he aboard?" Elham asked. *Maybe he changed his mind,* the soldier thought. *Maybe he won't come—*

"Inside," one of the men answered. "He arrived ten minutes ago, while you were below."

Elham gritted his teeth, then pushed open the metal door and stepped through onto the bridge.

Eight Somali pirates were kneeling on the floor in a circle facing inward, hands behind their heads. Most were teenagers, maybe in their early twenties at the oldest. He knew their type, arrogant and cruel as long as they were the only ones with guns. They weren't arrogant now and they'd had no practice at hiding their fear.

The bridge reeked of blood and *khat,* the foul weed that these Somali pirates chewed. They'd had two days' control of the ship during which to spit their juice all over the floor. Whether the blood belonged to any of the other pirates or to the missing crew, Elham didn't know yet. Somali pirate crews had general orders from their warlord patrons not to kill hostages needlessly, but they weren't always faithful to them and *Markarid*'s captain had been under specific orders not to surrender the ship.

Another burst of gunfire sounded from the deck, then a pair of screams erupted somewhere behind one of the deck cranes. His men fired again and the screaming stopped short. Ammunition was held cheap tonight.

Elham looked to the pirates and studied their reactions as they heard the violent deaths of their comrades. None of them soiled their pants, which surprised him. Several probably had done so earlier, before being brought to the bridge.

He was not here for them. Elham turned to the forward windows, through which he could see the entire forward deck of the ship. A man stood by the helm, midfifties, slim, gray throughout his beard. Hossein Ahmadi clearly was not a soldier. Both his clothing and his physique confirmed that. The man was smoking his own Russian cigarette and Elham knew where his men had gotten their supply.

"Dr. Ahmadi."

"Are we secure?" Ahmadi took a drag on his cigarette and exhaled the smoke through his nose. Only then did he turn to face Elham.

"Secure enough."

"What was their course?" Ahmadi asked, nodding his head slightly toward the prisoners.

"Bound for Eyl."

"Of course." Eyl was the major pirate haven on Somali's eastern coast. Dozens of seized vessels and a few hundred hostages were held there at any given time. Ahmadi turned and stared out the windows down at the smoldering hole in the middeck just forward of the conning tower. "And that?"

"A thermobaric round fired from an RPG. Several of the TBG-7V warheads were missing from the cargo hold. We recovered all but one."

Another drag of the cigarette. "How do you find the crew?"

"I find them not well. Eight dead and another six wounded. Fifteen more safe, but suffering from dehydration and contusions. We've moved them to the galley for treatment. This scum"—Elham nudged a pirate's head with the barrel of his rifle—"pitched the dead over the side and locked the survivors in the galley. I've ordered a second sweep to be sure, but I think we've found all of the crew that we're going to find."

"And the captain?" Ahmadi asked.

"Dead."

Ahmadi said nothing for almost a minute as he sucked the cigarette down to the nub. "He was the son of a dear friend," his voice almost flat. "And the pirates?"

"Besides this rabble there were twelve belowdecks. We executed eleven. Their remains are lined up on the deck for your inspection."

Ahmade frowned. "Only eleven?"

"The twelfth was the leader." Elham turned and shouted an order. Two members of his team maneuvered their way through the entry onto the bridge carrying another Somali by his armpits. They dropped him in a shivering heap onto the deck, where he groaned for a second, then started whimpering.

Ahmadi knelt by the man. "He found the cargo?" he asked.

Elham turned his head and looked out the forward windows. He'd known that question was coming and wished he could lie about the answer, but doing that would stop nothing in the long run. Perhaps it would have bought him time to get away from this mission but he'd never been one to avoid his duty. "One container breached in the forward hold," Elham said.

Ahmadi hissed through his teeth. "This one went through it." It wasn't a question.

"Yes. One squad discovered the damage while searching the hold for pirates."

"How did he breach the casings?" Ahmadi asked, furious.

"It seems that he used some of the other equipment we had stored below." Elham shifted his rifle in his hands and stared down at the captives kneeling on the deck. "Your orders?"

Ahmadi stood and looked around at his men. "Clear the bridge of this garbage and seal the hold. Change course, heading one-eight-five until further notice."

"We're not going home?" Elham asked. His surprise was an act. "We should return for a proper crew—"

"You know what this vessel carries?"

"Not precisely," Elham admitted. "But I know who you are, so I can guess."

"Then you know that there is too much invested here," Ahmadi answered. "Sargord, take charge of the ship and proceed on course to the destination port, best possible speed."

You mean you *have too much invested,* Elham thought. *You were stupid to send this ship and crew out so lightly armed.* This entire operation was a gamble not worth taking in his view, but he kept the thought to himself. Ahmadi was a connected man—connected at Tehran's highest levels—and crossing him would be unwise.

Ahmadi turned to the windows and stared out over the massive vessel. "Can you repair that?" he asked, pointing at the smoking hole in the deck.

"No," Elham told him. "Even if we had the engineers, we don't have the equipment or materials needed to fix something of that size."

"Hide it, then," Ahmadi ordered. "Cover it with something."

"Someone might see it before we can finish the job. Their satellites might have already spotted it," Elham protested. "We should—"

"Don't presume to tell me what we should do," Ahmadi said, cutting the major off.

Elham paused and thought carefully about his answer. "Very well. And them?" He nodded toward the Somalis.

Ahmadi stared at the captives for a few seconds, then shrugged. "We are fortunate that the security of the operation and justice demand the same thing, so let justice be done." Then he nodded at the pirate curled up on the floor. "Except that one. A commanding officer is responsible for the actions of his men, is he not?"

"Always," Elham agreed.

"Then we will leave that one to Allah."

Foolishness, Elham thought. Rumors were that Ahmadi was not a religious man. Elham had no problem believing that. He had seen Ahmadi's kind before. No matter. Elham wasn't an overly religious man himself, but in this case he was perfectly ready to accept God's judgment. These pirates had killed his countrymen. Mercy was for the merciful. Christians had that much right at least.

USS *Vicksburg* (CG-69)
Combined Task Force 150
The Gulf of Aden

Red sky at morning . . .

Captain "Dutch" Riley had always paid attention to that old adage. It wasn't true for every sea in the world, but old wisdom survived for a reason and technology didn't change a sailor's job as much as junior officers liked to think. A few hundred generations of sailors had lacked any better way to forecast storms than staring at the sky and Riley wondered which captain had finally cracked the weather code. Whoever that man was, he'd stood on the deck of his wooden vessel morning after morning, maybe for years, staring at the horizon until something clicked in his head. That was the key. Man had spent enough time connecting with the sea and sky around him to finally understand how his world worked. The sea was always trying to talk, but too many sailors weren't listening anymore.

It was just too easy to get disconnected from the sea these days, especially on the bigger ships. He'd gone whole days without seeing the sky as a junior officer on the *Bunker Hill* and the *Leyte Gulf*. Those days could turn into weeks, easy, on a carrier where stepping onto the flight deck was a life-threatening exercise. Riley didn't even like thinking about what life on a submarine would be like. So he walked the deck at dawn, enjoyed the slight rolling of the ship under his feet, and thanked heaven that he could suck in the fresh air whenever he felt like it and listen to the water.

Not that there was much to hear at the moment. The sky was clear today and the only breeze came from *Vicksburg*'s own forward motion. *It's September,* Riley reminded himself. *Another few weeks before the monsoons. Vicksburg* would be on her way home by then—

"Good morning, Captain." Riley turned his head without lifting his arms off the rail. Command Master Chief Amos LeJeune was a tall man, half a head taller than Riley, and thin with a frame built from a life of eating bayou food. He carried the usual second mug, which he delivered to his commanding officer, reserving his salute until the captain took the offering.

"Yet to be determined, Master Chief," Riley said, returning the salute. He took a swig of LeJeune's brew into his mouth—good stuff. "But the coffee's decent, so we're off to a good start." *Decent* was an understatement. He was sure he tasted chicory.

"Nice to see that I don't have to start digging out of a hole so early in the day," LeJeune agreed. The Cajun took a small swig from his own cup.

"Six months aboard today," Riley observed. "You miss the *Blue Ridge* yet?" The *Blue Ridge* was the command ship for the Navy's Seventh Fleet in the Pacific.

"The Hotel *Blue Ridge*?" LeJeune asked. "No, sir. She's a fine ship, that one. Good chilimac. But it's nice to be on a ship armed with something bigger than a .50 cal. Command ships run at the first sign of trouble and they do it proud. Thought it would be fun to ride toward the trouble for once."

"Sorry to disappoint," Riley said. "This isn't exactly a hotbed, is it?"

"Hot, anyway," LeJeune told him. "Not your fault, sir. Just luck of the draw on the orders. Not that I mind chasing pirates. Oldest naval duty that ever was. But I wouldn't mind pushing the button to launch a Harpoon at somebody who deserves it."

"Me too, Master Chief—"

"Sir!"

Riley didn't remember the name of the female seaman apprentice running toward him along the starboard rail. He'd met every member of the crew but it was tough to keep four hundred names in his head. These kids all came and went too fast.

The seaman slowed to a halt and saluted. "Captain.

Master Chief." Salutes returned, the seaman caught her breath for a second. "Sorry to disturb you, sirs. We've got a life raft, maybe three hundred yards off, passing port side aft. Can't see if there's anyone in it, but I don't have glasses." By which she meant *binoculars*. "Sorry 'bout that, sir."

Life raft? Riley thought. There hadn't been any reports of ships in distress in these waters. "Very well." He turned to LeJeune. "Master Chief, orders to the bridge, all engines stop. And get Winter up here. We might need the doc."

"Aye, sir." LeJeune took Riley's coffee mug and his own into one hand and threw the contents of both over the side before jogging off toward the ship's towering superstructure.

Riley faced the seaman again. "Show me."

"Aye, sir." The seaman turned and ran aft with her commanding officer behind.

That young lady has some good eyes, Riley thought. The seaman had underestimated the distance, easy to do on the ocean, where there were no landmarks to help the eye judge size or range, but seeing the raft at all had been a feat. It was a good five hundred yards away and he struggled to make the rescue craft out with his middle-aged eyes until someone fetched him binoculars.

A pair of petty officers guiding their own dinghy dragged the raft by a towline back to *Vicksburg*. Riley could tell from their body language that there was a smell coming off it that could wither a sailor's nose. They pulled alongside, Riley could see a single body in the raft and the bloating told him everything he needed to know about the castaway's current state.

LeJeune leaned over Riley's shoulder. "I think we're coming a bit late for this one, Captain," he offered.

"I think you're right," Riley agreed, following with a private curse. He looked behind him. Most of the crew on deck had heard the scuttlebutt and the few whose duties left them close enough wandered over to see the recovery, morbid though it was going to be. "Master Chief, clear these kids out of here. I don't want them to see this. Then call the officer of the deck. All engines ahead two thirds as soon as we've got this thing aboard. Get some breeze going to carry this smell off the ship."

"Aye, sir," LeJeune said, quiet enough for only Riley to hear. "We'll be seeing this in our sleep for a while." He turned to the assembled crew and began barking orders that Riley didn't hear for his focus on the corpse. Smart man that he was, LeJeune started herding the crew toward the far end of the fo's'cle.

The raft came aboard and the sight was something that Riley wished he could erase from his brain the moment he took it in. The carcass was that of an African man, he presumed, but Riley couldn't discern any more than that. The face was unrecognizable, the skin blistered, and the arms and legs were twisted at bizarre angles at the knees and elbows. *How long has this guy been out here?* he wondered. *A couple of weeks at least.*

The chief medical officer, Thane Winter, stepped up next to Riley and offered him an open tub of Vicks VapoRub. "Put some of this under your nostrils, sir, and breathe through your mouth. It'll help." Riley took the CMO's advice, then handed the tub over to the closest crewman and it began to make the rounds. Winter was right, almost. Riley could still smell the corpse but the mint odor lessened his stomach's urge to dredge up his breakfast. One of the other petty officers on deck wasn't so fortunate. The tub didn't get passed around fast enough and he lost his morning meal over the rail.

Winter pulled on a pair of latex gloves and stepped forward to examine the new passenger, passing through the other sailors who were retreating in the other direction to a safe distance. "I think he's dead, sir," one of the officers called out. It was a poor joke and no one laughed.

There's another candidate for med school, Riley thought, and silenced the heckler with a look. The few remaining sailors began to disperse of their own accord. Morbid curiosity couldn't survive long in the face of the smell, it seemed.

Riley felt the ship surge under his feet, the engines pushing her ahead. He saw LeJeune working his way back to the ship's bow. Winter stood and pulled the gloves from his hands. "Shot through both knees. And someone crushed his hands before they threw him into the raft. He couldn't have launched it and he certainly couldn't have steered it even if he had paddles aboard, which he didn't. No means of propulsion. No navigation or signaling equipment either. No food, just a couple of water bottles. He didn't even drink one of them. Probably couldn't get the caps off."

Riley winced. "Somebody wanted this guy to hurt."

"Somebody got their wish," Winter agreed. "He's also got burns under his clothes that weren't caused by exposure."

"Torture?" Riley asked.

"Maybe," Winter replied. "I won't know until I can do a work-up on him." Riley grimaced at the thought of keeping the corpse aboard.

"It wouldn't be the first time pirates got into an argument over the loot," LeJeune offered.

Winter shrugged. "This was a murder, Captain," he said. "We need to document the evidence, then transfer the body to Bahrain for autopsy."

Riley took a deep breath through his mouth, then stared back down at the body. "Okay. You can get everything up here on deck?" Winter nodded. "Good," the captain said, relieved. "It would take us a month to get the smell out belowdecks. Get your pictures and get 'em fast. Then call Naval Support in Bahrain and get me an answer within the hour. If they don't want him, we'll do a burial at sea. And make sure we're handling the body according to the local traditions."

"Aye aye, sir. I'll round up the chaplain." Winter marched off.

LeJeune watched the doctor go, and then turned back to his captain. "I'm afraid to ask, sir, but what're my orders?"

Riley gave the senior enlisted man a rueful look. "Somebody's got to get this guy into a body bag, Master Chief. Maybe it'll help keep the smell down."

"Aye, sir. That's what I thought." LeJeune jogged away to catch up with Winter.

Riley exhaled and looked down at the corpse. He finally saw the blood and vomit dried on the bottom of the raft. The body had covered the gory stain until Winter had shifted the bloated man and exposed it.

. . . *Sailors take warning,* Riley thought, finishing the adage that had started his morning walk on deck. *Can't wait to make this one somebody else's problem.*

DAY ONE

Kathryn Cooke didn't visit the Memorial Garden often. The water in the pond was surprisingly clear today and it rippled a bit as the waterfall rolled gently over gray rocks into the fishpond. The grass inside the low concrete shelf was growing again, and a Canadian goose was picking at the ground looking for breakfast, soon to be chased away by rain from black clouds that were moving in from the west. The Original Headquarters Building stood to the south a few meters away, the auditorium—called the Bubble for its shape—just behind her a few feet away. The Nathan Hale statue, worn and discolored by decades of abuse at the hands of the Virginia climate, was a bit farther to the east.

She closed her eyes and listened to the quiet sounds of the waterfall until she lost track of the time. It was a good spot to think when the weather was right—

"He was a terrible spy."

She knew the voice but it wasn't a morning to smile. "Jonathan," she said.

"Madam Director." His tone was overly formal.

Cooke finally opened her eyes and stared at the man now sitting on the bench beside her. Jonathan Burke, the chief of the Red Cell, didn't turn his head at all.

"Nathan Hale," Jonathan said, nodding at the weathered statue. "Brave man, bad spy. No tradecraft, no cover story, above-average height and facial scars made him unforgettable to the Tory officer in Boston who saw him. *Not* getting caught on his first mission would have been a small miracle. If it weren't for his pithy last words, which historians are certain he didn't say, nobody would've remembered him."

"So it's a monument to stupidity?" Cooke asked.

"No, to bravery," he conceded. "We need our heroes, even if they aren't always the smartest people." He snorted. "Anyway, you wanted to see me."

"Yes. But I hadn't told anyone yet, least of all you."

"So I saved you the trouble of a call," he said.

"You're annoying, you know that?" she asked.

"Being right covers a multitude of sins."

Cooke tried to let her anger drain away. Jon was arrogant but he earned his keep, even if he was too bold in calling her out. But she hadn't reprimanded him, had she? Not many people could get away with that and even fewer of that small group worked for her. "And how did you know where to find me?" she asked.

"You work in a building full of spies."

His isn't-it-obvious? tone bordered on insubordination, but Cooke let it go. Again. She usually did. It was his version of a sense of humor, but it was beyond her how this man could alienate so many of his peers and, at the same time, maintain a network of informants inside headquarters that reached all the way to the seventh floor. "And you have assets inside my office?"

"Surely you're not asking me to reveal sources and methods," Burke answered, his voice flat with mild sarcasm. "Besides, I'm told that women like a man of mystery."

"That was true before I came to work in a building full of spies. Here I've learned to appreciate the virtues of honest men. Not to mention humble ones," Cooke countered. "Where's your partner?"

"Kyra's at the Farm, renewing her field certifications. She'll be back tomorrow. Just has to requalify on the Glock and she's done."

"Generous of you to let her go," Cooke observed.

"Generosity is irrelevant." He looked annoyed. "Meetings with other analysts go more smoothly when half of the Red Cell is firearms-certified."

"I'm sure. You should've kept yours up-to-date. Days like this, you might need it in case I decide to send you to someplace very, very dangerous." Cooke repressed a smirk. "You know, when I first sent Kyra to the Red Cell, I didn't intend for you to keep her. The Clandestine Service spent a lot of time and money training that girl. Clarke Barron would like to have her back instead of watching her sit at a desk writing papers."

"Her choice," Jonathan said. "She can go anytime she wants. We've never made the rotation formal."

"Clarke thinks you're holding her down."

Jon shook his head. "They steal a dozen analysts from the Directorate of Intelligence every year. Barron's just mad that I might have brought someone back from the dark side."

"It's a good thing to have case officers with analytical training," Cooke observed. "It makes for better collection."

"It's a good thing to have analysts with field experience," Jon retorted. "It makes for better analysis."

Cooke sighed. Time to change the subject. "Have you read the President's Daily Brief this morning?"

"Not yet," Jonathan admitted.

Cooke nodded, picked up a binder sitting on the bench beside her, and handed it to the man. She motioned for him to open the notebook. "Three days ago, the USS *Vicksburg* pulled a corpse out of the Gulf of Aden a hundred miles off the coast of Somalia," she started. "African male, midthirties. The deceased was found in a life raft without any means of navigation or propulsion. The captain assumed that he was a Somali pirate."

"Probably a safe bet. Not many good reasons for Somali men to be that far out in the Gulf," Jonathan observed.

"The victim's knees had been shot off and his hands had been crushed. The bones were practically powder. NSA Bahrain performed the autopsy, but couldn't establish a time of death. He'd been out there awhile . . . exposure to the elements and such. Pages two through six. I apologize if you haven't had lunch yet." It was ten o'clock in the morning.

The next several pages were color photographs of the deceased. Jonathan studied each one while Cooke stared away in silence. He reached the coroner's report and read through the paperwork more slowly than she would have preferred.

After more than a minute, he looked up. "Burns under the clothes. Interesting."

"The *Vicksburg*'s chief medical officer thought it could be torture but he couldn't identify the tool used on him. There was no pattern so the CMO theorized it might have been some kind of chemical burn."

"You want me to find the ship he came from," Jon said.

"Nobody loves a pirate but someone really had a grudge against this one," Cooke explained. "I'm thinking that maybe his crew attacked a ship that somebody *really* didn't want captured."

"Maybe," Jonathan said. "Somali pirates seized the

cargo ship *Moscow University* back in 2010 and the Russian Navy took it back a day later. But it was just carrying crude oil . . . nothing illegal."

"Yes, but the Russians publicized that raid. Nobody has gone public with this one, and from the state of the body, the raid happened a while ago," Cooke pointed out. "This could be Iranians smuggling rockets to Hamas or Hezbollah . . . maybe the Russians running guns into a half-dozen African states. Lots of possibilities, none of them good."

"True," Jonathan admitted. "The time interval would make it tough to identify the ship."

"The analysts tell me that there's no way to find that ship without a starting point in time and space and a general course heading, none of which we have."

"You expected a different answer?" Jonathan asked.

"You don't sound surprised," Cooke countered.

"They'll look at this as a geometry problem," he explained. "Take the geographic starting point, multiply the number of hours since death by the maximum possible speed of the vessel and calculate the product of the equation. Pull out a map and draw a circle with the starting point at the center and the radius in miles traveled. Then they'll wait a month for the State Department to coordinate with a few dozen other countries to investigate every ship that's docked during the time frame at every port inside the circle. A general course heading would reduce the possibilities, maybe by half, but the problem set would still be prohibitively large." He turned toward Kathy and finally looked her in the eyes. "You want me to do better."

"Isn't that the Red Cell's job? To solve the puzzles that other analysts find impossible?" Cooke asked.

"Only as a favor to you. It's not actually in the job

description," Jon told her. "The geometry method is one approach to finding a ship. It isn't the only one, often not the best one, and its utility declines the farther out you get from the starting point in both space and time." He shoved the photographs back into the binder. "I'm taking this," he said, holding up the file. "I'll call when I have something."

"Thank you for doing this," Cooke said. "You could have made it unpleasant."

"The day is young."

He stood, then paused. Cooke looked up and was surprised to find him staring down at her. She smiled up at him. *Not here, not now.* There were a hundred office windows with a view of the garden.

"Jon?" Cooke said.

"Yes?"

"I've missed you."

Jon didn't answer for what seemed like a minute. "You know where to find me," he said finally. It wasn't a rebuke. "You should leave that office a little more."

"President Stuart only had a year left in office when he gave me the call. I thought they would replace me after the election," Cooke said. "I serve at the pleasure of the president."

"I never asked you to resign."

"No, you didn't," she said. "I just wanted you to know that hasn't gone unnoticed."

Jonathan smiled only slightly, then marched away on the sidewalk that wrapped around the Old Headquarters Building to the northwest entrance. Cooke closed her eyes again. After another five minutes, she gave up and walked in the other direction to the front doors.

The Farm
Somewhere in the Virginia Tidewater

The Glock 17 kicked up in Kyra Stryker's hands and she pulled it back down until the sights lined up with the target's head again. The trigger had a smooth five-pound pull; she sent another round downrange and the bullet punched through the paper right where she wanted. The slug sent up a puff of dust from the dry dirt backstop twenty feet behind, one of a dozen kicked up at that moment by other shooters standing to either side.

She had a rhythm going now, two shots per second, still loud enough to come thumping through her earmuffs. Her first trainers had taught her to aim for center mass and she put the last three bullets there just to prove she could do it right, but today she was pushing herself. The requalification shoot would be the one that counted and going for the head now would make the target's chest look a mile wide by dinnertime.

The Glock locked open, ready to receive another magazine, but Kyra had expended the four that she'd hand-loaded. The certification test would be for the Glock only, but Kyra tried never to miss a chance to fire something with a little more kick when the opportunity arose. She waited until the other shooters stopped, then ran out with the group to swap out her target for a fresh sheet. She wanted a pristine outline to work with for the other gun.

The Heckler & Koch 417 was a beautiful piece of work, a gas-operated battle rifle with a twelve-inch barrel and holographic sight. She pushed a clip into the body and chambered the first round. The weapon felt heavy for its size but that's what slings were for.

She took a breath, released it, and stifled the reflex to inhale again. She looked through the sight, picked her spot, put her finger inside the guard and pulled back on the trigger. The barrel erupted, flash and smoke, and the rifle kicked just hard enough to hurt.

She emptied that magazine, twenty rounds, every burst in the target's head, then the second and third. She liked this gun, had thought about buying one for herself, but her salary didn't allow it, not yet anyway. She could be patient. The Agency gave her enough time with its toys to satisfy her urge.

Her ammo expended, Kyra stretched her arms behind her back to work out the soreness in her shoulder. She would need a heat wrap on it tonight after a long, hotter shower and Kyra still wanted to hit the jogging trail that ran behind the student billets through the old-growth forest that lined the river.

She swept the empty magazines into her range bag and cleaned her station. Several of the other shooters, all men, she realized, were staring—half at her, half at her target. The bullet holes were all in nice, tight circles at the forehead and center mass of the thoracic cavity and Kyra had been shooting for fun, not for score. Still, she had done as well as any man here could've managed and better than most.

She realized that the closest gawker was speaking to her and had forgotten that she still had ear protection on and couldn't hear him. She pulled off the headset.

"What?" Kyra asked.

"I said, you're a SPO, right?" A security protective officer, one of the guards who kept the unwashed masses out of Agency facilities.

Kyra looked past the man and scanned the firing

line, where the other men had pulled down their ear protectors to hear her answer. She wondered if they hadn't been taking bets. Kyra looked at the man's face and she saw instantly that he was trying to project confidence, bordering on bravado, but a twitch around his right eye betrayed a sense of nervousness. He was wearing a tactical shirt and pants but both were relatively new, hardly worn. *Not an operator.* Those were all former soldiers and Special Forces who spent more time in the bush than in buildings, and they all came to the Agency with considerable weapons training. Her talent for observation had suggested it but the man's target confirmed it. The shot pattern on his target was respectable but not impressive. A case-officer trainee, then, like she had been a few years before.

That would make you more comfortable, wouldn't it? she thought. *If I had some good reason to be better than you?*

She shook her head.

"Then *who* are you?" the man asked.

She pulled off her safety glasses, dropped them and the ear protection into the bag, and then zipped it up. "I'm an analyst," she said.

Half the men on the line whooped, the other half cursed, and her interrogator grimaced as his face flushed red. He turned back toward his comrades and shuffled through the dust. She was sure he'd be on the business end of some late-night hazing now.

Kyra holstered the Glock, then slung the bag and the HK over her shoulder, and walked back toward the range house.

The jogging trail was a mile of wide gravel and cleared dirt through the pines and old-growth trees, with poi-

son ivy and Virginia creeper on the sides to keep run-
ners on the path. It started by the main road that ran
past the dining hall and her billet, bordered a field of
unexploded ordnance, or so the signs warned, then
curved west into the woods. The Virginia humidity
was still on the rise in late spring and the evening air
was cooler than normal for this time of year. It had
been getting dark when Kyra set out, but the moon
was full and she plowed on through the night. She'd
even decided to tackle the challenge course despite
the inherent danger of attacking such obstacles in the
dark. Broken ankles and torn ligaments were real possibilities, as was spending the night in the forest a mile
from her billet, crippled, until some other jogger came
along in the morning to help her back. But daylight
wasn't a luxury or even a friend in the intelligence
business . . . it was the enemy often as not, something
to be shunned. Darkness was the ally for those who
weren't afraid of it.

An intelligence officer who was afraid of the dark
was in the wrong business.

Kyra pushed through the course and made it back
to her billet in time to catch the bar with time to spare,
a hot shower notwithstanding. She'd missed dinner,
but she'd had the dining-hall chow enough times to
know that was no great loss and there were plenty of
all-night dives close by.

Kyra rested her elbows on the hardwood trim that
lined the bar counter, set her glass down on the granite top, and scanned the room. It was almost empty.
The flat-panel televisions were all tuned to news
channels that were recycling the same stories for the
second time since she'd arrived. The fireplace behind
her was framed by a pair of elephant tusks mounted

on wooden bases that sat on the stone hearth. She couldn't imagine how they had made their way to the Farm, or how the Agency had even allowed it, but she supposed that some cowboy from the Special Activities Center had smuggled them in. Three men were playing pool badly at a nearby table. One lonely soul was throwing darts at an old board to her left and Kyra hoped the young man didn't have aspirations of becoming a professional.

Her cell phone rang, a Bruce Hornsby song that turned the bartender's head. Kyra looked at the screen on the phone, then smiled. "Hey, Jon."

"You're at the bar, aren't you?" he asked without preamble.

"Yep." *Really, Jon? Where's the trust?*

"Beer?"

"Ginger ale," Kyra answered. *And proud of it.*

"Ginger ale and what?"

"And ice."

"Good for you." He wasn't being condescending, she knew. Kyra wasn't an alcoholic, but she'd come close and working a job where one's coworkers were hard drinkers was a prescription for trouble. Jon knew it and was being protective, which was a rare thing for him. She'd learned to appreciate it, slowly.

"How was the range?" he asked, changing the subject.

"It was good. I requalify on the Glock first thing in the morning."

"I heard you were shooting the place up with the heavy artillery."

Kyra half smiled and wondered who at the Farm was part of Jonathan's network of informants. "I wanted to play with something that had a bit more kick."

"The joys of life are in the small things, I suppose," he said. "You're wrapped up down there?"

Here it comes. She was surprised he'd taken this long to get to the point. "Just the one test left, yeah," Kyra admitted. "Why?"

"I need you back. The director gave us an assignment this morning," he told her. "We have to track down a ship."

"And you haven't found it by now?" Kyra teased.

"I have some thoughts, but I thought you might like a chance to look things over."

That's generous. It was also unusual, for Jon anyway. Jonathan didn't like letting a puzzle lie unsolved and he was stubborn and socially distant, so these kinds of gestures were as close as he ever came to admitting any affection for her, and they were rare. Kyra checked her watch. She couldn't get to Langley until well after midnight at the soonest. "I'll head out first thing after my range test," she said.

"Get here by lunch." Jonathan disconnected.

Kyra set the phone back down. *Well,* she thought. *That calls for something a bit stronger.*

She tapped the counter. "I'll take a Coke."

The rising sunlight was cutting through the river fog when Kyra decided it was time to leave. Then she stood there another ten minutes anyway. Jonathan could wait that long. If he complained, she would blame the delay on traffic. Route 95 north was always an iffy proposition and the Washington Beltway was forever a tangled mess. It would be a lie but the view here was worth a sullied conscience.

Kyra sat on a fat granite boulder on the shoreline, no coat, enjoying the morning air. She did love the

Farm. It was very much like home, Scottsville, which sat farther inland along a Virginia river like this one. This would be a fine place to end a career, teaching a new generation of case officers their trade. But that would be years away if ever.

She looked east along the trail and found the spot she was looking for. It was overgrown now with cattails and marsh grasses. Pioneer had sat there a year ago the day after she had exfiltrated him from China. He had lived here for three months after so they could debrief him and set up his new life. She had seen despair in the man's eyes that afternoon, the first time he had realized the full price he would finally pay for treason. To never go home again . . . she couldn't imagine it. Kyra had sat down beside him that afternoon for an hour, saying nothing because she spoke no Mandarin and he spoke almost no English. It occurred to her that this place, which felt so much like home to her, must have felt like an alien world to him.

The day they moved him out, she'd driven him to the airfield. He'd learned a little more English by then and was able to offer a broken farewell. They loaded him on the plane and she watched as it took off into a cloudless sky and disappeared. Now she wondered where he was. She knew the Clandestine Service wouldn't tell her anything. Pioneer was no longer an Agency asset but his case was compartmentalized as heavily now as it ever had been.

Kyra heard movement in the brush behind her and she turned. A family of white-tailed deer, unafraid of humans, was grazing near her truck, which she'd parked on the paved one-lane trail that doubled as a bike path along the shoreline.

Time to go, she thought, and this time she forced

herself to move. Kyra trudged up to her Ford Ranger and crawled in. The deer looked up when she started the engine but didn't run.

She drove out to the main road and it took five minutes to reach the main gate. Kyra rolled down her window and passed her badge to the guard at the shack.

"You coming back?" he asked.

"Not today," she said.

He filed her badge away in a box to be recycled. "Have a safe drive."

Kyra nodded and pulled out onto the highway and pushed the truck ten miles over the limit.

CIA Headquarters

The traffic had mostly stayed out of Kyra's way but the Agency parking lots hadn't been so cooperative. A failed twenty-minute search for something better left her parked by the Mail Inspection Facility and had given her more than a quarter-mile walk to enter headquarters.

Kyra navigated the crowd by the cafeteria, then finally bypassed it altogether through a stairwell by the library that opened into the 2G corridor. Kyra plodded down the empty hallway, swiped her badge against the reader, and the door to 2G31 Old Headquarters Building clicked open.

She didn't bother to announce herself. Jon's door was cracked open and the vault was small enough that he would hear her entrance.

"The file's on your desk," he called out from his office.

Kyra dropped her satchel by her chair then leaned over the desktop. A manila folder was laid open there, a photograph on top of the papers. She glanced at the picture and regretted it.

"And this couldn't wait until after I had lunch?" Kyra asked him, staring at the photo. A burned, bloated carcass of an African male looked back at her. Kyra was not squeamish, but someone had died slow and ugly. She skimmed over the *Vicksburg* CMO's description of the remains.

"Feel free to eat while we work," he said over her shoulder, missing her point entirely. Kyra looked up, startled. She'd been focused on the gory photo and hadn't heard him come over.

"Not a problem *now*," Kyra said. Any semblance of hunger was gone. "I think this guy is a little beyond help."

"True, but not the smartest observation you've ever had," Jonathan said. "And not the problem at hand. The starting assumption is that he's a pirate, tried to take a ship or actually managed it, and somebody dumped him back out into the Gulf of Aden. That's not usually how pirate raids go down, so she's wondering whether he didn't target a ship that someone really cared about."

"What if he wasn't a pirate?"

"Then this entire mess is somebody else's problem. But that would make him boring, so let's ignore that for now."

"Boring is good in this business," Kyra countered.

"Says the woman who just spent a week shooting automatic rifles. Anyway, it's the director's assumption," he pointed out. "And I like it because *it's not boring*."

"All right. No starting point in space or time?" *Of course not,* she realized. If they had that, any decent analyst could have found the ship. "So we have to deconstruct a scenario that we know nothing about, in reverse, and hope that it might provide some clues to what we should be looking for," she observed.

"Correct," Jonathan replied.

"And you waited until I got back to do this because . . . ?"

"I have my own thoughts but I want to hear yours," he said.

Kyra stared at Jon, focused on his body language. The fifteen months she'd been in the Red Cell had been more than enough time to learn that Jon didn't coordinate his analysis with anyone, even people he liked, who were few. *A training exercise? Or you need to prove something to someone?* "It's a red team exercise," Kyra said. "A decision tree. But decisions are subjective evaluations reached through education and cultural influence, which we don't share with the subjects who made them. So you're asking me to mirror image."

"Mirror imaging isn't entirely useless if you're aware that you're doing it," Jonathan counseled her. "Strategies often are culturally dependent; tactics, not so much. The more basic your options, the less they care what country you're from."

"Okay," Kyra conceded. She stared at the picture of the bloated corpse. *Funny how quickly you can get used to seeing that.* Her mind churned, Jonathan letting her sit in silence, totally comfortable and willing to wait on her. "So assuming he was a pirate engaged in a mission, there are . . . three possibilities for how he ended up in the life raft. First, his own crew did it, in which case the ship is probably still under pirate control and docked at one of the haven ports along the Somali coast. If that's true, NSA will probably identify the ship from phone calls between the pirates and the ship's owner. Or if the cargo really is that valuable or interesting, the pirates might offer the ship to any country or intelligence service willing to bid for it." She shuffled through the other papers in the file. "I take it there haven't been any intercepts or offers or we wouldn't be doing this. So we can probably discount that idea."

"I agree," Jonathan said. "And the second?"

"The ship's crew took the vessel back," Kyra suggested. "But if the crew had the will and the firepower to retake the ship, the pirates probably never would've gotten aboard in the first place. So that doesn't seem likely."

"And the third?" Jonathan said, sounding like a proud parent.

Kyra paused for a brief moment. "Someone retook the ship from the outside."

"Excellent," Jonathan said, smiling. "So how do we narrow the candidate list of countries?"

"Lots of countries in the area have military units that could've done it. The ones that don't could've hired mercenaries. So the real question is how the raid team got on board the ship." Her thoughts turned back to the hard landing she and Jon had made on the *Abraham Lincoln* off the coast of Taiwan the year before.

"A good thought," Jonathan said. "There are only three real possibilities for that. Airdrop from a cargo plane, fast-roping from a helo, or a rope climb from an assault craft. The first option would be the hardest. Parachuting from altitude onto a moving ship is doable but it's the riskiest option, especially if it's a night raid . . . leaves the men exposed to hostile fire for a relatively long period with no covering force."

"Fast-roping from a helo solves that problem. That's a short, fast drop while a door gunner lays down cover fire," Kyra said.

Jonathan nodded. "A small boat also is a common option, though problematic depending on weather and the size of the vessel you're boarding. If the target is a large cargo ship, that could be a long climb if you're under fire."

"The pirates did it," Kyra noted. "Unless Somalis have graduated to helicopter boardings."

"The crews of most cargo vessels aren't heavily armed, if at all. That usually eliminates the 'under fire' part of the equation."

"So if we assume a helo drop, they would've had to launch either from a nearby coastline or a vessel out in the Gulf that has a flight deck," Kyra said. "Combine that with a special forces capability and I'd be looking at Israel, Iran, the Saudis, or Pakistan . . . maybe India at the furthest. How many countries are part of Task Force 150? Any of them looking good for it?"

"Seventeen," Jonathan told her. "I looked it up. A lot of them are smaller European countries with no interest in smuggling anything through the Gulf worth a military raid to recover at sea. But the Russians and Chinese keep a presence in the area."

"I wouldn't put it past the Russians and I'll blame the Chinese for anything just for old times' sake. But I don't see how we can narrow it down any further just looking at the geography or naval presence."

Jonathan nodded and leaned back in his chair. "Neither NSA nor Naval Intelligence has picked up intercepts over the last two months from any of those countries that seem useful. So let's look at our theoretical raid on the ship. Assume a military team has retaken the ship and captured the pirates. What next?"

"I think at that point, the captain has two choices. First, return home. Second, continue to his destination. But in either case, the cargo ship would be late for port calls, assuming it had any scheduled."

"Which isn't an uncommon occurrence anyway," Jonathan told her.

Kyra stared down at the picture of the swollen corpse. *But you really made somebody angry, didn't you? Shot in the knees. Smashed hands. Burns everywhere.* She said nothing for several minutes. This was where she had the advantage over Jon—for all his logical skills, he couldn't read *people. I'm sure you made them mad just by taking the ship. But was that it? Or did you do something else when you got on board? Killed somebody?* "Why not just shoot him and toss him." She waved the picture. "This was cruel. He made somebody angry."

"Your point?" Jon asked.

"Maybe I'm mirror imaging too much, but special forces don't usually do this kind of thing. They're professional and efficient. Either detain the guy or just shoot him and be done with it. I don't know, maybe they were mercenaries. Or maybe our pirate here did something that really ticked somebody off. He killed someone . . . members of the crew or the raid team. Or maybe he broke into the cargo. If there was something aboard that justified a military raid and this guy cracked into it, then maybe the ship isn't just late for port calls. Maybe it's *missing* port calls altogether because it's hauling something the owners can't risk being discovered during a port call," she suggested. "Has NSA picked up any reports of a cargo ship missing port calls along the African coast for the last two months?" Kyra asked.

"See? Not boring," Jon said. He held out another folder, which Kyra took and opened.

"You had this figured out before you called me last night," she said.

"I had a theory," he admitted.

"Then why make me go through the exercise?" she asked.

"I thought you might like the privilege of briefing the Director."

"When?" Kyra asked.

"Ten minutes."

"You don't want the credit?"

"Call me generous," he said.

"You softie."

"Hardly. You'll be the one on the hook to answer the really hard question that you know she'll ask," he warned.

Kyra thought about that for a second. "How will we know we have the right ship?"

Jonathan nodded. "You might want to think about that one on the way upstairs." Kyra grinned as she walked out, missing his own rare smile as the door closed behind them.

CIA Director's Office
7th Floor, Old Headquarters Building
CIA Headquarters

"We have a theory," Kyra said, setting the binder down on the coffee table before Cooke and taking a seat next to the director. The first page was a color photograph copy of a cargo ship, with information from the Department of Treasury's Office of Foreign Assets Control listed to the side.

MARKARID (a.k.a. IRAN DEYANAT)
Bulk Carrier 43,150 Dead Weight Tonnage, 25,168 Gross Register Tonnage, Iran flag (IRISL); Vessel Registration Identification IMO 8107579 [NPWMD].

Builder Country SPAIN Company ASEA ordered Feb 1982 launched Aug 1982 delivered Nov 1983; Hull Form H1; Dimensions 119.50 x 29.06 x 11.72 m (654.53 x 95.34 x 38.45 ft); Cargo holds volume 54.237 m3 strengthened for carrying heavy cargoes; Speed 15.25 kt; Single engine/screw motor vessel.

"The MV *Markarid*," Kyra told her. "She's a dry bulk carrier owned by the Islamic Republic of Iran Shipping Lines. IRISL smuggles cargo for the regime and this particular ship's been banned by the UK and by Treasury's Office of Foreign Assets Control from docking at US and British ports. The NPWMD tag is the marker for Treasury's Non-Proliferation of Weapons of Mass Destruction Sanctions Program." Kyra realized that Cooke knew that fact as soon as she'd said it. Embarrassed, the younger woman pushed ahead and turned Cooke's binder to the second page, a map of the African east coast with a line drawn in red ink by hand and ruler tracing a southern course. "She put to sea seventeen days ago from Bandar-e 'Abbas," she continued. "Satellite imagery shows that she passed through the Strait of Hormuz and followed a southerly course for thirty-six hours before making a sudden turn southwest, here." Kyra pointed to a junction in the line. "If you extend that line"—which Jon had done with a ruler and a Sharpie. She traced the line with her finger—"you run straight into Eyl, which is a major pirate port on the Somali eastern coast. But two days later, she turned southeast away from Eyl and headed down the coast toward Madagascar."

Cooke studied the page. "You think she was hijacked off the Omani coast?"

"That's the guess," Jon confirmed. "Somali pirates have been charging farther north for years. Pirates might have taken the ship and the mullahs decided they really didn't want anyone looking at whatever was in the hold. Naval Intelligence reports that the Iranians launched a *Moudge*-class corvette from Bandar 'Abbas, the *Jamaran*, less than twelve hours after the *Markarid* changed course and that ship's course would've put it within helo distance of the *Markarid* within twenty-four hours. The *Jamaran* has a flight deck and usually carries a Bell 214 helo," he explained. "They could have sent out a team to take back the ship."

"And the boarding party decided to have a little fun or send a message, whatever, and put this guy out to sea." Cooke turned the book back to the autopsy photos.

"The sea currents around the area at the time roughly match to put the life raft in *Vicksburg*'s path if it was launched from the *Markarid* at the point of the course change," Jonathan observed.

"But this may not have been for 'fun,'" Kyra disagreed, tapping the pirate's picture. "The *Markarid* has missed three scheduled port calls over the last month."

"Missing one is common. Two is a problem and three is trouble," Cooke agreed. "So the cargo is too important to turn the ship around and too illegal to risk a port-call inspection now that the container is breached. I like it. Where is she now?"

"Her last known position was east of Dar es Salaam three weeks ago and heading south by southwest," Jon answered, pointing at marks near the bottom of the map. "After that, imagery loses her west of the Seychelles. I would guess she's well out in the Atlantic by now."

The Atlantic, Cooke thought. *Heading north again? Or west?* "The Suez Canal would've cut a few thousand miles off the trip. Kind of a tell that she didn't go that way," Cooke observed.

"The chances for inspection go way, way up in the Suez," Jonathan agreed.

"There's no real proof that we're right," Kyra admitted. "It is just a theory."

"But if this is right, I want to know what the mullahs are sending into my half of the world on a vessel flagged for smuggling materials related to weapons of mass destruction." Cooke looked up at the analysts. "One more question. If it is an Iranian ship, they've probably reflagged and repainted it by now. How will we know we have the right ship?"

Jonathan smiled and looked sideways at Kyra. The younger woman shot him a wry look. *You suck.* "Cargo ships keep smaller life rafts stored on the deck for easy access in case of an emergency. The *Markarid* will be the ship missing a life raft."

Cooke pondered that answer for a moment, then grunted her approval. "Very well, thank you."

Cooke hated to visit Jacob Drescher in the mornings. The senior duty officer was at his best in the dead of night and better still when some war or riot was keeping his staff busy and he was giving orders to his own troops. An appearance by the CIA director near his end-of-shift would trigger the man's sense of duty to stay in the office until he finished whatever tasking she would deliver. Only a direct order would prevent that and even then he would come in early that night to attack the request if the day shift hadn't finished the job.

The Ops Center was quiet, its usual state more often than not. The sun leaked in through the blinds in the back, not entirely closed. The monitor array that dominated the front wall showed morning news shows in three quadrants. The fourth showed Cooke's own schedule for the day. The Ops Center would have been a waste of resources if it couldn't reach Cooke no matter her location.

"Good morning, Madam Director." Drescher had sidled up to her while she was staring at her own schedule.

"Morning, Jake. Anything new?" She knew the answer. Drescher would have called or sent a runner if the answer had been yes. Most people seemed to have a muddy line about when events were important enough to disturb the Boss. It wasn't muddy for Drescher. The man seemed to know intuitively when it was time to pick up the phone and Cooke had learned to trust his judgment.

"No, ma'am. The world's quiet, mostly," the senior duty officer replied. "At least the parts we care about. Something we can do for you?" Drescher asked.

"You're off duty in an hour?"

"Unless you need me longer."

"I want you to find me a ship," Cooke told him.

"That's always a tall order." He respected the director too much to use the word *maddening* . . . hundreds of ships in constant motion en route to and from ports spread across millions of square miles of ocean. There was no way to assemble the entire picture fast enough before it all changed. "The MV *Markarid*?"

Cooke let out a frustrated exhale. "Jon came to see you?"

"No, it was that young lady he works with, but I'm sure he was the taskmaster. You don't think he'd go through the trouble to dig up those satellite photos, do you?"

"No, that would be 'boring.'"

"I've got a crew looking at all the African ports. They've already checked the Seychelles and are working their way down the eastern coast now. We're pinging the South African National Intelligence Service for anything they've got, and we've got a request in with NATO to poll the European ports and see if she's scheduled to dock anywhere in the EU," Drescher confirmed. "It's been tying up my manpower. I could use a few spare hands if you've got any to lend."

"I'll give you Jon," Cooke said with a smirk. "It's his theory. No reason he should just be an idea man and leave the real work to other people."

"That'll help," Drescher said. "What would help more would be the *Markarid*'s itinerary. I can't begin to tell you how much that would help."

"I doubt the Iranians will share," Cooke told him. "But don't be surprised if she's coming west."

"Yeah," Drescher admitted. "But it'll be the devil to

find her out on the open ocean staring at imagery. The Iranians are friendly with the Cubans and the Venezuelans, so we'll check those ports along with Africa and Europe. But I can't promise anything."

Cooke shrugged. "Maybe we'll catch a break."

"I'll call you when we've got something"—by which the man meant *don't wait up,* she knew. Jacob Drescher was a pessimist but Cooke knew he was right. Luck seemed to favor the enemy more often than not.

"Fine," Cooke said. "Now go home."

"Yes, ma'am."

DAY TWO

The Boeing 727-200 was not the most comfortable plane in which Dr. Hossein Ahmadi had ever flown. The craft was forty years old, making it only marginally younger than he was, and showing its age. The carpets were wearing thin and the interior plastics were discolored despite what he hoped were diligent cleanings by the maintenance crews. He would have much preferred an Airbus A320-200 or one of the Fokker 100s that Iran Air had managed to buy up the decade before, but he couldn't convince the head of the airline to give him one of its most modern jets when he was going to be the only passenger aboard. His influence still had some limits.

The operation would change that.

Ahmadi looked out the window and watched the Atlantic waters passing beneath the plane in the morning twilight. The *Markarid* was somewhere down there, close, if Sargord Elham had kept the cargo ship moving on schedule, but that was an open question. Ahmadi had ordered radio silence after that affair in the Gulf of Aden. Some of his critics in Tehran had whispered that he should have stayed aboard and sailed with the ship, which notion he had laughed off. Even his political enemies had to admit that his duties were too important for him to spend six weeks aboard a cargo vessel at sea and so he had delegated the task to lesser men. Would his opponents spend a day aboard such a ship with no comforts, much less two months? The answer was obvious and the argument ended there.

The flight from Tehran's Imam Khomenei International Airport had taken eighteen hours thus far, with two refueling stops adding almost three more hours to the schedule. It was an exercise in frustration and his patience was at its end. He had arranged for Iran Air to fly a Tehran–Damascus–Caracas route in years past that had allowed him to travel more directly but the security and cover stories surrounding those flights had been weak. Western intelligence services had seen through their purpose quickly and so Iran Air had terminated them. The route, though advertised commercial, had never sold a ticket to any common passenger. Those planes had been reserved for more special men and cargo, and Ahmadi despised the unknown idiots who had allowed their shoddy security to create this inconvenience for him now. Had that route been available, the *Markarid* itself wouldn't have been necessary.

Ahmadi turned back from the window. *That cursed Somali.* The fool's ignorant greed had almost derailed the entire operation at the start. The man's punishment had been deserved. In retrospect, a bullet to the head would have been better for operational security but not as satisfying. And that was the real point of punishment, wasn't it? Not to reform the criminal—a stupid expectation—but to make restitution to the offended. And in this case, the entire Islamic Republic of Iran had been offended, though only a few men knew it. How to make restitution to an entire country? Death was too quick. Even the pirate's prolonged suffering wouldn't measure up but it was all Ahmadi could exact at the time, so he'd left it to Allah to settle the difference in accounts. Ahmadi's only regret was that he couldn't drop the man's broken body on the desk of whatever warlord had funded him, to send a message that his ships were not to be touched.

The Boeing's pilot made the cursory announcement to prepare for landing. The plane had left the Atlantic and was now passing over mountains covered with shantytowns and tin-roofed shacks. A few minutes more and the wheels touched down on the Venezuelan runway. The pilot drove the plane onto the tarmac, then rolled it past the commercial concourses to a private hangar at the airport's far end where the Boeing stopped, the engines began spooling down, and the steward took his place by the door. He stared out the window, waiting for someone outside, then finally raised the lever and pulled the door open. Only then did Ahmadi finally move to leave.

The hangar was old, unpainted metal walls with a high roof of steel, rust and bird's nests, and brightly lit. The entire space was empty except for the plane and the two armored cars sitting near it. Ahmadi saw more black cars outside on the tarmac, doubtless the security team for his host, still kept at a distance because not all bodyguards could be trusted.

Two men in black suits stood near the base of the boarding ladder staring up at him. Ahmadi forced a practiced smile.

"Buenos días, estimado Señor Ahmadi. ¡Bienvenidos a Caracas!" one of them said. A second man translated the greeting into Persian. *Good morning, esteemed Mr. Ahmadi. Welcome to Caracas.*

"Mamnoon, President Avila. Salaam alaykum." Ahmadi replied in Persian. *Thank you, President Avila. Peace unto you.* He waited on the translator to do his work. He had learned some Spanish, enough to converse generally, but preferred to make his hosts

speak his language. Ahmadi could not have cared less whether Allah bestowed peace upon President of the Bolivarian Republic of Venezuela Diego Avila. He certainly had showed none to the man's predecessors. Hugo Chávez had died years before from metastatic rhabdomyosarcoma and had suffered tremendously before expiring. But the man had at least shown the good sense to invite Ahmadi's superiors to make use of his country before the cancer had eaten him alive, so perhaps God's hand was supporting these people after all.

Avila stepped forward as Ahmadi touched down on the concrete floor and took the Iranian's hand in both of his. "Señor Ahmadi, it is good to have you standing on our soil again. I take it your trip was free of trouble?"

Ahmadi had no desire to engage in pleasantries with this man and the translator gave him a few moments to consider the right words to seize the conversation. "It was," Ahmadi offered. "Have you heard from our friends?"

"We have," Avila confirmed. "They are inside our coastal boundaries to the northeast and will arrive tomorrow, late morning. But they are coming later than the schedule dictated. Engine troubles?"

"There was a minor problem after departure. I regret we could not inform you of the issue sooner but communication silence was necessary."

"I understand," Avila said. The man was fawning. He understood nothing, really, only that Ahmadi had something he wanted. "Your accommodations are ready now as requested. The driver will take you there. You may leave in the morning at your convenience and the head of the Servicio Bolviariano de Inteligencia will meet you dockside upon your arrival. I would accompany you, but it would be better, I think, if my presence did not draw attention to this." The Servicio—known as the SEBIN—was Venezuela's answer to the CIA.

"A shame," Ahmadi lied. "But I agree." Which he did. It was hard enough to keep the American intelligence services from looking in the wrong places, and the Israelis had eyes everywhere. Having an armored convoy and police escort leading Avila directly to the *Markarid* wouldn't help matters. "If you have nothing else, I will take my leave. It was a long flight."

"*Por supuesto.* Please come see me before your departure this time," Avila said. "When this is all complete, I think that a dinner together would be in order."

"Presidente Avila," Ahmadi said. "When this is all complete in a few days' time, *my* president intends to come dine with you. At that point, there will be much to discuss."

Avila smiled, surprised. "Excellent. My kindest compliments to your president, then."

"I will share them." Ahmadi pulled himself into the waiting car, closed the door, and laid his head back to rest during the drive through Caracas.

MV *Markarid*
The Caribbean Sea

The sun was rising behind the *Markarid*. *Thirty hours,* he thought. *Thirty hours and we're done.* They were inside the Venezuelan coastal boundary now so no hostile vessels, particularly American naval vessels, would approach.

Six weeks they'd been aboard. It hadn't been the

worst duty he'd ever performed, but it was one for which he and his men were not fitted. *Soldiers, not sailors,* he thought. Still, his men had performed well enough. Now there would be no complaints from their superiors, none directed toward him and his unit anyway. Ahmadi would be the target for any blame but he was a connected man. He would survive if the mission came off well and Elham had given the civilian a chance now to make that happen.

One of his sergeants approached and held out a piece of paper—the daily status report. Elham stared at the sergeant, then turned back to the ocean. "Just tell me."

"All ship's systems are nominal. No unusual communications requests. Surface contacts tracked and logged. We dock by noon tomorrow." The last was no surprise.

"The forward hold?"

"Still sealed."

Elham nodded. The hold had been closed for the duration. He didn't expect anyone to disobey orders and breach the seal, and no one had, but he made sure that all hands knew that checking it was a daily priority lest any of the surviving crew get stupid or curious.

"And our men?" By which he meant his actual team and not the *Markarid's* own crew members. It was surprising how quickly he, a nonmariner, had fallen into the pattern of thinking of everyone aboard as "his crew."

"The four who were in sickbay appear normal. No recurrence of symptoms."

That was good news. The ship's medic had insisted that they suffered from seasickness and prescribed Dramamine, but Elham knew from the start that the diagnosis was wrong. They had all taken the drug before boarding the vessel. There were other possibilities besides his worst-case scenario. Who knew what diseases those Somali pirates had carried? But those four had been the fire team that searched the forward hold, looking for Somalis during the raid.

It had been days before they could hold down solid food and none of them could control their bowels. The medic had labored mightily to make sure they didn't succumb to dehydration. They were all back on duty now, under orders to report to the medic daily for follow-up and to limit their contact with the rest of the crew. If the Somalis had infected them with some malady, Elham didn't want it spreading.

"Very good," Elham finally said. "Any problems with that?" He nodded toward the island superstructure where several tarps covered the crater in the ship left by the thermobaric RPG round one of the Somali pirates had fired off at the moment of his death.

"No," the sergeant confirmed. "The lashings held fine during last night's storm. We are still checking it every hour."

"Good." The hole was sizable, large enough that it wouldn't be repaired without a welding team, a dry dock, and more supplies than they had aboard. Even covered, he worried that any vessel could have seen at a thousand yards that the ship had taken damage, so he had ordered the crew to avoid contact with other vessels and populated islands. Ascension Island, home to a UK airbase, had been a particular concern some days ago, but they had passed far enough away that there had been no incidents.

"Your orders?"

Elham shook his head. "Prepare for docking and

unloading. After that's complete, the actual crew remains aboard until we receive further orders. Our men will provide initial security until I can hand off that responsibility to our hosts."

"The men are asking about shore leave," the sergeant noted.

"I'm sure." Six weeks aboard this barge had felt much, much longer. "Perhaps after the cargo has been relocated. Dismissed," Elham said. The sergeant saluted and walked away.

After the cargo has been relocated, he repeated in his mind. *You should have found a reason to scuttle the ship,* he thought briefly, then quashed the thought. That was treason . . . but was treason the smarter course here? His country was hated. Even their fellow Muslim states despised them. A few kept it hidden for the most part, barely, behind false smiles and closed doors but some like the Saudis didn't even bother with that pretense. The cargo in the forward hold would not change that for the better. It would earn them neither the respect nor the fear that Ahmadi insisted it would, he was sure. *We will be true pariahs now, to everyone.*

Elham pulled back from the portside rail. Such debate was pointless but he'd rarely had the luxury of so much time to reflect on orders while carrying them out. Time could be dangerous for a soldier in so many ways. He'd been drilled to obey orders as a younger man and taught the reason for it as he'd climbed the ranks. Questions were a hindrance to duty . . . and yet he'd never fully quashed that part of his mind that wanted to reason things out. It was a terrible habit for an Iranian soldier but he'd long since given up trying to kill it.

He forced his attention away from the debate going

on in his head. Elham had never truly been in control of this mission, no matter how free he'd felt on the bridge high above. Such was a soldier's life. Freedoms were always bounded by the whims of higher men. Decisions about cargoes and the fates of nations were not his to make and he was happy for that.

CIA Director's Conference Room

The room was smaller than some of the other conference rooms in the building but more ornate than most. That was fitting, Kyra supposed. The CIA director met with presidents and every other kind of dignitary here on occasion. Like the rest of the CIA director's office complex, no expense had been spared here. High-back leather chairs surrounded a real hardwood desk. Colored wooden seals of all the intelligence community agencies hung on the walls at eye level. The largest flat-panel monitor Kyra had ever seen hung between the U.S. and CIA flags standing in the far corners and it had taken her ten minutes to figure out how to drive the controller mounted on a touch panel rising out of the table.

Cooke entered, seven minutes later than promised, and Kyra knew better than to ask the reason. "Coffee?" Cooke asked without preamble.

"No, thank you. I've never had a taste for it."

"A tea drinker?"

"Only sweet tea on hot days," Kyra explained. "I'm a Virginia girl after all."

"You'd never have survived in the Navy," Cooke mused. "It was good to see you again this morning, Kyra." She poured her own cup, then seated herself at the head of the table.

"It had been a while, ma'am." More than a year, she realized. She knew Cooke and Jon made excuses to see each other on occasion, though not as often as either would prefer.

"You can stop with the 'ma'am,'" Cooke ordered.

"My apologies, ma'am. It's not optional. Southern upbringing."

Cooke shook her head, took her first sip, then set the mug on the coaster. "Show me what you've got."

Kyra pressed a button on the touch controller and a video feed appeared on the conference room monitor. Then she pulled a photograph out of a folder and held it out. Cooke accepted the paper, never moving her gaze from the screen. "I spent last night in the Ops Center with their IMINT team and we found this at 0330. That's our best candidate for the *Markarid*. We can't really confirm it's her . . . hard to see the name on the side of the hull when you're looking straight down and they probably changed it anyway," she said, deadpan. "But she's missing a raft from the starboard side."

Cooke's head turned at that bit of news. "Nice call," she offered. "What happened there?" She pointed at a spot on the photograph.

Kyra pressed a button and the satellite video magnified by a factor of two. "It's hard to tell. It looks like she suffered some kind of explosive damage to the superstructure, more than the crew could fix at sea. They covered it over with tarps and moved some cargo containers around to prevent anyone from getting a look at sea level. We're just guessing at that but I think it's a pretty good guess. The imagery analysts tell me that's fresh paint higher up, above the tarp . . . probably to cover some scorch marks. They also tell me there's not much aboard any legitimate cargo vessel that could tear up a hull like that . . . the worst thing they usually carry is fossil fuels, which would just burn the paint, not tear up the metal unless they did something spectacularly stupid."

"If they hosted a firefight, somebody might've gotten a bit happy with the high explosives," Cooke answered.

"That's what Jon thought when he saw it," Kyra conceded. "But it would take something bigger than a grenade to do that—" she said, pointing at the ship's damaged island. "At least an RPG round. I guess Jon has seen a few go off." She'd asked him for the particulars but the man had demurred.

"Where is she now?" Cooke asked. "Where are we looking?"

"Southwest of Grenada, almost due north of Caracas. She's inside Venezuela's coastal waters on a west-by-southwest heading. Extend the line and it looks like her port of call will be Puerto Cabello. If that's right, she'll dock by noon tomorrow. Drescher has asked the National Reconnaissance Office to keep a bird on her and let us know if she changes course, but they're not in a hurry to retask a satellite just to prove Jon's theory."

"I'm sure," Cooke said. There had been an unhappy note in the younger woman's voice. The director looked up from her coffee. "So what's on your mind?"

"I'm thinking maybe we could get coverage the old-fashioned way?"

"We should send someone down there?" Cooke offered.

"Yes, ma'am."

"Are you volunteering?" Cooke asked her.

"I wouldn't have suggested it if I wasn't willing to do it," Kyra finally answered after a second's pause.

"There's a difference between 'wanting' and 'willing.' Which is it?" Kyra pondered that for several seconds, long enough for the silence itself to tell Cooke that the younger woman wasn't sure. "Kyra, why are you still in the Red Cell?" the director finally asked.

"Ma'am?" The question had left her off balance.

Cooke stared at the younger woman long enough to make sure she had her full attention. "You weren't thrilled about becoming an analyst when I first assigned you to the Red Cell last year. The last time we talked down at the Farm, you weren't even sure you wanted to stay at the Agency. But you're still here and you're still working with Jon. I'm the CIA director, so I don't have career conversations with people at your level as a general rule. But you have two Intelligence Stars, both of which you earned within six months after you came on duty, and I'm pretty sure that's never happened before, so I'm making an exception. Not to put too fine a point on it, you're a very good analyst but you proved that you can be a better case officer and I don't want you working in a job where you're performing below your talents. People who do that usually just drag down their unit before they finally quit. So, again, why are you still in the Red Cell?"

Kyra felt her cheeks flush. She hadn't expected the CIA director to be quite so honest or blunt. She exhaled, a long, slow breath. "I can speak freely, ma'am?"

"Yes."

"I've been a case officer. In my first two field assignments, I got shot, assaulted, chased, and almost caught shrapnel from an antiship missile that would've hit the *Abraham Lincoln* very close to where I was standing if the CWIS gun hadn't shot it down. I admit, I don't want to spend my life behind a desk but every field op I've run came *this* close to getting me captured. That's not really what I signed up for. I thought I'd be working a cover job at an embassy or as a NOC, attending conferences, meeting with assets. I didn't expect people to try to kill me quite so often."

Cooke nodded. "I do understand that. I know those stars didn't come easy." The director stopped talking and Kyra waited for her to start again. The silence dragged out and became painful. Finally she spoke. "You know, when the World Trade Center came down, it became obvious that we couldn't go after terrorists and tyrants the same way we did the Soviets, but we couldn't change overnight and a fair number of people around here fought it when we started. For a long time we were too dependent on case officers who still wanted to work the cocktail circuits and meet with assets in hotel rooms over crab and caviar. Change isn't just hard, it's painful, and we're still not there." Cooke stopped for a moment, embarrassed just a little by the passion in her voice. Then she looked the younger woman square in her green eyes. "I don't mean to preach to you but we don't just need people who can work the streets, we need people who can work the street and the *bush*. Different worlds, different tradecraft. You proved in Caracas and Beijing that you can work the street. And your file says you can work the bush—your Farm instructors still can't figure out how you got away from the dogs during Hell Week. And a case officer who can do analysis too? That's just gold. You've shown everyone that you're up to it. We need people like you out there."

Kyra fumbled for a response and no good one came. "Have you had this conversation with Jon, ma'am?" she finally asked, deflecting.

That stopped Cooke in her tracks. "Why do you ask?"

"First, because he won't like it, you approving me for a field assignment, even if it's temporary," Kyra said. "'This is not a good idea,' and all that."

Oh, Cooke realized. *Have I had this conversation about* you *with him.* "That sounds like him," she agreed. "I can handle Jon. I presume there's a 'second' to come after that 'first'?"

"Ma'am, I know you two are friends." Kyra actually knew better than that but didn't want to be too bold. "I've shared an office with him for over a year and sometimes I feel like I barely know him. I know he's spent time in the field. He knew his way around the *Lincoln* like he's spent serious time at sea. But he gave up the field for a desk and never talks about why. He's an amazing analyst. He has a Galileo and a Langer Award . . . I've seem them. But he's one of the most disliked people in the building and he could be doing a lot more than he is. You said you don't want me working a job where I'm performing below my talents. What happened to him?"

"To be honest, I don't know. He was forward deployed to Iraq during the war, but he never talks about that with me. He came back, joined the Red Cell and never left, even when everyone else did," Cooke offered.

"He could do more," Kyra said.

"Yes, he could," Cooke agreed. "But right now we're talking about you, not him. Do you *want* to go? Do you want to be an operator or an analyst?"

"Honestly, I'm not sure anymore, ma'am. And I'm not sure how to find out."

"You know how," Cooke told her. "Your suggestion that we put someone on the ground is accepted. You've worked in Caracas so I'm sure the new station chief will be happy to see you come even if it's only for a few weeks. She's shorthanded right now anyway. Take the initiative. Get to Puerto Cabello, find some safe spot to hole up with line of sight on the dock, and report back what you see. I think the mission will be fairly low risk."

"'Low risk' is a relative term."

"True. But risk is the business, isn't it?"

"Yes, ma'am." Kyra stood to leave.

"When you get back, you tell me what you want. If you want to be a case officer or an operator, I'll make it happen for you. If not, I'm sure Jon would be happy to keep you . . . as happy as he ever gets about anything. You remember the first three rules from case-officer school?" Cooke asked.

"'Don't get killed. Don't get caught. Bring home the intel.'"

Cooke raised her coffee mug. "Go thou and do likewise." Kyra nodded and left the room. Cooke took a sip from her coffee mug and realized that it had gone cold.

Despite standing orders to the contrary, Cooke's secretary almost stopped Jon dead at the door. Cooke had told her executive assistant that she'd summoned the Red Cell chief but agitated men didn't get past the front desk as a general rule and the secretary had a button on her desk connected to the security station around the corner to enforce that policy. She let him in but not without a warning stare.

Cooke was sitting on her couch when Jon stomped into the office. He didn't bother to look at her or to close the door behind himself. The secretary, a woman of good sense, reached in and did it for him.

"What do you think—?" he started.

Cooke cut him off. "Whatever you're about to say, you're out of line." It came out a bit quieter than she had intended but had the desired effect, mostly. Jon stopped short, saying nothing. He turned away from her and stared out the windows. Already, this meeting felt different and Cooke didn't like it.

"I'm so glad to see my opinion matters to you," he said.

"This isn't about your opinion," she corrected him. "You're mad that I approved Kyra going to Venezuela."

"The Venezuelans almost killed her the first time she was there so you'll forgive me if that doesn't seem like a bright idea. We don't usually send people back into countries where they ran into that kind of trouble."

"Whether it seems smart to you or not is irrelevant, Jon. I'm the one whose opinion matters here. I'm the CIA director, in case you'd forgotten," she reminded him. "I don't have to discuss my ideas with you before I present them to anyone. But she volunteered, in case she didn't mention it—"

"She did."

Good for her, Cooke thought. Cooke had never thought Kyra was a coward. "A successful field op could get her career back on track."

"And why would choosing to be analyst be considered 'off track'?" He was angrier than she'd ever seen him. This was not going like she'd expected . . . too much on the defensive. Jon had never been this aggressive with her.

A soft answer turneth away wrath . . . where had she heard that? "She could be the best case officer of her generation. She could be running the Clandestine Service by middle age but not if she stays down in the

Red Cell," Cooke said. "And that wasn't fair. I've never pushed you to do anything you didn't want to do."

"And I'm doing fine."

"By your standards, Jon, not by mine," she said. "And not by a lot of other people's here on the seventh floor."

"I'm the one whose opinion matters there."

Cooke winced, hearing her own words turned on her. That was a first between them. "You don't think she can handle it?"

"I think this is a terrible way to find out. The failure mode on this could get real ugly, real fast—"

"It's a straightforward surveillance op," she protested. "Minimal risk—"

"There's no such thing as 'minimal risk' in field ops. We're kidding ourselves to think we can even quantify risk," he retorted, cutting her off. "But I thought you respected me more than this," he said. His voice had an edge that was both sad and sharp.

"My respect for you has nothing to do with this. It's not personal," Cooke assured him. She stood and walked over to him, closer than was professional, but the door was closed. She stared straight into his eyes to make the point.

"If you're determined to send her, she shouldn't go alone."

Cooke pulled back, surprised. *Are you asking to go?* Suddenly the operation seemed more dangerous than before. "You don't do field work anymore."

He answered nothing. Cooke tried to read him but he'd retreated into himself, which usually meant he wanted something he wasn't willing to ask for. She held her silence, giving him the chance to finally open himself to her, but she'd seen this play before. As always, she was the one to finally break the silence. *Another missed chance,* she thought. "Jon, the *Markarid* was your theory. I was hoping you'd come with me to the White House—"

"I don't care about the White House," he said, ignoring the professional temptation. "I've been there, I've briefed presidents and I don't care if I ever do it again, much less with this one," he replied, his voice heavy with contempt.

Cooke nodded slowly. "Caracas station is gutted right now. The SEBIN tore the entire operation open last year and we had to pull almost everyone out. We've been sending people in slowly but it's not even a skeleton crew. I'll call the chief of station down there. She's new to the place, but I can set things up," she said in surrender.

"It's still not a good idea." He started for the door.

"Jon," she called after him. He stopped and looked back at her over his shoulder. Cooke stood and walked over to him, put her hand on his arm to pull it away from the door. It took her another minute to figure out what to say, but he waited for her. "This is my decision," she said finally.

"I'll call you from Caracas." Jon pulled away, opened the door, and walked out, closing the door behind him. It saved Cooke from having her secretary see her exhale a long, sad breath.

The Oval Office
The White House
Washington, D.C.

The president of the United States was far younger than his predecessor and not much older than Kathy

Cooke herself. Rostow was just out of his forties, one of the boy presidents that the country liked to elect when it decided that vigor was a suitable substitute for experience. Cooke had known Harrison Stuart, been nominated to her current job by the older gentleman, and had come to like him during their infrequent meetings. He'd been a septuagenarian who exuded the calm of a man whose ambitions had all been realized. She had been as sorry as he was happy to see his term in office end. For once, she believed, one of the honest and wise men John Adams had prayed for had actually ruled under the White House roof.

Daniel Rostow felt like another animal entirely. He seemed to her like a man whose ambition could never be satisfied. The former governor of Oregon had been in the White House barely a year and his hunger for a legacy already was no secret at all. She'd watched him devour his intelligence briefings and she worried that he did so only because he was hoping each morning that the President's Daily Brief would bring him the tidbit that would finally give him the opening to write his name into history.

Cooke opened the lock bag while Rostow watched. "I apologize for the sudden request for a meeting, Mr. President. I appreciate your willingness to carve out a few minutes."

"Happy to do it," Rostow said. Cooke didn't believe it. The president's daily schedule was carved out in five-minute increments so agreeing to this meeting meant three others with donors and political allies had been canceled.

"Just don't let it become a habit." Gerald Feldman sat in a chair next to the president. Feldman had run Rostow's campaign two years before and then surprised the pundits by taking the national-security-adviser job instead of the chief-of-staff position everyone had predicted. The *Post* had openly questioned whether he wanted to be the next Kissinger.

"That depends on the world, sir, not on us." Director of National Intelligence Cyrus Marshall sat to Kathy's immediate right. The retired Navy admiral uncrossed his legs and leaned forward, anticipating the paperwork that his subordinate was about to dole out.

"Calm down, Gerry. This is the first time she's done this since we got here," Rostow said. "The world's been quiet." Cooke thought she heard a strain of disappointment in the man's voice.

"I appreciate your patience, Mr. President," Cooke said. "I promise, I don't do this lightly."

Rostow took the file that Cooke offered with duplicates going to the other men and he opened the folder. The picture of the Somali pirate sat on top. The briefing took five minutes and the president never looked up from the photograph, no emotion playing across his face.

"What's your confidence that the *Markarid* is the right ship?" Feldman asked.

"Our confidence is high," Cooke admitted. "The damage to the superstructure and the missing lifeboat are compelling."

"What are you asking for?" Rostow asked.

"A presidential finding authorizing a covert action. I want to send an officer to Puerto Cabello to put eyes on the ship and determine the nature of her cargo, if possible."

"Why not just use the satellites or a drone?"

"Can't read a ship's name on the hull from straight up," Marshall told him.

Rostow let out an exasperated laugh. "Billions of dollars per satellite and they can't read a vertical sign."

"The laws of physics are a cruel mistress," Feldman quipped.

"And the Venezuelans have a half-decent air-defense system, courtesy of the Russians and the Cubans, so sending out a surveillance flight would be problematic," Marshall added. "There is a carrier battle group in the Caribbean at the moment and the Navy could detach a sub to ID the vessel, but she'd have to hustle and she'd be running in close proximity to all of the cargo ships running around Puerto Cabello. That would raise the chance of an accidental collision. Getting someone on site to give us a ground-level perspective would be cheaper and easier."

"Cheap as long as they don't get caught. You had some trouble with that in Caracas last year as I recall. What's the risk?" Feldman asked.

"Low, we think. All of the dockyards in Venezuela are under government control, but Puerto Cabello is one of their largest so foreigners are a constant presence," Cooke said. "We expect no contact with the target."

"When will the *Markarid* dock?" Feldman asked.

"Imagery confirms that she's on course to arrive tomorrow, late morning. She'll enter the docks just before noon local time."

"Then you're wasting time, aren't you?" Rostow chided her. "Gerry, draw up the paperwork. Have it on my desk by lunch. Kathy, when can your team be on the ground?"

"They're ready to fly out today. I don't think we can get a team on site before she docks, but we hope they can get there in time to observe the unloading."

Rostow smiled, and Cooke wasn't sure she liked it. "Good," he said. "Give me daily updates after they arrive. Thanks for coming."

Marshall led Cooke out to the secretary's office and closed the door to the Oval Office behind him. "Well done."

"Thank you," Cooke replied. It was sincere. This director of national intelligence she liked. There were any number of people in this town for whom she could not say the same, including the two men in the office she'd just left. "I appreciate you supporting my request."

"Unlike my predecessor, I think it's important for CIA and the DNI to cooperate. From time to time, anyway." The gentle joke made Cooke smile for the first time in hours.

Cooke nodded. "I guess you've heard the stories by now."

"I got an earful from the Senate chairman when I was nominated," Marshall admitted. "They're afraid of you, you know." He nodded toward the Oval Office door.

"Afraid of me?" She hadn't heard that.

"Rostow's not a fool, Feldman even less, even if he does tend to politicize intelligence. The Hill likes you and that's never to be underestimated. But the truth is you took down the last director of national intelligence in a straight-up political knife fight . . . got Harry Stuart to fire his own appointee. That's not to be underestimated either. So, yeah, they're giving you some latitude."

Cooke repressed a rueful smile. "Your predecessor was appointing political donors as CIA station chiefs.

The one he installed in Caracas was talking too much to an asset who turned out to be working for the SEBIN. And then he sent a talented young lady on a mission that got her shot when she'd only been in the field for five months. That man was a fool that cost us our infrastructure down there and almost cost us a very good officer. Harry Stuart was just honest enough to call it for what it was."

"And you risked your job to snuff him. Bold."

"It helps to have a righteous cause."

"So it does," Marshall agreed. "That young lady . . . she's still with us?"

"I've assigned her to this op," Cooke said.

"Wanting to put her back on the horse?"

"She's been back on the horse, sir," Cooke replied. "She was the one who went into China last year and exfiltrated our prime asset after he was burned."

"I remember that report . . . that was a good read," Marshall said, honest respect in his voice. "Let me know when your team's in place."

"Yes, sir," Cooke said.

Leesburg, Virginia

Kyra set her bag by the front door and checked the wall clock above the entry table. Less than two hours until the flight. Dulles Airport was twenty minutes away and the Greenway certainly wouldn't be jammed at this hour unless someone was lying dead in the road. So long as the security lines weren't backed up, she would make the plane without having to rush if she left now.

She knew the flight time by heart. *Caracas.* She'd tried to keep the old memories out of her thoughts and failed for the most part, and the old anxiety had been rising inside her stomach all morning. Kyra ran her hand across her left arm and felt the scar that ran along the triceps. It was no thin line. The bullet had ripped through the skin and muscle there, taking much of both with it as it had passed out the other side. She hadn't even felt it at the moment. The adrenaline had been rushing through her, killing the pain then like the Vicodin had done for months after. Now it was a numb mass of scar tissue, visible from feet away whenever it was left uncovered. She always wore long shirts now, even in the humid Virginia summer. It was easier to explain that fashion choice away to her parents than to try excusing how she'd acquired that mutilation.

She had been trying to ignore the telephone on the entry table most of the evening as she packed her travel bag and secured the house. There was nothing left to do now, no good excuse for procrastinating about the call and the phone would not be denied any longer. Kyra picked up the receiver and dialed, hoping no one would pick up. She sat in silence while the call went through. She'd thought her mother would be home at this hour, but Kyra's wish was granted as a voice-mail system told her to leave her message.

"Hi, Mom, it's me," she said. And like that, it was time to lie. "My boss asked me to take a trip overseas today. We're having trouble with one of the software packages we're developing. The bug is in some code written by a foreign contractor and they're just not getting it fixed, so I have to go straighten things out. It's a mess and we're on a deadline. So I'm heading out for the airport and I'm not sure when I'll be back."

And the lie was done. Kyra hated it. Sarah Stryker

was a kind soul who didn't deserve to have her only child deceive her, and Kyra had been doing it for almost three years now.

She paused for a moment. She could almost hear her mother, as though the woman were on the phone speaking to her. The entire message didn't have to be a lie, she thought, but now she would have to tell the truth and that would hurt the other woman more than the lie she'd already told. "I know you wanted me to come down for a visit and try talking to Dad again this weekend. I think it's still too soon after what happened over Christmas . . . probably would just do more harm than good if I did come, but I won't be around this weekend anyway. Thanks for trying to help. Maybe when I get back. I'll call you in a few days. I love you. Bye."

Kyra hung up the phone, rolled her bag out onto the front step, and closed the door behind her. She started to lock the dead bolt when she heard the phone on the entry table inside begin to ring. She stopped for a second, then finished locking the door, seized her luggage and walked down the stairs toward her truck, the phone calling behind her.

DAY THREE

The *Markarid* sat unmoving under the stars, her engines finally cold. Elham had pushed the ship hard over the last day and Avila had arranged for the ship to jump the queue, allowing her to make up a few hours of the lost time and leave some angry captains anchored out in the Atlantic past their schedule times. They would have to wait. Their cargoes of machinery and foodstuffs were trivial.

Hossein Ahmadi stared up at the vessel, seeing her for the first time in weeks. He had seen her like this once before, when she had put to sea from the docks at Bandare 'Abbas. She looked no different now but for the gash ripped into her island superstructure and the new paint on sections of the hull and tower. He cursed the Somali pirates again.

"That is quite the hole." Ahmadi turned and saw Andrés Carreño approaching from behind. The director of the SEBIN walked ten feet ahead of the armed soldiers under his command. Carreño dressed like a businessman. The troops behind wore the usual tactical gear that made Special Forces of the world so hard for Ahmadi to distinguish one from another.

"An unfortunate incident in the Gulf of Aden," Ahmadi admitted. He offered no other details.

"Pirates?" Carreño asked, pressing the matter.

"Yes," Ahmadi said. A few times since that raid he'd wished that he'd put the gun to the Somalis personally. *But their leader received what he wanted in the end, now, didn't he?* the Iranian thought. For that, he was pleased with himself. The manner of the man's execution had entailed a certain irony.

"My apologies that your men had to remain aboard all day after docking. President Avila felt that it would be more secure to start the unloading process after dark."

"Likely right," Ahmadi admitted.

The ramp was in place and Ahmadi saw a man descending in the dark. He recognized Sargord Elham in the dirty light cast by the dockside lamps. The man was dressed not in his fatigues but in more casual clothes typical of a cargo ship's crew. *Wise of him,* Ahmadi thought.

"Dr. Ahmadi," Elham said, finally within earshot.

"Sargord. I received your report. My congratulations on your trip."

"Thank you. I have nothing new to report in the last twenty-four hours."

"Very good," Ahmadi said. He turned to the Venezuelan at his side. "Director Carreño, I present Sargord Heidar Elham of the Army of the Guardians of the Islamic Revolution. It was his unit that dealt with our . . . incident and safely delivered the vessel to your port."

"Welcome to Venezuela, and my congratulations, Sargord," Carreño said, offering the soldier his hand. "We have accommodations for your men at a secured location. Doubtless they're anxious for some food and companionship?"

"That would be much appreciated," Elham replied. "But we have four men who should receive medical attention. They fell ill after our intervention in the Gulf. They appear to have recovered, but given the circumstances a thorough physical is in order."

"Not at a public hospital," Ahmadi countered. "Director, I presume that you have doctors who can be trusted?"

"We do. I'll have one join us at the facility after our arrival."

"Our thanks. The pirates in the Gulf that the *sargord* skillfully dispatched managed to find the cargo before he could board. The casings were breached," Ahmadi said. He looked to his countryman. "Were there any further problems with that?"

"No," Elham replied. "But it was necessary to keep the forward hold sealed for the duration and we skipped some port calls to avoid any unplanned inspections."

"Understandable," Ahmadi assured him. "Someone will need to repair the containers before they can be unloaded. I regret, Señor Carreño, that your longshoremen would be the logical choice."

The intelligence officer frowned at the declaration. "My men?"

"Of course," Ahmadi said. "The *sargord*'s men are not engineers and the crew needs to be returned to Tehran immediately for debriefing and . . . isolation. They were not told of the cargo's nature and we need to make sure they don't endanger our operational security. We will need welders and other men with specialized tools and skills. We never expected any such need and so didn't bring either the men or tools aboard."

"You could have brought them on your flight," Carreño observed.

"To do so would have invited more scrutiny," Ahmadi countered.

Carreño grunted, then shook his head. "No, we

have no cleared men with those skills here. And conditions below could be dangerous—"

"Then I suggest you resolve those problems quickly," Ahmadi said, impatient.

Carreño bristled. "We are equals in this arrangement, not your subordinates. My men are no more expendable than yours."

"Of course . . . but your men are here. The equipment is here. We are already behind schedule and you know that timing is everything in this enterprise. It would take several days at least to bring men and materials over from our country and every movement risks drawing unwanted attention. And besides, this will give your countrymen the honor of unloading perhaps the most important cargo to ever come to your shores. I'm sure Presidente Avila would agree with me."

Carreño gritted his teeth and stepped closer to Ahmadi, anger drawn on his face. "This is not acceptable, Doctor," the SEBIN director said.

"And yet the schedule and security requirements demand it," Ahmadi replied calmly. "Please, feel free to call *el presidente* directly on this matter." His attempt at a Spanish accent was horrid.

"I will speak to him," Carreño said, his voice cold.

"I look forward to the conversation. But since you will doubtless need some hours to round up men and tools, I think we could at least begin unloading the legitimate cargo from the other holds if your people are ready," Ahmadi offered.

"The head longshoreman has already been aboard," Carreño said. He looked back toward the ship, not trying to hide his disgust. "He tells me it will take most of the night to clear a path to the forward hold anyway. The way your soldiers had to rearrange the containers on the deck to minimize anyone's view of that"—he pointed toward the tarp hanging from the island—"will slow them down."

"Then you will have the time you need to take care of the other arrangements." Ahmadi smiled. "You see, Director? Everything will come off as needed and your efforts will be much appreciated when this is all over. Now, please have your men secure the vessel." He looked to his fellow Iranian. "Sargord, please inform your men that their housing is being arranged, then join me at my car. We should discuss the voyage."

Elham nodded, then turned and began to climb the boarding ramp. Ahmadi smiled at Carreño and walked toward his car. The Venezuelan stared at the *Markarid,* angry, and then waved at his men. A small team moved to the boarding ramp and followed Elham up. The remaining soldiers began to fan out across the dock.

Simón Bolívar International Airport
Maiquetía, Venezuela

"Si se opone la naturaleza, lucharemos contra ella y la haremos que nos obedezca."

If nature opposes us, we will struggle against her and make her obey us.

Kyra had not understood why Simón Bolívar would make such a grandiose statement until she had seen the mountains here for the first time. Now, for the second time in her life, Kyra watched the Venezuelan coastal range erupt behind the Caracas beaches to her left as the Boeing 737-900 descended. This was a hard country from top to bottom, beautiful and brutal at the same time in so many places. With cliffs like those running across the northern border, it was little wonder the natives might feel that nature itself wasn't a friend.

The flight had been long enough to be uncomfortable, more so for Kyra than for Jon. She'd made this flight once before and knew the travel time, but it seemed so much longer and shorter all at once. She could hardly remember leaving the country the first time. She'd been shot days before that plane ride and painkillers in high doses played with the memory.

The airport bordered the Atlantic and the Boeing flew low over the water, reaching the tarmac only a few seconds after finally going "feet dry." Kyra and Jon deplaned and walked to customs where a Venezuelan military officer stood by the customs door leading into the airport proper, an AK-103 assault rifle in his hands suspended from a sling. Kyra tried not to stare, and instead turned her attention inward, curious about her own reaction to the sight. She had expected to feel anger. Instead, she felt numb.

The customs officer handed over her passport, offering no greeting, no *¡Bienvenidos a Venezuela!* which she wouldn't have appreciated anyway. She hated this country now.

Jonathan passed through the line behind her, speaking surprisingly good Spanish—he'd never said anything about a facility with the language. She wondered if he spoke others and what other skills he'd failed to advertise.

The Agency's Central Travel Office had arranged a car and the gas was cheap. She did the conversion in her head. *Twelve cents to the gallon.* Kyra's international driver's license was as fake as her passport, but that hardly mattered here. Venezuelan traffic laws were entirely theoretical. They existed but no one obeyed them and they were never enforced without some ulterior motive behind the traffic stop. The government had suspended a total of one driver's license in the last ten years.

She didn't need a map to find the embassy, which was another reason Jon was willing to give up the wheel. The Avenida La Armada led to a freeway, the Autopista Caracas–La Guaira, which curled through the ridges northwest of the city. Traffic was a mess; Kyra had expected nothing less and figured the drive would take the usual hour instead of the forty-five minutes she'd hoped for.

She took the off-ramp onto the Autopista Francisco Fajardo, and saw the artificial Guaire River snaking under the elevated highway. The buildings, even the graffiti, looked suddenly familiar.

She had faced the double agent on the bank of that river right . . . there.

The rusty bridge where the man stood that night was still in place over the muddy water, the bushes that covered the raid teams were still a nasty tangle, unmanaged and uncut. The streetlight where she'd started to run was still standing. She wondered if it still worked.

Kyra was surprised at how calm she felt, no shakes, no racing heartbeat. She felt so . . . detached? That was the word. Detached from that moment, like she could look at it all clinically now. The alley she had turned down for cover seemed closer to the bridge now than it had in the dark . . . but she must have been shot before she made it that far. *Maybe there?* . . . at the dead-end space before the alley, where she'd knocked that first soldier onto his back—

"Eyes up," Jonathan said. Kyra looked up and realized she was drifting left into the guardrail. She gently straightened out and veered back into the lane, no jerking of the wheel.

"You okay?" he asked.

"Yeah." She meant it, not that Jonathan would have known had she been lying. He was looking at her, intensely she realized, but reading personal cues was not his forte.

Kyra didn't look in the rearview mirror. She'd seen the site. It held nothing for her.

The U.S. Embassy compound sat in the center-east of the capital city, built on a twenty-seven acre rise in the Colinas de Valle Arriba neighborhood, overlooking the Las Mercedes shopping district a half mile below in the valley. The embassy itself was five stories, red granite with walls that caved in and out of the front at oblique angles like the architect had lost his ruler and resorted to a drafting triangle instead. Kyra had found it strange when she'd first seen it years ago, but had come to appreciate the design—

"That is the ugliest building I have ever seen," Jonathan said. "And they put it on a hill."

"It's all hills here, Jon."

"And the rum here must be excellent, judging by the architecture."

"It is, actually," Kyra admitted. She turned off the road to the parking lot in front of the building and began searching for a parking space. The cars were all American-made, a strange sight given the Fiats, Peugeots, Renaults, and Haimas they'd seen on the freeway.

"Had your share the last time you were here, did you?"

"The water isn't always safe to drink," Kyra told him.

"Convenient."

"I thought so," she agreed, smirking.

"So who's the station chief now?" Jon asked.

"No idea," Kyra replied. "I heard they cleaned house after Michael Rhead got pulled out last year."

"Which brought you no small satisfaction, I'm sure."

"I didn't cry for him," she said. She got out of the car and started walking for the front gate, where the Marine guards stood waiting to check their IDs. "Follow me," she ordered.

Jonathan obeyed, which was a rare thing.

Like third-world warlords, station chiefs could be happy tyrants who ruled with a fist and a smile and made subordinates take on the most menial tasks. So Kyra was surprised when they were asked to wait at the embassy lobby so the station chief could come down from her office to escort them herself. They found a padded bench and spent the time staring at the walls.

They sat in place for ten minutes. Kyra was staring at President Rostow's official photograph when she heard the footsteps on the tile floor. Then she felt her partner tense up in a way she'd never seen.

"Hi, Jon," Marisa Mills said.

Marisa Mills was a severe exception to the unwritten rule that chiefs of station were supposed to be nondescript. She was a tall woman with brown hair that fell to her shoulders and looks that probably drew slander about how she earned her assignments. Kyra watched Jon as pleasantries were stiffly exchanged and he seemed impervious to the woman's charm, but social graces had never been his strong point.

Not impervious, she concluded. *Active resistance.* No, that wasn't right.

Anger. Jon was trying to cover it and failing.

Kyra was sure that Mills knew it. The older woman seemed uncomfortable, intensely so. She was making an effort to be friendly to Jon, but the woman was proceeding with caution.

The trio marched through the embassy to the elevators and passed the ride up in silence. When the doors opened, Mills took the lead. Kyra stepped off, Jon trailing, and the last eighteen months of her life washed away in an instant. *Back again,* she thought. Kyra knew every turn, one turn after another with no hesitation in her steps.

Jon said nothing as Mills led them through the halls. Kyra wanted to ask him about Mills, how they knew each other, but the other woman was too close and would've heard any such question.

They approached a security door, no different from the ones at Langley, gray with a badge reader and a massive dial bolted into the metal. Mills swiped her badge, the door clicked open after a second's delay and she pulled it open.

Mills's office was typical of her position, large, with a view of the valley and shopping district a few thousand feet beyond the embassy wall. The desk was real hardwood, handcrafted by some local artisan, and Mills had cleaned out an entire drawer of her file cabinet for use as a tea shelf. Kyra saw that she kept no vanity wall in her office the way the men usually did, no pictures of family, just a few relics and photographs drawn from past assignments. A large photo sat behind the desk, Mills standing in some sand-swept village and looking attractive even in a brown tactical shirt and utility pants, surrounded by rough American men in Levi's and dirty shirts, all carrying automatic weapons or sniper rifles. Beside the picture was an engraved KA-BAR knife thanking her for her service to some Agency unit whose designator Kyra didn't recognize beyond the first initials of SAC. The Special Activities Center wasn't the most welcoming unit to outsiders, even fellow NCS officers. Some officers could work with them but only those with Special Forces training ever really were allowed to join.

"Director Cooke opened up your file for me," Marisa said, looking at Kyra. "Forgive me for asking, but how's the arm?"

Worried about whether I can carry my load in the field. Kyra turned and lifted her sleeve. Mills cursed in amazement. She leaned over the desk and touched the jagged lateral scar running across the younger woman's triceps where the 7.62mm round had torn out the skin and muscle a year before. "That must've been a bloody mess."

"It healed up okay. I was on painkillers for a while. Physical therapy took a few months," Kyra said. She thought about mentioning the psychological counseling but decided not to volunteer that story. She rolled her sleeve down.

"I'm sure," Mills said with sympathy. "They tell me you had a hand in taking down the last station chief down here?"

"That was Director Cooke, ma'am. She just used my case to pull the trigger on him."

"Wish I'd been there," Mills said. "I never met my

predecessor and I'll crack his head if I ever do. That jackass destroyed this station's asset networks, tech ops, you name it. I had to send most of the staff back to the States because we didn't know whether their names had been leaked to the locals. It's going to take another year to get this place back on its feet."

"I would've thought that the NCS would have this place back up and running by now," Kyra told her.

Marisa shrugged. "Venezuela has never been a high-priority target and the Agency moves at the speed of government. I had seven people in station, counting myself, until last month, when *el presidente* decided to randomly accuse half the embassy of espionage just because. He declared a dozen people persona non grata and got lucky. He named my one case officer and the only Global Response man I had . . . couldn't have done better if Michael Rhead still was passing him names. Heck, I actually launched an investigation to see if we were penetrated, but with only five people left to question, it only took me two hours. Avila just got lucky. So now I've three techs, two reports officers who have no reports to write . . . and now I've got you."

She fell back into her chair, looking suddenly tired. "Sorry, not your problem. But you need to know that we don't have a lot of resources in place right now, so it's good to have someone who's been on the ground here. We need the help."

Jonathan said nothing, nodding only slightly, grunted, tried to half smile, and failed. It was as close as he usually came to *you're welcome*. Mills exhaled, leaned back, then stared at him. "And now they're sending me analysts to run field ops," she said. Her smile announced that she wasn't truly annoyed at the thought. A proper station chief should have been cursing Kathy Cooke's lineage and sanity by now, if not outright refusing the orders. *You know we're analysts but you're not even putting up a fight . . . station chiefs don't like sending analysts into the field.* She'd been there before. She looked over at Jon and decided to let him handle the answer. *She's giving you an opening . . . trying to get you talking?*

If so, he didn't take the opening. Mills leaned forward again, opened a file, and pushed it gently to them. "I think this is already a wasted trip. The *Markarid* finished docking procedures not long after you got on the plane and the locals got busy right after dark." She pulled out two satellite photos from the folder and laid them side by side on the table. "This was taken two hours ago."

Jon lifted the photo and held it so both he and Kyra could see. The *Markarid* sat in her berth, lit by halogen lamps and overrun with dockworkers and, presumably, soldiers scattered in random fashion. A security cordon sealed off a nearby warehouse and access to the ship. A line of five-ton military cargo trucks sat dockside.

"And this was taken after you landed at the airport," Marisa said, touching the second picture. Kyra looked down at the photograph. The *Markarid* was in the same location, but there were no men to be seen. The security cordon was absent now and the cargo trucks gone.

"You don't have images of the actual cargo?" Jon asked.

Marisa shook her head. "Whatever they pulled off that ship, they did it when we didn't have a bird overhead. They knew exactly when there would be a blind spot in our coverage and timed that bit of the operation to match. Sorry, Jon, but that cargo is gone and we don't have a clue where it went." She sat back in her chair. "But to be fair, you probably couldn't have gotten close enough to do us any good anyway. The government took control of the major ports over a decade ago and they block off whole sections of the docks from time to time."

Jonathan took the papers and scanned the new satellite imagery, with Kyra looking on. He'd fallen into his professional mode now, all emotion gone from his voice and face. He held one of the photos inches from his eyes.

"I'd still like to get out there," Kyra said. "The dock is cleared, no soldiers or anyone else. If they've already unloaded whatever it was that they cared about, I might be able to get in there now. They might have left something behind that would tell us where they went." She looked at her partner, who was still staring at the picture. The silence was unlike him and she wondered whether he wasn't using this development as an excuse to stay quiet.

"I'd be surprised if you find anything. This was a precision operation," Mills countered.

"Everyone makes mistakes," Jon said finally.

The comment shut Marisa down instantly. *No answer for that?* Kyra thought. *Precision strike, Jon.* She watched the other woman's face carefully. The chief of station held a good poker face, giving away nothing . . . but she was staring at Jon. The senior analyst stared back, some unknown message passing between them.

"You remember where the garage is?" Marisa said finally, not looking at Kyra.

"Yes, ma'am," Kyra said.

"You can pack up down there." She finally turned

her eyes to Kyra. "We keep ops gear in the storage room in the back. Once you get out there, I want updates on the hour. You run into any trouble, back off and come home."

"I'll leave tonight . . . less chance that I'll run into anyone on the docks in the wee hours."

Marisa nodded her approval, then focused on the man in the room again. "Jon, why don't you go get some chow, then set up shop next door. I don't have a deputy yet, so you can take that office."

Jon sat in his chair for a minute and Kyra could almost see his brain processing the order, something conflicting. Finally he grunted again, scooped the papers, and made for the hall.

Kyra focused on Marisa as the older woman watched Jon march out of the room. The station chief's face twitched a bit and it took her several seconds to refocus on the young woman still in the room. "Just us case officers and girls now. I'll walk you down to the garage," Mills said. She stood and followed Jon's path out into the hallway, Kyra trailing behind, and the station chief caught the younger case officer's gaze. "Jon is a direct one, isn't he?"

"He won't cop to having Asperger's, but it's the current theory," Kyra offered.

"How long have you known him?"

"Almost two years," Kyra said. "How long have you?"

"Picked up on that, did you?" Mills asked. She sighed. "Ten years. We met in the Sandbox."

Iraq, Kyra realized. "And how long were you dating?"

Mills's eyebrows went up. "Did he—"

"No, he didn't." Kyra stopped her.

"You guessed."

"Not really. As a general rule, station chiefs don't drop everything and escort DI analysts through an embassy, suggesting you had a special reason for doing so. We sent a travel cable in advance, you would've read it, seen his name, and known he was coming; hence your reason. Jon's pucker factor went up ten notches when he saw you, and given his usual disdain for authority, that's an unusual reaction unless the other person is someone he knows and dislikes. Jon doesn't care for people in general but his actual dislike is earned," Kyra said. "You wouldn't be a station chief unless you had significant time in the NCS, and you wouldn't be the station chief *here,* cleaning up Michael Rhead's mess, unless you were very, very good at the job. In the NCS, that means you're both charismatic and ruthless, even more than usual since you're a woman. I would know. But you have no wedding ring and there are no pictures in this office of anyone resembling family or a long-term boyfriend or girlfriend. Either would give you a reason to hold him at arm's length when you met us in the lobby, but you didn't do that."

Kyra opened the stairwell doors, eschewing the elevators, and the two women began the march downward. "Given how you persisted in trying to be friendly with Jon despite his hostility suggests you know why he wasn't warming up to you and you feel some responsibility for it. All of which means that you had a previous relationship with him, a close one, and you flipped the off switch, probably because it was standing in the way of your career."

Mills smiled, not in a perfectly happy way. "I see why he likes you."

"What makes you think he does?"

"I've only met one other person who does what you just did and he just left the room," Mills told her. "He's been teaching you observation and logic but he can't read people like you can, even people he knows well. That's beyond him. You have a talent he doesn't, so when you master the other bits you'll be better than him at this business and I suspect he knows it. He wouldn't waste his time with someone who didn't have that potential. As you said, he doesn't care for people. His dislike is earned but so is his tolerance."

"We've been through some business together," Kyra confessed.

"That business with China, I assume," Mills said. "Anyway, we didn't know that ship was coming until it was practically throwing towlines onto the dock. So the best I can do is send you out with some general kit and pray. Are you good with that?"

"Yes, ma'am," Kyra said. "I volunteered for this. I'm not going to back out now."

"Good woman," Mills said. "One more question. How long were you down here before the Chavistas shot you?"

"Six months."

"Do you know who you were supposed to meet on that bridge?"

"Does it really matter?"

Mills smiled, sympathetic. "Maybe not." She pushed open the stairwell door on the bottom level, which led to a long hallway. She pointed at one of the doors. "Welcome to the garage."

The CIA garage was separate from the regular embassy motor pool for reasons that had nothing to do with elitism, much smaller, and housed a far wider variety of vehicles. Several of the vehicles were SUVs and trucks, not the town cars and vans the State Foreign Service officers had at their disposal. Kyra preferred that. Her upbringing in central Virginia had left her partial to vehicles built for unpaved roads. She'd learned to drive on dirt trails bordering the James River and had bent the axles on three vehicles before she'd started college, all to her father's frustration.

The darkened shop was full of autos but devoid of people. Marisa flipped a switch and the fluorescent lamps brightened the space with a harsh, unnatural light.

"There's your ride." Marisa pointed to a far corner occupied by a Toyota 4Runner that had seen a few minor collisions. It made sense not to fix every scrape, Kyra supposed. New cars, unblemished, driven by Americans, would draw attention. Curiosity from the locals was never a good thing and the dirt and dents would turn no heads.

"It'll do," Kyra said. "Wish I had more time to prep."

"You and me both. Gear is on the table," Marisa said without sympathy. She waved a hand toward a table by the corner.

Kyra stared at the inventory laid out on the plywood slab. "They haven't given you the latest and greatest here, have they?" she asked.

"Rhead pretty well gutted the entire operation down here," Marisa replied. She leaned against the Toyota. "HQ set up a task force that still hasn't figured out just how far it all went and they didn't want to risk Avila's boys laying hands on any of the really good stuff until they could be sure we were battened down. So the NCS took the best gear home and left us with this.

They swear we'll get a full load-out when the station gets built up again, but they're in no hurry. So take whatever you'll need."

Kyra looked over the weapons. "These jokers shot me once. I'm not going out without a gun again."

"As long as you're smart about it," Marisa told her. "Shouldn't need anything bigger for this than a side-arm."

Kyra stared down at the guns, then hefted a Glock 17. "My favorite." She looked over the table and another weapon turned her head. "You mind if I take that one?"

"I can live with that," the chief of station said. "Just don't get caught with it. There's a hidden panel under the floorboard." The woman paused, trying to find the soft way to serve up hard news. "If you get in trouble, I have no one to help you. You're up on the personnel recovery protocols?"

"I am," Kyra assured her.

"For the record, you're *Arrowhead* on this one. Do *not* get seen, do *not* get caught. They tried to bag you once. I'd hate to serve you up on a platter after what you went through to get away from them the first time."

The deputy station chief's office was embassy standard, only a little larger than Jon expected, furnished with a hardwood desk and a large couch. That position was unfilled so it was little wonder Mills had looked tired. She was probably doing a tremendous amount of the grunt work usually reserved for lesser bodies. It didn't help that the computers took all day to boot up. He'd waited almost fifteen minutes before the computer had finally finished its business. He supposed that the servers needed time to establish secure connections with Langley—

"Jon?" He saw the chief of station standing at the door.

"You've got a few minutes before she leaves. The girl knows how to pack a bag but the commo gear is giving her fits. You know those old units," Mills said, her attempt at humor weak and she knew it. "Did you see the opplan?" she asked him.

"I read the file," Jon said. "Doesn't look complicated."

"Simple is better."

He said nothing and made no effort to move the conversation. "I was hoping to talk," Marisa said, finally uncomfortable with the silence.

"You had five years to start a conversation. I don't see any reason why you'd want to now," he said.

"Because today we're finally together again?"

"Not a great reason in the age of the telephone," he said.

"You hate phones."

"Yes, I do," he admitted. "But I make exceptions and use them from time to time."

Marisa shifted her weight on her feet, nervous. "Your hair is longer. You're going gray," she told him.

"I should be. I earned it."

"We might all earn a few gray hairs on this one," Marisa said, trying to shift the conversation to something less personal.

"I did tell Kathy Cooke this wasn't a good idea," he conceded.

"You're having meetings with the director?" Marisa asked, surprised. *And telling her that you don't like her decisions?* That was the real question she'd wanted to ask but she held it back.

"We know each other," was all he said.

Kyra appeared at the door. The conversation was finished and Marisa felt a sharp pain in her chest, something she hadn't felt for some time. "Kathy Cooke is a smart woman. I'm sure it'll come off okay," she said. Then she fled the room as slowly as dignity allowed.

"That was sweet," Kyra said a few moments later, slight sarcasm tingeing her voice. She had changed clothes, her blue jeans and casual shoes gone in favor of khaki pants and boots that were going to be warm in the equatorial heat. At least she had chosen a plain tee instead of some heavier long-sleeved shirt. Her dirty-blond hair was tied off into a single ponytail that fell just to the top of her shoulders. She looked every bit the foreign tourist come to hike through the backcountry. "Are you going to tell me what went on between you and Miss America there?"

"Eavesdropping, were you?" Jon asked her.

"I'm a spy. I get a pass," she replied.

"I don't suppose you'll just leave it alone?"

"You can tell me now or I can keep hounding you over the comm when I'm out in the woods. Surveillance is boring. I'll have nothing but time."

"We got close. I became an analyst and she took a job at headquarters. Then she left. Nothing more to tell."

Kyra studied her partner with an odd expression. "That might be what happened, but it's not what happened."

"What are you talking about?"

"For an analyst, there are times you suck at it," Kyra told him. "Women can read each other. You know that moment when you're in a crowded room with a woman and you finally figure out that she might be trying to send you signals?"

"Yes." His tone said otherwise.

"By the time that moment comes, the woman's been throwing herself at you and humiliating herself in front of every other girl in the place for at least a half hour. I've spent less than that around Mills and I can tell you that she cares what you think about her . . . and she's scared." Kyra grinned, a wicked smile that unnerved the man.

"That makes no sense at all," Jon said, frowning.

Kyra shook her head, amazed that he couldn't see signs that were so simple. "I know I just blew up your mental model for dealing with Mills, so I'll just say this—she's that girl who always had a date in high school anytime she wanted one, so she never learned to appreciate any single relationship. Everything came easy because she was pretty so she ended up with no self-confidence and she's been spending her life ever since trying to prove she's more than what people see. You probably treated her different, the way she always wanted, and she didn't realize it until it was gone. Now she's wondering whether she screwed up."

Jon nodded, clearly not understanding what he'd just heard. "You're heading out?" he finally asked, almost desperate to turn the conversation. He looked out the window. The sun was getting low in the sky now.

"I wanted to say good-bye before I left," she said, confirming his suspicion.

"This is still—"

"—not a good idea, I know," Kyra told him, finishing his sentence for him. "You said the same thing about China and Pioneer last year. That turned out okay."

"Just because something turns out okay doesn't mean it wasn't a stupid plan."

"Maybe," she conceded. "But have faith. I do."

"Faith in what?"

Kyra held up an earpiece headset for him to see. "That you'll be here if something does go wrong." She leaned down and kissed him on the cheek before he could pull back, something she had never tried. "Thanks for caring," she said quietly into his ear. Then she made for the door and was gone before he could protest.

Puerto Cabello
Carabobo, Venezuela
75 km west of Caracas

Of those men, only a very small group of officers knew what we were going to do that night, the troops didn't know a thing. In other words, their superiors had decided these men would risk their lives for a political enterprise about which they knew nothing.

Hugo Chávez said those words. He had been talking about the night he had tried to overthrow the government by force in '92, but Carreño thought it odd how they could have applied to what had just happened on the dock. *El comandante* truly had been a prophet even if God had struck him down too early.

The truck bounced under him as Carreño sliced into the Cohiba with a stainless-steel cutter, put the tobacco roll to his mouth, and lit it off with a small torch. All three objects were gifts from the Castros, which was fitting. Venezuela had kept Cuba's economy afloat on a sea of free oil for almost two decades. Free cigars and the tools to properly enjoy them were all they could offer their patrons in return for financial salvation.

His friendship with the revolutionary brothers had paid Carreño other dividends over the years. The Cuban intelligence service had performed the occasional service, improved his standing with his superiors, at least the ones who weren't rivals. He had cleared those lesser men out of his path, sweeping them aside through brazen operations against the Americans that had made his political enemies look like fools.

His operational record had been perfect until that single failure, that one exception that still rankled. His influence in the government now would be second only to Avila's had that little operation gone right. That fool Rhead had been drunk on his own ego and swallowed the information that Carreño had fed him without question. He had led the CIA station chief like a chicken to the axman's stump. Avila had wanted an American intelligence officer in custody . . . no more randomly accusing Americans who worked at the embassy of espionage as a public distraction from the government's failures or to earn a bit of momentary support from the masses. A live CIA officer, provably a spy, in jail, undergoing a trial that would have lasted months would have given Avila a more lasting card to play.

What had gone wrong that night, Carreño still wasn't sure. Rhead hadn't shown for the meeting on the bridge over the Guaire River and the Venezuelan had no idea who the woman was who had come in his place. She'd stood under the streetlamp where he couldn't see her face. It had unnerved him for the briefest moment and in an instant he'd made a single error, waving the woman over instead of giving her the appropriate signal. She'd caught it and she had run faster than anyone Carreño had ever seen in his life. Two dozen men hadn't been able to catch her on foot and a dozen more in cars had lost her in the Caracas streets.

The operation had revealed Carreño for the double agent he'd played for more than a year. Rhead was a fool but his CIA superiors were not. They recalled him a few months later, and most of his staff were gone by the summer. The SEBIN lost their window into the CIA's operations in the country. They went totally, utterly blind and even the Cubans hadn't been able to help them change that for the last year. He didn't know who was running CIA operations in his country now but whoever had taken charge was very, very good. His people were watching the embassy, using every resource they had but the Americans were making no mistakes. An entire year's work and Carreño was no closer to prying open the CIA's networks now than he had been at the beginning.

Avila was still angry with him for that failure and that wouldn't change until he could show *el presidente* something that satisfied him. Close ties with the Castros kept Avila from firing him, but not from assigning him the occasional duty like this one, which was beneath him. This operation with the Iranians— this could give him that success he needed to squelch Avila's anger, but he should have been overseeing it from a distance, staying just close enough to move the pieces but far enough away that he could blame failure on some junior officer. Instead, he'd had to stand there watching dockworkers unload cargoes of scrap metal, fertilizer, and tractor parts, all legitimate goods that happened to be in the way of the containers he actually cared about. A recruit could've done it but Avila justified the assignment by claiming the national interest was far too important to entrust to anyone but his chief spy.

He took another long drag on the Cohiba and let the smoke mix with the anger in his chest. They were minutes from the facility now and the real work could begin. Ahmadi had been right about one thing—if this operation came off well, this truly would end up the most important cargo ever unloaded onto a Venezuelan dock. And as the Iranian had predicted, Avila had approved using Venezuelan men and tools to unload the cargo without question. Carreño wasn't entirely unsympathetic to how the operation would end for them, but perhaps Chávez was speaking to him now, telling him that every man had his role to play. For some, they would do their part, never really knowing why they had been called to give their lives in the service of their country. Perhaps that gave their sacrifice some noblility . . . they fulfilled their duties through faith alone and not for any sure knowledge of what the purpose of their lives really was. Didn't God ask the same? Perhaps that's why he had taken Chávez too young, so the man's words could come back to Carreño this very day, to help him endure to the end and teach him patience at the same time.

The Venezuelan intelligence chief would have to ponder that. He didn't believe that the Iranians really worshipped the same God, doubted they believed it either, but someone above had blessed this operation. Despite the mistakes Ahmadi's people had made, letting their ship get taken by savages, they were still so very close to the end. He had just a few more days to endure; this unpleasant business would be short, and in his pocket there was no shortage of Cohibas to help him pass the time. Then Avila would have no more reason to ever assign him such duties again despite his position . . . and perhaps one day he would replace Avila in the Palacio de Miraflores. That alone would make this all worth it.

Autopista Valencia/Route 1
Puerto Cabello
Carabobo, Venezuela
200 km west of Caracas

Three hours behind the wheel revealed more of the country than Kyra had seen during the six months of her first tour and she felt the resentment toward her former station chief rising with each mile. This was a beautiful land, with large stretches that looked so much like the James River Valley, where she'd spent her childhood. Only the small shantytowns that stood every few miles along the roadside reminded her that this was not home.

The freeway turned north at the town of Valencia and carried her toward the ocean for twenty miles, then turned east, bending back toward Puerto Cabello. The Atlantic met the shoreline only a few hundred yards to her left and the port town finally opened up before her five minutes after the eastward bend.

The architecture of the city was unremarkable, mostly low buildings of old concrete and brick with no semblance of any coherent design to the whole. A few high-rise buildings towered above the rest in the northern district that jutted out into the bay on an angular delta. The twilight sun did nothing to improve the look, with harsh shadows and darkening faces on the buildings giving the scene a threatening look . . . or maybe she was just projecting her own thoughts on what was an average town. There was no doubt that the bullet that had torn up Kyra's arm had stripped away the love she'd once felt for this country. She had no trouble believing that the cities, the actual buildings themselves hated her as much as the people seemed to in her mind.

Kyra used one hand to extract a smartphone from the military pack she'd confiscated in the garage. She placed the Bluetooth headset in her ear and told the phone to call Mills's office.

U.S. Embassy
Caracas, Venezuela

The phone took its own good time connecting the call and encrypting the feed, long enough that Jon was sure Kyra would be getting impatient. "You're not there yet," he finally said without preamble.

"Are you tracking me?" Kyra asked

"Of course. There's not a phone made these days that doesn't have GPS."

"How's the scenery?" Marisa asked, leaning close over Jon's shoulder. He didn't move.

"Jon thought Caracas was ugly," Kyra said. "This is worse." She held up her phone and switched on the video, streaming the feed to him for several seconds, then turned off the camera.

"I've slept in worse places. You'll survive," he assured her.

"We've scoped out some possible sites for you to

leave the truck and sent them to your phone," Marisa
cut in. "The freeway should take you around the docks
to the south, then curve back to the northeast. Imagery says the *Markarid* is docked at a quay in the port's
north end. Stay on the highway after you pass the port
and you'll go north past a fuel storage field. There's a
delta on the other side of that where you can park.
Don't go past it if you don't find a good spot . . . there's
a naval base just up the road."

"Marvelous." She'd be within spitting distance of
the Venezuelan military. Kyra pressed another button
and the phone displayed an overhead map, her location marked by a moving blue dot. "What's the distance to the target?" Kyra asked.

"About a half mile across the water," Marisa said.
"Walking around the beach, probably twice that."

"Sounds like a plan to me," Kyra agreed.

"Don't be afraid to bag it and come home," Jon
offered.

"It's a little late for that, Jon."

"It's never too late to walk away from stupid," he
said.

**Embassy Suites Hotel
Valencia, Carabobo, Venezuela
32 km south of Puerto Cabello**

"Enter."

Elham pulled the door open and walked past the
SEBIN guards who had kept him in the hall for the
last ten minutes. He felt no contempt for those men.
He had stood a post his share of times for men not
worth protecting and he was sure the soldiers outside
felt the same about Ahmadi.

Ahmadi's suite was the largest in the hotel and at least as large as Elham's home at the military base back in Tehran. The decor was suited to Western tastes, of course, but Ahmadi hid his distaste masterfully if he felt any. The doctor sat at a square dining table, moving sausages onto a plate already filled with pastries and polenta. He had forgone water for wine to drink and a small bowl of *quesillo* flan sat by his plate. The civilian was a man at ease in these surroundings.

"*Asr be kheyr, Sargord Elham.* Or perhaps *sobh be kheyr?*" Ahmadi welcomed him.

Elham looked at his watch. "*Sobh be kheyr.* It is past midnight."

"Yes. The jet lag never seems to work in our favor, does it? We'll pay for that come the morning," Ahmadi mused. "Would you care for some breakfast?" He waved his knife over the food.

"No, thank you." He and his men had finished the last of the lavash bread, feta cheese, and quince jam they'd found in the *Markarid*'s small mess hall before leaving the dockyard a few hours before. It was a small meal, the last one they'd have before having to inflict Venezuelan food on their stomachs. He was in no hurry to do that.

"I presume the convoy has arrived?" Ahmadi asked.

"On schedule," Elham confirmed. "Carreño's men are surprisingly efficient, if unhappy about working under our guidance."

"'Our guidance,'" Ahmadi said, smiling as he pronounced each word, sarcasm in his tone. "I was not aware that soldiers had such talents for diplomatic words."

"It's a necessity. The Quds Force spends much of its time training foreign fighters," Elham told him.

"Teaching requires a certain skill with language. Students learn best when they feel valued and respected."

"Indeed," Ahmadi replied. "You finished your review of the security of the operation?"

"Unbreached," Elham said. *Except for your order to throw that pirate overboard.* Ahmadi's cruelty repulsed him. Elham had done some repellent things in his time, but out of duty alone. The civilian's choice to torture the Somali had been pure indulgence. *What do you truly care for security? Only that you're not embarrassed.* He didn't say it . . . that need for diplomatic language again. "The cargo arrived at the facility. I watched them secure it before leaving to come to you. The *Markarid* has a nominal security detail aboard and the dock has been emptied. Carreño has refused to let any of the longshoreman near the ship until we can guarantee there is no residual danger to his countrymen. That will require some diplomacy of its own."

"Irrelevant," Ahmadi replied. "I could not care less what happens to the rest of the cargo. But I will have another crew flown here and they can take the *Markarid* home again. What did you do with your unwanted guests?"

"We loaded them into a cargo container and moved it into the warehouse by the dock. Our hosts are arranging a train to carry the container to a suitable site for disposal, far from here. Carreño has promised to wrap up that detail, not by choice of course," Elham replied. "But we have another problem."

"Oh?"

"Some of the longshoremen are sick. Some of my men suffered the same problem during the voyage but they recovered. I can't say whether the same will be true for these men."

"You think they should be eliminated?" Ahmadi asked.

"Security hinges on the details. The best way to manage some risks is simply to never take them." *Like throwing sick pirates overboard in life rafts,* he thought but decided not to say. "Others are easily solved, if one is prepared to take steps from which other men shrink. The longshoremen need to be secured for the long term, certainly. Of course, it's possible that their medical condition might solve the problem for us. If not, their executions might be necessary."

"You sound unhappy about that," Ahmadi observed.

"I do what duty requires," Elham answered him. "Whether I enjoy it is unimportant."

"And Carreño is unwilling, no doubt. You need me to come."

Elham nodded. "Carreño will be unpleasant to manage on this. We secured his people with the rest of our guests, and I warn you that the smell is both quite impressive and unmistakable. We got to enjoy it for most of the voyage. I will not be sorry to see this particular problem behind us."

"On that we agree." Ahmadi wiped his mouth with the napkin and tossed it onto the emptied plate. "Very well. Tell the guards to bring the car."

The Puerto Cabello Dockyard

"That's it," Kyra said. She was lying prone behind the tree line, looking though a Leupold spotter's scope from her bag mounted on a small tripod. The *Markarid* was surprisingly large given the distance, a testament to how long the cargo ship truly was. Half of the space between her and the vessel was Atlantic water, the other half sand and scrub, nothing to obstruct the view. Kyra held her phone up so she could see the screen next to the ship docked in the far distance and flipped through the color photographs, swiping through them with her finger. The vessel matched the pictures down to the rust pattern on the hull.

An adaptor cable connected the scope with her phone, which was streaming the video to Jon. "The name in big English letters is kind of a giveaway," Jon said in her ear.

"The international language of commerce. Convenient," she said. Staring through the optic, she panned from the ship's fo'c'sle aft, then stopped and swore quietly. "Check out the ship's island. You see that?"

The gaping hole was covered by a tarpaulin sheet badly tied down and the ocean wind kept the corner waving in the air. Underneath was a dark void, a hole directly into the corridors behind with twisted metal and mangled pipes in view, burned paint and scorched stains around the edges.

"There's your RPG hit. I'd bet money that was a thermobaric round," he said.

"You think that's what the Iranians are smuggling in?"

"Sure. But the question is whether it's the only thing they'd be smuggling in," he said. "The Venezuelans could buy those from plenty of countries. They wouldn't be worth a raid at sea."

Autopista Valencia/Route 1

The SUV was not nearly so large or comfortable as the town cars Ahmadi preferred, but his choice of expensive vehicles was limited in this part of the South

American backwater. Public attention was risk, but surely he didn't have to settle for this. Then the truck ran over a badly maintained section of road and Ahmadi reconsidered. These country roads would destroy a better car's suspension, and perhaps his spine along with it. Maybe sacrificing a bit of luxury in return for saving one's back was the wiser choice? Still, it grated on him.

He sighed and turned to the soldier riding next to him in the backseat. "You've impressed me with your performance on this operation, Sargord," Ahmadi said. "You seem like a man who is too smart to be a soldier. Surely you have higher ambitions?"

Elham ignored the implied insult. "I am a career soldier, not a conscript. Most of the Quds Force are. There is no career soldier who doesn't aspire to the higher ranks," he said carefully.

"Ah. The leader of the Guardians of the Revolution . . . I suppose that would be a worthy calling to have," Ahmadi said. "So we are both cementing Khomeini's revolution in our own ways. You fought the Americans in Iraq?"

"I did," Elham confirmed.

"You killed many?" Ahmadi asked.

"Not directly. I trained insurgents to make roadside bombs out of the artillery shells we supplied. My students were very effective in that regard. A few others were promising marksmen and I taught them to be snipers."

"Do you regret it? Not taking a more direct hand in the affair?"

"No," Elham said. On that point, he didn't care for diplomacy.

The Puerto Cabello Dockyard

Kyra finished packing the Leupold back in the truck, then secured her Glock and a pair of extra clips in the concealed carry pocket of her pack. She shoved the smartphone into one of the other pockets. A few other odds and ends consistent with her cover as a tourist hiker were scattered throughout the bag, but the gun alone ensured that no cover would stand up if she were searched.

She was not going to submit to a search. Kyra had faced down the SEBIN before. She knew she could outrun them, if nothing else, though that had been in a city. The Caracas traffic had given her more obstacles than the local security service could overcome. That was absent here. The terrain near the dock would be too open for an extended chase and running in sand would be a futile maneuver. She would have to stay hidden this time and pray that the dock was as empty as it had seemed through the scope.

She touched the earpiece. "I'm heading over. Everything still clear?"

"Lots of activity on the west side of the port, but nothing on the eastern end by the ship. The bird is showing a few guards by the gangplanks so I don't think you'll be getting aboard. And they can see the front of the warehouse, so you'll want to stay away from that side of the building. I guess everybody else has standing orders to stay away until further notice."

Kyra nodded automatically, a gesture she knew Jon couldn't see even as she made it. His report was both good news and bad. The light security by the ship would better her chances of getting in and out but almost certainly proved that whatever the Iranians had smuggled in aboard the *Markarid* was gone.

"Let's hope they stay there," she said. She pulled the pack over her shoulder, closed and locked the truck, then started the trudge around down the delta's shoreline toward the dockyard.

Autopista Valencia/Route 1

"I find that surprising," Ahmadi said, leaning back and adjusting his belt. The man's stomach reached over his belt, his belly surely as soft and white as a pillow under his shirt judging by the size. "To be so close to our greatest enemies with so many opportunities to kill them . . . and you have no regrets that you didn't get to shoot even one?"

"It's a poor soldier who lets killing become an indulgence and not a necessity."

"Shouldn't a man take joy in his work?" Ahmadi smiled. "Did you know that I was part of the '79 Revolution?"

"No."

Ahmadi stared at the passing fields, his memories becoming more real to him than the vehicle in which he was riding. "I was in the crowd outside the American embassy that day . . . the fourth of November. I had abandoned my graduate work at Oxford to come home and support Khomeini. The shah had fled our country and was dying in America. One of my friends was the first over the wall . . . brave one he was . . . would that it had been me. In that moment, I could see it all so clearly, what was about to happen. I knew we would overrun the building, taking prisoners and using them to bargain for the shah's return. I helped cut the chains off the gates and was one of the first inside."

"You helped take the hostages," Elham realized.

"Oh, I did more than that," Ahmadi admitted. "I lived at that embassy for the next year. I helped guard the Americans, I interrogated them. I pulled the trigger of a rifle in mock executions in the basement. The American staff there . . . they were such weaklings. A few refused to break, but the rest? Crying like women at a funeral before we even tied the blindfolds. More worried about their lives than what it would mean for their country if we succeeded in forcing Carter to deliver up the shah."

"You failed in that," Elham observed.

Ahmadi shrugged. "Allah took His justice before we could take ours. Who am I to complain when the great Judge of Heaven renders such judgment? I went down to the basement that night and watched another interrogation and wondered what good the Americans were to us then. It seemed so very unjust that such people should be a superpower."

"You still feel that way?" Elham said. The answer was obvious.

"I've come to see they can be cunning people," the civilian admitted. "They can be complicated people—at times capable of great feats and true bravery, at other times, so self-indulgent, so weak-minded. They have no single religion so they have no moral center, which makes them unpredictable. But always cunning when they need to be. That is the only reason to fear them."

"True enough, I suppose, though I think we're not that different," Elham said, surprised by his own candor. Ahmadi had enough connections at home to put an end to higher ambitions with a single remark.

"And how do you see them?"

"I've found the Americans to be . . ." He paused for a moment, picked the word carefully. ". . . determined," he finished.

The Puerto Cabello Dockyard

The satellite image showed a dirt trail running through the woods from the south side of the storage field below the paved road to the southern end of the dockyard warehouses. Kyra found it without trouble and marched across packed dirt in the dark for almost an hour, staying close to the tree line so she could disappear into the shadows if anyone approached. It was almost midnight now and the waxing moon was her only light. It was enough for most of the walk. Her night vision was undisturbed until she approached the dockyard, where some of the large lamps finally grew bright enough to interfere.

Kyra reached the edge of the paved yard. Another fuel storage depot was off to her right, large white towers that reflected the moonlight and brightened the open space. A large warehouse sat directly in front of her five hundred feet to the west. The *Markarid*'s berth and warehouse were northwest of her position with a fence running between the two mammoth storage buildings.

She pulled a night-vision monocle from her satchel and scanned the yard. She saw nothing, then touched her earpiece. "I'm here. You sure I'm alone?"

"Still three guards by the gangplank, but that's a hundred yards from the warehouse. Anyone else there is inside a building with a heavy roof," Jon replied.

Kyra nodded, then calmed her breathing. There

was no cover story she could offer that would explain her presence away once she entered the dockyard. The Glock and a hard run would be the only things between her and prison.

That's more than I had last time, she reminded herself.

She ran north along the trees for almost a hundred feet, then west, skirting the edge of the fuel storage depot. She had to skirt a smaller building, some kind of office, she guessed, but the lights were off. She reached the fence. It wasn't topped with barbed or razor wire. The longshoremen had erected it for organization, not security. Kyra ran parallel to the barrier until she reached another darkened shed. She mounted the building quietly, then went over the fence and landed in a crouch.

"I'm over."

"I see you," Jon said in her ear.

"I'm going to try the warehouse. I'll see if I can get a look at the dock from inside. If there's nothing there worth our trouble, I'll pull back."

"Roger that."

Kyra crept along the building's metal wall, occasionally stepping around stacked wooden pallets and forklift tires. The warehouse itself was at least five hundred feet long, two hundred feet wide, easily bigger than a soccer field. The main doors on the east side were chained shut, which didn't surprise her. She hadn't expected her luck to be that good. She moved around the perimeter, stopping to listen and testing every door until she found an unsecured window. She slid it open a foot, then squeezed herself inside.

Autopista Valencia/Route 1

"You respect the Americans?" Ahmadi asked.

"I have no particular feelings toward them, hate or admiration," Elham confessed. "I'm just a soldier and I want my country to prosper. If the Americans stand in the way of that, I will do my part to remove them from the road. That is the definition of duty. An American general once said that a man can do no more but should aspire to do no less. But where does the road lead that our leaders have chosen for us to travel?"

"You surprise me again. I was not aware that soldiers were ever philosophers," Ahmadi mused.

"Soldiers spend a lot of time thinking about the causes for which they're asked to die."

"You question our leaders?" Ahmadi asked.

Elham considered his answer, but only for a few seconds, lest Ahmadi get the wrong idea. "Leaders are just men and even the best are fallible. Even when Allah speaks, we are sometimes slow to hear or we misunderstand the divine message. So I obey my orders, but not out of any particular loyalty to any particular leader or even all of them together. I simply trust that our country has Allah's favor and He will make everything right. If our leaders do their jobs well, they push forward His work. If they do their jobs poorly, Allah's will rolls forth anyway, perhaps just a bit more slowly. My calling is just to do my part."

"Sargord, you are a diplomat after all."

The Puerto Cabello Dockyard

The warehouse was completely dark inside. Kyra had to scan the space with the night-vision monocle to get her bearings. She listened for voices or movement, heard nothing, and then started to move. The building was also mostly empty of cargo, which surprised her. There were open shelves in the back, storage bins for hand tools, compressors, gas cans, and other equipment. More stacks of pallets were scattered randomly around, the occasional chair and card table set together where some longshoremen took their lunch or played cards. It was her father's garage on a massive scale. The dust kicked up by her boots was visible in the green light of the night-vision camera.

"Still with me?" she whispered.

"Yes, but your signal isn't great," Jon advised.

"I'm in the warehouse . . . metal roof."

She padded forward as quietly as her boots would allow. The massive space had pieces of equipment here and there, scattered around in no organized way she could identify. One green cargo container, covered in streaks of rust red, sat near the main doors to the west. A forklift was parked a dozen feet away, its metal tines lowered to the ground. Kyra looked around again, the monocle turning the warehouse interior a sickly olive color. She closed her eyes and listened hard again for almost a minute, but heard nothing.

She made her way to the front and approached the metal box. "Only one container in here," she reported. "Don't know if they unloaded this one from the ship."

"That's strange. Port warehouses are usually full. They might be reserving that one for special cargo," Jon said. "Can you get the box open?"

Kyra pulled out a Maglite from her bag and clicked it on, the red light helping to preserve what little night vision she had. She played over the container. She approached the door . . .

Then it hit her, a horrendous odor, stronger than the smell of diesel fuel and oil, rolling out of the box into the warehouse. It was possibly the worst thing she had ever smelled. It staggered her and she wondered why the owners had bothered locking the enormous metal crate. No one in their right mind would open it out of pure curiosity. She couldn't remember ever having inhaled anything so evil and her stomach heaved, almost out of control. Kyra clenched her jaw shut, forcing the bile back down.

"The smell—" She was breathing through her mouth. Even so, Kyra could *feel* the odor in her throat. *This is the mission,* she told herself, but her stomach took no comfort in the thought.

"Can you open it?" Jon asked.

A padlock sealed the container door. "I think so . . . give me minute." She knelt on the floor, opened her bag, and rifled through it. She pulled out a steel sheet, the size of a credit card, with lockpick tools laser cut into it. She popped out the two pieces she needed, tucked the card into her thigh pocket and set to work, inserting the torsion wrench into the padlock, then the half-diamond pick. Opening locks wasn't her specialty and it took her two minutes and far more silent profanities to get the lock open. Done, she put the tools back in her shirt pocket, pulled the handle, and swung the door open.

U.S. Embassy
Caracas, Venezuela

"What is it?" Marisa said. She leaned over Jon's shoulder to see the monitor. He didn't flinch.

The station chief stared at the screen until Kyra's flashlight played over the contents.

The Puerto Cabello Dockyard

The metal box trapped the light, magnified it. The container only held two cargoes.

In the back, shapeless black bags, stacked in no orderly way, each one roughly the size of a man—*No,* Kyra realized. *Exactly the size of a man.*

In the front, men, a dozen, still alive. They were curled up on the metal floor, covered in their own bile and excretions. The sight caused Kyra's stomach to heave again, harder this time, and she barely held it down.

She forced herself not to stumble backward. "Jon?" she asked, using his name and breaking communications protocol. "You seeing this?"

One of the men reached up at her with a shaking hand. *"Ayúdame,"* he begged weakly in Spanish.

Help me.

U.S. Embassy, Caracas, Venezuela

"Yes," Jon said simply.

Marisa looked at him, surprised. There was a gentleness in his voice she'd hadn't heard for years. She'd never known him to show sympathy often.

"How many?" he asked.

The Puerto Cabello Dockyard

Kyra didn't want to open her mouth to answer. "Eleven body bags, I think," she spit out as quickly as she could. "Twelve men in the front. They're still alive and they're not Africans. I'm pretty sure they're Venezuelans . . .

the accent is right." More of the men had raised their arms to her, some pleading, others too weak to even say a word.

"Eleven . . . counting the one the Navy pulled out of the Gulf, that's a good ballpark number for a pirate team," Jon said.

"We have to help these men," Kyra said. She knew the answer.

"Arrowhead, this is Quiver," Marisa announced, touching her own headset microphone. "There's nothing you can do for them."

"I can't just leave them like this—"

"Arrowhead, you have no way to move them out. Even if you could help them back to your vehicle, somebody is going to come back for that container," Marisa said, trying to be patient. "If they open it and find any of those men missing, they'll know somebody was there. I know this feels wrong, but if you want to help anyone, all you can do is get the intel. You have to get what you came for and get out. That's the only way you can help anyone."

I know. Kyra refused to say it.

"I hate to ask this, but you need to open one up in the back and get some footage," Marisa said.

"Are you serious?" Kyra asked. It was as close to begging as she'd ever come.

"We need confirmation," she said.

Kyra muttered a curse too low for the smartphone to record. She entered the container, her sense of smell objecting, almost violently, and she stepped over the grasping Venezuelan men. She knelt down before the closest bag.

"Arrowhead?" Marisa called out.

"Yes?" she gasped, trying not to breathe.

"When you open it, don't puke. Whatever you've got to do, you hold it down."

"I can't promise that," she said, gasping for air. The smell alone convinced her that she wouldn't be able to hold down her dinner when she pulled the zipper. Whatever she found inside—

"If you puke, they'll know you were there," Jon advised.

"I doubt that." She'd felt the men's bile pulling on her boots. But Jon was being logical again. *And here I thought you were actually worried about me. So much for sympathy.* "Do my best." She put her flashlight in her teeth and tried not to inhale. She aimed the smartphone with one hand and reached for the cadaver bag with the other.

U.S. Embassy
Caracas, Venezuela

Jon and Marisa watched Kyra's hand grasp the zipper as the Venezuelan men groaned and pleaded in the background. She tugged, the zipper caught for a moment, and Kyra had to wrestle it for leverage with one hand. It finally came, sliding open fast, and the corpse inside was exposed to the light.

For a half second, they saw it—an African male, his head massively bloated from the gases of decomposition trapped under his skin and open blisters covering his face and lips. His hair was patchy, bald in spots, with sores on the scalp where the follicles were absent. They couldn't tell his age for the swelling—

The smartphone and flashlight swung away from the corpse in opposite directions, the picture went dark and they heard Kyra heaving, trying desperately to keep her jaws clenched shut. The young woman needed almost a full minute to control herself, and they heard her trying to suck in air.

The smartphone and flashlight swung back onto the corpse and Kyra held the picture for a full five seconds. "That enough?" she pleaded.

"Jon, hostiles inbound," Marisa said. She pointed at the IMINT feed on the wall monitor. A pair of vehicles had passed through the gates to the dockyard and were approaching the warehouse.

"Yeah, that's enough," Jon said. "You'll have company in one minute. We can get stills from the video. Close everything up."

The Puerto Cabello Dockyard

Kyra nodded and did as she was ordered. She stepped over the men until she stood outside the container door and tried to breathe fresh air in through her nose. It didn't help. The odor was trapped in her sinuses now and she wondered if she would ever get it out. She turned back and looked down at the men, still reaching up to her but too weak to move otherwise, even to drag themselves out of the box. Tears began to flood out of her eyes. "¡Lo siento!" she said, her voice breaking. *I'm sorry.*

She finally got fresh air into her lungs and her mind finally focused in that moment. She began scanning the warehouse, desperately searching for any way to help the men still crying out, but there was nothing. Whoever was approaching was coming for them and she wondered if God Himself would forgive her for what she had to do next.

She heard a sound . . . a motor, a heavy one rising as it approached the building.

"Lo siento," she cried again, quiet, then she grabbed the container door.

"¡Señorita, no! ¡Ayúdanos, por Dios!" one of them men pleaded weakly. *By God, help us!*

With her conscience yelling at her louder than the men, Kyra closed the door and threw the handle, cutting off their pleadings. The tears were flowing now, falling in the dust on the floor. She sobbed, her chest heaving, and she moved like a machine, refusing to listen to her emotions. She set the padlock, then twisted the head on her Maglite, killing the light, and the space went dark for a few seconds—

—and then she could see again. A moving light streamed under the warehouse door, then stopped as whatever truck had approached came to a stop outside.

Kyra ran for the rear of the warehouse, moving through the shelving and equipment scattered about the back.

Metal struck metal at the warehouse front and one of the sliding cargo doors began to open. Kyra judged the distance to the window and knew she wouldn't make it through and out before the men entered the warehouse, the lights from whatever vehicle they had filling the space.

She looked back to the door. If the truck was *there*—

She turned, ran, and slid down behind a pallet stack near the back that sat at an angle to the truck lights and the cargo container. It wasn't a solid barrier, but the wooden frames would break up her outline and any shadow she would cast behind. The cargo container sat an angle to her . . . she could still see the container door. She set the smartphone against the bottom of the stack, as close to it as she could, aiming the camera to the front, and darkened the screen.

The door slammed open and the full lights of a five-ton cargo truck flooded into the building, lighting up everything to the back wall. The only dark space for fifty yards in any direction was found in the shadows cast by the cargo container, the pallets, and the forklift.

Buried in shadow, Kyra pulled open the concealed carry pocket on her bag and pulled out her Glock. She wiped her face with her gun hand, trying to clear her eyes and she clenched her teeth, forcing herself to stop crying.

U.S. Embassy
Caracas, Venezuela

"Stay down," Marisa muttered. She and Jon stared at the screen, the image transmitted by Kyra's phone still coming through, steadier now because it was resting on the floor.

Jon said nothing. Kyra didn't need the distraction.

The Puerto Cabello Dockyard

The men entered the building, talking in Spanish phrases. She saw three . . . four . . . five . . . realized there would be more outside. Several carried assault rifles. *Soldiers.* She looked through the pallet stack, trying to identify uniforms but saw only dark silhouettes cut out of the truck lights.

They approached the cargo container and the closest man opened the door. *"¡Madre de Dios, qué olor!"* *Mother of God, that smell!*

Most of the other men recoiled, muttering in agreement, covering their faces with their hands or collars to no good effect.

Three men approached and the gaggle of soldiers parted to let them have a clear view. Two of the men weren't dressed for the occasion. Both wore suits, European cut. The man on the left was medium height and kept a thin cigar clenched in his teeth. The man in the center was the shortest of the three, overweight, with a beard. The last man, farthest to the right, was dressed more casually, tactical pants and work shirt, but carried an assault rifle, a model Kyra couldn't identify.

The trio walked forward, staring inside the container.

"You see the problem," Elham said in Farsi. Carreño didn't speak the language and hated it when his visitors did, but Elham didn't care for the man or his frustrations.

"These are longshoremen?" Ahmadi asked.

"Yes, the crew that repaired the cargo breach and unloaded the body bags you see behind them," Elham replied. "Our hosts had intended to assign them other duties and then remove them one by one under less obvious circumstances. But they became sick too quickly and now they are too weak to assign any duty at all. If they're released, they might find their way to the hospitals, which would certainly cause a security breach. But having so many go missing at once will raise questions."

"I understand," Ahmadi said. Then he switched to Spanish as he turned to Carreño. "I don't understand your problem. The solution here seems obvious."

"I would prefer to try to give them some medical

treatment . . . ease their suffering. Some might recover. We can remove them to some location where they would present no danger—" Carreño told him.

"That cannot be allowed. Every man here is a possible security leak every minute they draw breath," Ahmadi replied.

"You would just execute them?"

"It's not the ideal answer to the problem, but the only one that I see. You can always call *el presidente* if you disagree."

Carreño shook his head. "No. I had hoped that we might avoid this but I will not bother *el presidente* with it."

"I think that is a wise choice, my friend." Ahmadi nodded and turned to the Iranian soldier at his right. "Sargord, please make sure the job is finished, then call me." Not waiting for an answer, he started walking back to the car. Carreño frowned then nodded to the soldiers milling around the container and followed Ahmadi out the door.

Kyra pulled herself quietly into a crouch, the Glock pressed against her forehead. The men argued, their words mostly incomprehensible to her. She was too far away to make out the discussion, part of it in Spanish, which she could understand, part of it not. The smartphone would record the noise. With luck, some tech from the Agency's Directorate of Science and Technology would be able to enhance the audio track and tease out the words.

The two men in suits finally walked back to the vehicle. One of the soldiers barked a command in Spanish. Two soldiers stepped up to the container and raised their rifles and pointed them into the box. She heard the men inside pleading and begging, their cries indistinct to her ears. *Please, no—*

U.S. Embassy
Caracas, Venezuela

"Oh, no," Marisa protested quietly. Jon said nothing. She grabbed his hand and squeezed. He squeezed back, surprising her.

The Puerto Cabello Dockyard

The guns chattered and the muzzle flashes lit up the warehouse like strobes. The gunfire echoed off the metal walls and Kyra could hear some of the rounds bouncing around the container. Small holes appeared and the truck headlights streamed through them. It lasted less than five seconds, the echoes a bit longer, then the warehouse was quiet again, the still air broken only by the sound of a car driving away on gravel.

The soldiers moved forward, slinging their rifles over their shoulders. Several laid out more body bags on the warehouse floor and they began to load the dead longshoremen inside. The minutes crawled by, too slow, and Kyra caught herself quietly praying, something she hadn't done for quite some time. The soldiers began hauling the bodies out to the truck, two men to a corpse. She heard grunts, curses, a thud as a body bag was dropped. The job went on for almost fifteen minutes more.

"*¡Terminado!*" someone exclaimed. "*¡Afuera, ya, antes de que me ahogué!*" *Finished! Outside, now, before I suffocate!* The Spanish resolved itself to English in Kyra's mind automatically.

The warehouse went dark again. The soldiers were moving for the door. The man in khakis carrying the bullpup rifle pulled his own phone out of his pocket. Kyra risked a quick look around the pallet and saw him for an instant before he passed behind the cargo container. She watched as he stopped, waiting for his call to connect. Finally he began to speak, and Kyra couldn't understand a word.

**U.S. Embassy
Caracas, Venezuela**

"What is that?" Marisa asked. She leaned in, trying to hear the soldier's foreign words through the tinny speaker of Jonathan's monitor.

Jon twisted his head, listening.

"That's not any language I know," Marisa finally said.

"It means 'the job is done,'" Jon said. "In Farsi."

The Puerto Cabello Dockyard

The cargo truck's engine started up as the last man walked out the door and closed it behind him. Kyra exhaled but didn't move until the light under the door finally swung away and she heard the truck rumble off in the distance. She put the Glock back in her satchel, then recovered her smartphone. She walked slowly to the front of the container. The soldiers had closed it but not locked it. She pulled the door open, then pointed her smartphone at the pools of blood covering the floor, shooting video for several seconds. Then she closed the door, touched her headset, and began to walk toward the rear of the building.

"Still with me?" she asked quietly.

"We're here," Marisa said through the speaker-phone. "You okay?"

"No," Kyra said. "They killed them all."

"We saw," Marisa said.

"Did you see that last guy? He was carrying an assault rifle . . . some kind of bullpup I've never seen before." She reached the window and climbed through, her boots quietly grinding gravel as she put her feet down outside. She closed the window as far as it would allow. Then she sank to her knees and sat in the gravel, her back against the wall.

U.S. Embassy
Caracas, Venezuela

Jon shrank Kyra's video feed to a small window and began typing furiously on the keyboard. "You've got access to Intelink?" he asked Marisa.

"Yeah," she assured him. "We weren't gutted *that* badly."

Jon grabbed the mouse and started clicking links, cursing the slow connection. He finally found the page he was looking for on the classified network. "Did his rifle look like this?" He clicked another button and shared his screen with Kyra's phone.

The Puerto Cabello Dockyard

She looked down at her phone and stared at the photograph. "I think so, yeah. What is that?"

"It's a KH-2002. They also call them Khaybars. It's a Chinese design, ripped off from the M-16, but they're made in Iran," Jon told her. "That guy was a member of the Revolutionary Guard . . . probably Quds Force."

Quds Force? Kyra thought. She looked down the road past the storage field and saw the taillights of the cargo truck in the distance, turning onto the paved road that led to Route 1. *The SEBIN were bad enough.* "Jon, he made a phone call when they finished up," she whispered.

U.S. Embassy
Caracas, Venezuela

"We're on that," Marisa told her. "Are you clear?"

"Looks like it," Kyra said. "They're already on the freeway, heading south. If they don't exit, they'll end up heading west."

"Noted," Marisa replied. She checked the wall monitor. "Overhead says you're clear back to the dirt trail. You go find someplace safe to hunker down for the night, and that doesn't mean the truck. Get back into town. Find a hotel. Check back in when you're there, then go to sleep and get some breakfast. I'll have new orders for you in the morning."

The Puerto Cabello Dockyard

"Yes, ma'am," Kyra said. "I don't think I'm going to sleep very much."

"Understood," Marisa replied after a short delay. "Do your best."

Kyra ended the call, then looked around. There was no movement, no sound. The silence around the complex had an edge to it now, like the dark was alive and watching. *An intelligence officer who was afraid of the dark was in the wrong business? Idiot,* she cursed herself. An intelligence officer who wasn't afraid of the dark was a fool.

She worked back to the fence, climbed the barrier, made her way back through the shadows by the storage field to the trail, and didn't relax at all when she entered the forest.

U.S. Embassy
Caracas, Venezuela

"In the old days, you and I would've had a betting pool on where they're going," Marisa announced, trying to lighten the tension.

"They're going to the CAVIM explosives factory in Morón," Jon announced. "I assume that you have a file on that somewhere."

Marisa said nothing for a good ten seconds. "You want to explain that conclusion?" she finally asked.

"Let's assume the man with the bullpup was Quds Force. That means we have an Iranian cargo ship docked at a Venezuelan port with Iranian special forces soldiers in the group. Therefore whatever they smuggled in was part of a joint operation between both countries," Jon replied. "Ever since Hugo Chávez and Mahmoud Ahmadinejad first allied back in 2001, both countries have been opening joint commercial operations all over Venezuela . . . almost twenty years now. A tractor factory in Ciudad Bolívar . . . a cement plant near Ciudad Guyana on the Orinoco River . . . lots of buildings. If any of them are cover facilities used for joint operations like this, whatever cargo they unloaded from the *Markarid* is probably headed for one of them. Now assume that to minimize the possibility of a security breach or accident, they had the *Markarid* dock at the port closest to the destination," he said. He rifled through a pile of papers, extracted one, and held it out to her. "This one at Morón is operated by the CAVIM, the *Compañía Anónima Venezolana de Industrias Militares,* the state Military Industries Company."

"Morón's only twenty minutes away," Marisa protested. "It's a straight shot west on Route 1. Those cargo trucks have a range of a couple hundred miles, fully gassed. No reason they couldn't be going south—"

"Where is the next closest joint facility?" Jon asked.

Marisa stepped out to her office and returned with a map. She unrolled it across the table behind Jon's desk. "An ammunition factory in Maracay. It's another CAVIM site, thirty miles southeast of the dock."

Jon searched through his stack and pulled out another paper. "There was a pair of very large explosions at two different locations at that factory in 2011," he said. Marisa took the paper and scanned it. "Some analysts suspect the fires were meant to cover up a weapons transfer to FARC terrorists in Colombia, but they put the factory on everyone's radar in any case. I doubt Avila would use it now for joint operation with the Iranians that he wanted to keep out of sight. After that, the next closest facility is a bicycle factory in Cojedes, two hundred kilometers southwest, which appears to actually *be* a bicycle factory," he told her. "But the explosives factory is another story. In 2007, Iran Air and Conviasa partnered to fly an air route from Caracas to Damascus to Tehran, but, funny enough, no private passengers could ever seem to buy a ticket on those flights and the passengers who did board in Caracas never passed through immigration or regular security. Once it hit the press, the air bridge shut down in 2010. But there was a report that CAVIM sent shipments to Tehran from the explosives plant aboard that flight, but everything went diplomatic pouch, so it wasn't subject to search."

Another long pause. "Is that what you were doing in here all afternoon?"

Jon shrugged. "I had three hours to kill after Kyra left. Figured I might as well get smart on these people. Heaven knows you don't have anyone else down here to go through this stuff." He smacked a pile of papers he'd stacked next to the computer.

"Yeah." Marisa was reluctant to agree, but there was no denying the truth. She smiled. "Back in Iraq, you always did clean out the Rangers and the Deltas with those betting pools of ours," she admitted. "I presume you'll be wanting satellite imagery of the factory in Morón?" she asked.

"That would be marvelous," Jon said.

"Heaven help *you* if you're wrong and we lose those trucks," the chief of station warned.

"We've already lost those trucks, unless there's a satellite overhead. So if they're at Morón, I'm going to look like a big freakin' hero."

"You'll deserve it," Marisa admitted. "Any idea who those two civilians were?"

Jon brought up the video, cued the soldiers' entrance into the warehouse, then began stepping through it frame by frame until he got a still frame with good lighting, the men's faces identifiable in the car lights.

"I know this one—" Marisa pointed at the man with the cigar. "That's Andrés Carreño, head of SEBIN." She took off her headset, patiently wrapped the cable around the muffs, then cursed and threw it across the room.

"Problem?" Jon asked.

"Kyra told you about that night she got shot?"

"Not in detail."

"Carreño was the double agent she was supposed to meet. He almost got her killed," Marisa told him.

"Does she know?" he asked.

"I asked her. She evaded the question but I don't think we can take the chance. If he's involved, she's done with this operation."

"Headquarters will override you," Jon said.

Marisa frowned and stared down at him. "Why?"

"Because I know who this one is." Jon pointed at one of the men on the screen, the shorter, fatter man of the trio. Marisa stepped forward, leaned in, and saw that Jon was pointing at the man who had given Carreño his orders. "And when the president finds out who that is, he's going to order us to stay on the target."

CIA Operations Center

Jacob Drescher pressed the F9 key on his keyboard, forcing his in-box to reload. The list of field cables didn't change and he fell back in the chair, trying not to sigh in frustration. The rest of the night shift did not need to hear his exasperation.

He looked out over the bullpen. All heads were down except for two officers standing by the coffee machine, reloading on caffeine and quiet gossip, and one heading into the annex room to wrestle with a photocopier. As a rule, Drescher preferred the quiet because that meant a quiet world beyond the fence at Langley. Tonight he knew better and the incongruity was quiet torture, but he refused to take it out on his people.

He looked at the clock. Barely a minute had passed. He pressed F9 anyway.

The list changed, a new entry at the top. *There we go.* Drescher double-clicked the cable and it filled the screen. He scrolled past the addresses and endless crypts and code words to the part that really mattered, and that bit he read in silence. Then he read it again.

This just turned into a bigger mission, he thought.

Director Cooke was at home but he doubted she was asleep. Drescher picked up the phone and dialed. "Madam Director, this is the Ops Center. Going 'secure voice.'" He pressed the button that encrypted the call.

DAY FOUR

Cooke stared at the iPad, disgust drawn across her face. "You've confirmed their identities?" she asked.

"I woke up some senior analysts in the wee hours. Once they got enough coffee in themselves, they called it," Drescher confirmed. "The White House is going to want to see this."

"I know," Cooke said, resigned. She looked up and Drescher watched her stare at the ceiling. "Call the Multimedia Production Group," she said. "I need one of their video specialists for an hour."

The Oval Office
The White House
Washington, D.C.

AHMADI, Hossein;
DOB 09 Jun 1960
(Individual) [NPWMD]; list of affiliated
organizations follows:

*ADVANCED INFORMATION AND COMMU-
NICATION TECHNOLOGY CENTER*

(aka AICTC), No. 5, Golestan Alley, Shahid
Ghasemi St., Sharif University of Technology,
Tehran, Iran;
Website www.aictc.ir [NPWMD].

MINISTRY OF DEFENSE LOGISTICS EXPORT

(aka MINISTRY OF DEFENSE LEGION EXPORT; aka MODLEX), PO Box 16315-189, Tehran, Iran, located on the west side of Dabestan Street, Abbas Abad District, Tehran, Iran; PO Box 19315-189, Pasdaran Street, South Noubonyand Square, Tehran, Iran [NPWMD].

PENTANE CHEMISTRY INDUSTRIES

(aka PENTANE CHEMISTRY; aka PENTANE CHEMISTRY INDUSTRIES COMPANY; aka PENTANE CHEMISTRY INDUSTRY COMPANY; aka "PCI"), 5th Floor, No. 192, Darya and Paknejad Blvd, Cross Section, Shahrak Gharb, Tehran, Iran [NPWMD].

JOINT IRAN-VENEZUELA BANK

(aka BANK MOSHTAREK-E IRAN VENEZUELA) Ahmad Ghasir St. (Bokharest), Corner of 15th St., Tose Tower, No.44-46, Tehran 1013830711, Iran [IRAN].

MALEK ASHTAR UNIVERSITY OF TECHNOLOGY

(aka DANESHGAH-E SANA'TI-YE MALEK-E ASHTAR)
Shahid Baba'i Highway, Lavizan, Tehran, Iran . . .

It was a long list.

"We have high confidence that the subject in that video is Hossein Ahmadi," Cooke said. "He's Iran's version of AQ Khan. He's currently in charge of the Iranian nuclear program and answers directly to the Iranian president . . . maybe to the supreme leader, but we're not sure. The Iranian government has always been fairly opaque. But we do know that Ahmadi is the most serious nuclear proliferator in the world at the moment. He's not in Khan's league, but he still sells technology and nuclear fuel to lots of people we don't like." She set the iPad on the coffee table in front of the president. The video was frozen on the picture of the Iranian.

Rostow picked up the tablet and replayed the video. She could tell the precise moment he saw the SEBIN soldiers shoot their rifles into the cargo container. Rostow clenched his teeth and his eyes narrowed. "Do you think he's shipping weapons of mass destruction to Avila?" The president of the United States had too little worry and too much relish in his voice for Kathy Cooke's taste.

"We have no evidence of that, sir," she corrected him. "One of our officers confirmed that the vessel was, in fact, the *Markarid*. She penetrated the warehouse in Puerto Cabello at great personal risk, where she collected the intel on Somali pirates that you saw and determined that Ahmadi and Andrés Carreño were on-site. Carreño even appears to be deferring to Ahmadi, which I'm fairly sure wouldn't happen without President Avila's explicit consent."

"Those Venezuelans they executed . . . we don't know why they were sick?" He'd watched the video four times. The sight of the Somali pirate in the bag had almost cost him the eggs Benedict the Navy stewards had delivered to the Oval Office that morning.

"No, sir," the CIA director confirmed. "Our Office of Medical Services examined the video but couldn't determine a cause for their condition."

"Exposure to nuclear materials?" Gerry Feldman asked. The national security adviser flipped through the other pages on his own tablet. "Any chance the ship was smuggling chemical weapons? Or that the group just got food poisoning?"

"Ahmadi hasn't been known to traffic in chemical weapons," the director of national intelligence advised. Cyrus Marshall had stayed silent, as was his habit, letting his subordinate take the lead and offering his own comments at the moments they would have the most influence. "Every intel report we have on him says that he deals in nuclear technology and materials. Any chemicals that he smuggles are related to the nuclear fuel cycle. But if he is moving chemical weapons, then he's branching out into new markets and that wouldn't make me any less worried. And I doubt the Venezuelans would let Iranians shoot their own citizens over a case of food poisoning."

"So these dockworkers"—Rostow tapped the iPad—"weren't puking because of bad food. They were tossing up breakfast because they'd been exposed to something nasty, maybe even a significant radiation source. And these soldiers"—another tap on the iPad—"killed them and disposed of the bodies because they were *evidence*."

"That seems likely, sir," Cooke confirmed.

"And the Venezuelans didn't have a problem with

Ahmadi ordering them to shoot their fellow citizens on the spot?" Rostow asked, incredulous.

"It seems that Carreño did, though he didn't argue the issue very hard," Cooke said. "The audio we were able to extract was faint, so the transcript isn't complete, but what we did get suggests that Ahmadi overrode him."

"Hossein Ahmadi is no small-time operator, Mr. President. Ahmadi wouldn't come to Venezuela for some shipment of guns or even minor nuclear tech. He could delegate that to somebody else," Marshall said, not looking up from the computer on his lap. "If he's down there, wielding that kind of influence, then President Avila is serious about either putting together his own nuclear program or becoming a supplier to Ahmadi. The Venezuelans are sitting on top of huge reserves of uranium in the Roraima Basin and they were giving the Iranians mining access as far back as '09."

"Could they be putting together a program just to build some reactors for power?" Rostow asked.

"Hugo Chávez announced back in 2010 that his government was taking the first steps toward building a 'peaceful nuclear program,' as he called it," Cooke admitted. "They'd signed an agreement with the Iranians two years prior to cooperate on developing nuclear technology. But both countries are signatories to the Non-Proliferation Treaty and shooting dockworkers doesn't inspire confidence that they're trying to comply." She shifted on the couch and set her tablet back on the low table that sat between her and Rostow.

"And your people didn't pick up on Ahmadi making any visits down there before?" Rostow asked her.

"Unfortunately, sir, our entire operation in Venezuela was gutted eighteen months ago by the former chief of station."

"That was the Michael Rhead fiasco?" Rostow asked.

"Yes, sir," Cooke confirmed. "We were able to convince President Stuart to remove him, but not before he'd exposed several of our people to the SEBIN. As a precaution, we had to transfer most of our people out of country and start a review of every asset we had. We didn't know which Venezuelan assets we could trust. We've been rebuilding but we can't just replace the entire case-officer corps en masse and it'll take years before we can rebuild our asset networks. Until that happens, our coverage down there will be spotty at best."

"I understand, but your people caught this and that was no small feat given what you're working with," Rostow said. The man sounded sympathetic and Cooke started to wonder whether she hadn't misjudged him. "Your team is still on-site?"

"Yes, sir."

"Kathy . . ." he started, then paused for dramatic effect, she thought. "Do your people know where the *Markarid* cargo is now?"

"No, sir, not for certain. We have a possible lead but we need time to run it to ground. We suspect it could be somewhere at the CAVIM ordnance factory in Morón."

"If that's correct, I take it you'd agree that we need to know what Ahmadi has shipped to that facility?"

Cooke carefully parsed the words and looked for hidden meanings. She found none. Still she spoke with caution. "If we can confirm that's the destination, it should be a priority target, sir," she concurred.

Rostow nodded, smiling. "Your officer is still in the field?"

"Yes, sir. We're going to task her to conduct surveillance—"

"I don't think surveillance will cut it," Rostow said. "Ahmadi isn't going to leave that cargo sitting out in the open for every satellite in orbit to see. We need somebody to get inside that facility."

Cooke froze, alarmed. "Sir, we have very little intel on the CAVIM facility beyond just the general lay-out and none on the interior of any buildings on-site. Trying to send a team in blind would be exceptionally dangerous. There would be a very high probability of failure."

"How much time would you need?" Feldman asked.

Cooke turned to the national security adviser. *You should tell him that this isn't a smart idea,* she thought, and then had to suppress a tiny smile. *I sound like Jon.* "Months, at least. A year would be better."

"Months?" Rostow asked, clearly not liking the an-swer. "Kathy, we don't have months. If the cargo is there, Ahmadi could move it at any time."

"Sir, that one officer is the only field officer we have in-country. We don't even have a Global Response unit that could pull her out if she got in trouble. We have no insiders to feed us intelligence on security, floor plans, nothing. Even under optimal conditions, an operation like this takes—"

"I don't want to hear months, Kathy. I don't even want to hear weeks. Ahmadi could be on a plane out of the country tonight. We need to know what's inside that facility and we need to tie Ahmadi to it."

"I understand, Mr. President, but—" Kathy started.

"No 'buts,'" Rostow interrupted. "I've read the CIA

mission statement. 'We go where others cannot go, we do what others cannot do.' It's time to live up to that. I know it's dangerous, but I need your people to find a way in there. If the Iranians are moving nuclear material or weapons of mass destruction into this hemisphere, we need to know now and we need to stop them."

There it is, Cooke realized. *He wants his own "thirteen days in October."*

"Gerry, amend the presidential finding," Rostow said, ending the discussion. "The CIA has forty-eight hours to determine whether the *Markarid* cargo is inside the CAVIM facility. No 'best guesses' or 'high-confidence' estimates. I want some confirmation with hard evidence and I don't care how you get it."

"Sir," Marshall protested, finally intervening. "That's not real—"

"Cy, we're talking about possible weapons of mass destruction here. I'm not going to put the national security of the United States at risk because CIA wants to be cautious. The debate is over. Kathy, if you can't get behind this, you can resign."

And there's the trap, she thought.

Cooke considered the options, then made her choice.

She balled her fists and put them on the couch to push herself up. "Mr. President—" she began.

Marshall put his hand gently on her knee, stopping her from getting up. "We'll get it done, Mr. President," he assured Rostow, cutting her off.

Rostow turned his head and stared at the DNI with a poker face that Cooke was sure he used to mask frustration. Then the president smiled at her and Marshall and nodded, cool. "Thanks for coming. I want daily reports from you personally on this until further notice," he ordered.

"Yes, sir," the DNI replied.

The Oval Office door closed behind them and Cooke and Marshall started for the West Wing entrance, brushing people aside as they marched through the building. Cooke refrained from cursing the president only because she was moving through hostile territory and anything she said would be reported.

They reached the West Executive Avenue entrance and Marshall pulled the foyer door shut behind him.

"What was that?" Cooke demanded before the door clicked.

"You're not going to fall on your sword on this one," Marshall told her. "I'm from Oregon so I got to follow Rostow up close when he was governor back home. This is what he does when he wants to clean out an agency. He gives them an impossible tasking for reasons that will sound good to the public, and if they refuse, he fires everyone who protests and replaces them with his people. If they try but fail, he fires them for incompetence and does the same thing." Marshall stopped talking to catch a breath, then leaned against the wall. "Kathy, as long as you're at Langley, you can act. This president thinks CIA is responsible for half the evil in the world, so if you quit, he'll have a clear path to putting in a hit man who'll pull out the long knives and gut the place. It'll take the Agency twenty years to recover. It'll be like '76 when Jimmy Carter put in Stansfield Turner."

Cooke nodded and slumped. "He fired eight hundred field officers in one night. They called it the 'Halloween massacre.'"

"And Rostow wouldn't bat an eye if it happened again," Marshall replied, agreeing with her sentiment. "But they like you on the Hill. If you're holding the office and acting in the best interests of the country, he can't just dump you without drawing political fire. So, can you get a team down there?"

"Even if I could, they wouldn't be any better prepared to penetrate the factory than the one person already on-site," Cooke replied. "One person, a dozen, it doesn't matter, they're all likely to get captured or killed."

"Get back to Langley and work on the problem. I'll help any way I can."

"Thanks." She pushed open the door and walked out to the parking lot.

Feldman closed the Oval Office door behind the CIA director and the DNI, then turned back toward the president and leaned against the wall. "I thought you had her."

"I *did* have her," Rostow groused. "Did you see her face? She was going to resign and Cy stopped her." The president threw himself back into his chair and gritted his teeth. "I've squeezed her for all the political capital she's worth. Earned me plenty of goodwill with Congress, especially the intel committees, and the feminists were ready to throw me a party. But we need a clean break from Harry Stuart . . . get our own man in her seat, someone who knows how to take orders." The president grabbed the iPad off the table and started the video playing again. "What do you think about this?" he asked, smacking the tablet.

"Yeah, that was some good porn," Feldman agreed. "If the Iranians are moving nuclear material down there, it would be the Cuban Missile Crisis all over again. Nobody's going to stand for the mullahs smuggling radioactive material over here. The world almost blew up the last time someone tried to move nukes into Latin America. Nobody wants a replay of that."

"We can't prove that's what they're doing."

"Maybe we don't need to," Feldman offered. "Saddam didn't have any WMD in '03, but he refused to play ball, so everyone assumed he did and the entire country lined behind George Bush for war. We just have to do the same thing here but we don't invade. The longer Avila holds out and refuses to play ball, the worse he looks."

Rostow heaved himself to his feet, wandered back to the Resolute desk and sat on it, dropping the iPad on top. He began swinging his legs as he thought, gently hitting the antique with his shoes on the backswing. "Avila wouldn't want a war with us. Castro at least had the Russians backing him and Krushchev had ICBMs and the whole Soviet Navy. The Iranians don't have a fraction of that firepower. They couldn't back up Avila even if they wanted to." Rostow smiled and hit the iPad with the flat of his hand. "It's perfect . . . all the political upside of the '62 crisis with none of the risk."

"And everyone on the Hill lines up behind you or they end up looking weak on national security." Feldman stared at the Oval Office ceiling, running the possibilities through his head. "You'd have to call Avila out in public," he said finally. "Demand that he give up the cargo and Ahmadi. You get both of those and your political capital would go through the roof. We'd be able to push Congress on everything, not just foreign policy. This could break the dam open, grease the skids for everything we want to do in the first term. And nobody will be able to touch you on the national security issue during the reelection campaign," Feldman said. He slapped the table with his hands like it was a drum.

"But we'd need some real proof if we're going to force Avila's hand," Rostow said. "Kennedy had pictures of the actual missiles and Adlai Stevenson used them to pin Krushchev's boy to the wall in the UN Security Council. Zorin couldn't wriggle out of it . . . 'Don't wait for the translation, yes or no' and all that."

Feldman thought for a minute, then shook his head. "Forget it, it's a pipe dream. Cooke's people will never get into that factory. But you've still got proof that Ahmadi is down there and video footage of him at the site when they executed those workers. That's juicy stuff."

"And maybe we get him to cough up Ahmadi to save his own hide. We take down the 'next AQ Khan.' They'd be showing that on the History Channel for the next ten years," Rostow said.

"Yeah," Feldman agreed. "But that video's classified, so we can't just release it to the press corps."

"How do you want to handle it?"

"You don't need to know," Feldman advised. "I'll take care of it."

The George Washington Parkway was the most beautiful drive in the District and Cooke watched the scene without seeing as it passed to her right. Getting lost in thought was one of the luxuries that having a driver afforded her. In her younger days, she'd spent hours at a time in Moscow watching for surveillance, which amounted to looking in the rearview mirror more than at the road ahead while memorizing license plates. It had made her wish that she'd been there during the Cold War when fewer Muscovites had owned cars. After the Soviet Union had fallen, the number of cars on the Moscow roads had climbed steadily, making life tougher for U.S. intelligence officers trying to ply their trade. She'd been skilled at surveillance detection years ago but it was one skill that she had allowed to atrophy with no regrets.

Cooke lifted the handset to the portable STU-3 mounted between the front seats. She dialed and encrypted the call. "It's Cooke," she said without preamble. "I'm ten minutes out. The president has given us forty-eight hours to figure out whether the *Markarid* cargo is at the CAVIM factory."

"Well, that's unfortunate." Drescher's sense of humor was dry for Cooke's taste but it seemed to fit the situation now.

"I want a task force on this . . . all of the directorates at the table, and I want you to run it. The first meeting is in twenty minutes, my conference room."

"Roger that. See you soon." Of all his traits, Cooke liked most that Drescher knew when a conversation was finished.

"Thanks." She hung up the phone.

Palacio de Miraflores
Caracas, Venezuela

The Miraflores Palace had begun its long life as the family residence of Joaquín Crespo, one of Venzuela's past presidents who knew not Bolívar, or so Diego Avila thought the Bible might have phrased it. Crespo was a warlord, a member of a corrupt elite who had either forgotten or ignored Bolívar's legacy and tried to extend his betrayal by installing an ally in the president's office as his successor through a fixed election. The masses had rebelled, Crespo had moved to put down their uprisings, and some righteous mobber had used a rifle to put an end to his perfidy and his life at the town of Cojedes.

A righteous end for an oppressor, Avila thought, *but the man knew how to build a house.* It was a shame that it was only the president's official workplace and not his residence, but Avila would not break the traditions that Chávez had laid down. The edifice was a piece of exceptional workmanship, white brick, red-tiled roofs, immaculate, with a Japanese garden. The neoclassical building stood out in the surrounding sea of gray apartment buildings that looked like they belonged in old Soviet Moscow. Avila had been a carpenter before Chávez's revolution, which skill let him appreciate the expert work of the palace builders. It was the finest house he would ever work in, though the fortune he was amassing in office would provide him an excellent residence in which to retire in Ciudad Bolívar, the home of his youth. But that was years away and he had no plans to leave Miraflores despite what his political opponents were promising their followers about the next election. Venezuela belonged to the Chavistas, now and forever. They would not allow the moneyed elites to take control again and bring their corruption back. The revolution was eternal.

Avila strode across the courtyard, pausing to light a small cigarillo, a cheap brand that he'd favored since his teenage years and had never found wanting, though his other tastes had matured since his youth.

Lunch today would be *pabellón criollo* with shrimp and scallops and a bottle of Pessac-Léognan, all waiting for him in the Boyacá room.

And it would wait longer still for him. A functionary ran up to him with a secure cell phone in hand, holding it out. Avila took it, stared at the screen, then held it to his face. "Andrés, *amigo mio,* what is the good news?"

"The dockyard has been *sanitized,*" Carreño told him, a bit of anger seeping through his voice. "The *Markarid* will sail as soon as our friend can arrange for his government to send another crew."

"That was unfortunate, but it's done now. All else proceeds as planned? No other security issues?"

"None," Carreño said.

"And there is still no sign that the Americans or some other intelligence service has been tipped to the operation?"

"None," Carreño said. "After their station was gutted last year, I don't think they're in any position to give us such trouble."

More good news. This conversation might have a good end after all, Avila told himself. "And I presume the American embassy is being watched?"

"As always."

"Good," Avila said, finally satisfied. "Where are those unfortunates now?"

"At the CAVIM facility. They will be buried behind the tree line of the ordnance test field. I have given orders to have the job complete by morning."

"Good. That is good," Avila said. "Stay well, my friend." He disconnected the call, then dragged on the cigarillo and resumed his walk to lunch.

Posada Santa Margarita Hotel
Puerto Cabello
Carabobo, Venezuela
200 km west of Caracas

Kyra had no idea whether the hotel room cost more than the Agency per diem allowed and, for the moment, didn't care. The bed was soft, the room as modern as any hotel back in the States, and she hadn't slept on the plane. The adrenaline and caffeine pills had kept her going through the night but she'd faded as soon as she'd laid her head on the mattress.

Her smartphone sounded and Kyra slept through it. It sounded again, then a third time before the noise finally penetrated her dreams. She turned, half conscious, and managed to wrap her hand around the device.

Kyra looked at the clock on the wall opposite her bed: *1100 hours.* Still, she'd slept less than six hours and could've slept six more. But the Venezuelans had impressive coffee and she decided that she was going to find some before she went out to wherever Jon and Marisa wanted to send her next.

She deactivated the lock screen, then stared at the phone until her vision finally focused. She tapped the link embedded in the decrypted e-mail and a map appeared with a location indicator standing out in the center. She zoomed the map out and ordered the handheld computer to show her the route and distance. It was less than twenty minutes away, but the phone was assuming she would be driving the entire route. That wasn't going to happen. She spent ten minutes staring at the satellite view. The marked facility was surrounded by high hills and a dense forest that went for miles.

"You suck, Jon." She dropped the phone on the bed. She was at least going to do herself the courtesy of a shower and a decent lunch before marching off into the trees again.

"Do you think she took it well when she woke up?" Marisa asked.

"Doubtful," Jon replied.

"How do you know?"

"Not because I've ever been with her in the morning, if that's what you're suggesting," Jon said, a tinge of annoyance in his tone.

"So you always skipped out before she woke up?" Marisa teased. She suppressed a laugh when she saw the murderous look that crossed Jon's face. "C'mon, Jon, she's a pretty girl. You can't tell me you haven't thought about it."

"No, and not your business," he warned.

"Lighten up, Jon. You never could figure out when I was teasing you."

"I figured it out. I just didn't care for it," he said, his voice cold.

Marisa's smile died. She opened a file folder and laid the contents on his desk . . . satellite photos. "Maybe this'll make you happy."

"The CAVIM facility?" he asked, picking them up.

Marisa nodded. "They came in five minutes ago, about the same time you were sending your partner on a hike through the woods. And it gets better." She walked around behind him and leaned in close over his shoulder, pointing to a line of dark squares on one photograph. "Five-ton cargo trucks. Same type and number as the ones at the dock by the *Markarid*. There's no way to tell whether they're the same cargo trucks, but it's something."

"It's not *inconsistent*," Jon said. "Theories are difficult to prove but easy to disprove. Too many analysts get invested in their theories, so they latch on to the data that backs up their ideas and downplay or ignore the information that contradicts them . . . confirmation bias. That doesn't happen when they look for evidence that disproves the theory. And this"—he held up the photo—"doesn't disprove the theory."

"So what's the next step?"

"Gather more data," Jon said. "Analysts can never have too much data."

CAVIM Explosives Factory
Morón, Carabobo, Venezuela
220 km west of Caracas

The hike was well over a mile, closer to two, from the back road where Kyra had hidden the truck. The undergrowth there was thick, a double blessing. The weeds hadn't been run down, suggesting that no one had driven down that path in weeks at least, and the taller biomass had given her more than enough material to camouflage the truck, hiding it behind a woven wall of branches, leaves, and other greenery. Her vehicle would be unrecognizable to anyone passing by on the larger road a hundred yards east. She'd walked the distance and stared at her work to be sure. That task done, Kyra had entered the cab one last time and pulled out a panel in the floor. She extracted a Hechler & Koch HK416 and some extra magazines and sealed them up in the scabbard of a larger backpack, an Eberlestock, which held some Meals-Ready-to-Eat, an evasion map and compass, a survival blanket and medical kit, a change of clothes and other supplies. The Glock she hid in a holster in the small of her back under the tail of her khaki shirt. Then she loaded a Canon camera with a high-power telephoto lens, strapped on the pack, and started off to the west.

It took her over two hours to reach the hilltop, stopping every few hundred yards for a minute or two to listen and observe. She was a mile from the closest road and the sun was dropping fast now. There was no question she would be sheltering underneath the trees tonight. She couldn't have made it back to the truck before dark and didn't want to try. The pack wasn't overly heavy and she was in very good shape, but her legs burned anyway from the constant need to shift her balance on the uneven terrain. The HK and its ammunition added eight pounds to her load, but she didn't begrudge herself that. If there was a security patrol in these woods and she had to lose everything else to run, the rifle was staying with her. The camera and commo equipment were a different story.

Scouting around the summit, just below the brow, she found a small depression with a decent opening through the forest that promised a good view looking out and down. She took another hour to erect a cover over the dip and a shallow trench around it, giving her a low ceiling of branches and leaves over her head for the inevitable rain that would come if she had to stay long enough. Anyone in the valley looking up wouldn't see it, either with eyes or with optics.

The CAVIM factory was not a single building, but a string of small complexes spread out over a square mile. Each set of smaller buildings was connected to the rest by several roads that twisted through the forest. Jon had updated her map by the time she'd gotten out of the morning shower, marking a clutch of warehouses where the SEBIN had parked the cargo trucks. It was the largest assemblage in the area and the one closest to a chemical processing plant, its nature obvious even to her untrained eye. Her phone had a theodolite app and Kyra had put it to use, marking waypoints on the topographic map.

She imagined there had to be some kind of security cordon, certainly patrols, but how far out they would go, she didn't know. The map said that the hilltop she'd chosen would be just under a mile on foot from the target building if she had to work her way down the hillside, half that as the crow would fly, and it would be a steep climb. So she hoped that whatever security guards went out would find it too troublesome to climb to the summit.

The sun would be down in less than a half hour and she turned to the real business. She pulled out the Canon, affixed the telephoto lens, and set up her pack as a rest for it. Kyra laid herself prone and stared through the camera to get her first good look.

The convoy was there, unmoved since the satellite photo had been taken that morning. She couldn't see into the trucks but they were surely empty. The enemy, as she'd long since come to think of them, hadn't shipped the cargo this far just to leave it out in the open. She pressed the shutter and recorded the moment, then moved the camera and stared down at the factory, comparing the buildings to the imagery on her phone.

Kyra panned left, then froze as she saw movement.

By one of the warehouses, north of the trucks, a dozen men were milling around on the ground, some sitting, all carrying bullpup rifles like the one she had seen the night before. *Iranian Quds*. That was worth a call and sharing a bit of live video.

She pulled out her smartphone and unlocked the unit. The cell signal was surprisingly strong. *They have their own cell tower here?* That seemed likely and made her smartphone unsafe to use—if the SEBIN were here, they might detect an unexpected call routed through the tower.

For this, we have a solution. Kyra pulled the LST-5 satellite radio from her pack. It had added more than its fair share of the weight in her pack, almost nine pounds. It didn't seem that heavy, but one of her Farm instructors had once told her that anything gets heavy in the mountains . . . ounces equaled pounds and pounds equaled pain. The Agency had newer, lighter comms gear. This was an old model, not even classified tech anymore, War on Terror surplus. Kyra had seen one like it in the Agency museum, where any uncleared visitor could study it. She supposed that this was another case of the Clandestine Service trying to prevent any more technology from falling into the wrong hands while Caracas station was rebuilding.

Setting up the radio was simple, programming the crypto a bit harder. "This is Arrowhead."

"This is Quiver," Marisa replied, her voice distorted.

"I'm at checkpoint Apple."

"Roger that. Any trouble?"

"Trouble no. Something interesting, yes." Kyra connected the Canon to the data buffer, plugged it into the transceiver, turned on the camera's video feed, and the camera obediently began streaming its picture to the embassy.

U.S. Embassy
Caracas, Venezuela

"There are those rifles again," Marisa observed. "Quds Force. Congratulations."

Jon ignored the compliment. "Convoy, incoming," Kyra's voice announced. Somewhere more than a hundred miles away, the field officer moved the camera to the left and the picture shifted.

A trio of dark SUVs turned off the highway to the warehouse road. The darkened window by the driver of the lead car rolled down as it approached the line of soldiers holding out their hands, signaling it to stop. The guards held it at the cordon for less than a minute before scrambling to let it through and the vehicles all rolled slowly past smaller buildings before stopping in front of the chemical factory. The doors opened and more armed soldiers crawled out of the first and last cars. The driver of the middle SUV stepped out, then opened the rear door and held it for the passengers inside.

Three men climbed out, the first a bearded man in a European-cut suit as black as his beard, including the shirt and tie. Even at long range, through the scope Kyra could see the jowls hanging from his jaw and a paunch hanging over his belt. The man was no soldier, not even remotely fit enough for that job. This was a man who enjoyed his comforts. "There's Ahmadi," Marisa said. "That should get the president off Kathy Cooke's back."

"Good luck with that," Jon replied.

The second man was dressed down and unfamiliar,

tactical pants and boots, with a pistol holster strapped to a thigh rig on his right leg. The third man also wore a suit, this one not so bespoke as Ahmadi's. He put a Cohiba to his mouth and lit it off.

"Uh-oh," Marisa said quietly.

"What—?" Jon started.

"Jon—?" Kyra said over the transceiver, her voice rising. Jon could hear the woman nearly hyperventilating over the speaker.

"Problem?" he asked

"That's Andrés Carreño," Kyra's voice declared.

Marisa looked down at Jon and covered the handset microphone. "She knows."

CAVIM Explosives Factory

On the hilltop, Kyra couldn't take her eyes off the man in the valley below. "I saw his face, just for a second. He was standing on a metal bridge over the Guaire Canal and all the lights were out. He finished a cigar and I saw his face when he lit another one. It was him . . . matched the face in the file." Her voice quivered slightly and she clenched her teeth, hoping Jon hadn't picked it up.

U.S. Embassy
Caracas, Venezuela

Marisa reached down and covered the microphone on Jon's headset. "Keep her calm," she advised. "She needs to detach. There's nobody there to help her if she has a panic attack."

"She won't let that happen," Jon said. "She's been through worse."

"You sure?" the station chief asked.

"Yes."

CAVIM Explosives Factory

There was a long pause before Jon spoke again. "Did you ever hear what Churchill said about being under fire?"

"No," Kyra replied.

"'There is nothing more exhilarating than to be shot at without result.'"

"His boys put one in my arm. I say that was a result," Kyra noted. She was suddenly conscious of the scar running across her triceps, could feel its full length on her arm. She felt her hand starting to shake. She let go of the camera carefully, trying not to disturb it, rolled onto her back, and looked at the ceiling of her shelter, clenching her fists.

"He took his best shot at you and you got out," Jon reminded her. "Now he's the one in your scope and he doesn't even know it. Keep that in your head and he won't worry you so much."

"My rifle doesn't have that kind of range." Kyra let out a long breath.

"I'll bring you a bigger one," Jon said.

Kyra finally smiled, feeling some of the tension in her shoulders ease. That was as close as she'd ever heard him come to telling a joke. She rolled back onto her stomach and took control of the camera again. "Any idea who the other two are?" she asked.

"One of them is Hossein Ahmadi," Jon replied. "No idea about the guy with the pistol. But anyone with Ahmadi is worth some pictures."

"Already done," Kyra said. Headquarters would

have to enhance the lighting in the pictures but the screen shots would be more than good enough for some DI analyst to confirm identities.

Carreño smoked his cigar as he trailed behind the Iranians, the lit end giving Kyra something to follow in the growing dark. The trio walked through the front doors of the chemicals building and the guards closed the doors behind them.

"Quiver, Arrowhead," Kyra said, finally returning to protocol. "Did you get all of that?"

"Yeah, we got it," Jon said. He checked a live satellite feed of her position, saw her body appear on his screen as an orange blob lying prone. "Shut down for the night. We'll contact according to schedule with anything new. The birds overhead don't show anyone in your sector."

"No patrols?"

"Some, but they all seem to be down at the valley edge. Nothing at your altitude."

"Thanks. Catch you in the morning." Kyra switched off the transceiver and the phone went dead.

The dark had finally settled, the only lights now coming from the halogen lamps at the factory's fence, which cast hard shadows that reached out even to her shelter, a mile away. It was a strange relief. Every guard's night vision would be destroyed. No one would be able to see past the tree line in any direction and she was buried in the trees well enough that a roving patrol would have to practically step on her to find her. She was as safe as she could be until morning.

She crawled outside her blind, sucked in fresh night air, and stared up through the forest canopy at the stars. The facility lights blotted out the dimmer ones, but the Milky Way still stretched out across the sky above her. *Like home.* For a moment, she felt like she was in the Blue Ridge Mountain foothills, sitting on the bank of the James River on a warm April night.

The memory lasted only a second before her mind cut through. Home was a long way north and a mile below were men who would kill her without thinking twice.

Kyra crawled back into the shelter and laid her head down on her pack. It occurred to her that Jon hadn't actually told her to get some sleep. He was not the kindest man she'd ever known but he was not condescending, and for that, this one night, she was grateful. She knew sleep wouldn't come tonight. She closed her eyes anyway.

DAY FIVE

Feldman dropped prints of Kyra's photos on the Resolute desk. "There's your connection. Ahmadi is at the CAVIM site. Whatever he brought is in there."

Rostow didn't bother to pick up the pictures. He leaned over and gave them a cursory glance, then looked up. "I want pictures of the cargo, not more of the guy who brought it there."

"Not going to let Cooke off that easy?"

"Not a chance," Rostow replied.

CIA Director's Office

Drescher caught up with the CIA director as she stepped out of her office. "You talked to the White House?" he asked.

"I did," she confirmed. "The CAVIM photos bought us zero currency with them."

Drescher grimaced and stepped in behind her as they walked down the short, narrow hall to the conference room. "That's not unexpected, I guess."

Cooke nodded, pushed the door open to her conference room and stepped inside. It was full this time, every seat at the table taken except for her own. Two dozen computers were now mounted on the desk and around the walls, with cables snaking over the floor in secured bundles. Stacks of papers sat by each workstation with several legal boxes in the table's center.

Drescher took a seat by the door without being

asked, ready to drive the computer. "Good morning," Cooke announced to the room. A dozen quiet replies came back, repeating her words. "There is no time for pleasantries on this and I will not repeat myself or answer questions. Your office directors chose each of you here at my request to support an ongoing operation that has been ordered personally by the president. You are all senior officers. There's not a person in this room under a GS-14 who hasn't been on the job at least a decade, so this is possibly the most experienced team you will ever be part of during your career in this building. Until further notice, your office is either here or the Ops Center. The operation is compartmentalized, so you will either sign the paperwork in front of you in the next thirty seconds or you will leave this room and not return. Understood?"

Every man and woman in the room signed the papers. "Thank you," Cooke said. "Thirty-six hours ago, an agency officer operating out of Caracas station in Venezuela tracked an Iranian cargo ship to the Puerto Cabello dockyards. We don't know what cargo she was carrying, but our officer entered a warehouse in the dockyard and recorded the following video."

Drescher darkened the room and played the footage on the monitor on the front. The room remained silent except for a single quiet gasp when the soldiers fired into the container. Ahmadi's face appeared on the screen and Drescher froze the movie on that frame.

"That man, as some of you know, is Hossein Ahmadi. The officer who recorded this video tracked Dr. Ahmadi and, we hope, his cargo to the CAVIM explosives facility in Morón, twenty-two kilometers west of Puerto Cabello." Drescher advanced the presentation to an overhead satellite photo of the area. "At this moment, the officer is sitting on a nearby hilltop over-looking the facility, conducting surveillance," Cooke finished. "Lights."

The room brightened and all heads turned back toward the director. "Dr. Ahmadi is, as of this moment, the most serious nuclear proliferator in the world. You will find his bio in the file in front of you and all of the intelligence the Counterproliferation Center has ever accumulated on him and his network is now avail-able to you. Because of Ahmadi's known activities, the president is concerned that his cargo could be nuclear in nature. We believe it is inside the main chemical production facility at CAVIM. The president has given us thirty-six hours to determine what that cargo is."

This drew protests that she stifled with a look. "I understand your concerns and I sympathize. We have our orders and it's not your place to question them. It is your job to help us carry them out and determine how we can take Ahmadi off the board. So I want you to find a way to penetrate that building. I want the lay-out analyzed and the security system dissected. I want to know if there's a hole, a weakness, a malfunction-ing camera, a way to hack into the computers there, *anything*. I want you to review every Venezuelan asset Caracas station ever worked going back to the found-ing of this Agency to see if anyone still living might know a way in or if any past asset might work there now. If you find something, you are authorized to run, not walk, down that hallway to my office. My secretary has standing orders to admit you no matter what I'm doing or who I'm meeting with. Understood?"

Heads nodded. "I realize that this is an exception-ally difficult assignment," Cooke said, finally relenting from her hard line. "It might not even be possible, but we will not fail because we did not try. Thank you for your service. Get started."

Everyone rose and the legal boxes were open with papers coming out before her hand reached for the door.

U.S. Embassy
Caracas, Venezuela

1. POTUS COMMENDS STATION FOR ITS EFFORTS THUS FAR AND EXPRESSES HIS RELIEF THAT ARROWHEAD WAS NOT DETAINED BY HOST COUNTRY SECURITY SERVICES.

2. POTUS FURTHER COMMENDS STATION FOR IDENTIFYING SUBJECT AHMADI AND CONFIRMING THE POSSIBILITY OF ILLEGAL CARGO SHIPMENTS INTO VENEZUELA.

3. DUE TO THE IMPLICATIONS OF INTEL RECOVERED THUS FAR BY ARROWHEAD, POTUS ORDERS COS CARACAS TO DETERMINE THE NATURE OF THE MARKARID CARGO WITHIN FORTY-EIGHT HOURS. POTUS RECOGNIZES THAT WILL INVOLVE INCURSION INTO TARGET FACILITY BUT POSSIBLE DANGER POSED BY THE CARGO JUSTIFIES ANY RISK INHERENT. C/CIA HAS ESTABLISHED A TASK FORCE TO EVALUATE ALL OPTIONS . . .

"It *is* a direct order from the president of the United States," Marisa noted.

"It's a stupid order," Jon said. "Either he's a complete idiot, he thinks the Agency has some invisible ninjas, or he's intentionally setting us up to fail. None of those speaks well of him. The only way into that place would be for DoD to invade the facility and take it over."

"We've seen that happen before, haven't we?" she asked. "Arrowhead?"

"I'm here." Kyra's voice came through the table speaker, the encryption stripping it of its natural timbre.

"You're the one on-site. Opinion?"

CAVIM Explosives Factory

Kyra stared at the headquarters cable on her iPad screen in disbelief. *Forty-eight hours?* She looked at the time stamp—more than a quarter of the time was gone. *This is politics,* Kyra realized . . . but Cooke knew how to play political games. The young officer had seen that.

"He's right. It's stupid. I've been staring at the place all night," she continued. "There's no covert in-and-out into the main building. At a minimum we'd need an asset who could get us the security layout, if not just do the whole job for us with some tech ops support. I'm assuming we don't have that?"

"You assume correctly," Marisa confirmed.

"Then I've only got one other option," Kyra said.

"Explain," Marisa ordered. She looked down at Jon, who had straightened his back and was making no effort to hide his disbelief.

"Do you have an overhead of the site?" Kyra asked.

Jon brought one up on the wall monitor. "Roger that."

"Southwest corner, quarter mile east of the trucks, where the fence butts up against the open field," Kyra said.

The base was a mile long at its widest point and it took Jon several seconds to find and focus the image on the location and increase the magnification. "What about it?" Marisa asked.

CAVIM Explosives Factory

"There's no way into the actual building, but we're the Red Cell so I figured we should start looking outside the box. It took me two hours, but I noticed a pattern. Patrols run along the fence line north and south, but not to the west through the field. There's no human security there, no road, and I think I know why. Do you see it?" In her hidden blind, Kyra focused the telephoto lens on the camera at the field west of the fence.

U.S. Embassy
Caracas, Venezuela

Jon and Marisa stared at the field. It was enormous, brown and patchy with large round clumps of foliage missing from the high grass, like some large animal had scooped out handfuls of vegetation. "Oh, there is no way—" Jon started.

"I don't see it," Marisa admitted. She squinted at the screen, wondering whether there was some minute detail Jon had found—

"Arrowhead, there is no way you are going through that field," Jon ordered.

"Why not?" Marisa asked.

"Because it's an ammunition test range," Jon told her. "These"—he drew circles around the missing foliage with his finger—"are blast craters, probably mortar strikes judging from the size. And there's probably unexploded ordnance in there. That's why SEBIN doesn't patrol it. They don't want their own men blown up and those unexploded shells are security enough. It's like a minefield."

"I hate mortars," the chief of station said.

"Right there with you," Jon said. Marisa looked at him again, smiling. She was surprised to see him nod at her, a brief acknowledgment of that moment the decade before when they had come so close—

"I wouldn't have to traverse the full length of the field," Kyra advised. "See that camera on the southwest corner post?"

"Yeah," Marisa assured her.

"It's pointed into the tree line and hasn't moved all night. I don't know if it's jammed or just not built for it. But judging by the angle, I'd bet it can't see into the field more than twenty-five yards off axis, right about where that tree fell into the field along the edge. I could move through the woods to that point and enter the field and crawl along the perimeter. I'd bet there won't be any ordnance that close to the edge or to the fence. Assuming the fence isn't electrified, I could go over or cut through," Kyra said.

"That's not bad," Marisa said quietly.

"The failure mode on that plan is ugly, but even if you manage it, what's the point?" Jon asked. "You still can't get inside the plant."

CAVIM Explosives Factory

"Look at that shack fifty yards north of the fence corner," Kyra ordered. She swung her camera left and focused on the small building.

"We see it," Marisa replied through her earpiece.

"There's a junction box on the building's south wall. Cables from all of the security cameras on the western fence run to it, and there's an air-conditioning unit on the west side, too big for a building that size, so it could be there to cool some computer equipment on the inside," Kyra reported. "Nobody's come in or out all day. I'd bet that's a security junction for this end of the base. If I can get in there with some gear, I might be able to tap the security camera feeds and see what else is going on, maybe even inside some of the buildings. We might get lucky."

"Give us a minute, Arrowhead," Jon told her.

U.S. Embassy
Caracas, Venezuela

He hit the speaker mute. "There's no way," Jon said. "Risk the patrols, crawl through a minefield, and 'we might get lucky'? You can't approve that."

"We've got nothing else," Marisa told him.

"Then we push back against the order," he protested. "You at least have to call headquarters—"

"Jon, the orders were twelve hours old when we got them," Marisa advised him.

"Screw the deadline!"

"I can't just refuse to follow an order from the president of the United States!" Marisa said, her voice rising.

"Disobeying stupid orders—"

"You don't get to decide when the president of the United States is being an idiot! If you want to do that, quit the Agency and start a blog!" Marisa managed to refrain from yelling, but only just. "And even if he is stupid or malicious, he's not wrong! Jon, if Ahmadi is smuggling nuclear material into this half of the world, we have to know. When was the last time anyone tried that?"

Jon glared at her. "Nineteen sixty-two."

"Darn right, nineteen sixty-two. And the world almost ended. The only reason it didn't is because the Russians are rational. The mullahs in Tehran, maybe not so much," she reminded him. She reached out her hand and put it on his. He didn't pull his away, but he didn't look at her. "We have to know before they move that cargo even if we have to risk some people."

"This isn't 'some people,'" he protested. "She's not some random warm body out there who you never have to talk to—"

"I know she's your friend and I wish I didn't have to recommend the option to the director, but I think I do," Marisa broke in.

"You're going to get her killed."

"I truly hope not." Marisa pressed the button again, turning on the microphone. "Arrowhead, this is Quiver. If approved, when can you proceed?"

CAVIM Explosives Factory

Kyra's heart hammered against her ribs. "I'd have to return to the truck, grab some gear. And I couldn't move before nightfall anyway." She checked her watch. "Three hours?"

"Copy that, Z–minus three hours," Marisa came back. "Get your gear, check in when you get back. I'll give you the green light or not."

"Roger that." Kyra shut down the phone and stared at her watch again. *Three hours.* The risks in her plan suddenly felt so much larger than they had just a few minutes before.

Kyra grabbed the HK, then crawled out of the blind and started to run down the back side of the mountain. Two miles to the truck, two miles back.

U.S. Embassy
Caracas, Venezuela

Marisa touched the speakerphone and shut it down, then dipped her head, trying to catch Jon's eye. "I am sorry," she said. She couldn't tell whether he believed her. "We've got three hours. I'll call the director. If the task force can come up with a better option, we can still call it off—"

"They won't," Jon said. "Kathy will have to approve it and Kyra will run down that mountain straight at the enemy like she always does."

Marisa was afraid to answer. There was no question that Jon knew both women better than she did and the station chief desperately wanted to know how. But the man refused to open up and she couldn't ask him all of the questions that had been backing up in her mind for a decade now. "I'm sorry I don't have anyone to send her for backup—"

"Yes, you do," Jon told her. He threw down the headset.

CIA Director's Conference Room

She wasn't used to seeing the room like this. The conference room was usually clean, the space swept by security after every meeting to make sure that none of the Agency's most sensitive information could ever leak to the next guest, who could be a reporter, a Hollywood actor, even a foreign intelligence chief. Now

Drescher's task force had taken over the room and papers were everywhere. The map of the CAVIM facility on the table was so large that Cooke wondered where they'd found a printer big enough to run it off. Smaller maps were pinned up, photographs and intelligence reports scattered around the rectangular hardwood table, and the conversations were a chaotic mass of overlapping arguments that quieted only a little when she entered.

Drescher saw the director enter through the rear door and he broke loose from the small group he'd been directing to make his way to meet her.

"I heard you got a call from the station," Cooke said.

"Ten minutes ago," Drescher confirmed. "Somebody down there came up with a plan. They'll be sending us a cable in an hour or so, but for now we've just got a verbal brief. It's bold."

"Show me," Cooke ordered.

U.S. Embassy
Caracas, Venezuela

"Jon!" Marisa was practically yelling at him as he ran down the stairwell. "Jon, stop!"

He ignored her orders, then finally obeyed once he reached the bottom of the stairwell, turning and shoving his finger in her face. "Don't you tell me that it's too dangerous to go. Not after you practically gave her the green light."

"You're not a field officer."

"You know I can handle myself."

She couldn't deny it. "It's dumb to put you both at risk," she said.

"If it's too risky for both then it's too risky for one," he said. "If you really believe that, call her and pull her back." He pushed the door to the garage hard enough to slam it open against the concrete wall and stomped toward the equipment alcove.

"Jon, at least wait until we hear from Headquarters! The director might not even approve the plan—"

"If she does and I'm still here, there won't be time for me to get out there before Kyra goes in."

"And what if Cooke tells you to stay?"

"I don't plan on being here when you finish talking to her."

"This is insubordination!" Marisa told him, fuming.

"Lead, follow, or get out of the way. I don't care which," Jon told her. He grabbed a backpack and turned to the gun locker.

CIA Director's Conference Room

"That's not bold, it's crazy," Cooke announced. She stared down at the hand-drawn lines marking boundaries, fences, and buildings on the map. The rest of the room had finally gone quiet when Drescher started briefing the director. "Does anybody think it will work?" she asked the room.

Drescher shrugged. "All the real security is a half mile north around the chemical plant itself. That's the place with all the heavy patrols and cameras pointing every which way. It doesn't look like they're too worried about somebody getting through the fence that far from the main building. We don't know the specs of the security cameras along the fence line so we can't calculate their field of vision, but the point of entry into the ordnance field is as good a guess as any.

Assuming she doesn't get blown up, the real question is whether she can tap the feeds coming off the rest of the camera network from inside that shack. Not to mention the feeds could be encrypted. Still a lot of variables that we can't control inside the president's time frame."

"Is anyone going to come up with anything better?" Cooke asked.

"Not likely," someone called out, a face and voice that Cooke didn't know.

"We've got more intelligence gaps on this factory than a sieve has holes," another analyst agreed. "We can't begin to plan anything because every possible option has so many failure modes that we can't get past the first step. We just don't know that much about the place. We might as well be calling this Operation Flail."

"Can't argue with that," Drescher agreed. "Give us a year and we'll tell you everything about that place down to the brand name on the toilets. Give us one day and this plan is probably the best you're going to get. There's no way we could have come up with it. Station could because they've got eyes on the target."

"Any way we can help her out?" Cooke asked.

"Track the patrols using thermal imaging," another person suggested, this one a case officer who'd run a few field ops of her own. "Call them out if they start moving on that sector. That's about it."

Cooke nodded silently. "You're with me," she told Drescher.

"Yes, ma'am," Drescher replied. "Keep working," he told the room. "I want this place torn apart. You miss *nothing*. You overlook *nothing*. We've got an officer on a mountain ready to go into that place and if she gets killed or captured, it will *not* happen because we missed a better option. You get me?" The room muttered angry assent as Drescher and Cooke walked out the door.

"President's a flamin' idiot," someone muttered.

U.S. Embassy
Caracas, Venezuela

"I used to be able to change your mind," Marisa told him. "When did that change?"

"When I couldn't change yours when it counted," Jon told her. He zipped up the pack, scanned the garage, and set his course for a Toyota 4Runner. "I wanted you to stay."

"I thought about it," she told him, hopeful that it might make a difference.

"I don't care what you thought about. I care what you actually did," he told her. "Intentions count for nothing."

"Things have a bad habit of going sideways whenever we're together," Marisa protested.

"They've always gone sideways for me even when you weren't around. But we're not together so you don't have to worry about that," he said. Jon threw his pack inside the truck.

"I'm the station chief, Jon. It's my job to worry about it."

"Just keep feeding me the intel until I get back with her."

"Jon, wait." Something in her voice stopped him . . . quiet surrender. He'd heard that from her a few times, not often, years before.

Marisa held her face in a rigid mask as she walked

over to a tall cabinet, opened it with a key, and pulled out a long black case and a PRC-148 radio. "You should take these." She gave him the radio, then laid the case on the workbench. She flipped the locks and lifted the lid.

Jon stared down. "I thought you said they took all of the good stuff," he told her.

Marisa shrugged. "I didn't let them have *everything*. And if you're determined to run back out into the field, I figured you could do something useful with it."

"I don't know if I can use it. I haven't used one since al-Yusufiyah."

"Please don't go."

Jon turned his head far enough to see her out of the corner of his eye. Marisa had never surrendered easily to him but he knew it when he saw it. She looked at him, her head bent low, trying to catch his gaze.

"Jon, you didn't used to be mean. I don't like it. But I saw it coming. That's why I left. I couldn't stand to watch that happen to you."

"You couldn't stop it. Nobody could," he said. He closed the lid on the black case.

"What do you mean?" she asked.

Jon looked sideways at her, sucked in a nervous breath, and she could tell he was deciding whether to talk. She didn't give him the chance. "Jon, don't do this. I don't want you to go through it again—"

"I don't have time for this." He suddenly lifted the long case and put it into the truck behind the seat, then threw himself into the driver's seat and buckled himself in. "Mari, if this op goes south and Kyra and I have to run, there still might be an opportunity to turn all of this to our advantage," he offered.

"How so?" she asked, both sad and grateful for a reason to talk business.

"I assume the SEBIN monitor cell-phone calls?" he asked.

"Yeah, they do. They can't break the encrypted ones but anything in the clear gets heard," she assured him.

"Just be ready to call me on an open line if she gets blown. Then get ready to start watching some overhead imagery." Marisa looked at him, suspicious. "Just trust me."

"You're thinking three moves ahead again, aren't you?" she asked him.

"It's my thing."

"I hate your thing, Jon," she told him.

He finally smiled, that small half grin she remembered. She walked to the far wall, pressed a button, and the garage door rolled up. Jon pulled out, stomping on the gas as the truck touched the asphalt outside. She followed him out, and watched him go until the truck passed through the embassy gates and rolled out into the Valle Arriba.

CAVIM Explosives Factory

Kyra kept her distance from the truck, watching for a half hour, then closing her eyes and listening for another five minutes. She saw no signs of movement, heard no sounds, and crept down the hillside slowly. There was nothing, no signs that anyone had disturbed the truck. She finally shifted some of the camouflage she'd erected and let herself in. The tech ops bag was behind the driver's seat. She closed the door, replaced the foliage, and sprinted back into the woods.

She reached the summit this time in an hour. Kyra wished that she could take the HK but had to settle for the Glock. For this she would have to travel light and quiet. She applied camo paint to her face, an act that would mark her as a spy every bit as much as the sidearm or her other gear. She was beyond cover stories now. There would be no talking if this went badly, only gunfire and a mad race through the hills that she would probably lose.

There was a large, flat rock ten yards from the blind. It was almost beyond her strength to move it, but she managed to shift it a few feet. She dug out a hole large enough for her radio minus the antenna, placed it inside, and moved the rock back over it, leaving a small space open underneath facing the valley. The antenna she left on the ground. She covered the opening with some netting and biomass that she scrounged from the hillside, then stood back and looked at the work. It wasn't perfect, a little too obvious to her eye, but she knew what to look for. If someone stumbled across the antenna, they could trace the cable to the pit under the rock, but the odds were against that in the dark. It was more important that no light from LST-5's LEDs leaked out through the makeshift cover. That job was done and the covered hole would serve well enough.

The PRC-148 that Kyra strapped to her vest only had a four mile range, so she programmed it to talk to the LST-5, which would transmit it back to the embassy. That done, she secured the headset, wisps of her dirty-blond hair falling back over it. Finally ready, Kyra sat under the thin clouds and looked up at the sky until the sun had vanished and the Milky Way was stretched out across the sky. *Time to go . . .*

In a moment, her heart was pounding so hard that she could feel it against her ribs and her breathing had picked up, her lungs pumping air at a furious rate. Adrenaline surged through her system, hitting her so hard that she could feel the drug driving her to the edge of panic.

Kyra tried to detach herself from it all and pushed the memories aside of that moment aboard the *Lincoln*. She sat herself on the ground, legs crossed, arms folded, and focused her mind on the quiet scene above her. There was no Battle of the Taiwan Strait here, no Phalanx guns ripping the air apart as they tore antiship missiles from the sky. No shrapnel pinging against the hull armor or tearing through sailors on the deck.

Her breathing slowed, her heart less so, but after long minutes it finally began to obey.

Kyra opened her eyes. She turned on the PRC-148. "Quiver, this is Arrowhead," she said.

"This is Quiver," Marisa said.

"I'm ready. Do we have a green light?"

"Affirmative."

"Moving out," Kyra said.

She stood and marched down the hill, careful and deliberate.

There were no trails here, just trees and undergrowth thick enough to slow her progress to a crawl. It wasn't so different from the Farm, but she couldn't just hack through it. The growing dark was her friend but noise was her enemy now, so she moved slowly, choosing her steps. Kyra took an hour to reach the tree line. She was moving in a crouch by the time she arrived, trying not to disturb the small trees or the weeds. The sentry lights mounted above the factory's security fence were throwing sharp shadows along the forest edge and movement would attract the eye.

She had misjudged the distance to the fence. Crouching behind the broken stump where the trunk had fallen out of the forest into the ordnance field, she saw that she was still a hundred yards from the fence but the security camera was pointed into the woods, as she'd thought.

The only thing that might see her coming from this angle would be human eyes. She spent another half hour watching in order to judge that risk and saw the occasional guard wander through the western end of the facility, more to smoke and relieve themselves than to watch for threats.

The sun was finally down, the moon taking its place, large on the horizon. It wasn't going to get any darker than this. *As good a time as any.* She touched her small earpiece. "Quiver, Arrowhead. In position." She kept her voice to a whisper. The radio strapped to her chest reached out to the antenna back on the hill, and the signal went out to some satellite orbiting above.

"This is Quiver." Long pause. "Can you hold?"

Kyra kept the curse to herself. *If we're going to do this, let's do it.* "Why?"

Another long pause. "You have a friendly inbound."

Kyra frowned. "Who?" *Did Langley send someone after all?*

**U.S. Embassy
Caracas, Venezuela**

Marisa stared at the wall ahead, her mind twisted in knots. *We didn't assign Jon a code name.* The radios were encrypted and the chances were excellent that the Venezuelans couldn't break the cipher and listen in . . . but the Iranians were in town and she didn't know their capabilities.

"A friendly," Marisa repeated.

CAVIM Explosives Factory

Okay, so you don't want to tell me. "ETA?" Kyra asked.

"Sometime in the next two hours."

That doesn't work. "If I'm not clear to go, I should withdraw from this position and try again tomorrow," Kyra advised. "I don't know how long I'll need to reach the destination and I have maximum time to proceed now."

Hiding behind the stump, she felt like time was stretched out and the answer took too long to come back, though it was only a few seconds. "Godspeed," Quiver said. "I'm on the line."

Kyra laid herself on her stomach in the dirt. Her heart was a hammer again, pounding hard enough that she could feel it in her stomach.

She pulled the Leatherman from the pocket on her sleeve, extended the blade, and began to move forward behind the tree, crawling in the dirt.

Autopista Valencia/Route 1
50 km west of Caracas

Jon's smartphone rang. "What?"

"She's on her way in. Already at the field and moving. Where are you?" Marisa told him.

"I just passed Maracay, near someplace called Mariara."

Marisa stared at the highway map on the wall. Still ninety kilometers away. "You're at least an hour out, not counting your time running uphill. You still in shape, old man?"

"Good enough," he said.

"Hey, Jon? Nobody ever gets pulled over in this

country for speeding. Ever." Marisa hung up. Jon dropped the phone in the seat, put both hands on the wheel, and let the truck have all the gas it wanted.

CAVIM Explosives Factory

Kyra reached the top of the fallen tree. She was well out into the field now, at least fifty feet in, and only moving a few feet per minute. She probed the dirt gently, but didn't expect to find anything. This wasn't a minefield after all, or so she hoped, and she expected any unexploded ordnance to be sticking out of the ground where she could see it.

Unto the breach, as Jon would have said. No, that wasn't right. Jon would've been yelling at her to turn around. *Sorry, Jon.* Kyra took another breath, then slowly pushed herself out into the high grass.

A small crater appeared just to the left. A mortar shell had hit the dirt here. *If there's a hole, it means the shell went off, right?* She fought down the fight-or-flight response that rose up in her mind, crawled carefully down into the hole, then up the shallow side.

Seventy-five yards to the fence.

The field was missing chunks of grass, whether from the ordnance or some toxic chemicals scattered over its surface she didn't know, but it gave her a twisting path forward. Kyra pulled her body through another narrow channel in the grass, careful not to brush it with her legs or boots, lest it wave to any guards standing at the fence. The little trail turned left, Kyra twisted her body to follow the bend—

An 81mm mortar shell stood out of the ground, less than a foot from her face.

Kyra stared at the metal tube. It was green, an oblong teardrop that narrowed at the tail to a set of fins, with rust growing on the skin.

CIA Director's Conference Room

Cooke entered the room. It was silent now, all eyes on the wall monitor. Fifteen people sat around the room and no one dared speak. The screen was streaming a live satellite feed, a thermal image of someone crawling on their stomach toward a compound of buildings and lampposts.

The director moved behind Drescher, who didn't look up. "How's she doing?" she asked.

"Fifty yards to the fence, give or take. No patrol in the area," he said, not taking his eyes away from the picture. "She just backed up and reversed course. I guess she saw something she didn't like."

"Ordnance?" Cooke asked.

Drescher shrugged. "Could be."

"Any idea if there's a patron saint of spies?" she asked quietly.

"Saint Joshua," Drescher advised. "One of the twelve spies sent by Moses to explore Canaan. He's also the patron saint of literature and reading."

"How do you know that? You're a Mormon. Mormons don't have patron saints."

"I was a missionary in Italy back in the day. Two years on the ground in Liguria," Drescher said. "The Catholics kept trying to convert me, God bless 'em. They didn't get the message that's what I was supposed to be doing to them."

The secure line phone in the corner rang. He picked up the receiver. "Drescher."

U.S. Embassy
Caracas, Venezuela

Marisa enlarged the satellite picture, looking at the
larger compound. A vehicle was coming down the
northern fence line. "Arrowhead, hold your position.
Security patrol incoming, northern road. ETA one
minute." *Hurry up, Jon,* she thought.

CAVIM Explosives Factory

Kyra slid past another intact mortar shell to her right
when Marisa's warning sounded in her ear. She turned
her head and saw the incoming vehicle's headlights
streaming between the trees and shacks ahead to her
left. Another blast crater was directly in front of her,
within arm's reach. She probed the dirt, found nothing, and pulled herself forward, her body descending
into the shallow depression. It wasn't deep enough to
completely swallow her, but she hoped it would lower
her profile in case anyone looked into the field.

The truck rolled past and curved off onto some side
road. The sound of the engine dropped in pitch as it
moved away from the field.

"All clear," Marisa's voice said in Kyra's ear.

Kyra clawed at the dirt to pull herself out of the low
crater, then pushed herself forward, multitool in hand,
stabbing the dirt gently every few inches. The closer
she moved toward the fence, the fewer unexploded
artillery shells there should be, right? She wasn't convinced that any logic applied here. She stopped as her
tool touched something metal in the loam. Shrapnel
from one of the shells that had actually worked? She
moved forward a few inches, and then she saw it . . .

a grenade, half buried in the dirt. *Couldn't we have just stuck with the mortars?* she thought. Mortar shells were easy to see. Grenades might as well be mines.

She looked up through the grass and tried to gauge the remaining terrain between her and the fence. Twenty-five yards? Kyra pushed herself to the right, away from the grenade, and started probing the ground again.

CIA Director's Conference Room

Drescher uttered something Cooke had never heard come out of a Mormon's mouth, some strange variation of a curse that rhymed with the real thing but still qualified as family-friendly. He spun around, grabbed for a television remote, and brought up one of the cable news networks in the back of the room, the volume set low. He wanted the task force watching the operation on the big screen, not some pompous politician on the small one.

A news anchor was talking. Cooke knew the journalist, had met most of the big ones in fact. The networks had climbed over each other two years before to score the early interviews with the first female CIA director in U.S. history. In the end, Cooke had given time to most of them, at least the ones from reputable outlets. More than a few of the interviewers barely had the brains to read their teleprompters, but this one, a late thirtysomething blonde owned dual degrees in journalism and law from Princeton and was smarter than most. She also had a reputation for being able to score interviews with Rostow almost at will, which said as much about the president's libido as the anchor's ambition.

". . . We warn our viewers that this video contains graphic footage. Viewer discretion is advised." The camera cut away from the anchor . . . to the inside of the Puerto Cabello dockyard.

"Oh, no," Cooke said quietly.

**U.S. Embassy
Caracas, Venezuela**

Almost there. Marisa looked up at the clock. Kyra had been moving through the field now for almost an hour, pushing herself ahead, one agonizing foot after another. Kyra's path through the field had been a torturous series of turns, not a straight line more than five feet at any point. The girl couldn't possibly have memorized the route. Any run back would be an exercise in desperation, prayer, and luck.

CAVIM Explosives Factory

Kyra reached out to touch the fence, then thought better of it. Was it electrified? She'd bypassed four mortar shells and a dozen grenades to get here and it wouldn't do to grab a charged fence now.

There was no telltale buzz. She looked for posted signs, though she didn't trust the Venezuelans to bother with such niceties, then realized the signs would be facing into the compound, not out. *Moron,* she thought.

She scanned the fence line at ground level as far as she could see. Ten feet to her right, there was a depression directly underneath the metal where some rodent had dug its way in, and the tiny invader was nowhere to be seen. *Not electrified,* she thought. But she had reached the barrier too far to the south. A cut here might get noticed the next time some soldier walked out to relieve himself.

The first of the small corner shacks was maybe a dozen yards to her left. She pushed off again, crawling in its direction, probing the ground as she went. Kyra didn't expect to find anything dangerous *this* close in, but stabbed carefully at the dirt anyway.

She reached the fence span just a few feet from the corner where the fence turned north again. She looked up and saw the camera atop its post, looking placidly out into the woods. *You just keep looking that way,* she muttered inside her head. She pulled out the wire cutter in her pack.

CIA Director's Conference Room

"Hostile inbound, fifty yards north," one of the analysts commented. He didn't need to say it. Everyone saw the infrared shape wandering south from one of the larger buildings near the top of the screen.

Cooke ignored the quiet banter going on at the conference table. The video had finished playing and the anchor was now interviewing a talking head from the Brookings Institution, an expert on arms control and proliferation.

". . . Well, Jenny, one of the men in the video appears to be Dr. Hossein Ahmadi, long regarded by the CIA and other spy agencies as a key figure in Iran's nuclear enrichment program. Our analysts here at the Brookings Institution also believe one of the other men could be Andrés Carreño, the head of Venezuela's SEBIN intelligence service," the man said. "To see those men together at the scene of a massacre like that one could have truly disturbing implications."

"Like what?" the blond anchor asked, trying to project gravitas. The woman clearly didn't know Hossein Ahmadi from Adam.

"It could mean that Venezuela is complicit with Iran's attempt to develop a complete nuclear fuel cycle, and possibly nuclear weapons. Both Iran and Venezuela signed the Non-Proliferation Treaty in 1968 and ratified it in 1970. And despite its revolution and change in government in 1979, Iran has never withdrawn from the treaty, but over the last two decades, Iran has repeatedly refused to comply with its treaty obligations. It has constructed nuclear facilities that it declared to the IAEA only after their existence was revealed by other means—"

"You mean after the U.S. intelligence community found them," the anchor said, cutting in.

CAVIM Explosives Factory

"Hostile inbound," Marisa warned.

I see him, Kyra thought. The man was in uniform and carried no rifle, but there was a pistol hanging from a holster on his belt. He reached the fence but made no move to unzip his fly. Instead, after a few seconds of stargazing, he pulled out a pack of cigarettes, extracted one with his teeth, then lit up.

Motion always attracted the eye. There was tall grass between her and the soldier, not enough to completely hide her but enough to break up her outline. A lamppost towered above the shack to her immediate north, casting a shadow that fell on her and stretched out into the field another five yards.

The man took a long drag, then turned when he

heard feet shuffle through the gravel that passed for the road between the small cluster of buildings. A friend wandered his way.

Great. It's a party.

CIA Director's Conference Room

"Right. This could be confirmation of old rumors that the Iranians are mining uranium from Venezuela's Roraima Basin and shipping it home for enrichment, which would violate several UN sanctions," the Brookings analyst replied. "Another possibility, one I think we all hope wouldn't be the case, could be that Iran is now trying to smuggle illegal nuclear materials into the western hemisphere."

The room exploded.

"Get me the NCS director now!" someone yelled. Hands fought for the few secure phones in the room while keyboards started to clatter. Drescher was on his feet, barking orders and dispensing with pleasantries as he did so.

"Stop!" Cooke yelled. The room went dead silent as fast as it had descended into chaos moments before. "We have an officer in harm's way *right now*," she said, pointing at the monitor on the wall. "Our first priority is to get her out. If the SEBIN are watching the news, security is going to lock that facility down at any time. You work that problem *first*."

Behind them, on the larger screen, two men stood by the CAVIM fence line talking, animated, their cigarettes glowing more brightly on the infrared image every time they sucked in the smoke, giving the burning tobacco a fresh infusion of oxygen. Kyra's thermal outline was maybe thirty feet to the left of the pair.

CAVIM Explosives Factory

They were standing almost where she had first reached the fence. If she had stayed there, they would certainly have seen her.

Go back to work, she mentally ordered the men. It took fifteen minutes for them to finally obey Kyra's command. They finished their first cigarettes and consumed a second while talking about the vulgar things they had done on their last leave, then threw their smoked-out butts onto the gravel road and walked slowly north again, passing out of her sight. The sound of their boots crunching on the small rocks finally died.

"Charlie Mike, Arrowhead," Marisa said quietly into her ear. *Continue mission.*

Kyra cut into the fence, snipping one link after another in a perfectly vertical line. When she judged that the height of the broken line was right, she set to work cutting metal at ground level, a foot on either side of the vertical gash she'd just made. It only took a few cuts. She evaluated her work, an inverted T, then pushed herself forward on the ground. *Quiet now,* she thought as she pushed the severed fence to the sides.

Then she was through.

Kyra drew her Glock and sidestepped to the edge of the shack, the gun in both hands pointing down, and she looked around the corner.

The next shack up the road was . . . twenty feet? "All clear?" she whispered.

"Two hostiles one hundred yards north of your position and still walking away. The same ones who had a party by the fence while you were lounging around. Anyone else in the area must be inside a building."

Kyra took a deep breath, then pushed off and ran,

moving as quietly as her boots would allow. The cover of the second shack seemed to arrive slowly. She reached it after a few seconds, then crouched, her back against the metal wall, and she closed her eyes to listen.

Nothing.

She realized she hadn't heard Jon's voice over her earpiece during the entire op. *Where are you?*

CAVIM Explosives Factory
Chemical Production Facility

Andrés Carreño walked out the front door past the SEBIN guards standing their posts. Seeing them standing at attention, he held his tongue and swallowed his curses at Avila for assigning him this duty. Words spoken in anger could last long in this country and travel to the most inconvenient places.

He hated the chemical plant. The smell always lingered in his nose for days, killing his sense of smell and affecting the taste of his food. It seemed especially noxious tonight. The Venezuelan spy chief pulled the tobacco roll from his pocket, lit it with the torch, and sucked in as much smoke as the small tube would give up in three puffs. He exhaled, looked up at the stars, then started to walk south.

Palacio de Miraflores
Caracas, Venezuela

"Señor Presidente!" The pounding on the door was insistent, almost panicked. Avila dragged himself from his bed, leaving behind the young lady, not his wife, who was sharing it this evening. He stumbled over, pulling on a shirt and pants, then opened it.

A staffer stood in the hall, a young man whose name Avila had never bothered to learn. "What is it?" The functionary thrust a piece of paper at the head of state, which Avila took. His eyes refused to make sense of the blurred words and he had to force them to function.

What—? Avila cursed and shoved the paper back at the staffer. "Where is Carreño?"

"We don't know, Señor Presidente. No one can reach him. He was at the Morón facility within the last hour but no one can find him now," the younger man said, afraid to be the messenger of that particular piece of news.

"And Ahmadi?"

"At his hotel in Valencia."

"He must be moved," Avila said. "That location is no longer secure. Set the television in my office to this foreign news network, then call the defense minister. I want him here within the half hour . . . and find Carreño!"

The young man ran off, trying to balance his dignity against the president's anger.

CAVIM Explosives Factory

The door to the security hub faced the road, east, and there were no windows on the south or west side that Kyra could see. She leaned out from behind the shack, giving her cover just far enough to see that there was a padlock on the door, ten yards away. *No one inside.* There was a camera on the roof corner closest to her position, but it was pointed at the road. As long as she stayed close to the fence, Kyra guessed, she'd be able to stay behind, then under its field of vision. There was a series of toolsheds twenty-five yards to the north but she could see they were empty. The closest building that could have occupants was a hundred feet away, with no window looking south.

She took a breath, expelled a prayer, and ran for the security annex, staying in the grass. There were no yells, no shots, and then Kyra was behind the building. *Keep going.* She crept around the south side, keeping the building between her and the two soldiers who were, doubtless, far out of earshot now, but they would be able to see farther than they could hear. She moved under the camera, staying close to the east wall, and finally stood in front of the door.

"Quiver, Arrowhead. Door is padlocked. Trying to open it now."

She inserted the torsion rod, then the pick, and started to work the tumblers.

CIA Director's Conference Room

On the monitor's thermal image, several guards ran out from the CAVIM factory.

"Oh, there we go," Drescher said. "Someone was watching the news."

Cooke looked at Drescher, murder on her face. "You want me to call the White House?" he asked

She took five seconds to answer. "Not yet," she finally said. "But soon. We have more immediate priorities." Cooke looked toward the screen. "Call Jon and Mills."

CAVIM Explosives Factory

The padlock dropped open. Kyra lifted it, swung the latch out, then replaced the lock. The doorknob turned easily in her hand and she moved inside and closed the door in a single movement. No yells. No shots. She'd made it inside. Getting back out to the fence would be no easier—

One thing at a time.

The darkness was broken by the system status lights on a series of rack-mounted servers and other gear. It was cooler here than outside, with the air suffering from the processed smell of air-conditioning. The small building had no windows, but light could still leak out from under the door. She pulled the Maglite from her pouch, turned it on, and swept the room with the red light.

"I'm in," she said.

The only furniture was a chair parked in front of a desk with a monitor sitting on it, which connected to a CPU underneath. The desk sat next to the rack, which stood taller than Kyra's head and was full of single mounted servers and other equipment, not all of which she could immediately identify. She swept the south wall—

There you are.

The video cables reached to the floor from a junction box on the wall. She leaned in, trying to squeeze herself into the space, and found the box where the wires connected in the rack.

Kyra dropped to one knee, pulled her satchel over her head, set it on the floor, then unzipped the top and pulled out the iPad, a set of cables, and a tool kit. Then she extracted the little black box.

Carreño walked slowly. The cigarro reached the end of its short life; he dropped it, reached for one of its brothers, then decided against it. His supply here was limited and he didn't want to burn through them all in a single night.

He passed a pair of SEBIN soldiers walking north, who saluted him as he passed. He returned the salute, sloppy and hardly caring. He saw the southern fence a few hundred feet down the gravel road. He'd go that far, maybe then smoke another cigarro, and return. A half hour's walk total. Maybe longer if he moved slowly.

Kyra pushed the cable head into the iPad port, then launched the app. The room lit up from the new picture, causing her to suck in a nervous breath.

The iPad screen split into eight boxes, each showing the feed from a different camera. She swiped the screen and the eight boxes scrolled off, replaced by eight more. Then again and again. Kyra had access to the take from at least thirty-two different cameras through the facility, some inside buildings, which ones she didn't know.

She pressed a button on the screen and started recording.

U.S. Embassy
Caracas, Venezuela

Marisa watched as the heat signature in the shape of a man entered the frame, walking south at a slow pace. She checked the clock. *Ten minutes since entry.* "Arrowhead, Quiver," she announced. "One hostile moving your way. He's in no hurry. You've got maybe five minutes until he reaches your position. Time to start packing up."

"Roger that."

The secure phone on Marisa's desk began to ring. She let it go to voice mail. It rang again. Finally she picked up the receiver. "This is Mills."

CAVIM Explosives Factory

She'd only been recording the camera network feed for ten minutes, but a quick check showed that the tablet's storage was filling up fast. *Thirty-two cameras . . . ten minutes per camera . . . three hundred twenty minutes . . . five hours twenty minutes of total footage.* She wouldn't be able to record more than a few minutes more before the computer ran out of space to store the feed.

Kyra waited another three minutes, then closed down the recording app, unplugged the cable, and began to retrieve her gear.

The southern fence and the signs warning of unexploded ordnance were less than a hundred feet away now. Carreño wondered whether anyone had ever been so foolish as to ignore the warnings and climb the fence. Bored men did like to drink after all. Booze and machismo were a bad combination.

The work sheds were behind him now. The only buildings between here and the end were a storage shack that held nothing important and the small security annex, little more than a relay point for the camera network.

He looked over at the security building, squinting.

The padlock hung from the latch. Was it open? He couldn't tell from this distance. Carreño frowned and moved toward the building.

U.S. Embassy
Caracas, Venezuela

Marisa looked at the telephone receiver in her hand in disbelief. She grabbed the mouse, zoomed the picture on her screen out, widening the angle of the satellite feed. Soldiers were rushing out of the CAVIM chemical factory, more from other buildings, running for trucks, jeeps, any vehicle that would move. "Oh, no . . ." Then she saw movement near the facility's southern end. She narrowed the picture again. One man was walking directly to the security hub.

CAVIM Explosives Factory

Her gear was packed. Kyra slipped the satchel strap over her head.

"Arrowhead, Quiver. Hostile inbound on your front door, ETA ten seconds, and you're going to have a lot more behind him in two minutes. Do you have another exit?"

"Negative," Kyra advised.

"You have to get out now," Marisa ordered. "When you do, run for the fence."

"What's—"

"Don't ask, just do it."

"Roger that."

The padlock *was* open. He looked at the base of the door . . . no light streamed out. Someone had left the door unsecured after leaving. *Incompetents,* Carreño thought. He pulled the padlock out of the latch, ready to secure the door again.

Best to be sure, he thought after a moment.

He tossed his cigarro onto the gravel, replaced the padlock, and pushed the door open. It swung into darkness; he stepped inside and went blind, his eyes seeing only the dark until the lights from the server rack began to focus. He touched the light switch on the wall to his right. The room went bright, blinding him again just as he saw something in the corner of his eye—

The elbow hit Carreño hard enough that he spewed blood on the wall as his head snapped to the right. He stumbled off balance, then turned back toward his attacker. He swung wild, the vision in his left eye blurry from the strike. He missed, but the swing gave him time to pull the pistol from his belt holster under his coat. His attacker was an unfocused blur but at this distance he hardly had to aim—

Kyra's own vision was taking too long to adjust to the light, was still blurry, but she saw the intruder go for his belt and then there was a gun in his right hand. She struck out with her left, hitting his gun with her palm and driving away from her body, then grabbing it with her hand to control the weapon. She leaned in, putting her weight behind her arm, driving the pistol toward the ground. She struck forward, driving her right forearm into the man's throat, compressing his windpipe, and he began to gag. Then she dropped her arm, grabbing the rear of the pistol with both hands, and twisted it to the side.

Carreño felt the gun being torn from his fingers. Panicked, he pulled the trigger.

The gun jerked in Kyra's hand, shooting off to her right, and she went deaf, her ears ringing from the shot. The man jumped back, trying to rip the gun away from her. Kyra ran forward with him and swung her hands to the right, moving the gun to the side. She kicked forward and caught him between the legs, giving him a blow to the testicles that threatened to lift him off the ground. She threw another punch, this one with her left hand that caught him square in the nose, drawing blood again and forcing his eyes to shut from the pain. Kyra twisted the gun hard, this time finally pulling the weapon from his hand before he could fire.

The Venezuelan threw his head up, catching Kyra just under the jaw with his skull and knocking her back. She couldn't keep her hand on the gun. It hit the server rack, then the floor, but she couldn't see it. The man charged forward, blind, hoping to knock her on her back. He was coming in low, trying to put his shoulder in her stomach and fold her in half. She'd have no leverage and he'd have her on the floor.

Kyra rolled backward under him. She grabbed his shirt with both hands as she went down and brought her legs up, putting her feet on his stomach. He was out of control now. He'd thought to tackle her, but now he was flying forward with Kyra fully underneath him. She pushed up with her legs; the man went airborne over her, and smashed into the wall behind.

Kyra twisted on the ground, pushing herself back to her feet. The SEBIN officer behind her made it onto his feet a second after she did. The second was all she needed.

Carreño forced his eyes open as he dragged himself to his feet. His vision was sharper now. His attacker—

—was a woman. He was getting thrashed by a woman.

No puede ser.

The woman's boot caught him in his stomach, compressing it into his spine, and the air rushed out of him. Carreño tried to suck in a breath as he fell backward onto the wall. His knees buckled and he slid to the floor. His diaphragm refused to move and he felt like he was choking. He clutched at his abdomen, trying to protect it, helpless.

Kyra drew her Glock and pointed at his head. The man held out his hand, pure instinct, trying to put anything between him and the gun. "*No, por favor,*" he gasped, looking at her face.

Kyra stared down at him, finally able to stare at his face. Even with the blood gushing from his nose, she recognized him.

Andrés Carreño was lying at her feet.

Cold anger erupted inside her chest, a calm rage that took control of her.

Kyra kicked him in the ribs, knocking him backward. Then she was on him, beating him with the gun. It was stupid, she knew, to engage him again at close range on the floor . . . he could grab her, grab the gun, but she couldn't control herself, like she was a spectator in her own mind. He tried to block one of her swinging arms, missed, and she caught him in the temple with cold steel. The nausea rose in his gut so fast he couldn't hold it down. Carreño vomited onto the floor.

"Arrowhead! Arrowhead!" Kyra heard Marisa yelling in her ear. The sight and smell of Carreño's bile on the floor cut through her fury and Kyra took control of herself, forcing her emotions down. She pulled back

and scrambled to her feet, still covering the SEBIN
director with her pistol.

"This is Arrowhead," she said, trying to catch her
breath. Her heart was pounding too fast.

"Status?"

"One . . . one hostile . . . incapacitated," Kyra told her,
her chest heaving. "It's *him*." The adrenaline was surging
through her again, the panic attack starting to rise.

**U.S. Embassy
Caracas, Venezuela**

The station chief scrolled down the map on her screen.
SEBIN soldiers were everywhere and spreading out in
all four directions. At least twenty were moving south,
only a few hundreds yards from the security hub.

"Understood. Leave him and get out immediately.
Do you copy?"

CAVIM Explosives Factory

Leave him? Carreño was in her sights and she was
furious, angrier than she could ever remember being.

There was murder in her heart, Carreño's quivering
body seemed to fill her vision and the Glock was light
in her hands, the tritium sights over the barrel glowing
a faint white.

The panic was gone, displaced by a cold, dark calm.

**U.S. Embassy
Caracas, Venezuela**

"Arrowhead, do you copy?" Marisa asked again, her
voice more urgent now.

CAVIM Explosives Factory

Kyra stared at Carreño's bleeding face through her sights. The anger was like a living animal, trying to rip control of her hands away from her and make her put a bullet through his brain.

It would be so easy to surrender.

She breathed in deep . . . then moved her finger off the trigger.

It was the hardest thing she'd ever done.

U.S. Embassy
Caracas, Venezuela

It was a very long pause, one that seemed to stretch out time. "Roger that. Understood," Kyra said, her voice calmer now.

Marisa looked at the screen. "Hostiles approaching your area, three hundred yards and closing on your position. You have ninety seconds. Fall back."

CAVIM Explosives Factory

Kyra kept the gun on Carreño as she moved to the only exit. She stepped outside and closed the door behind her. She took the padlock, threw the latch, and locked Carreño inside.

Her knees quivered, the rage inside her chest turning on her now, screaming at her for fighting it. She felt weak all over, her whole body shaking.

Then she heard the voices, all yelling in Spanish, orders and curses. She looked to her right, north, and saw the line of soldiers moving in her direction. Headlights broke over the low ridge behind the men and jeeps came tearing down the road, sliding side to side on the gravel as their drivers swerved to avoid hitting their own men.

Kyra ran for the fence.

The first bullets hit the ground to her left and she heard some ricochet off bricks and metal. She turned right and sprinted to put the shack between her and the soldiers. A few more rounds hit the building as she threw herself behind it. The adrenaline was making it hard to think now, and to keep her hands steady.

The jeeps were close now, less than fifty yards away. She could hear the engines growling as they approached, at least two of them. She looked around the corner, saw them approaching the security hub, four men in each jeep. She saw her inverted T-cut in the fence. It was ten feet away.

She was out of time. The soldiers were too close now. She'd never make it through.

She had three clips for the Glock, seventeen 9mm rounds each, with one in the chamber—fifty-two shots.

Dozens of soldiers were on foot, running to this position. The men in the jeeps were yelling into their radios, calling for dozens more, all with automatic weapons, thousands of rounds. She wouldn't even be able to stop them from flanking her on either side.

Her mind went suddenly clear again and she felt a peaceful calm settle over her.

She closed her eyes, then set the Glock on the ground and prepared to step out from behind the shack, arms raised.

I guess I'm going to end up in Los Teques prison after all.

* * *

Kyra's head jerked as she heard the supersonic crack of the .50mm round as it hit the lead jeep in the grille six inches above the bumper. The monstrous round tore a hole in the metal and steam and fluids blew out of the engine in a violent gush. The bullet ripped into the engine itself, cracking the block and throwing shrapnel in every direction under the hood. Only then did Kyra hear the deep boom of the gunshot as the sound wave finally caught up to the supersonic slug. The driver, blinded by the steam, stomped the brake pedal into the floor and the jeep's last act was to crash to a halt.

The second .50 hit the trailing jeep a few inches below the line where the hood met the grille, killing it as dead as its brother, and Kyra heard that gunshot a moment later. Two more rounds hit the vehicle in quick succession. The passengers got the message, threw themselves out of the vehicle onto the ground and stumbled for cover in any direction they could find it. The other SEBIN officers all did the same, and Kyra heard the first yells of *francotirador!*

Sniper.

"Arrowhead, this is Sherlock," Kyra heard over her headset. "Fall back. I'll keep your friends occupied." Another bullet hit the lamppost light to make the point, sending sparks and shattered glass into the grass below.

It was Jon's voice.

Kyra grabbed her Glock off the ground and sprinted for the cut in the fence.

CIA Director's Conference Room

The room exploded in cheers and Cooke saw Drescher smiling, the first time she could ever recall the man looking pleased with anything.

"Do we have clearance to fire on the Venezuelans on this op?" he asked.

"No," Cooke admitted. "But I'll deal with the president if he has a problem with it."

"He will," Drescher said.

CAVIM Explosives Factory

"Sherlock, this is Quiver. Don't kill anyone if you can avoid it."

"Quiver, Sherlock. Wasn't planning on it. Please don't tell the bad guys."

"We're the ones who broke into their facility. I think that makes us the bad guys," Marisa said.

"Fine by me. Bad guys don't have to feel guilty about property damage." Jon pulled the trigger on the large rifle and sent another slug downrange.

He was lying prone in Kyra's shelter, the Barrett sticking out from the crude woven roof she had lashed together. He kept his eye on the scope and swept the optic over the CAVIM fence line. Kyra had pulled herself through the T-cut and was dragging herself to her feet now. A SEBIN soldier swung his rifle over the tail end of his murdered jeep, trying to line up on the running girl. Jon pulled his own trigger, smooth but quick, and the Barrett yelled at the soldier in the valley below, tearing another hole in the jeep's hood. The Venezuelan leaped back, throwing himself onto his back, wetting himself as he did. He scrambled behind the jeep, out of Jon's line of sight.

Kyra ran to her right along the fence line for the edge of the forest. There was no sense running back through the ordnance field now. Five seconds and she was clear of the explosives range, then she turned and sprinted for the hill. She holstered her Glock and accelerated through the brush, ignoring the plants and small trees as they tore at her legs.

"Quiver, Sherlock," Jon announced. "Arrowhead has cleared the facility. I need a readout on any other hostiles in our area."

"They're all headed your way," Marisa told him. "Everyone is coming to the party. Evacuate the area as soon as practical."

"Roger Wilco. By the way, now would be a good time for you to make that phone call."

He pulled the Barrett's trigger, this time shooting at no one in particular.

U.S. Embassy
Caracas, Venezuela

Phone call? Marisa asked. Then she remembered. *What are you up to, Jon?* She pulled a cell phone out of her desk and dialed his number.

CAVIM Explosives Factory

"Arrowhead, Sherlock," he called out over his headset. "Suggest you head straight for the truck. We need to evac this area now. I'll meet you there. Over."

"I copy, out," Kyra said, gasping her response. He watched her turn through the scope, running in a horizontal line along the hill now away from his position. It would still take her another fifteen minutes to get to the vehicles if she could keep up her pace. Jon swung the rifle back to the base. The SEBIN soldiers were still cowering behind every building and car they could find. Jon emptied the Barrett's clip at them as fast as it would fire.

There was no time to break down the antenna. He pulled the cable out of the satellite transceiver and shoved it under the rock, then threw the antenna into the trees. Then he slung the rifle over his back, drew his Glock, and ran down the hillside.

The tree branches clawed at her face. Kyra knocked them aside but they tore at her, slowed her down, as if they were trying to hold her for the SEBIN soldiers she could hear in the distance. They knew she couldn't be far. Jon and the darkness were her only allies now.

Her lungs ached, her legs burned. Her boots felt heavy, getting heavier with each step. This wasn't like racing through the Caracas streets as she'd done the year before. Then the ground had been hard, smooth pavement, and she'd been able to see every obstacle as the SEBIN had chased her. Now she could hardly see the next few feet, the ground was soft and soaking up what little energy she had left. She was close to the truck, another half mile to go, but the terrain was uneven and it would be like running twice that distance.

The soldiers sounded closer now, but it was impossible to judge distance by sound in these hills. She heard dogs barking and wondered if they were wild or if they were SEBIN themselves, tracking hounds that the Venezuelans had called out.

She forced herself up a small ridgeline, then down, around another, and finally she saw the road where she'd left the truck. She couldn't make out the blind she'd built around the vehicle in the dark, and the moonlight wasn't penetrating the tree cover well. She felt a second wind rush into her chest and she accelerated, reaching the wide gravel trail and leaving the brush behind.

Kyra turned right and ran down the road a hundred yards until she found the pile of brush and branches that she'd heaped on her ride. There was another truck there . . . the Toyota 4Runner from the embassy garage. Jon must have driven it here, she realized. She looked down and saw the skid marks on the road and the crushed plants that led to the tires. He'd slammed his brakes and slid the truck to its parking spot, then gotten out and run for the woods.

Hurry up, Jon. She fumbled for her keys, then started the hardest job of the night.

She sat in her truck, the engine off, waiting for her partner as she heard yells and barks from the forest, growing a little louder with every minute.

The smartphone finally rang in Jon's pocket. "It's me," Mari announced.

"We're compromised," Jon said, telling her the obvious. She wasn't the audience for this call. "Contact the other teams and tell them to fall back." He ended the call and threw the phone into the woods as far as his arm could manage without causing him to break stride.

CIA Director's Conference Room

"Yes!" Cooke was practically yelling now.

"What other teams?" one of the analysts called out.

"He's kicking the hornet's nest, kid," Drescher told him. "All of them at once."

"You two!" Cooke pointed at a pair of analysts. "I

want satellite coverage of every joint facility in-country that the Venezuelans and Iranians have ever set up, right now! Get NRO and NGA on the phone. If they have an issue with it, tell 'em they can call me."

CAVIM Explosives Factory

Jon finally came crashing through the trees. Kyra jumped out of the Ford as he ran for his truck, pulling his rifle over his head without breaking stride and setting it in the truck bed. "Got any M67s?" he asked, out of breath.

"Good to see you too." Kyra turned back to the Ford, leaned the seat forward, and searched behind. She found the grenades hidden under her seat and tossed one to him. Jon tossed his keys in return, pulled a knife from his pants, flipped the blade and cut a strip of cloth from his shirt as he ran to his own truck. He pulled a small oil can from the back, opened it, and doused the cloth in motor oil, then tied the strip around the grenade, knotting it down hard and pinning the spoon to the body.

The yells of the soldiers and the barks of dogs were louder now.

Jon depressed the cigarette lighter in the truck's dash, waited for it to heat, pulled it out, and touched it to the cloth band around the grenade. It took a few seconds for the flame to ignite, black smoke rolling into the air. Jon pulled the pin out of the grenade, tossed the burning load into the Ford, then he threw Kyra the keys and ran behind her for the other truck. Kyra crawled into the driver's seat, brought the Toyota to life and put the gas to the floor before Jon's door was closed. The SUV crawled up the low embankment and the tires dug into the gravel, spinning out for a few seconds, then found traction and the truck jumped, speeding as the wheels clawed against the small rocks. Kyra cranked the wheel hard left when they reached the main road, rubber on asphalt, and the truck started picking up real speed.

Jon turned his head and looked back.

The cloth strip wrapped around the explosive in the Ford burned through and broke. The spoon on the thermite grenade released, allowing the aluminum powder inside to mix with the iron-oxide filler. The chemicals ignited, heat erupting inside the small can and racing to four thousand degrees in seconds. Molten iron began to spill out and the burning aluminum oxide flashed, brighter than a flare, lighting up the night for hundreds of feet in every direction. The burning compounds ignited the upholstery and began burning through the seats, the floor, and then the truck body below. It took twenty seconds for the fire to hit flammable fuels and a small explosion burst out from under the vehicle, scorching the brush beneath.

"Nice," Kyra said, seeing the pyre burning in her rearview mirror.

"It'll draw the search parties," Jon told her. "If they don't figure out in the next few minutes that we had a second truck, they'll assume we're still on foot. That'll let us put some distance between us and them."

"We can hope," Kyra said. "Where are we going?"

Jon shook his head. Kyra sighed and let out a long breath. She pressed the gas, sped up, and drove along the dark road, heading east.

Puerto Cabello, Venezuela

They drove in the dark and silence for twenty kilometers until Kyra saw a cut in the woods that was lightly overgrown with brush. She pulled off onto the trail and found a string of decrepit concrete buildings a quarter mile off the road, shops abandoned by their owners, how long ago she couldn't tell. The village was both too small and too far from Puerto Cabello to be properly called a suburb, but she could see the glow of that town's lights above the trees, maybe ten kilometers distant and still bright enough to wash out the smaller stars above.

One of the cement shacks had a rusted garage door that Jon opened with difficulty and Kyra shuddered at the grinding sound as the door's wheels ground against the metal tracks. She pulled the truck inside and killed the motor. Jon closed the door, easier this time with gravity's help, and the quiet of the forest around them invaded the truck. There were no lights, no sounds of motors in pursuit.

"I think we're clean," Kyra offered.

"I think you're right." Jon ran his hands through his hair, then dropped his head back against the seat. "I guess I've slept in worse places."

"Like either of us will be able to sleep after that," Kyra said. She opened her door, stepped out, and reached for her pack in the truck bed.

"You'd be surprised. The body tends to collapse after intense stress is relieved."

"I'm not there yet," she told him. Her hands were shaking, whether from the stress or the adrenaline finally burning off, she didn't know. "I got it, Jon. I was right. That building at the south end was a security shack. The video cameras connected to the base system there and I was able to tap the line and get video from the rest of the base. We've got to upload the file. It's almost twenty gigabytes . . . almost filled up the iPad's storage. It's going to take a while to transmit."

"I left your transceiver on the hill."

Kyra stopped, then cursed. "You didn't bring one?"

"Just a short range unit so I could talk to you. I was in a bit of a hurry going out the door. Can you get a cell signal out here?" he asked.

Kyra checked the iPad. "No."

"We should keep our heads down tonight," he suggested. "We can try to move into Puerto Cabello tomorrow . . . get close enough to get a call out."

Kyra nodded, suddenly too tired to come up with another plan, much less argue with Jon's. She leaned over. "Thanks for coming. Saved my tail." And she kissed him on the cheek for the second time in three days.

"You got lucky," Jon said.

"Better lucky than good any day."

"Luck can't outrun stupid forever," he told her.

DAY SIX

CAVIM Explosives Factory

The truck was a smoking hulk, wisps of charred rubber and upholstery rising in the air like strings. The metal frame was still hot and the vegetation beneath was a black waste for several meters around. Even identifying the make and model would be difficult.

Elham stared at the burned wreckage and suppressed the frustration trying to rise in his chest. Emotion was not helpful at such moments, a lesson the SEBIN soldiers encircling the area clearly had not learned. Elham knew curses when he heard them in any language.

One of his own subordinates walked over, his Kaybhar rifle slung across his back, a cigarette hanging from his mouth smoked down almost to the nub. "What news?" Elham asked him.

"From what I can discern, there was a second vehicle here; we can tell that much from the tracks. But the trail disappears at the road. They went east but beyond that, we know nothing," the soldier said.

"Where is Carreño?" Elham asked.

"The infirmary," the soldier replied. "He encountered one of the spies in a small building at the southern end of the facility and received a fierce beating for his trouble. The rumor is that he was thrashed by a woman."

Elham looked at the man, surprised. "A woman? Then he is more pathetic than I believed," he announced.

"Indeed. These latinos talk forever of their manliness, but a woman puts one of them in the hospital?

And we're trusting *them* with the security around the operation?"

"That is not our decision to make," Elham said, failing to keep the disgust out of his voice. "Why was the woman inside that particular building?"

"The SEBIN won't tell us what the building is for, but our men scouted the area and one of them managed to look inside. It appears that it was a security access point. It is possible that the woman might have been able to access the facility computer network or the security feeds from there."

Elham grunted. "She couldn't penetrate the chemical plant, so she attacked a weaker point that let her see inside the building anyway?"

"It's a possibility. We don't know for sure. I doubt our hosts will tell us anything. They don't want to admit their failures."

"You're surely right," Elham agreed, then exhaled a long, slow breath. "This has the feel of a military operation. A spy infiltrates while another provides overwatch from the hill with a long rifle. And the floorboards of that truck are melted out, so it was burned with some kind of thermite grenade."

"The SEBIN are convinced it was CIA or American Special Forces."

"They might not be wrong," Elham conceded. "But we cannot discount the Israelis. In either case, until we can prove otherwise, we must assume the worst case, that the woman has identified the cargo and its location. We have to find her and her companion."

The soldier nodded in response. "They only have one truck now. They must be traveling together."

"I agree," Elham said. "These spies must be caught, but I don't trust these SEBIN to execute that mission." He looked around the forest and back up the hill. "Have a squad assemble near the southern fence by the ordnance field in two hours. I have to report to Ahmadi, and then I want to search the hills around the southern perimeter. Given the direction of the shots, the shooter must have been there."

"Yes, sir." The soldier walked off to fetch a radio from their own vehicle. Elham turned back to the smoking truck frame and studied the carnage. *This operation might be entirely compromised,* he thought. If the woman had accessed the network, she might already have transmitted the data to . . . who? *Who are you?* Elham thought. The frustration rose in his chest again, begging to run free. He dismissed it. Enough mistakes had been made and he could not count on these new opponents making any of their own.

CIA Director's Conference Room

Drescher walked in, a stack of Styrofoam trays in hand, which he set on the table. "Breakfast, ladies and gentlemen, courtesy of the director's chef. Poached eggs Erato with crab and hollandaise. Bagels and lox for the kosher among us. Either way, it beats a load of sugar bombs and coffee from the Dunkin' Donuts in the cafeteria."

"Don't be so sure about that," one of the junior analysts muttered as he fought his way through the crowd to the table and took his tray.

"Gratitude, children, gratitude," Drescher counseled. "I've been gone fifteen minutes. Somebody tell me something new?" The group muttered, mouths full of food, but it was apparent no one had anything to report. The senior watch officer frowned, scanned the group, and noticed one analyst in the far corner, disconnected from his surroundings. He was a young black man, business-casual dress, focused on his computer screen. Drescher wandered over and looked past his shoulder at the monitor.

"What've you got for me, Holland?"

The analyst looked up for a half second, then put his eyes back on the screen. "The records of all the companies that secured bonds to cover any IRISL cargo ships transiting to Venezuela in the last year."

"And?" Drescher asked.

"I don't know if it's worth anything."

"Show me," Drescher ordered.

Holland pointed at the screen. Drescher leaned over and stared at the records, then squeezed the younger man's shoulder. "For that, you get to miss breakfast. Come with me."

CAVIM Explosives Factory

The SEBIN director's phone sounded in his pants. He lowered one arm to retrieve the phone and the doctor wrapping the bandage around his torso was forced to stop for a moment until his patient lifted the phone to his ear.

"Carreño." The SEBIN director sounded weak.

"This is Avila," came the basso voice through the phone. "Where are you?"

"I'm in the medical building at the Morón facility."

"You've seen the news?"

"I have," Carreño admitted. To deny it would have been feckless.

"The Americans have penetrated the project," Avila said. It was an admission of the obvious, meant not to educate his subordinate but to knife him in the ribs.

"I'm aware. I encountered an American spy last night inside the facility." At least he assumed she had been American.

The phone went silent for several seconds. "And you captured this spy?"

"No," Carreño told him, another admission that would have been equally feckless to dispute. "She caught me by surprise as I entered the south security hub—"

"She was inside the security hub?!"

The SEBIN director hung his head only because he knew the president couldn't see the act of disgrace. The doctor finished wrapping his ribs and taped the bandages in place. "Yes. We attempted to detain her, but a sniper in the woods covered her escape. Our patrols executed a search but failed to find them. But their vehicle was burned."

"So they're on foot now?" Avila asked.

"No. We found a second set of tracks once the sun rose. We are searching a ten-kilometer radius."

"And you're sure she was American?"

"No," Carreño admitted. "Some of the Iranians feel she might have been Israeli."

He heard Avila let out an angry hiss. "Israeli? The Mossad? They are more vicious than the CIA, if such a thing is possible," Avila sneered. "Fix *this*, Andrés. The Iranians will be nervous."

Carreño was quite sure that *nervous* wasn't the appropriate word. "We will deal—" he began, but the call disconnected before he got the second word out of his mouth.

Palacio de Miraflores
Caracas, Venezuela

Avila pushed the phone away from him on the ornate desk and slumped in his chair. Carreño was again proving to be a disappointment and the president wished again that the man didn't have such close connections with the Castros. Venezuela had few partners and fewer patrons in the world and could spare none of them. The Cubans certainly would not sever their ties if he removed the SEBIN director, but they had other, more subtle ways of expressing their displeasure. And now that the American media had played that tape, all of Venezuela's allies would be exercising caution—

Avila turned at the sound of frantic pounding behind him. He nodded at one of the security guards standing watch and the man opened the door. An aide hurried inside.

"Pardon my interruption, Señor Presidente—"

"What is it?" Avila snapped.

"The crowds," the man said. "Some crowds have formed up—"

"I know," Avila told him. "I *ordered* it. The Tupamaros—"

"No, sir." The aide shook his head. "It's not as you think, sir. These are not Tupamaros or any of the revolutionary militia."

Avila gaped, walked to the window, and looked through the blinds. A small mob had formed outside the *palacio,* signs in hand. He couldn't hear them but they were clearly yelling at the soldiers holding them away from the gates. "Who are they?"

"Civilians. Locals." The worry in the aide's voice was infectious. "And they're not just here. We have reports from Maracaibo, Puerto Cabello, Ciudad Bolívar in the southeast, and several other port towns. They emerged after the American broadcast."

"What are you saying?" Avila asked, perplexed.

"Sir . . . they are protesting *you.*"

Avila turned his head and looked at the bureaucrat, murder on his face. "How large are the mobs?"

"Not large yet," the aide replied. "A few hundred in the larger towns."

Avila nodded. "Contact the television stations. I want no coverage of this at all. *None.* There will be no 'Arab Spring' here . . . do you understand?"

"Yes, sir. But what about the foreign media? We cannot control them."

"If you find anyone with a camera on the street, find a reason to arrest them. I don't care, but smash the camera," Avila ordered. "I don't want these people organizing. And make sure the Tupamaros take their place at the American embassy. I want that nest of spies cordoned off. Contain *this.*"

"Yes, sir," the aide said, not at all convincing, as he fled the room.

Embassy Suites Hotel
Valencia, Carabobo, Venezuela
32 km south of Puerto Cabello

Hossein Ahmadi watched the television replay the warehouse video again. He'd lost count of the times the American news network had shown it. He thought his anger couldn't rise any higher in his chest and found that he was wrong. Each viewing fed his rage until he could hardly control his hands every time the scene came on the television screen.

Someone rapped the door. "Come," he said through clenched teeth. It could only be Elham. He'd summoned the *sargord,* who was the only soldier with standing permission to disturb him anyway.

Elham entered and closed the door behind him. "You've seen this?" Ahmadi said.

"Yes," the *sargord* answered.

"How did the Americans film this?" Ahmadi knew the answer but his mind didn't want to accept it.

"They had someone in the warehouse, obviously. Not twenty meters from where we stood," Elham replied.

"How could you not see such a person?" Ahmadi demanded.

"The question applies to you as well," he answered, turning the question back on the civilian.

"But you are in charge of security for this operation!" Ahmadi said.

"No, I am not," Elham corrected him. "My men and I were not privy to any of this until we were pulled from our beds to retrieve your ship and ordered to bring it here, despite the fact that we are not sailors. You allowed the *Markarid* to be taken over by a pirate crew by refusing to assign an armed crew when she sailed. The Venezuelans took charge after the ship arrived and Carreño was in charge of protecting the dockyard and the ammunition factory. But the security on *your* operation has been poor from the start."

"You cannot speak to me that way!"

"I can speak to you any way that I wish, provided that I am prepared to accept the consequences of my choices. And given that your poor choices are heaping consequences on me that I didn't choose, I am quite prepared to tell you what I think." He pointed at the television. "My face is in that video as well. Neither of us will escape this unscathed. We will both find ourselves answering unpleasant questions when we return to Tehran, but you more than me, I think."

Ahmadi clenched his fists and his teeth, breathing hard. He needed a target for his rage and the *sargord* wasn't providing a good one. He cursed in Farsi, then took his phone from the hotel room desk, set the speaker, and furiously dialed. The call rang numerous times before someone finally picked up.

"This is Avila," the other man answered.

"Your man's incompetence has endangered us," Ahmadi said without preamble.

"We are dealing with it," Avila said, defensive. "I will be making a statement later today—"

"This is going to take far more than a *statement* to correct!"

"Surely, but our dear *comandante,* God rest his soul, showed us how to deal with American spies. Trust me now, brother. Don't fear this. God gives us opportunities from adversity. With this, we will finish the revolution that our leader began almost twenty years ago."

I don't care about your fool revolution! Ahmadi raged silently. The Venezuelans were infidels, the same as the Americans. "Useful idiots," as Saddam had once phrased it. "We must move the cargo," was what Ahmadi finally told him.

"I agree, but we cannot yet. The cargo has been opened, so we must finish the job there first and only then will it be safe to move, I'm told."

"How long?" Ahmadi asked.

"Two days."

"Get this done," Ahmadi said. "Or my superiors in

Tehran will have to reassess our alliance." He turned off the phone.

Elham wondered whether Ahmadi truly had the influence to carry through on the threat. *Probably,* the soldier thought. The other man was a narcissist but he had no reputation back home for making idle threats.

National Security Adviser's Office
West Wing, the White House
Washington, D.C.

The size of Gerry Feldman's office belied the power of his position. The national security adviser's work space sat in the corner opposite the Oval Office and was larger than most in the West Wing, but there were interns on Wall Street with more space and better views. The furniture was government traditional, the desk of average size, fake wood over particleboard and buried under a landfill of paper. Feldman preferred to hold his meetings in one of the conference rooms or even the Oval Office itself, where the surroundings lent themselves to intimidation. But some conversations needed to go unnoticed by the staff and this was one of them.

Feldman had braced himself to see righteous wrath all over Kathy Cooke's face, but the CIA director was calm and he was sure that should worry him far more. She was sitting to the side of the couch, legs crossed, an iPad resting on her lap. Cyrus Marshall was doing all the talking. There was no frustration on her face, no fidgeting, no attempts to break into the conversation. The woman was picking her moment and Feldman felt himself growing more tense every second the moment didn't come.

"You should have run it by us, Gerry," the DNI said. "You can't go public like that without warning. There's damage control—"

"We didn't leak it—" Feldman began.

"Don't give me that, Gerry!" Marshall protested. "That video wasn't twenty-four hours old. How many people do you think even know it existed, much less had access to it?"

"Cy, I'm telling—"

"It was you," Cooke interrupted.

"Excuse me?" Feldman retorted.

"Before we delivered the video, I had one of our video specialists insert a unique numerical code on a single frame of each copy of the video so we could trace it in the case of a leak," Cooke said. "We recorded the footage televised last night and identified that code. It matched the one we delivered on your iPad."

Feldman glared at the woman and let out an exasperated breath. "You didn't tell me that."

"That would have defeated the purpose," Cooke replied.

"My staff—" Feldman started.

"The captain of the ship is responsible for the conduct of his crew," Cooke answered before he could complete the sentence. "So whether you released it personally or gave explicit or implicit directions to one of your staffers, the responsibility still lies with you."

"You are not seriously trying to threaten me," Feldman said, anger creeping into his voice.

"Mr. Feldman, you released that tape last night because you and President Rostow expected that the CIA was going to fail to carry out your order to locate and identify the *Markarid* cargo," Cooke said. "You're looking to squeeze some political capital out of this and given your assumption that we would fail, you saw no point in waiting to start."

Cooke took the iPad off her lap and laid it on the table, folding back the brown Corinthian leather cover. "Your assumption was wrong. Our officer penetrated the CAVIM facility. But your broadcast triggered a security lockdown and we lost contact with her during the escape. We're trying to reestablish contact now and retrieve her intel. But you have your crisis and now we all have to manage it," Cooke continued. "And I'm going to lay down some ground rules for exactly how we're going to do that."

"Now you wait a minute!" Feldman ordered. "You don't get to dictate terms—"

"Yes, sir, in this instance I do," Cooke warned, her voice rising in anger. "You didn't clear the release of that information with us—"

"The president gets to decide whether to declassify—"

"Yes, he does. But your reckless advice that he do it without talking to me first endangered our officer!" Cooke slapped his desk in anger. "While the networks were busy last night telling the Venezuelans that we had penetrated their program and had an officer within a hundred feet of their team, that same officer was inside the CAVIM facility trying to retrieve the intel that you and the president demanded. She was attacked and escaped only because a second officer arrived and used a sniper rifle to pin down the entire security contingent long enough for her to get away."

"You did not fire on foreign nationals on their own soil!" Feldman protested.

"Yes, we did," Cooke said, calm as the morning. "And you're not going to issue so much as a reprimand for it because that team recovered video footage from CAVIM that might identify the *Markarid* cargo. And if that senior officer hadn't used that rifle, not only would the operation have failed, the team might now be in a SEBIN detention facility with President Avila using them as propaganda tools against you. So if you attempt to punish those officers or my agency, I will be forced to plead our case to the House and Senate Intelligence Committees and use the embedded code on the footage in support. Given that they weren't told about the covert action at the warehouse before it occurred, I suspect the committees weren't very happy to hear about it from cable news."

"No, they weren't," Feldman admitted. He'd been avoiding calls since the broadcast. "But the law allows us to inform them after the fact in exigent circumstances—"

"I'm sure they'll be excited to hear why these were exigent circumstances. I have to go to the Hill later today to talk about that," Cooke advised, pointing at the tablet. "Just as I'm sure they'll be thrilled to hear about how an ill-advised White House leak almost cost a decorated CIA officer her life and possibly the intel needed to stop Iranian proliferation of who-knows-what into our half of the world. Details like that tend to leak to the *Post* too. And before you threaten me with jail, I won't have to do that. The Hill will do it for me and you know it."

Feldman leaned forward, anger in his own eyes. "So what are you asking for?" he finally said.

"I'm not asking for anything," Cooke told him. "I'm telling you that if another shred of classified information about this operation leaks, Congress will hear every gory detail about last night's operation before the next broadcast is done. I have people in harm's way down there, two people who I happen to know personally and care about, and it will be hard enough to get the job done and get them home without you"— she pointed her finger at the spot between his eyes— "trying to sacrifice them in exchange for a few points in the president's next approval poll."

"You don't dictate terms to the president of the United States," Feldman told her.

"I'm just laying out the consequences of a particular choice you might choose to make, sir," Cooke said. "And I *will* fall on my sword for this one if necessary," she finished. Cooke stood and walked out, not caring whether Marshall followed.

The DNI had shared his car with his subordinate, so Cooke's exit from Feldman's office had been fine theatrics but she could hardly leave the White House without him. Marshall found her waiting for him inside the West Wing entrance foyer, just past the Secret Service desk. "You didn't mention that the broadcast gave your people an opening to figure out where the Iranians have the rest of their covert infrastructure down there," he said.

"If I told him that, he would've used it to justify the whole thing, never mind that they had nothing to do with it," she replied. "It was just fast thinking on the part of a very creative officer." *Good job, Jon.*

"That never stopped a politician from taking credit for an accomplishment before," Marshall noted.

"No, it didn't," Cooke agreed. "But they can't take credit without going public, so I'm not sure they wouldn't leak that part too."

"Yeah, maybe."

"You said there was no way her people could pull off something like this."

"No, *you* said that. I just thought you were right," Feldman admitted. "We're going to have to step a little more carefully with Cooke after this. She's thinking ahead."

"Yeah. I cut her loose now and the Hill really will start asking some hard questions." The president shook his head, cursing. "We'll tackle that later. Has Avila said anything about the broadcast?"

"He did," Feldman confirmed. He opened a folder and pulled out a pair of typewritten pages. "State sent this over through the Situation Room an hour ago. Avila delivered his rant on that show of his, *Aló Presidente.*" Feldman botched the accent badly but Rostow didn't know the difference. He picked up the papers, leaned back in his chair, set his legs up on the Resolute desk, and scanned the translation.

Jefes de estado, jefes de gobierno que pueden estar escuchando, estimados ciudadonos de nuestro patria amado. Muy buenos días a todos y a todas. (Heads of state, heads of government who may be listening, and esteemed citizens of our beloved homeland, good morning.)

Ladies and gentlemen, yesterday the American media showed you a video that they said proved we were murderers. Was there anything to indicate where it was filmed? No. Was there anything to indicate when it was filmed? No. And

why not? Because this video that they showed
is a fabrication, a lie from the first to the last
moment. They say the CIA filmed it. I say the
CIA staged it. They are the killers, with a long
history of trying to overthrow the governments
of Latin America. They have tried to topple this
government since the first days when our beloved commander took it away from the corrupt
imperialist puppets who had held it for so many
years. And they are still trying now.

The United States government has launched
an open attack, an immoral attack, against the
nation of Venezuela.

Those who did this were CIA killers, terrorists.
But Venezuela is fully committed to combating
violence. We are one of the people who are
fighting for peace and an equal world.

We want to save the planet from the imperialist
threat. And hopefully in this very century, in
not too long a time, we will see this, we will
see this new era, and for our children and our
grandchildren a world of peace.

*Dios está con nosotros. Un buen abrazo y que
Dios nos bendiga a todos. Muy buenos días.* (God
is with us. I embrace you all, and may God
bless us all. Good day.)

"I guess that's a 'no,' as far as giving up Ahmadi," Rostow said.

"You expected anything different?" Feldman asked.

"Not really. But we've got to crank up the pressure on Avila now. He's not playing ball. We need to crucify him," Rostow said.

"We can't let him move that cargo or Ahmadi out of the country. We lose track of them and he'll squirm out of this."

"Yeah," Rostow agreed. "Call the SecDef. Then call the ambassador to the UN and tell her to get the Security Council to call a special session."

Feldman grinned. "You want to play Adlai Stevenson?"

Rostow just smiled. "Tell Kathy Cooke that I want her there too. If we have to keep her around, she might as well be useful for something."

Puerto Cabello, Venezuela

The morning light finally reached into Jon's sleep and he opened his eyes. The humid air was reaching under his shirt, turning his skin clammy, and he knew there would be no more rest now. The sun was already well above the horizon and approaching the higher branches of the trees that he could see through the shack's broken windows. The stress of the previous night had driven him to sleep far longer than was usual.

He was sitting upright in the truck bed, having fallen asleep there. He'd volunteered to take first watch. Kyra needed the sleep. The woman had been near staggering around by the time she'd given up trying to find a cellular signal and she fell unconscious within a minute after he'd convinced her to lie down in the truck bed. But Jon had never planned on staying awake through the night. If the SEBIN were going to find them, they'd have managed the feat within the first hour after their escape from Morón. Two hours later, Jon had heard no vehicles, no voices, no helicopters, and he let himself go. Still, he'd slept sitting up, the Barrett beside him.

He felt a weight on his lap and he looked down. Kyra's head was resting there. Sometime during the night, the young woman had curled up and started using his legs as a pillow. She probably hadn't even been awake when she did it . . . wouldn't remember having done it when she woke up. *I guess I can't tell Marisa that I've never been there when she woke up now.*

He shifted his legs slightly, which accomplished the task. Kyra opened her eyes slowly, realized where she was, and moved off Jon's lap, her cheeks flushed red from embarrassment. "Sorry," she offered, groggy, her voice slurring a bit.

"No need to apologize," Jon said. "You didn't snore. I'd want an apology for that."

Kyra smiled, pulled herself upright, and folded her legs against her chest. She scanned the building, getting her first look at their surroundings in daylight. "We're not in prison. That's something."

"It's a lot, actually," Jon agreed.

"So what's the plan?" she asked him.

"Breakfast and a bladder dump," Jon said. He heaved his body over the side of the truck, then reached back and opened the toolbox mounted under the rear window for the small one-man gas stove stored there. "Then I'm going to find some way to call Mari. We should get back to the embassy. We can upload the video from there."

"So it's 'Mari' now? You two make up?"

"Not really."

Kyra grunted. He stared at her but she looked away. "You okay?" he asked.

"That's a dumb question to ask after last night."

"'Okay' is a relative term," he said.

Kyra didn't look up from the truck bed. "He was there . . . Carreño. He was the one who came into the security shack while I was inside," she told him. "I caught him by surprise when he came in. Got him on the ground and had my gun on him. I could've put two in his head. My hands were shaking but at that range I couldn't miss."

Jon just nodded slowly, no sign of surprise at her admission that she'd wanted to murder a man. "My dad was in the Corps. I was twelve when he decided that I needed to learn how to handle a gun. He started off that first lesson with this speech about how 'one day, the Good Lord will come again and remove that seed of evil that lives in us all, but until then, we need *guns*.'"

Jon's voice took on a southern accent as he repeated the words. Kyra had never heard him talk that way but it sounded oddly natural coming out of his mouth. "And then he told me something that I never forgot. He said, 'Don't you never point that gun at anyone unless you're gonna kill him, 'cause there are two kinds of people in this world . . . those who've killed people and those who haven't. Once you become the former, you cain't never go back to being the latter.'" Jon pulled out the gas stove and closed the toolbox. "I'm glad you didn't join that group."

"Did you ever kill anyone? When you were in Iraq?"

Jon avoided her gaze as he set the stove up. Kyra could tell he didn't want to answer the question. She was surprised when he did. "Mari and I were assigned to Task Force North in '06," he finally said. "We spent time hunting Abu Musab al-Zarqawi together . . . worked the case for a couple of years, taking apart insurgent networks. I found some evidence that the Iraqis were smuggling munitions through a Syrian border town and shipping the goods to a transit point in al-Yusufiah . . . right in the middle of the Triangle of Death. The Rangers and Delta Force launched a raid on the place . . . big fat mansion right in the middle of this dirty little town. We were on a roof-top doing overwatch when things went pear-shaped. A couple of mortar crews started dropping rounds on the teams. The sniper team near us took a round. I grabbed their rifle and found that first crew on top of a mosque. Then I put a .50-caliber in one of them . . . hit him center mass. The round must've punched right through his heart. His body seized up for a second when the bullet went through him. It left a hole big enough for me to see daylight through the scope."

He stopped talking and ran his hands through his hair. Kyra had been with him long enough to know his body language. *This hurts,* she knew, but she didn't say anything. Maybe he needed to get it out.

Jon started again after a minute. "I didn't even think after that. I shot his partner in the face and watched his head bust apart like a fat melon. I guess their friends didn't like that much. They zeroed us . . . put a round on the roof behind us, missed us by a couple dozen feet. Mari was on her feet when it hit. The shock wave would've blown her off the roof if I hadn't grabbed her. It was five stories down."

"Knight in shining armor, Jon," Kyra said. "She didn't stand a chance after that."

Jon fiddled with the gas stove, screwing a fuel canister to the intake. Kyra watched his face. Jon had always been a hard target, even for her, and she wondered how Kathy Cooke had ever cracked that wall. Kyra read body language like most people read English but her partner still was a cipher most days. But today, this morning, she saw pain in his eyes. "She's not the kind to settle down. Mari hung around Langley for a couple of years, punching her tickets at headquarters until she got offered her first chief-of-station post. I was done with the field, she wasn't, and that was that."

Kyra nodded. "You were a pretty good shot with that rifle last night. It's at least a half mile from the hill down to the base," she offered, trying to shift the subject to something less painful for him.

"Not that good . . . but good enough, I guess. It helped to have a big scope," Jon demurred. He smiled at some memory. "My father made me practice on his old M1 Garand for hours, dry-firing in the living room. He always said, 'You gotta be able to focus on that target, 'cause when the bad man is on the move, that cold shot might be the only one you get.'"

"What's a cold shot?" Kyra asked.

"When you fire a rifle, the barrel heats up and expands. The more rounds you fire, the more it expands. That expansion causes each bullet to wobble a little bit more and the gun gets a little less accurate each time you fire," Jon explained. "Doesn't matter at close range, but over a long distance it can make the difference between a hit and a miss. So 'when the bad man is on the move,' you might only get the first round you shoot when the barrel is cold. Miss that and the target gets harder and harder to hit each time you pull the trigger. Doesn't help that he knows you're shooting at him then either." Jon finished setting up the stove and set it on the tailgate. "Where'd you learn to shoot? Did the Agency teach you?"

Kyra rested her head on her knees and stared at the man for a long minute. "You know I grew up near Charlottesville? A little town on the James River called Scottsville?" she asked.

"You've mentioned it."

"Everyone out there hunts, even the girls. The first day of deer season, half of my school was always off in the woods. I had a boyfriend when I was fifteen . . . cute guy named Matt. He took me on one of his hunting trips and gave me one of his twenty-gauge shotguns." Kyra looked around at the forest. "I was so anxious to shoot that gun that I pulled the trigger on the first animal I saw. There was a raccoon up in this pine tree, and I lined up on it and shot it. But it didn't drop. It turns out that I'd crippled it and it just hung there off this branch." She stopped, realized that tears were starting to flow. She wiped them off with her sleeve, then turned away from Jon and looked off in the woods. "After a few minutes, I guess it just got too weak and fell to the ground. It still wasn't dead. It tried to crawl away from me, but it couldn't use its back legs. Matt had heard the shot and finally showed up. I was shaking so bad that he had to put it down for me."

Kyra turned back, looking at Jon and away from the trees. "I know it's not the same as shooting a man, but I never wanted to shoot another living thing after that. But I signed up with the Agency and they put a gun back in my hand down at the Farm. I got comfortable with them again . . . even got back to where I really liked them. I told myself that shooting that dumb animal had freaked me out just because I was a kid and now I wouldn't have any trouble pulling the trigger on someone if I had to."

"And then you had Carreño on the floor," Jon said. He was no good at reading body language, but he didn't need it to know what was running through the woman's head.

She nodded. "That man almost got me killed. I've got a scar on the back of my arm two inches long because of him. I hate him more than I've ever hated anyone, and for one second, I really wanted to put him down. I couldn't do it."

"There's a difference between killing someone because you have to and killing him because you want to," he said. "You decided not to murder a man. That doesn't make you weak."

"Then what does it make me?" Kyra said.

"It makes you someone with a conscience. As long as you've got that, you can always get righteous again if you go off the road," he said.

Kyra sat in the truck bed, legs pulled to her chest, pondering that. Jon had the water boiling on the stove before she finally spoke again. "I think the op is done," she said.

"I think you're right. Which makes it all somebody else's problem now," Jon said. "What're the options on the food?"

Time to change the subject? Kyra rifled through the Meals-Ready-to-Eat that she'd found in the truck cab behind the driver's seat. "There's not much here that looks like actual breakfast . . . just some MREs. Pork rib or chili with beans is as close as it gets."

"Pork rib. You really don't want me to eat the chili."

Kyra pulled the plastic pouches out of the box.

U.S. Embassy
Caracas, Venezuela

Jaime Reyes slowed his car and exited the freeway onto the side road that led to the Colinas de Valle Arriba district. He enjoyed this part of the drive the most. The rest of Caracas was nothing special. He'd seen far prettier cities during his twenty-two years with the State Department and not many worse. Buenos Aires was a particular favorite, even if it wasn't truly the Paris of South America as it had once been called. But Caracas was fast becoming the Pyongyang of the continent, he thought—a crowded city filled with unfinished construction projects, crumbling infrastructure, and violence that the government wouldn't acknowledge. Almost twenty years of Hugo Chávez's Bolivarian revolution had taken it on a downhill slide from a modern municipality to second-world status, fast falling to the lower rungs on the ladder.

But it was his last assignment before retirement and for that he wasn't sorry. Reyes had had his fill of traveling and living abroad, of learning new languages and cultures. He hadn't had to do that for his assignment to Venezuela . . . the real reason he'd taken it. He already spoke the language, understood the culture, which wasn't much different from the rest of the continent. He could handle everything but the food. He was tired of fighting the food. His intestines weren't as resilient as they'd once been and he was having too many disagreements with his stomach about what constituted a good meal these days. It was time to go home for good, to spend some time with his daughters. His oldest was about to make him a grandfather for the first time, his ex-wife had abandoned the family for the bottle, and he wanted to be there when his grandson came into the world.

Reyes made the last turn off the main road onto the trail that led to the embassy—

What—? Reyes slowed the car to a stop. The group of men was standing in front of the embassy gate, crude signs in hand, mostly sheets with crude letters painted by hand. Several were yelling at the Marine embassy guards standing inside the compound. *Stupid protesters,* Reyes thought. They must have come in response to the news broadcast from last night. *Like we had anything to do with that. Don't blame us when your own people let a bunch of thugs come into your country and shoot your own.*

The men spotted his car and a number of them started to move toward him, sticks in hand. Reyes stared at them, decided they meant business, and put his car in reverse. He hit the gas, and only then looked in the rearview. He tried to slam the brakes but was a second too slow and the car hit one of the men who had formed up behind him, knocking him to the ground. Reyes heard him scream in pain, genuine or not he couldn't tell. The rest of his comrades began screaming and cursing and banging on the car. The men from the gate reached his vehicle and joined their fellows. Reyes locked the doors.

Get out of the way! He gunned the engine, hoping to scare them into moving. They didn't move, so he put the car back in drive and let it jerk forward, hoping that would frighten them. The crowd jumped back, not to the side, angrier than before. One of them produced a baseball bat, put it to his shoulder, and swung, connecting with the right-front headlight and smashing it out.

The crowd got in close now, rocking the car. Reyes went for his cell phone, trying to call embassy security for help, but fumbled it and lost it under the seat. He leaned down in desperation trying to find it—

—and heard the loud *crunch* as the *caraqueño* with the bat shattered the driver's-side window. Glass exploded into the car, striking his face. Reyes sat up on reflex and then the men's hands were clawing at him, pulling at his seat belt. One of them, a teenager, leaned into the car, reaching across him, trying to unbuckle the belt. Reyes punched him in the face, bloodying the boy's nose, then grabbed his hair and smashed his face against the shattered window frame. The boy yelled out in pain and retreated, only to be replaced by another, this one smart enough to unlock the door. It swung open and then there were a half-dozen hands ripping at his clothes and trying to pull him out. Someone's fist connected with his own nose and pain exploded from his sinuses backward into his head and he saw stars. Stunned, he felt blood pouring out of his nose onto his suit, and then someone did manage to unlock his belt and he felt the mob pull him out onto the concrete. He tried to curl up, but a foot connected with his head and his ears started to ring louder than the Spanish and English curses being thrown as fast as the blows.

Then someone else screamed in pain, the yells and curses taking on a sense of panic, and the attack stopped. Reyes managed to open an eye and saw . . . boots. Strong hands grabbed him under the armpits and he heard someone shouting Spanish orders in a bad accent at the crowd. The Marines from the gate had come out, guns drawn. One of the protestors was on the ground, someone who had been foolish enough to take a swing at one of Marines and been made to eat asphalt for his trouble.

One of the guards lifted him up. "Can you walk?" he asked.

Reyes nodded, groggy, and the Marine shifted to support the older man and they jogged as fast as the consular officer's weak legs would allow. The other Marines fell back in a line between them and the crowd advanced forward as fast as the Americans were retreating. Then they were inside and Reyes heard someone slam the gates shut behind him.

Marisa ran through the lobby doors, following the small crowd that had run down from the upper floors of the embassy. She finally broke through into the large foyer, pushing aside some of the gawkers who'd assembled to watch the scene. A man was sitting on the bench, clothes torn, a blood-soaked rag being held to his nose by one of the Marine guards.

"What happened?" she asked a second Marine standing over the bleeding civilian.

"We've got a mob at the gates . . . attacked him in his car. They pulled him out onto the street. Would've beat him to death if we hadn't gone out for him."

"How big was the mob?"

"No idea," the Marine replied. "A few hundred, maybe, but getting bigger by the minute. Buncha cockroaches, coming out from everywhere, faster than I could count."

"Where's the local security?" she asked.

"What local security?" the Marine replied. "That buncha morons are probably getting paid off by the local cops. Wouldn't be the first time the government paid some gang to take care of their dirty work."

Marisa turned and ran for the stairs.

The crowd outside the perimeter was large, maybe a thousand bodies by Marisa's estimate, but it could've been more. The Marines were holding them back with a show of force but she didn't know whether they had permission to fire or even if their weapons were loaded. The mob was raucous, bordering on chaotic, and the screams and curses were audible even from this distance. Young men were burning U.S. flags, others were heaving bottles over the fence, a braver few were grabbing the gates and trying to shake them off the hinges. No doubt more than a few of them were Bolivarian militia, the civilian forces that the government called out when it needed some intimidation while keeping its own hands clean. A few others might have been from the armed gangs that ran the slums in the 23 de Enero neighborhood . . . maybe La Piedrita, maybe the Tupamaros. She hadn't seen any guns in the crowd, but she was too far away to tell.

One of her few junior officers ran into the room, paper in hand, which he shoved at the station chief. Marisa scanned it, then picked up her secure phone and dialed a number she'd hoped to never use. It rang only twice before someone picked up. "Director's office."

"This is chief of station Caracas. I need to speak with the director."

"Hold, please."

Marisa didn't have to wait long. Someone apparently had orders giving calls from Caracas station priority.

"Marisa, it's Kathy Cooke."

"Madam Director," Marisa acknowledged. "We have a situation developing down here, ma'am . . . a serious mob outside the embassy. They've already assaulted one of the state officers downstairs as he was trying to get in to work. It's not a riot yet, but it's close. They're calling the rest of the staff, telling them to stay home. An hour ago there was nobody out there. Then the sun came up and now I'm looking at a thousand people."

"You think Avila organized it?"

"It wouldn't surprise me, ma'am," Marisa replied. "Probably some Bolívars, maybe some of those gang-bangers the government lets run loose. I can't see any guns from my office window, but that doesn't mean anything and could change in a hurry anyway. Whoever they are, we're locked down here. The Marines aren't letting anyone in or out."

"So our friends can't get back?" Cooke asked.

"They're probably safer hunkered down in the woods right now. They couldn't reach the gate, and even if they could the Marines wouldn't open it now. Some idiot could make a run through it and we'd have Tehran '79 all over again," Marisa said.

"Can you get the team to a safe house?" Cooke asked.

"I don't know," Marisa replied. "Ma'am, it's not just here. I'm holding a report from the ambassador. His people are getting calls from AmCits all over the place. People are getting roughed up, threatened, and a lot are calling to find out whether they should get out of the country. It's not on the news back home?"

"Not yet," Cooke told her. "I'll check with SecState and see what he wants to do."

"Yes, ma'am," Marisa replied. "But if the SecState decides to evacuate the embassy, we'll have to find another way out of the country for our friends."

"We're already thinking about that," Cooke reassured her. "If all else fails, I have some good friends in a five-sided building who might want to give their people a chance to stretch their legs. Anyway, stay safe, keep your staff inside and we'll get back to you ASAP."

Cooke disconnected from the other end and Marisa cradled the receiver. Out at the fence, a young man determined to prove his machismo tried to scale the gate and a Marine moved forward, ready to bash the protester's fingers with the butt of his rifle. The *caraqueño* protester jumped back and his friends screamed at the *yanqui* Marine, hands waving wildly in the air as another pyre of flags lit up behind them.

A mob is only as smart as the dumbest guy in it, Marisa thought. *And there's no shortage of dumb guys out there today.*

CIA Director's Office

Cooke hung up her own phone and leaned back. She hadn't slept the night before . . . in fact, hadn't slept in two days now and the fatigue was catching up with her. She'd done this before, but she wasn't a young woman anymore. Discipline could only carry her so far, caffeine a little farther, and neither as far as they once did.

"Ma'am?" Drescher was at the door with one of his team behind him, but she couldn't remember the younger man's name.

"Come in?" Cooke asked, sounding more tired than she'd intended.

"Ma'am, this is Marcus Holland," Drescher said. "He's got something you should see."

Holland looked up at Drescher, who just nodded his head at the CIA director. The young analyst swallowed, nervous. "It's a pleasure to meet you, ma'am," he said. "I work down in the Counterproliferation Center and I'm the primary analyst who's been following Hossein Ahmadi. I'm the one who ID'd him on the video. I mean, I know his face. You should see my cube downstairs, ma'am. I've got so many pictures of him pinned up it looks like a shrine. All I need is some candles," he stammered. "Anyway, I've been on that account for almost eleven years now—"

"That's a long time to work one target, Mr. Holland," Cooke observed, politely interrupting his narrative.

"He's a big target, ma'am. He needs to go down, ma'am."

"I agree. What do you have to show me?" Cooke asked. Her patience was fading along with her mental faculties.

The young analyst laid a folder down on the desk. "We always suspected Ahmadi was dealing with the Venezuelans but we've never had any evidence. But once we found that ship, I figured that he must have some other front companies that we don't know about yet. So I started looking for them." He pointed at the top sheet. "The MV *Markarid* is owned by IRISL. If we assume that Ahmadi has been shipping supplies and equipment using IRISL vessels, there have been five vessels that made the same trip in the last year. All of them sailed directly from Iran, some with no stops, some with just one or two. I tracked down which companies contracted those vessels to see whether there was a connection and found that they all secured bonds for those trips through one bank."

"Which suggests that they could be front companies acting in collusion," Cooke observed.

"Yes, ma'am," Holland said, clearly pleased that the director had reached the same conclusion as he had. "I'm still trying to figure out where they fit into Ahmadi's network, but I believe he probably created them just for this one series of operations. That would fit with his known method of operation. He compartmentalizes his operations pretty much like we do . . . pretty good tradecraft. Anyway, if we can get the bank records for some of those companies, I think we might be able to identify some of the accounts that Ahmadi is using to finance his proliferation network. We probably can't get anything on the ones incorporated in Iran—"

"But two of them are incorporated in Venezuela," Cooke said, reading off the report.

"Yes, ma'am. Joint companies, running their money through the Iran-Venezuela Joint Bank, another one of those pet partnerships that Hugo Chávez set up with Mahmoud Ahmadinejad back in the day."

Cooke smiled, feeling a new rush of energy surge out of her bones into her body. "What do you need?"

It was Drescher who spoke up. "A call to the secretary of the treasury."

"That, I can do." Cooke picked up her phone again.

CAVIM Explosives Factory

Elham knelt down by the crude shelter on the hilltop. *The shooter was here,* he thought. *How long was he watching?* That a sniper had been in position long enough to build a shelter worried him. The Iranian had built such shelters himself, but only when he was planning on staying in place for days at a time. Once he had waited in a single spot for two weeks for his target to arrive. Patience was a sniper's tool every bit as much as his rifle.

His squad was inside the tree line below, where the hill began to slope down sharply, but there was a good break in the trees here. He could see the entire facility in the valley below, including the chemical factory and the security hub a half mile to the south. *He must have watched from here,* Elham thought. In every other spot on the hill there were trees obstructing the view.

The soldier looked to his right, moved some of the grass with his hand, and found the spent brass he'd hoped the shooter had left behind. *Sloppy, not to clean up. Or he had to leave in a hurry?* Probably the latter, he decided. Once his partner's security breach had been detected, he would have had to flee the site as soon as she was in the woods and he could no longer see her to provide cover fire.

Elham lifted the shell. It was very large, a .50-caliber, like his own Steyr. That was not a surprise. The shooter had killed several vehicles with his gun and nothing smaller would have done the job reliably at this distance.

But he didn't kill anyone, Elham considered. *Because he wasn't skilled enough? Or he didn't want to?* A human would have presented a smaller target, but even hitting the front of a moving jeep at this distance took considerable skill. *I think you didn't want to hit anyone. Why?* Elham wondered. Political consider-ations? Or personal? It had to be the former. A sniper who wouldn't kill? That made no sense to him.

He must have lain prone, the soldier thought. He pulled his Steyr rifle over his back, then laid himself into the dirt, pushing the weapon's stock against his shoulder. *Yes, here, like this,* he thought. It was the most stable position to make an accurate shot over that distance. *The angle is right. The berm was the rest for his gun.* Elham raised his head, then rested his hand atop the stock and his chin on that. The feeling that swirled inside him was strange, like he understood this shooter, a man he'd never met. It told him nothing about where the other sniper was now, but he knew this other soldier had skills that he could respect.

One of the other soldiers came jogging up the hill, the incline steep enough that he covered the distance no faster than he could have done walking. The man was carrying some piece of metal in his hands. Elham pushed himself back onto his knees and stood, slinging the Steyr back over his shoulder. "What do you have?"

"An antenna." The man handed over the equipment, a long, slender rod with several more rods screwed onto it at right angles down its length. "I recognize the type. The Americans used them in Iraq and Afghanistan during the wars."

"Yes, I've seen them," Elham agreed. "Did you find any other equipment?"

"A military pack with some survival equipment and a cell phone, halfway down the hill, that direction." The soldier pointed away from the facility. "It's a common model, available at any number of stores. It's fairly new, no rust, so it's not been there long enough for the rain or humidity to corrode it. We suspect the shooter lost it when he fled."

"A common cell phone wouldn't have worked with this," Elham said, hefting the antenna. "You found no other communications gear?"

"No, sir. The cable connected to this was cut, and it looked like the antenna had been thrown down the hill, so he probably took any radio he had with him."

Elham shrugged. "Probably right."

"First the warehouse, now this," the soldier remarked. "This entire operation is penetrated. The Americans or the Israelis could have an insider in the chemical factory."

Elham considered the suggestion, broke it down in his mind. "I don't think so. If they had someone that close, they wouldn't have needed to send an operative into the base to the security hub. No, if they have an asset inside the program, it's not someone that close. But there has been a serious breach, that much is true."

"Do you think setting that pirate adrift somehow led them to this site?"

Elham considered the question. "I can't imagine how anyone could have connected the two, but stranger things have happened before."

The soldier scanned the hilltop. "I can't believe the SEBIN didn't patrol up here. You can see the entire valley floor from here."

"Yes," Elham replied. "They probably suspected that the trees provided enough cover to make it unsuitable as a surveillance site."

"Fools," the soldier spat. "They have no one who thinks like a real sniper. I'd sleep in the trees if I had to."

"Agreed," Elham told him. "Finish the sweep and let's start down. It'll be growing dark soon."

"Yes, sir."

Puerto Cabello, Venezuela

Kyra sat in the truck cab, the iPad on her lap and plugged into the truck's charger. The video file seemed endless. There had been thirty-two cameras and it turned out that twenty-five of them were positioned in the facility's interior . . . the SEBIN had mounted more cameras inside the various buildings than out. *They were more worried about their own people than they were about anyone coming in from the outside,* she realized.

Kyra looked at the digital clock on the truck radio. It was late in the afternoon now, Jon was trying to get a cellular signal long enough to make a call and had been working on that task on and off since breakfast, muttering to himself most of the time. Some of his ramblings had contained a few choice profanities that Kyra swore to remember and deploy at some appropriate future moment.

She turned back to the iPad. She'd scrubbed through more than half the footage now. Most of it was mundane, images of offices and entranceways, many of which were empty. Other cameras had captured large industrial spaces, filled with valves and pumps with workers milling around the machines.

After another hour of tedium, Kyra reached the end of yet another camera's feed, the twenty-first, and she began to fear that she'd captured nothing useful. *Maybe they didn't have a camera on the cargo?* she thought. It was possible that the cargo was so sensitive that Carreño and his masters didn't want any record at all—

The next clip of footage began to play out on the iPad screen.

That's it.

"Jon?" she called, her voice quavering.

Jon clambered out of the back and took his place in

the driver's seat. Kyra handed him the iPad. He stared at the screen, no expression on his face.

"What now?" she asked.

"We find a phone," Jon said.

Kyra reached up and tested the ledge. It didn't move and she carefully put her entire weight on it, lest Jon's ascent had weakened it. The stone held and she looked down for a toehold large enough for her boot. "When we were in China, I seem to recall that you told me that going out on the street was a stupid idea," Kyra offered. "How's this any different?"

"When we were in China, you didn't speak the language and there were actual streets with people on them," Jon answered.

Kyra only grunted in response, shifted her satchel to the other shoulder, and took his hand so he could help her clamber up the outcropping. The trees had finally given way to a steep hillside whose surface was rocky enough that only weeds could grow on it. She turned back and saw the abandoned string of buildings where they had left the truck, at least two miles away now. They had stayed inside the woods, where the canopy of the trees would give them cover from an air search. Only one helicopter had flown over and that at least a mile to the east. She had questioned the wisdom of leaving on foot, but Jon worried that their truck would be identifiable. It would also restrict their travel to roads where the SEBIN were more likely to be looking. Kyra had found no serious problems with his logic but her body was arguing the decision now all the same.

Another ten minutes' climb brought them to the summit. Puerto Cabello appeared to the north, maybe five miles distant. "Try it now," Jon suggested.

Kyra pulled her phone, turned it on, and stared at the screen. "One bar," she advised. "Better than none." She pressed a button. The unit dialed but the call refused to connect the first time, then the second, finally getting through on the third.

"This is Quiver." The encryption almost hid the anxious tone in Marisa's voice.

"Quiver, this is Arrowhead."

"Good to hear from you, Arrowhead. A lot of people are worried about you two."

"We're good," Kyra said. "We also have the intel from the facility and think we've identified the cargo."

"Can you transmit it from your location?"

"Unlikely," Kyra told her. "The signal here is weak and it was a two-hour hike to reach this position. I'll be surprised if the signal holds long enough to transmit the whole file."

"Where's your comms gear?" Marisa asked.

"Back at the CAVIM site. We didn't have to time to recover it before we had to bug out."

"Understood. Can you get me anything useful?" Marisa asked.

"Maybe some screen shots?" Kyra offered the phone to Jon, then dug the iPad out of her satchel.

"What did you find?" Marisa asked.

"Quiver, Sherlock. It's a nuke," Jon said. "One warhead, partially disassembled."

**U.S. Embassy
Caracas, Venezuela**

Marisa stared at the monitor on her desk as the image from Kyra's iPad resolved itself slowly in her browser. The CAVIM security camera had been mounted high in the corner of the room, facing toward the center of a large machine shop stocked with drill presses and lathes and other advanced tools she couldn't identify. In the room's middle was a large stainless-steel table mounted on wheels. The table was clear except for a conical device, partially assembled, parts lying around it in organized fashion.

Dear God in heaven, she thought; whether this was the start of a prayer she wasn't sure.

Puerto Cabello, Venezuela

"We'll still need the full video," Marisa finally advised after more than a minute's wait. "Otherwise Avila will just claim that we photoshopped the images."

"We're sitting on twenty gigabytes of security footage from the CAVIM site," Kyra said, taking the phone back from Jon. "Maybe we can load up and head into Puerto Cabello or some other town . . . find an Internet café—"

"I'd advise against that," Marisa said. "I don't think a pair of Anglos are going to get a warm welcome in any major city at the moment and I don't want to risk losing the footage to a street mob."

"I guess the word got out about the op," Jon remarked, leaning in to listen on the small speaker.

"Not the op you're thinking," Marisa corrected him. "The White House leaked the footage that Arrowhead recorded in the warehouse and CNN put it on the national news. You can thank the national security adviser for the chaos at the facility last night."

Kyra snarled, too angry to even utter a proper curse. "Any chance we can make it back to the embassy?"

"Don't even try and that's an order. The barbarians

are at the gates. There's a mob outside that's already assaulted one Foreign Service officer and the Marines are looking for a fight. The ambassador is going to order nonessential embassy personnel back to the States if it gets any worse, but the mob isn't letting anyone out so the DoD is prepping to evacuate everyone by helicopter if the order comes down. The rest of us are banned from leaving the compound. We're sleeping on couches here. All other AmCits have been advised to leave the country and more than a few tourists are sitting in holding cells. Avila's people have even arrested some journalists. So I don't think it'll end well if you show your faces out there. Just hold your position and check back every four hours. We'll figure something out. You still have enough gear to last for a while?"

"Yes, but not as much as I'd like," Kyra said. "I left my pack on the hill and Sherlock torched my truck last night . . . didn't have time to move much over."

"We needed a diversion," Jon offered in his defense.

"I'm in a forgiving mood," Marisa replied. "His practical joke worked. The locals bit hard. Security sweeps went out from four other facilities less than an hour after he called. We've got every one of their covert facilities pegged now. So, nice work," Marisa said. A few hundred miles away she hoped it made him smile, but wasn't optimistic.

Her pessimism was justified. Jon just grunted, making Kyra grin. "Sherlock says, 'You're welcome.'"

"No, he didn't," Marisa replied. "But thank you anyway. We'll find out a way for you to deliver the intel."

"We do have another option," Jon said.

"What's that?" Marisa asked.

"We can try to recover the comms gear from the CAVIM site," he said.

"I think that would qualify as one of your 'stupid ideas,'" Marisa replied after a delay.

"Probably," he admitted. "But maybe worth the risk if that's really a nuke." He tapped the iPad.

"We'll consider it. Hold your position. We'll get you out soon."

CIA Director's Conference Room

"This is Drescher." The watch officer set his pen down on the desk to give Mills his full attention.

"Mills, down in Caracas," the station chief replied. "I'm sending you a file. You'll want to have some analysts from the Counterproliferation Center go over it first, but you might want to call Kathy Cooke in."

"She's in a meeting with—"

"I think you'll want to pull her out," Mills interrupted.

Drescher's eyebrows went up. "What do you have?"

"Arrowhead found something on the security footage. And you need a bigger task force."

The Oval Office

Drescher's briefing had been terse and the single image from Kyra's iPad spoke for itself. A group of analysts from the Counterproliferation Center and two other departments had filled in enough blanks that Cooke felt justified in interrupting the president's private luncheon with the first lady with a call two minutes later. Rostow's inclination had been to dismiss her with prejudice but Cooke's manner had convinced him, hostility notwithstanding, to clear his schedule for the next hour. Cooke obviously disliked him but she was not suicidal, he supposed.

Feldman and Marshall passed into the Oval Office ahead of her and she closed the door behind the last staffer out. "Whatever it is—" Rostow started.

"It's more important than whatever you were talking about," Cooke said abruptly. She set her folder on the coffee table, pulled out the stapled packets, and passed them out. "This is the information that our officer recovered from the CAVIM facility night before last."

Rostow flipped through the pages, then stopped at the still images, marked over with technical notations. He looked up in disbelief. "You're not serious."

"I am, I assure you. We've had analysts from our Counterproliferation Center and the Office of Weapons Intelligence, Nuclear Proliferation, and Arms Control study the photos along with some engineers from our Directorate of Science and Technology. We've also sent it to the Department of Energy for review, but our people concur. That"—Cooke said, pointing at the device in the photograph—"is a nuclear warhead in the final stages of assembly."

"The last estimate I heard from your people was that the Iranians wouldn't have nuclear weapons for another few years!" Rostow protested.

"Analysts' estimates have always varied," the director of national intelligence corrected him. "That's been true for us, the Brits, the Israelis, and everyone else with a stake in the game. But given their rate of progression in acquiring equipment and expertise, there was never any question that Iran was going to get there eventually. The only real question was whether they would have the will."

"So much for our push to open talks with them about easing sanctions," Feldman muttered. "Better to make them feel like they wouldn't need nukes than to keep playing these hide-and-seek games."

"I'd have to disagree with that, sir," Marshall replied. "Threat equals intent plus capability. Intent can change quickly and without warning, so if you want to make sure the threat is zero, make sure the capability is zero. Letting hostile countries develop capability while hoping their intent stays peaceful is rarely a winning strategy."

"Defense without offense is the art of losing slowly," Cooke agreed.

"Enough," Rostow ordered. "So this isn't an ammunition factory either?"

"It's *also* an ammunition factory," Cooke corrected him. She reached over and turned the binder pages to a second set of images. "The footage shows that they've converted just one floor of the building for nuclear assembly. We can't confirm what they're doing with the rest of it."

"How long before that thing is assembled?" Feldman asked.

"It's difficult to tell from the image, but it could be as little as a couple of days. After that, Ahmadi could load it up and move it out on anything as small as a jeep," Cooke told him.

"And then we'll never find the thing again," Feldman said. "We can't let that get out of the country. And we sure can't let them mount it on some missile."

Rostow nodded. The president's face had gone white and he looked shaken to Cooke. "Assemble the National Security Council. Meeting in the Situation Room in twenty minutes." He stared Cooke directly in the eyes. "You know I'm going to release this to the UN."

"I understand that," she replied.

Rostow furrowed his brow. "You're not going to even try to argue with me about it."

"This is one case where the world really does 'need to know' what's going on," she said. It was a rare thing to hear that phrase invoked in reference to the general release of information rather than keeping it secret. *Jon would find that ironic,* she thought.

USS *Vicksburg*
21°21' North, 68°17' West
150 miles north of the Dominican Republic

By choice, Command Master Chief Petty Officer Amos LeJeune spent most of his time below with the enlisted men, coming up to spend time in the command centers only as necessary. He couldn't complain about the view, but was happier to see the outside world from the deck where he could feel the sun. But captains lived on the bridge and Riley was no exception. The commanding officer stood facing a monitor that showed *Vicksburg*'s current position in the western Atlantic.

LeJeune approached the captain and took the offered printout. The time stamp on the message fell within the past hour. "We're being chopped to the Fourth Fleet."

"Really? And who else is joining our little party?"

"*Harry Truman,* for starters," Riley told him. "Fifteen ships total."

"That's a lot of metal to be moving around the ocean. Did the rear admiral care to explain why we'll be delaying our arrival at home?"

"He did," Riley said, surprising the petty officer. "You saw the news last night?"

"That story out of Venezuela?" LeJeune nodded. "It's all the news networks have been playing all day."

"The president's just ordered a blockade. I guess he doesn't want that Iranian gentleman to leave." Riley scrolled the electronic map southwest until it stopped over a small point of Venezuela's northern coast. "We're assigned here, southeast of Curaçao. Half the fleet will be in place by tonight. We'll be one of the last to show for the party, on station by tomorrow night. I have no idea how long we'll be here."

"Mighty close to Aruba," LeJeune noted. "A shame we won't be making any port calls."

"I think most of the crew would just settle for home," Riley said.

"Most of the crew has never been to Aruba," LeJeune countered. "I'll let 'em know. 'Ours to do and die.'"

"Very well."

LeJeune handed the orders back to the captain and left the bridge to the officers.

DAY SEVEN

CIA Director's Conference Room

"Who's Marcus Holland?" the courier asked from the doorway. Drescher pointed to the far corner where the analyst was sitting and the courier made her way around the table, ogling the mass of papers covering the entire space as she did. "Delivery from Treasury," she said.

Holland snatched the office envelope from her fingers, tore it open, and a CD in a jewel case slid out into his hand. "Yeah, baby," he said. He looked up at the courier. "Thanks." He swiveled in his chair, pulling the disc out as he turned, then grabbed a laptop from the conference table and slid the CD into the tray. The laptop considered the disc for several seconds, then opened a file window.

Drescher caught the young man by surprise as he leaned over the analyst's shoulder. "Any joy?" he asked.

"Treasury actually coughed up the data. That's something. Usually getting stuff like this takes a couple of months. The director must have pulled out the *big* machete to go through the red tape," Holland said. "Ask me again in a few hours."

UN Security Council
United Nations Conference Building
New York, New York

Cooke had never set foot in the Security Council chamber. No CIA director had since George Tenet had taken a seat behind Colin Powell, lending his authority to the case that Saddam was still pursuing weapons of mass destruction. The intelligence failures revealed after that had made any intelligence chief a liability to have in this room. But Cooke had understood Rostow's reason for ordering her attendance the moment he'd called. He would make the presentation and, if events to come turned out to his liking, he would take the glory. If they didn't, her presence behind him would give him cover. The media would assume she had misled the president of the United States and she'd have to resign in disgrace, which wouldn't bother Rostow at all.

The council chamber wasn't the largest auditorium she'd sat in, only a few hundred feet square. Drescher had told her that the Norwegians had designed and paid for it. She looked behind the central table and studied the Per Krohg mural on the wall that overlooked the circular table—a phoenix rising from the ashes. The artist had meant it to depict the rise of peace in the aftermath of the Second World War. *If that's true, that bird is still having a terrible time trying to climb out of the fire,* she thought.

The U.S. seat at the circular table was at the one o'clock position and Rostow was already there, talking to the British prime minister, who was the council president this month. Feldman took his place next to Cooke, the secretary of state and ambassador to the UN both to the left of him. The chamber was full to capacity, with some functionaries crowding at the doors and sitting in the aisles. The room was large enough to seat a few hundred and often the chairs were not all filled, but all of the players at the table were heads of state today. The world had noticed the U.S. Navy moving to cut Venezuela off from the rest of the planet, which had lent credence to the rumor that

Rostow was going to present something disturbing to the council. Cooke wondered whether Feldman had passed that tidbit to the *Washington Post* or if Rostow had done it personally.

The British prime minister pounded his gavel against the table and the room went silent. "I should like to inform the council that I have received a letter from the representative of Venezuela, in which he advises that the head of state of the Bolivarian Republic has declined to attend the discussion of the item on the council's agenda."

The audience muttered at that unwelcome piece of news and Cooke heard Feldman cursing under his unpleasant breath. Rostow turned back and looked at Cooke, frustrated. She held his gaze, returned his stare, and gently shook her head. *I guess Avila's not following the plan,* she thought. *Hard to have an Adlai Stevenson moment when Zorin doesn't show up.* She held herself still in her seat, knowing the news cameras in the gallery could see her sitting behind Rostow, but she searched the room. *Avila's not here. His ambassador isn't here.* She searched the room and saw none of the faces she expected. *The Iranians aren't here,* she realized.

"The Security Council will now begin its consideration of the item on its agenda," the UK prime minister said. "The purpose of this meeting is to hear a presentation by the United States. I call on His Excellency Mr. Daniel Rostow, president of the United States of America."

Rostow leaned forward in his seat and opened the leather binder on the table before him. "Mr. President, members of the council, honored guests, I would like to begin by expressing my thanks for the special effort that each of you made to be here today," he began. "My purpose now is to share with you some disturbing information the United States has obtained regarding a conspiracy between the Bolivarian Republic of Venezuela and the Islamic Republic of Iran to traffic in illegal nuclear materials in violation of the Treaty on the Non-Proliferation of Nuclear Weapons to which both countries are signatories, and in violation of sanctions that this council has imposed on the latter country."

The silence in the room died in an instant, forcing Rostow to stop as cries and yells rent the air. A hundred different conversations mixed with excited utterances and the UK prime minister had to gavel the room back to attention.

Rostow nodded toward the council chairman, then started again. "The material I will present to you comes from a variety of sources. Some are United States sources and some are those of other countries. Some of the sources are technical, such as photos taken by satellites. Other sources are people who have risked their lives to let the world know what President Avila and his Iranian counterpart are doing. To protect our intelligence sources and methods, I cannot tell you everything that we know, but what I can share with you is deeply troubling."

Puerto Cabello, Venezuela

"But why would the Iranians build their nukes *here*?" Kyra asked out loud. "It would be a lot easier to maintain security on their home soil." She stuffed the last of her garbage into the MRE pouch and tossed it into a garbage hole they'd dug.

"I could only guess."

"Your guesses are usually pretty good."

"Maybe they aren't building them in Iran because everyone is looking for them in Iran. Nobody was looking for them here," he said. Jon cleaned out the last of his dessert pouch while he thought. "Chávez was already courting Iran before the September eleventh attacks. Then he was ousted for a few days in a coup in 2002 and the U.S. didn't lift a finger. After that he probably thought that he was an unwritten charter member of the 'axis of evil,' so he started making alliances with every anti-U.S. ally who would talk to him . . . Iran, Libya, Syria. But Chávez was smart enough to see that he was only three hours away from the U.S., so maybe he figured he needed a little insurance after we invaded Iraq and Gaddafi decided to come clean on Libya's WMD program. The threat of chemical weapons hadn't deterred us from taking down Saddam and biological weapons are big bags of hurt to manufacture and maintain, not to mention you can't control their spread after release. That left nukes."

Jon cleaned up the remnants of his breakfast and tossed it into the hole. "Iran had the same problem. There were rumors they had a covert weapons program called the 'Green Salt Project' since the days of Khomeni, trying to get uranium hexafluoride for a bomb, and they'd gotten some help from AQ Khan. But after September eleventh the risks of getting caught building one went way up and their facilities were getting outed. Ahmadi could bring Iran's nuclear production infrastructure to the table and Chávez had uranium deposits in the Roraima Basin. Iran had the means and Venezuela had raw materials. Avila's people mine and ship uranium to Tehran, where it's enriched, then Avila ships the fissile material back here for final assembly where no one is looking. While we're looking all over Iran for nuclear facilities, Avila builds them in our backyard. No aspiring nuclear power has ever built its infrastructure outside its own country, so no one considered the possibility until you took that video."

UN Security Council

"I hesitate to reveal this information to you, but I believe that circumstances compel it and there is historical precedent of a U.S. president declassifying even the most highly sensitive information during a crisis of an exceptional nature," Rostow said. The crowd shifted in response and the president hesitated, playing to the group. "In the first video you saw two days ago, a U.S. operative penetrated a Venezuelan warehouse and witnessed officials from both countries colluding to commit murder. One of those men was Dr. Hossein Ahmadi, who our intelligence collection confirms is a nuclear proliferator. We will make some of this intelligence available to the members of the council immediately after this session. Dr. Ahmadi's appearance raised fears that his presence on Venezuelan soil was a sign of a larger operation. I must report to this body now that those fears are confirmed. Less than twenty-four hours ago, another highly sensitive U.S. operation recovered video footage from a Venezuelan facility near the town of Puerto Cabello, where Dr. Ahmadi's presence was also recorded. The facility is an ammunition factory jointly constructed in 2007 by both the Venezuelan and Iranian governments. The still photograph you see behind me is taken from that video, which was filmed by the facility's own security cameras."

The lights in the room dimmed. Rostow turned and pointed at the graphic that appeared on the enormous screen behind him above the table—the single frame of the video, the warhead in pieces, with labels overlaying the image, identifying the parts.

"Our analysts have confirmed that the device depicted in the image is, in fact, a nuclear warhead of advanced design."

The crowd gasped and erupted again. Cooke looked at each of the permanent council members in turn. They were hard to see, the light in the room mostly coming from the image hovering above the council table and the small lights above the individual seats. The French and British were silent, slack-jawed, staring at the screen. The Chinese delegates were quietly talking. The lone Russian, Moscow's ambassador to the UN, was staring down, his eyes closed as he listened to the translation through his headset. Then he jerked upright, eyes open now, and he twisted his head to look up at the photograph.

I guess the translator finally caught up, she thought.

Puerto Cabello, Venezuela

Jon stopped talking as a helicopter butchered the air in the distance with a low, throbbing cry, rising over one of the lower hills to the west, then riding down the tree cover to the valley. It was ten kilometers from their position, by his estimate. It turned north and headed for the coast.

"If that's true, they'd need more than one facility," Kyra said. The woman was lying flat on her back, staring at the sky. She set down the Glock that she'd pulled from her holster at the sound of the aircraft. "Puerto

Cabello is a long way from the Roraima Basin. I can't imagine they'd want to move illegal uranium a few thousand miles overland to ship it out from here." She paused and then she laughed. "That's why you told Mari to warn other teams on an unsecured phone."

Jon nodded. "I was hoping the SEBIN would intercept the call and send out security sweeps from any other illegal facilities. When they did, they gave up every covert facility in the country."

UN Security Council

It took the Security Council chairman more than a minute to finally restore order. "I'm sure that everyone here is asking how these two countries managed to accomplish this undetected. Our intelligence agencies have been working to piece the entire conspiracy together and the time line is telling," Rostow said when the crowd finally hushed to let him speak. Cooke turned her attention to the gallery. Half the crowd was focused on Rostow, the other half looking down, tapping on their smartphones. *Journalists,* she realized. *The story is already out.*

The picture on the screen behind the council changed to show a map of Avila's country, with a half-dozen points marked, satellite photos of each location inset to show factories and facilities. "In 2007, these two nations created a joint enterprise named VenIran that began a series of construction projects on Venezuelan soil. One of these includes the ammunition factory near Puerto Cabello, where the photo I just showed you was taken. Another is a 'tractor factory' in Ciudad Bolívar along the Orinoco River. A cement factory in Monagas. A car assembly plant in Aragua.

All of these were revealed as part of the nuclear infrastructure during the operation. I cannot reveal to you how this was accomplished, as the sources and methods involved are far too complex and sensitive."

Thank heaven for small favors, Cooke thought. For once she was grateful that the man was a shameless liar.

"With those and other facilities in place, in November 2008, both countries signed a secret 'science and technology' agreement formalizing cooperation 'in the field of nuclear technology,'" Rostow went on. "That same month, the Iranian company Impasco received a 'gold mine' concession in the heart of the Roraima Basin in the southeastern state of Bolívar, which sits along the Venezuela-Guyana border. I would suggest that if you think it's gold they're after, you should think again."

Puerto Cabello, Venezuela

"So you were just making things up as you went along?" Kyra asked.

"Something like that," Jon admitted. "I had no idea whether it would work, but I figured if your op was blown, there would be no reason not to try. But if Mari's right, we should have a map of their nuclear infrastructure now. It'll take a while to figure out what each facility is for; the CAVIM chemical plant has got to be the hub . . ." Jon trailed off.

"What?" Kyra asked. She'd seen the man cut himself off in midsentence before. The tic usually heralded some unpleasant conclusion.

"The ammunition factory . . . part of the facility is a chemical plant."

"Yeah."

"And those pirates burned to death," he said. "The ones in the cargo container."

"Yeah, it sure looked like it." Kyra zoned out the world and focused on his face, watching the theory play out in his mind, one logical connection joining another and another, latching on to each other in a steady trail. "If Ahmadi was smuggling nuclear material, that would make sense."

"Not if he was smuggling processed uranium. Even weapons-grade uranium is only weakly radioactive . . . all the isotopes are unstable. It decays by releasing alpha particles. Anything blocks alpha particles, even your skin. It can't burn you from the outside. You'd have to inhale it for it to kill you."

He was staring past her into space now, his hand pressing against his forehead like he was trying to squeeze the thoughts out. It usually meant the logical leaps were coming too fast for even him to track and he had to slow down his mind.

"All the nuclear weapons ever designed have only used two kinds of fissionable material . . . uranium and plutonium. You want plutonium if you can get it because you only need ten kilograms of the stuff to create critical mass, but you need three times as much uranium. More bang per kilo, as it were, but making it is complicated," he replied, trying to organize his theory as he spoke. "And at weapons grade, neither one would burn you to death in the time it takes to cross the Atlantic."

"So what cooked the pirates?" He'd have the answer, she was sure.

"Plutonium is a by-product of nuclear reactors," Jon said. "U^{238} goes in and nuclear waste comes out—

spent fuel rods made up of U^{234} and trace amounts of plutonium^{239} and a laundry list of nasty isotopes that emit beta and gamma particles that can cook a human being in short order. That's why they have to bury the stuff behind some serious shielding for a few million years. But with the right equipment, you can extract the plutonium from the fuel rods. You need a reprocessing facility to do that and one key element of the reprocessing cycle is nitric acid."

"And they set up shop in a chemical factory," Kyra replied, repeating his assertion. Her own mind was racing now, trying to follow his leaps and conclusions. "The Venezuelans mine the uranium and ship it to Iran, where it's processed and run through a reactor to produce spent fuel rods. Then they ship the fuel rods and other parts for the warhead back here," she realized, "and the Venezuelans reprocess the waste to extract the plutonium."

"Which they use to make the nuclear 'pit,'" Jon agreed. "Except this time, a group of pirates took the ship and broke into the cargo hold. They cracked open one of the fuel-rod containers and got a lethal dose. The Iranians took the ship back and locked the bodies down in the hold, except for the one they threw overboard—"

"Why do that?" Kyra asked. "That makes no sense."

Jon shook his head. "I don't know. It was a stupid act, but that's not the point."

"The point is that the CAVIM facility isn't just a chemical factory," Kyra said. "It's a nuclear reprocessing plant." She looked at Jon and realized that she'd reached the end of his analytical process. "The Iranians aren't shipping nuclear warheads into Venezuela. They're making the nuclear warheads *here*."

UN Security Council

"And in December 2008, the Republic of Turkey intercepted an IRISL vessel carrying cargo destined for this so-called tractor factory." Rostow's list of allegations was getting tedious now, coming one after another in an endless stream of criminal charges, but Cooke kept herself rigid. The audience was alternately locked on to the American president or their laptops and tablets, and the CIA director could hear the combined sounds of dozens of reporters and spectators clicking away at their keyboards. "But the cargo didn't contain tractor parts. It contained large quantities of explosives. Now, why would a tractor factory need explosives? It's a shame President Avila isn't here to tell us, isn't it?"

Puerto Cabello, Venezuela

"You'd need them to build an implosion weapon," Jon explained. "You surround the nuclear core with explosives in a very precise pattern. They go off simultaneously, forming a perfectly spherical pressure wave that compresses the core, forcing it to critical mass. Inject a little tritium or deuterium at the right moment to enhance the fission reaction and you've got a bomb with more explosive yield than either Fat Man or Little Boy."

"Convenient that the CAVIM factory produces explosives," Kyra observed.

"Isn't it?" he agreed.

UN Security Council

The audience had fallen silent. Rostow had finally stopped speaking, using the dramatic pause in his presentation to enhance the effect of its blistering rhetoric.

The U.S. president said nothing for almost ten seconds, then leaned forward, his voice low and measured again. "After my recent broadcast, President Avila of Venezuela released a statement declaring his country's innocence and accusing my country of imperialism. He accused my country of hypocrisy and of faking the evidence presented. Well, President Avila," Rostow said, staring directly at the network cameras in the back of the room, "let me say to you, sir, that the evidence released then and the evidence I have released now have not been faked or fabricated in any way. It is you, sir, who have deliberately and cynically deceived this body and the world about your efforts to help Iran evade its obligations in pursuit of nuclear weapons. It is you, sir, who is trying to upset the balance of security in the world. You and Venezuela, in concert with Iran, have created this danger, not the United States. The world has seen how far a Venezuelan chief of state is willing to go in order to deceive this body."

Rostow leaned back, pulled off his glasses, and dropped them on the table, exaggerating the weariness implicit in his gesture. "Mr. President, members of the council, I have ordered the United States Navy to establish a blockade of the northern coast of Venezuela and prevent any ship or aircraft from departing the country. We cannot afford to allow President Avila the opportunity to smuggle Hossein Ahmadi or any illegal nuclear materials out of the country. I ask this council to pass a resolution supporting that action. I further ask this council to pass a second resolution imposing economic sanctions on Venezuela if it does not immediately comply with its obligation under the Treaty on the Non-Proliferation of Nuclear Weapons and open its nuclear sites to IAEA inspectors immediately. I am submitting draft resolutions to that effect today."

The UK prime minister nodded slowly, then leaned forward to his own microphone. "The draft resolutions are accepted for review. We will take a ten-minute recess and then reconvene." He slammed the gavel on the wooden desktop.

The audience erupted; arguments and conversations broke free in a dozen languages, and more than a few members of the crowd ran for the doors, cell phones pressed to their ears.

Feldman spun around in his seat. "Where's Avila?" he growled.

"Caracas, I presume," Cooke replied.

"Why isn't he *here*?!"

"We have no intelligence that answers that question," the CIA director replied.

"That isn't acceptable," Feldman told her.

"It's the only answer I can give you. But if you're asking for a theory, I'd say he's not here because he had a good idea of what the president was going to say and didn't feel the need to defend himself . . . possibly because he's close to becoming a nuclear power and there's nothing the UN can do to stop him before he gets that warhead put together." She pushed herself up and began to button her jacket. "If you don't need me to be a show prop anymore, I have to get back to Langley. I still have people down there and we need to get them out."

"Don't try to bring them home just yet, Kathy. This isn't over and I don't need you diverting resources that we might need—" Feldman began to order.

"We all serve at the pleasure of the president." Then Cooke leaned over, putting her face inches from his. "But I'm going to protect my people, Mr. Feldman," she told him.

She turned her back to the men, made her way around the center table, and walked out of the Security Council chamber. The director of the Central Intelligence Agency was quite sure she would never see it again.

Caracas, Venezuela

The American Marines had broken out the riot gear now. The television on the hotel wall showed the U.S. military guards standing in a line, making a show of force for the mob that certainly numbered in the low thousands now. The scene shifted to show the crowd on the other side of the gates. The protest signs they carried were crude, offering the usual insults and making the typical demands. They'd burned a few flags, but having run out of those they had begun to express their anger through violence, and the bricks and bottles were now coming over the wall at a steady clip. The heavy metal barrier was holding the crowd back despite their best efforts to shake it free from its hinges in the masonry—the U.S. State Department clearly had learned a few things about security and construction since losing its embassy in Iran to the locals in '79—but it couldn't restrain them forever. Only a few *caraqueños* had tried to climb the walls, mostly young, stupid boys anxious to prove their manhood to their peers and nearby girls, but they'd had the sense to retreat when the soldiers had moved toward them. That couldn't last. One of the boys would finally try to outdo his fellows by staying on the wall too long and then things would get interesting.

"Like your own revolution, no?" Avila asked. Ahmadi and the soldier, Elham, stood inside the room, staring at the television. The crowd below seemed to offer no fascination for the Iranians, he saw. *Well, it isn't their country,* he supposed. The future of their mutual enterprise was at stake, admittedly, but the protests and sporadic violence signaled their triumph, he was quite sure.

Ahmadi grunted. He could hear the yells from the streets below even here on the top floor of the residential tower where the Venezuelan president had arranged to hide him from sight. "It does remind me of my younger days," he admitted. "The day we took the Americans' embassy in Tehran was the real moment we saved our country from the West. It is strange how easy it was in the end. The Americans are like shadows . . . frightening until you finally touch them and realize that their image was their power all along. A little courage is enough to break their hold."

Avila smiled and leaned on the balcony rails, placing his forearms on the metal guard. "Our *comandante* Chávez first tried to take power in 1992, when he staged a coup against *el presidente* Carlos Andrés Pérez. The plan was to take Miraflores, the Ministry of Defense, the military airport, a few other important sites. But he was betrayed by defectors and trapped inside the Military Museum. This . . ." Avila raised his hands in a sweep over the protests twenty floors below. "This is what he had hoped to see. And some civilians did rally here and in other cities . . . Maracaibo, Valencia. Still, it all fell to pieces. The *comandante* was captured and went to prison. But God's will was done and he emerged victorious. The coup earned him the people's loyalty and they elected him president seven years later. But his revolution truly began that night of the coup."

"You were there?" Elham asked.

"I was," Avila told him, pride on his face. "Would that I had been a soldier and had been taken with him that night, but I was just a factory worker then. But when I heard of his move on the capital, I ran out and joined the civilians who moved against the city center in Valencia. The troops came against us and we fought them. I escaped arrest, but I knew that God had called me that night to join the Bolivarian revolution. I moved to Caracas, and when the *comandante* was freed, I devoted myself to his cause. He was more than a leader, I think. He was like a prophet, blessed by heaven to return freedom to this country."

"And how many died in your coup?" Elham asked.

Avila shrugged. "A dozen soldiers in the actual attack. A few dozen more when they were called to suppress the crowds. They killed almost a hundred of us. But you are right, *hermano*. Their courage was enough to bind the movement together." The president slapped the metal rail standing between him and the empty air beyond. "And now Chávez's dream is made real. The revolution will never end, but here, today, it becomes *final* . . . irreversible."

"But not all of these people are protesting against the Americans," Ahmadi said. "I'm told that a good many are against you." *And me,* he didn't say.

"We have experience handling protests," Avila said, waving a dismissive hand at the crowd.

Ahmadi nodded, then looked back at the city below. "And President Rostow's address to the UN doesn't worry you?"

"What can they do now?" Avila said.

"They do have a fleet off your coast," Ahmadi observed.

"And what will they do with it? What will they shoot with it?" Avila asked. "We will harass them and they will do nothing . . . perhaps turn some ships away from our ports, but nothing else. You will see. As you said, their image is their power. Even when they put up a line around Cuba during 1962, they wouldn't attack the island itself. They knew what the price would be. And when the weapon is assembled, we will announce it to the world and the Americans will leave. No doubt there will be a period of upheaval. The Americans will try to rally the world against us, to impose sanctions or some other punishment. But our brother Castro has survived sanctions for decades. Your own country has survived sanctions for decades. We will persist and the Americans will have to accept what is."

"I think you will find that the Americans do not like to accept 'what is.' They much prefer to define the rules by which everyone else must play. They're stubborn that way," Elham told him.

The door to the room opened without warning. Carreño stomped in and tossed a leather briefcase on the desk before collapsing himself on the cushions. "You have good news, I presume?" Avila said, more an order than a question.

"No," Carreño said, ignoring the directive. "My motorcade was attacked leaving Miraflores."

Avila's eyes widened and his mouth tightened. "Explain."

"We were pulling out of the gates. A few people in the crowd had thrown rocks, bottles, garbage, but someone threw a Molotov, which hit the car. My driver was able to evade and get us away—"

"They knew who you were?" Avila asked.

"They didn't *care* who I was," Carreño told the president. "We were just some officials leaving the *palacio* and they tried to kill us. It could have been you and they would have done the same. And this is spreading, Diego." The SEBIN director called the president by his first name, too worked up to care about protocol now. "The reports are that the crowds in the other cities are still growing. Attacks on the troops are getting more violent. We are taking casualties."

Avila nodded, his teeth clenched. The intelligence officer knew his chief of state well enough to see that he was embarrassed by the news. Weakness before allies was not to be tolerated. "I don't want these groups coordinating."

"We can shut down Internet service…the phone companies will follow orders. We can send soldiers to occupy them if they won't," Carreño suggested.

"We should shut down the entire cellular network," Avila replied.

"That would make it difficult to coordinate with the gangs and other civilian allies."

Avila grunted. "Very well. Leave it up for now. But if the situation grows worse, it will have to come down."

"Yes, sir," Carreño said, suddenly tired.

USS *Vicksburg*
11°22' North 67°49' West
75 miles north of the Venezuelan coast

Captain Dutch Riley stepped through the hatch onto the *Vicksburg* bridge. "Captain on the bridge," the officer of the deck announced.

"Report," he ordered.

"We have a contact bearing one-eight-three, ten thousand yards on course zero zero zero, speed twenty-five knots," the lieutenant replied. "Sir, she's approaching the red line and will cross in four minutes at her present speed. Signal bridge reports she's a warship, likely a *Lupo*-class frigate. I've ordered a course change to intercept, speed thirty knots. What are your orders?"

"Very well. The XO is in the CIC?"

"Yes, sir."

Course zero zero zero, Riley thought. That was no navigational error. *Due north. She's going to run the line.* "Set Condition One, then ask him about it," Riley ordered, nodding his head toward the approaching vessel.

The junior officer looked up, surprised that the captain was declining to take immediate command. "Aye aye, sir," he said, trying to suppress a smile. The OOD turned on the 1MC. "General Quarters, General Quarters, all hands man your battle stations. General Quarters, General Quarters, all hands man your battle stations. Damage Control, set Condition Zebra." Then he took a deep breath, switched off the shipwide speaker, and raised the mic again. "Venezuelan warship, this is USS *Vicksburg*. State your intentions." He held the mic to his chest, keeping a mental countdown as he waited for the answer, which didn't come in time, and so he lifted the mic to his mouth and repeated himself.

Venezuelan Missile Frigate *Almirante Brión*

Captain Rafael Loyo of the Bolivarian National Armada of Venezuela fought down the urge to tell the American his real desires in profane terms and restricted himself to his orders. Whether the admirals in Caracas were actual fools or just playing at it for some higher purpose, he didn't know, but regardless, he didn't like them using his ship this way. *My ship?* he thought. It wasn't really, he knew, but every captain liked to think so. The days were long gone when pirates sailed these waters and captains acted alone for months, sometimes years at a time, without orders from their superiors. In those days, a ship truly did belong to its master and commander. Now a captain was never truly alone and the admirals above and far away used ships like pawns. A disobedient captain could be removed on a whim, whisked away by helicopter within hours of even questioning an order. He wanted desperately to disobey this one, but there was no point to it. The admirals would have their way and the American blockade line would be tested, whether with the *Almirante Brión* or another vessel.

Vicksburg? Loyo ransacked his memory and came up with nothing. One of the junior officers finally handed him a vessel recognition card—Ticonderoga-*class guided missile cruiser*. The American ship was four times the size of the *Almirante Brión,* bigger, heavier, a severe mismatch in every way but speed. His own ship was a *Lupo*-class missile frigate, built by the Italians to counter the Russian Navy ships in the Mediterranean, then later upgraded by the Americans before Chávez turned so completely hostile to them. The *Brión* was no ship to be trifled with, but it was now badly outmatched, not nearly the equal of the vessel he was approaching. At best, with luck and God's blessing, she might actually manage to sink the *Vicksburg*. She had a pair of Mark-32 torpedo tubes, American designed, and the ordnance to go with them. If Loyo fired first at close range, he might prevail. But the *Vicksburg* would surely savage his own ship in short order, sending her to the bottom in the time it took the torpedo to transit the space between them. One antiship missile from the American ship would kill his entire crew and they did not deserve that fate. They were a good crew, mostly boys who should not have been pawns in this stupid game of machismo that the politicians were trying to play with the rest of the world.

Loyo would not fire first. He would not be the man to plunge his country into a war the Americans could win very, very quickly.

He looked down through the forward windows at the foredeck. His men were at their stations, guns manned, but his sailors were untested. Venezuela hadn't fought a naval battle since . . . when? The War of Independence in 1824? Certainly not in his lifetime. None of his men had ever fired a gun in anger and now they were facing down the most powerful navy in all of history? The admirals and politicians expected this crew of untested young men to embarrass the Americans? He would count himself fortunate if one of those nervous teenagers on the deck didn't do something foolish out of pure fear.

"*Vicksburg,* this is the Bolivarian National Armada ship *Almirante Brión,*" Loyo replied over his own mic. The Venezuelan sailor rankled at having to answer in English. It was another sign of which navy truly ruled these international waters. "I am engaged in the defense of Venezuelan coastal waters per international law. You are in violation of our territorial sovereignty. Withdraw immediately." *Foolishness,* he thought. They were well past the twelve-mile line that marked the end of Venezuela's territory and the U.S. captain surely knew it. He didn't need a GPS to tell him that.

At this distance, a sextant and compass would've been more than enough to figure that out. *They will not run.*

USS *Vicksburg*

"You have got to be kidding me," Riley muttered, too quiet for anyone else on the bridge to hear.

"*Brión,* this is USS *Vicksburg,*" the OOD said. He took a deep breath, excited that the captain was putting his trust in him, terrified of speaking even a single word wrong. "We are in international waters and are engaged in the enforcement of the Venezuelan quarantine per orders of the president of the United States and UN Security Council resolution twenty-five eighty-seven. You are hereby ordered to remain inside the zone or you will be fired upon. Heave to or reverse your course." He looked to his commanding officer for approval. Riley nodded at him and watched the young man's confidence start to swell.

The response was immediate. "*Vicksburg,* this is *Almirante Brión.* You are in Venezuelan waters. You will withdraw or we will seize your vessel in the name of the Bolivarian Republic of Venezuela for violations of our national laws." The Venezuelan captain's English was accented, heavy to the point of being unintelligible through the speaker.

"*Brión,* this is your last warning. Reverse course or you will be fired upon," the OOD ordered.

Venezuelan Missile Frigate *Almirante Brión*

The Americans were holding their ground, as Loyo had believed they would do. Both vessels were well out into the open oceans, both their captains knew it, and *Vicksburg*'s captain must have thought Loyo a fool for disputing that reality. But his orders were clear and Loyo intended to follow them. He could hardly expect his own men to follow his orders if he was willing to disobey those he was given.

"Steady as you go," he ordered the sailor at the helm.

"Steady as you go, course zero zero zero, sir."

"How long to the quarantine line?" Loyo asked.

"Two minutes, ten seconds, sir," the helmsman answered. The younger man's voice quavered a bit as he said it.

"Very well." *He's afraid,* Loyo knew. *I don't blame him. I'm afraid.* But perhaps his leaders were right and the Americans wouldn't fire. Any fight now would be one-sided and perhaps the fear of appearing as bullies before the world would stay the Americans' hand.

Maybe, Loyo thought. He would know in two minutes.

USS *Vicksburg*

"They're holding course and speed, sir," the OOD reported a minute later. "They'll cross the red line in fifty-five seconds."

My responsibility if we have to fire, Riley thought. The first shot in a conflict should never be laid on the shoulders of a subordinate, he believed. The younger officer had performed well but it was time for Riley to take back his command. "Very well. Lieutenant, once she crosses the red line, put one shot across her bow with the five-inch gun."

"Aye aye, sir," the officer of the watch said, relieved

that the captain was finally taking charge. "Forty-five seconds."

Venezuelan Missile Frigate *Almirante Brión*

"Distance to the *Vicksburg*?" Loyo asked. He stared at the American vessel through his binoculars. She was some distance away, but even so, she was large enough for him to see the five-inch gun swivel on the foredeck.

"Thirteen-point-five kilometers. Ten seconds to the red line, Captain," the helmsman announced.

"Sir, shall I target the *Vicksburg*?" the gunnery officer asked.

Target them? Loyo thought. *I suppose we must.* The *Vicksburg*'s guns were surely trained on his vessel. Loyo nodded. "Very well." Loyo counted backward in his mind. *Diez, nueve, ocho, siete, seis, cinco, cuatro, tres, dos, uno . . .*

"We have crossed the red line, sir."

For a moment, Loyo thought the Americans would do nothing, that his superiors had been right. The U.S. Navy would not fire. The quarantine was an illusion and the *Vicksburg* and her sister ships and the aircraft flying between them in a thousand-mile line were all an empty show of force. Then anger began to surge in him, fury that the Americans had tried to oppress his country again, to intimidate them into acting out of cowardice. But he and his men were not cowards. He felt a bit of pride swell in his chest, that he and his men had braved the danger despite their fears—

The *Vicksburg*'s five-inch gun roared, fire and smoke tearing into the blue sky. The round struck the water just ahead of the bow, missing the *Brión* by only tens of meters and spewing a geyser into the sky that flew as high as the ship's bridge. The officers on the bridge began to yell, alternately asking for orders and hurling them around, contrary directions given as discipline started to break down in the face of real hostile fire.

It's over, Loyo thought. The Americans were not hesitating, they were not backing down . . . no sign of weakness. *We cannot fight them and win—*

USS *Vicksburg*

Riley had heard his ship's gun fire before, but never in anger, only in drills. It sounded the same this time, but he felt no joy in it now. *Heave to, you idiot,* he ordered the other ship's captain. Whoever was in charge of the *Brión* had to know how badly he was outgunned. *You obeyed your orders, you made the good show, now don't be stupid—*

"Sir!" the officer of the deck yelled. He pointed out the window.

The *Brión's* OTOBreda 127mm deck gun flashed orange and red. It was a strange thing, to see the sight without hearing the noise of the gun, and it took Riley a second to realize the cause. The sound was slower than the light.

The sound wave was also slower than the round the gun had just fired. They wouldn't hear it before it hit.

"Come right, steer course one one five! All engines ahead full!" Riley ordered.

"Come right, steer course one one five, all engines ahead full, aye, sir!" the OOD repeated, confirming the command.

Riley grabbed the 1MC. "All hands, brace for shock!" He felt *Vicksburg's* four General Electric turbine engines surge under his feet, trying to squeeze out the few horsepower that they hadn't already been throwing into the water. The two propellers chewed into the Atlantic and the ship began a hard turn to port—

The round hit the *Vicksburg* just aft of the island, ripping into metal and armor, sending a small fireball and white smoke back out over the water. Riley heard the dull thud, followed by the scream of his wounded ship as the steel plating was torn and the entire vessel shuddered under the blow.

Venezuelan Missile Frigate *Almirante Brión*

No! Loyo thought. The explosion on *Vicksburg*'s superstructure seemed impossibly large given the distance and he knew without question that American sailors had just died. He prayed to God that it wasn't so but the shot had hit the ship a solid blow. He'd seen it rocked in the water and was sure he would be able to see the hole in the armor when the smoke cleared . . . assuming he lived that long.

"Who fired?!" he yelled. He knew the answer before he'd asked the question. The OTOBreda gun was controlled by a single console, operated by one crewman who controlled the entire firing sequence. "I didn't order you to fire!"

The crewman, barely more than a teenager, looked out, terrified. *He panicked,* Loyo realized. *The Americans fired and in his terror he fired back.* But now that the *Vicksburg* was wounded, fired on by his ship in international waters, the Americans had cause to return fire in kind, and the *Ticonderoga*-class guided missile cruiser carried ordnance that would crack a *Lupo*-class ship in half.

Loyo grabbed for the radio mic. "*Vicksburg,* this is

Brión! Do not fire! Repeat, hold your fire! Our shot was an accident! An accident!" He doubted the American captain would believe him.

In his panic, Loyo failed to realize that he was yelling in Spanish.

USS *Vicksburg*

"XO, return fire, all guns!" Riley ordered. "Then ready the Harpoons to fire on my order." Riley's executive officer was in the Combat Information Center.

"Return fire, all guns then ready Harpoon launch, aye sir," the XO replied over the radio. *Vicksburg* had two five-inch guns and they both roared almost before the executive officer had finished confirming the order.

The ship shuddered as both guns went off at once and Riley watched the forward gun spew its spent metal shell out of the turret. The reload would be automatic and take a little more than a second. He heard the speaker come alive again, the captain of the *Brión* yelling something, but Riley didn't speak Spanish and didn't care now what the man had to say anyway. His rules of engagement allowed him to respond "in kind" and the Venezuelans weren't going to get another shot.

Venezuelan Missile Frigate *Almirante Brión*

Both of *Vicksburg*'s five-inch shells connected with the Venezuelan ship. The *Almirante Brión* heaved under the captain's feet and Loyo heard men scream in terror as the vessel bucked in the water. Fire erupted from the foredeck and the captain heard the screech of tearing metal as shrapnel scattered across the deck. Loyo wasn't sure where the second round had hit, surely aft of the island, and he prayed the explosion wasn't near the waterline. Men and bodies took flight, some pitching out over the rails into the water, others sliding across the deck, coming to rest against bulkheads and whatever else blocked their paths.

The men of his bridge crew were lost in their own yells and panic, their drills and training hardly remembered. The fire control officer was paralyzed by his own fear and terror at what he had started. Any order Loyo gave would take long seconds for the men to carry out now, assuming that enough of them could control themselves long enough to hear him and obey.

He lifted his binoculars and looked out across the water at the enemy vessel. *Vicksburg*'s five-inch guns flashed again and Loyo knew that more of his sailors were about to die.

He also knew that the five-inch guns weren't *Vicksburg*'s heaviest weapons. A single Harpoon missile would end this fight in seconds, maybe cracking the *Brión* in half, maybe not, but surely sending her to the bottom with every sailor aboard who couldn't stagger to the deck and throw himself into the sea. He couldn't let that happen. There were too many young boys aboard, too many men who deserved to go home today. Could he sink the *Vicksburg* before she fired? If the captain gave the order to launch his torpedoes, were there enough men belowdecks who would hear and obey to carry out the order? Maybe he couldn't stop this at all. If his ship was to die, he might be able to sink the American ship too—

Loyo felt a heavenly calm settle over him. *No,* he thought. Even if he gave the order, a Harpoon would cover the distance in a fraction of the time it would take his torpedoes to reach the *Vicksburg* and his men would die. If they managed to fire the torpedoes before the Harpoon struck, the *Vicksburg* would be crippled, possibly sunk, either way unable to perform rescue operations even if the captain were so inclined, and men would die all the same.

The second pair of five-inch shells hit the *Brión*, tearing into the steel plates, one round hitting the superstructure, and Loyo lost his footing as the entire island shuddered, as though some giant's fist had struck his ship. The deck was hidden by dark smoke now, and Loyo could smell it in the air. Electronics were burning, the insulation on the wires melting.

Vicksburg's guns flashed again. There was only one choice to make and he had to make it now. The next five-inch shells might kill his radio and all hope of ending the fight while some of his men lived.

Loyo picked up the mic, cleared his mind, and made sure this time that he was speaking in English.

"*Vicksburg*, this is *Almirante Brión*," he said calmly. "We surrender."

Two more shells from *Vicksburg*'s deck guns slammed into the *Brión*'s hull, ripping holes in the hard metal, one of them near the waterline.

USS *Vicksburg*

"Cease fire!" Riley ordered.

"Cease fire, aye," the XO confirmed. Down in the CIC, the fire control officer slammed his hand down on the controls and the guns obeyed their captain.

The bridge crew turned to their captain, waiting for his next command. Riley looked out at the Venezuelan ship.

The *Brión* was almost hidden by a cloud of black

smoke. Oil and fluids were burning somewhere below-decks and he could see the flames through the gaping holes in the hull. She'd taken six hits from his five-inchers and would've taken at least that many more before a Harpoon would've closed the distance and torn her in two. Riley wondered for a moment how close the fire control team had been to launching the antiship missile he'd ordered.

He lifted the mic to his mouth. "*Brión*, this is *Vicksburg*. We accept your surrender. Heave to and prepare to receive boarding parties."

"Understood, *Vicksburg*. We will receive your boarding parties. Please understand that we fired on your vessel by accident. Repeat, we fired by accident. Can we render any assistance to your crew?"

Riley's eyebrows went up at the question. *They want to help us? It took some humility for the man to make that offer,* he realized. *Their captain is telling the truth. Maybe we've got a chance to back everyone down here.*

He turned on the radio. "*Brión*, thank you for your offer. Your concern is much appreciated. We will discuss mutual assistance after our boarding party has come aboard your vessel."

"Understood, *Vicksburg*. Standing by to receive your launch."

Riley flipped the switch on the 1MC. "This is the captain," he said. His voice echoed throughout the passageways and across the smoking deck outside. "I have accepted the surrender of the Venezuelan warship *Almirante Brión*. Their captain reports that they fired by accident and has offered their assistance. We will maintain general quarters until we confirm non-belligerence." The captain could imagine how well that bit of news was being received belowdecks by the crew. "Your performance during the fight was exemplary. Well done. Let's show them how Americans can be gracious in victory. Boarding parties to the deck in one minute. All departments, send damage and casualty reports to the bridge immediately. Master Chief LeJeune to the bridge."

It took LeJeune less than thirty seconds to obey the order.

"How does it look?" Riley asked.

"We're okay, I think. One clean hit to the island. We've got wounded; looks like four casualties and we took some damage to the multifunction radar."

"Status of the casualties?" Riley asked.

"I'm not sure, sir. I saw them as I passed by them running. At least one critical that I saw, judging by the burns. Two others look serious. We'll have to evac them out."

"Very well," Riley acknowledged. "Make it so."

"Not going to seize the ship, sir?" LeJeune asked, nodding his head at the *Almirante Brión*. "You're passing up your chance to be a commodore for a few hours," he said, a bit of dry mirth in his voice.

Riley pondered that for a minute. "No," he said finally, too quiet for the rest of the bridge crew to hear. "He never fired a shot after that first salvo and he says that was an accident."

"You believe that?"

"If it gives us the chance to avoid a shooting war and killing a lot of Venezuelans kids, I'll choose to believe it," Riled responded. "We'll help patch them up and then send them home under their own flag. Tell Doc Winter to get over there and help take care of their wounded after he's prepped our own for evac.

We'll airlift anyone he can't treat here over to the *Truman*."

"That's generous," LeJeune conceded.

"Maybe the sight of two wounded ships helping each other out after a misunderstanding might get everyone to calm down a bit," Riley said.

"Maybe, assuming it really was a misunderstanding," the master chief agreed. "But the politicians aren't always so good at connecting compassion with common sense."

Puerto Cabello, Venezuela

The stars were out, the lesser ones near the horizon disappearing in the light that the port town was throwing into the sky. Jon stared at the darkness just over the town where only a single point remained. *Mars,* he thought. There was a red tint to it. Or perhaps the color came from the smoke. Several pyres rose from Puerto Cabello: four, and one had started in the last hour. All were too large to be campfires set by tourists on the beach, and if Marisa had been right, there wouldn't be any tourists on the beach now anyway. He closed his eyes, hoping to pick up some stray sound from the port city that might give him some clue about what was happening, but all was silent. *Humidity muffles noise,* he knew, and this country had more than its share of humidity.

He turned his back to the city lights and searched the now-darkened valley floor for any sign of Kyra. The young woman had left hours before to fetch the truck. He'd wanted to accompany her, but she'd insisted on going alone. *You're better on the Barrett,* she'd said. *The hill's defensible and you can cover me.* Neither was true.

There was no defensible position against an enemy that could bring in helicopters and lay down fire from the air, and the forest canopy kept him from seeing her once she reached the base of the hill. But he couldn't argue with her assertion that it made no sense for them both to get arrested if someone was waiting for them at the abandoned shack. So she'd left all her gear but her gun, climbed down, and walked into the woods. He'd stared through the Barrett scope at the cluster of buildings where they'd left the vehicle, looking for some sign of her until growing darkness had made that futile. Now he hoped to see truck headlights through the woods from that direction, but there was nothing. That made sense, too. Kyra would probably be navigating with her night vision alone, fearing that headlights would be visible from the air. There was no sound from her engine either. At this distance, the humidity was probably stifling that too.

He could call her on the PRC-148. She was carrying hers. Without the antenna or transceiver, the radios were only good for line of sight and he could see far enough, but he didn't want Kyra to think he was looking over her shoulder.

Jon took up the cell phone instead. He dialed the one number in its memory, the call went through on the first try, and he waited for the encryption to start up.

"This is Quiver."

"Quiver, Sherlock," he told Mari. "Just checking in."

"Good to hear your voice," she said. "What's your status?"

"Arrowhead has gone back to move the truck closer to our position. She left three hours ago, still isn't here," he reported. "She should be back soon. How are things at your place?"

"Some of the locals weren't thrilled to hear that Avila is trying to take the country nuclear," Mari said. "Somebody threw a Molotov cocktail over the wall a half hour ago. Not sure what things are like outside the walls. None of the media are showing what's happening. I think the president here has shut that down. We're just getting snippets and cell-phone video from bloggers. But from what we can tell, there are some pretty ugly riots going down across the country."

"I think that's going on here too," Jon said. "I see smoke columns going up from the city closest to my position."

"Roger that."

"Anything new on the bad guys?" he asked.

"POTUS made an appearance before the UN and called them out. The Security Council approved his request for a blockade. He doesn't want them moving their package out of the country. The ambassador is working the phones with the Colombians and the Brazilians to make sure their borders stay closed, but it sounds like Guyana isn't cooperating . . . some greedy autocrats are holding out for some bribes in return for their help. Whoever thought Western security would hinge on Guyana? Anyway, congratulations. You set off the sequel to the Cuban Missile Crisis."

"It gets better," Jon said. "I'm pretty sure the base where Arrowhead found the package has a nuclear reprocessing facility hidden away somewhere. Probably under the chemical plant."

"Was that on the video?"

"No. But it's a logical deduction. I'll spell it out for you when I see you. For now, just tell the folks back home. Someone there is bound to be smart enough to work backward from the conclusion to figure out my reasoning," he replied.

"You're not a weapons analyst. How do you know this stuff?"

"I've written a few Red Cell papers on proliferation," he replied. "If the facility isn't here, it's at one of the other sites. And if that's right, then all they need is a single nuclear reactor, even a small one, and they've got everything they need to run the nuclear fuel cycle."

"I believe you. You were always right."

"You always found that annoying," he said.

"Yeah, I did, but the arguments were fun," she admitted. "Until that day in the sandbox. You were different after that. I always hoped you were going to get over what happened, but you never did."

"That's the funny thing about Asperger's. It turns out that when a memory gets dredged up, you get all of the emotions that came with it the first time . . . they don't fade. Combine that with an eidetic memory and time doesn't heal a thing."

U.S. Embassy
Caracas, Venezuela

Marisa closed her eyes as that revelation sank in. *He never told me.* No, that wasn't right. *You didn't stay long enough to find out, did you?* "How do you get past them?" she asked quietly, trying to be careful. Words felt dangerous now, each one a weapon primed to go off if she picked wrong.

"You try hard to never think about them . . . or you replace them with something better. Whichever works," he told her.

"Is that what you've been doing since I left?"

Marisa asked. "Replacing them?" *Of course he was,* she thought. *How could he not?*

Jon said nothing and silence filled the time, giving her the answer. "Jon, Syria was coming apart. Assad was breaking out the chemical weapons. The Special Activities Center doesn't always let us tell families or friends where we're going. You know that."

"I do. But that doesn't explain why you didn't tell me you were coming back. I found out you were in D.C. when I read about it in an intel cable."

She shifted the phone headset to the other side of her head, used her newly freed hand to lock the window shades open, and looked out at the city as her mind sifted through the answers she could give. Small pyres of smoke were rising in a dozen columns, from the shantytowns that covered the mountain hills to more than one spot between the residential and commercial towers surrounding the Plaza Bolívar in the city's heart.

"I didn't know how to help you—" she began.

"So you just left?" he asked. "That certainly didn't help."

"I didn't know what else to do." It was all she could find to say.

"Almost anything else you could have done would've been more helpful than leaving," he told her.

Now it was Marisa's silence that hung in the air. "Does it ever help when the other person says they're sorry?" she asked finally.

"No," Jon said, plain and fast enough to cut. "That's the funny thing about emotions, especially the rough ones. They don't care why they were born and they're never in a hurry to die. All you can do is live with them until you can learn to ignore them.

And all the excuses and apologies in the world don't change that a bit."

"I'm—"

A Marine appeared in her doorway, a member of the Embassy Security Group. "Just a second, Sherlock," Marisa said, using his unofficial crypt again, a signal that the conversation had gone from personal to professional. She covered the phone with her hand. "What is it?" she asked the sergeant.

"The ambassador just received orders from Sec-State, ma'am. We're evacuating the embassy. You and your people are to sanitize and secure your spaces, then report to the lobby in one hour. Choppers will be landing behind the building and all personnel will be relocated to the quarantine fleet, where you'll board a transport for Washington."

Marisa sat, stunned into silence. She finally forced herself to speak. "I have people in the field. I can't leave them out there."

"You can't stay here, ma'am. You won't do them any good if the mob comes over the fence and you get taken."

Marisa nodded. "Understood. Tell the ambassador the rest of my people will be ready to ship out. I'm staying here until my people are safe or the situation becomes untenable." She put the phone back to her ear. "Jon . . . SecState is closing the embassy. We're being evacuated."

"How long?" he asked.

"One hour . . . not enough time for you and Arrowhead to drive back, even if you could get inside the gates, which you can't. They're going to relocate us to the fleet. I'm staying here until they drag me out. Once I get to whichever ship we land on, I'll talk to the captain and see if we can't arrange a personnel recovery mission for you. If you have to move, get to a safe house." Marisa paused. "Arrowhead knows where one is in Caracas."

"Roger that," Jon said. "Don't forget about us."

"I never have," Marisa said. Jon disconnected. She stared at the phone, then dropped it on her desk. She started to stack the classified folders on her desk. The chief of station could already hear the industrial shredders in the next room warming up.

Puerto Cabello, Venezuela

Jon turned the phone off. The sky was full of stars now, the sun entirely gone. He could have forgotten that he was in a hostile land if not for the smoke that broke up the lights of Puerto Cabello on the horizon. He was still watching the sky an hour later when the growl of the truck's engine finally cut through the silence.

DAY EIGHT

Elham watched Presidente Avila as the chief of state read the intelligence report for a third time, disbelief on his face. Carreño and Ahmadi both stood in silence on the other side of the antique desk. None of the senior men had spoken a word in five minutes. The soldier turned back to the window and stared at the manicured garden below. The sun was behind the office towers now and soon would drop below the hills to the west. Dark shadows were stretching out behind the buildings with bright sunbeams cutting through the spaces between them. Farther away, an American Sikorsky SH-60 Seahawk helicopter glided over the skyline, descending toward the embassy that sat out of sight beyond the trees that surrounded the complex. Smoke was rising out past the gates, some of it black as ink. The locals were burning tires now, some not too far from the presidential offices.

Avila had made a great show of machismo when they had finally arrived, calling them *hermanos* and boasting that matters were proceeding as planned. That last claim was a lie. Getting here had been tedious, the motorcade having to move slowly through the streets clogged with protesters. The crowds had been mixed, some among them turning on each other with their words, some with their fists and whatever weapons they could find lying about. An unhealthy number had attacked the cars, requiring the SEBIN guards to assault more than a few men to clear a path to the gates. The *presidente* was like so many other civilian leaders Elham had served over the years, assuming that the world would happily comply with their grand designs and having no contingency plan when events refused to go as they willed. If nothing else, the Americans certainly had shown themselves to be a disobedient bunch.

"They fired on our ship," the *presidente* finally muttered. "I had not thought they would fire."

"Actually, our ship fired first," Carreño corrected him. "The captain claims it was an accident but the American vessel then opened up with all guns and beat her into submission. Why they didn't put a missile in her, I have no idea. A single one would've finished our vessel. The *Brión* would have been sunk in short order had she not surrendered." It was not a pleasant statement but it was an honest one, though not the kind that Avila usually liked to hear in this room. "The Americans boarded, helped the wounded and repaired the damage to the navigation system, then sent her on her way back to our naval base at Puerto Cabello."

"There must be some way we can play this to our advantage," Avila suggested.

His voice reeked of desperation to Elham's ears and the soldier found his patience was exhausted. "You have nothing," he said. Carreño and Ahmadi both turned toward him, surprised to hear the Revolutionary Guard soldier interject himself into the conversation.

"Elham—" Ahmadi started, caution in his voice.

"They have denied you victory at every level," Elham noted. "Had they sunk her, you could have claimed American aggression had cost Venezuelan lives and there would have been no witnesses to contradict you. Had they left her adrift with wounded sailors, you could have yelled about American arrogance or cruelty. Had they seized her, you could have cursed the Americans for seizing Venezuelan property and holding your men. Now they have beaten you with both guns and charity. And the UN Security Council has agreed to their quarantine of your coast, denying you even the claim that they are acting as imperialists. I believe the Americans would say that you have no leg to stand on."

"You speak out of turn, Elham," Ahmadi said, his words tinged with anger.

"And when would my turn come?" Elham asked. "I have been a soldier for more than twenty years and if I have learned one thing, it is that the lowest-ranking man in the room is usually the one who sees the truth most clearly. The higher the rank, the more one is concerned with how the situation makes him look before his peers and the world instead of how to solve the problems at hand. And the problem is that we are all trapped here now with an illegal weapon of mass destruction that the world won't tolerate."

Avila dropped the paper and pushed it away from him. He leaned back in his chair, lifted his chin, and puffed up his chest. "No, the Russians will help us," he began. "They are our allies too. We have conducted joint naval exercises with them—"

Are you truly that stupid? Elham thought but didn't say. Patience gone or not, he still had some small sense of propriety left in him. "The Russians in the Security Council abstained from the vote to cut your country off from the civilized world," Elham pointed out. "They are happy to take whatever you give up freely but they are not prepared to risk anything for you. If they won't even cast a vote in your favor, they certainly won't send warships to face down the United States Navy." He finally turned away from the window and looked to his countryman. "We are on our own here, you and I. Our hosts cannot protect us, not from the Americans and certainly not from the Israelis who will be coming. This country will be crawling with CIA and Mossad within days."

"That is not true," Avila protested. "The Americans have no power here! They cannot touch you so long as you are under our protection. You can stay here indefinitely. Our patience is greater than theirs—"

"Is it?" Ahmadi asked. "Even if that is true, the question is what will the Americans do when their patience runs out? And the Israelis will have no patience whatsoever in this matter."

Avila looked up at his intelligence adviser, desperate for some good solution. "What do you think, Diego?"

Carreño scratched his beard, then pulled up a chair and lowered himself into it carefully, trying to avoid touching his tender ribs. "I think we must strengthen our position."

Avila leaned forward, anxious. "What do you propose?"

The SEBIN director made a show of pondering the question for several long seconds before answering. "First, we must move the weapon. Clearly, it is not safe where it is. The Americans know about the facility—"

"The Americans know about all of your facilities," Elham interrupted.

Avila leaped to his feet and pounded on the desk with a closed fist hard enough to crack a knuckle. "That is not possible!"

"It is not only possible, it is certain," Elham corrected him. "The American shooter on the hilltop spoke to his superior as he fled, no? Yet the call was made on a common cell phone, which we found. He used no encryption. Why not? To be certain that you would intercept the call, which you did. And what did you do? Order security sweeps at every facility in the program. Do you really think the American satellites didn't see that?" The look on Avila's face delivered his answer. "You were outmaneuvered, *presidente*," Elham told him.

"Even if that is true, we can still win," Carreño said, cutting in. It never hurt to help a superior preserve his sense of machismo in the presence of allies, especially ones who were dubious and wavering. "As long as the Americans and their allies don't know where the cargo sits, we will still have a path to victory. They can't go about the country randomly striking at sites hoping to destroy it. Eventually the world would turn against that and the American public themselves always tire of long military operations. Uncertainty would be our greatest tool."

"Yes. Yes!" Avila agreed. "How soon can it be moved?"

"Assuming we want to finish construction first, we could have it ready for transport by tomorrow," Carreño said. "Do you agree?" he asked, turning to Ahmadi.

"I would," Ahmadi said after a slight pause. Elham grunted in disgust.

"I would also suggest," Carreño continued, "that perhaps we should consider seizing the American embassy."

"To what end?" Elham asked, incredulous. *Madness,* he thought.

Carreño twisted in his chair to address the Iranian soldier. "Two years ago, the last *presidente* ordered me to run an operation to capture an American spy on our soil. The mission failed, but the goal was to hold up the criminal to the world as a useful diversion away from the start of this operation. We wanted to put the United States back on its heels and we need that now. We may not find these spies in the countryside, but the Americans must have any number of spies in that embassy . . . but only for a few more hours. They're evacuating their staff and if we hesitate, they will slip past us on one of those helicopters. But even if we don't catch their real spies, anyone we could grab could be accused of such and no one will accept American denials outright. And if we have prisoners"—Elham noted that the man declined to use the word *hostages*—"the Americans will have to proceed much more slowly."

Elham watched Avila nod slowly, as though Carreño's words were the wisdom of God Himself. "I think that would be good," the *presidente* agreed.

"What do you think, doctor?" Avila said, turning to Ahmadi.

"I . . . I think it might work," the Iranian said. "We seized the American embassy in Tehran in my youth. If their president now is as weak as their president then, it could give you some considerable leverage."

"And if he isn't?" Elham said.

"Do we know how many members of the embassy staff remain?" Avila asked, ignoring the question.

"No idea," Carreño admitted.

"Then move quickly . . . tomorrow morning, I think. We want the cameras to see it . . . but kill the cellular network when the order is given. We don't want the

Americans warning their *asesinos* in the countryside,"
Avila ordered. "You see, my friends," he said, turning
back to Ahmadi and Elham, "this will work itself out
in our favor. Watch and see."

You are a fool, Elham thought. The man was choosing to believe his own fantasies instead of dealing with
realities. *You want the Americans to tire of this quickly
but you want to kidnap their citizens? Fool* wasn't a
strong enough word.

CIA Director's Conference Room

Holland stuffed the last Krispy Kreme donut into his
mouth, his fourth of the morning. The sugar crash
would hit him before ten o'clock and it would be terrible, but for now it kept him going. The last file of bank
records appeared on his screen and he started to filter
through the account numbers, then stopped to rub
his eyes. He'd been staring at spreadsheets throughout the night and his vision was rebelling, refusing
to focus on any more of them. He squeezed his eyes
shut, then opened them and shook his head. Finally
the laptop screen sharpened and he began to scroll
through the numbers again.

U.S. Embassy
Caracas, Venezuela

The morning sun was to the Marines' backs, pouring
its rays square into the faces of the mob. *Small favors,*
Corporal Charlie Mansfield thought. *If I gotta stand
here decked out at the crack of dawn without a cup
of coffee, the least you morons can do is go blind.* He
shifted his feet slightly, trying to relieve the discom-

fort. He and his brothers from the Corps were standing in a line, twenty feet behind the embassy's main
gate, all dressed in riot gear. The *caraqueño* mob on
the other side had been mostly quiet during the night.
It took a dedicated protester to shout curses at dirty
Americans in the dark hours before the dawn. Many
of the mobbers had stretched out on the grounds outside, finally submitting to nature's demand for rest,
but sleep had come hard as Seahawks from the U.S.
Fourth Fleet descended over them at least twice an
hour throughout the night. The helos had landed behind the embassy, each taking up a load of passengers,
then rising over the building and passing low back
over the protesters on its way out to sea. Mansfield
didn't know whether the pilots had been doing it on
purpose to annoy the crowd but he couldn't say that
he disapproved.

He heard boots on the asphalt behind him and
turned to see another Marine approach at a slow jog,
one of the guards stationed inside the building. His
fellow leatherneck slowed to a stop, dispensing with
the salutes that would've required Mansfield's setting
his gear on the ground in order to return. He leaned
in close so the corporal could hear through his riot
helmet. "Last Seahawks from the fleet are prepping
for launch, ETA one hour. They'll touch down on the
back field and keep the engines warm in order to evac
us if it comes to that. Everything quiet?"

"No trouble so far this morning. But it's early.
That'll change," Mansfield replied. The other Marine
nodded and jogged off back up the hill toward the
embassy.

It took another fifty minutes to fulfill Mansfield's
prophecy. The mob stood quiet most of that time, a

few of the younger groups singing patriotic songs and starting to wave their signs and flags, hoping to inspire some zeal in their tired comrades. It seemed too early for that yet . . .

. . . and then Mansfield felt the emotions rise in the air. Something changed in the crowd, some kind of excitement moving through them in a wave. The murmurs and Spanish curses began to rumble through the air and the sergeant could feel the anger spread like a morning fog. *This is going to be ugly,* he thought.

The Molotov cocktail came over the wall from the middle of the crowd. Mansfield couldn't see who'd lit the bottle that landed just in front of the Marine guard line, close enough to burn. They stepped back a few feet. The next homemade munition followed a few seconds later, this one passing just over the heads and exploding behind the Marines, spreading its payload across the black asphalt.

The crowd's yells would've been deafening now if not for the helmets. The Venezuelans were pressing themselves against the gates, hands and fists reaching through the bars, and Mansfield spoke more than enough Spanish to know they were screaming death threats—

It happened in an instant. A roar went up from the crowd and suddenly the men in front were grabbing at the bars, trying to shake them from their hinges again. The younger *caraqueños,* impatient with that approach, began to scale the gates and the wall.

This is it, Mansfield told himself. *They're coming over.* Some had tried before, ones and two. Now they were trying almost by the dozen.

The corporal stepped forward and raised his tear-gas launcher to his shoulder. The crowd didn't recoil, started yelling louder instead. As the first youth reached the top of the gate and stood straight up, waving his comrades forward, Mansfield pulled the trigger, heard the launcher utter a loud thump, and felt it press against his shoulder. The CS grenade struck the teenager square in the chest, white smoke trailing, and the young man pitched backward, falling into the bodies below. The rest of the Marine line followed Mansfield's lead, more CS grenades sailing over the wall into the crowd, pouring out their white smoke. The yells turned to coughs, then gagging, tears flowing as the vicious aerosol attacked the crowd's tear ducts. One of the protesters sucked in a lungful and immediately vomited onto the ground, collapsing to his knees. Someone grabbed one of the grenades and threw it back inside the compound. Mansfield returned the favor and sent another canister over the wall to replace it. *I can do this all day, morons,* he thought, though he knew it wasn't true.

"Get ready to fall back," he ordered his men. The president had denied them permission to use their guns and without that, intimidation had been their only defense and that was failing fast. Mansfield checked his watch. *I hope those Seahawks aren't late,* he thought. *We don't have ten minutes—*

It was the shouting that finally woke Marisa. The couch had been disturbingly comfortable, a sign of how tired she really was. The sunlight was breaking through the slats of the window blinds in her office, forcing her to squint until her eyes could adjust, a process that was taking a little longer every year. But the loud voices in the hallway drove her to sit and force her mind to focus faster than she normally preferred to do. There was no coffee in the pot to help this morning. *Gonna have to do it the old-fashioned way,* she thought.

She managed to get her feet on the floor just as a Marine sergeant threw her door open. "Report to the back field, now!"

"What's happening?"

"The barbarians finally decided to storm the gates, ma'am. The boys outside hit 'em with tear gas and ran them back, but that won't keep 'em away long and we don't have permission to shoot 'em. The last Seahawks are inbound, ETA four minutes. If you're not aboard in five, I can't promise you won't end up on the business end of a long rope," the Marine told her.

"Understood," Mari said. The sergeant turned back to the hall and she heard his boots pounding on the thin carpet as he moved to the next room to make sure it was clear. The chief of station reached for her phone. It would take her sixty seconds to reach the rally point the Marine had identified. That meant she had three minutes to make two phone calls.

CIA Operations Center
7th Floor, Old Headquarters Building
CIA Headquarters

"This is the senior watch officer," Drescher announced, pressing the headset to his ear.

"This is chief of station Caracas," Marisa announced. "The Marine Security Detachment advises me that the embassy is about to be overrun. I am abandoning the station and will be evac'ed by helicopter to the U.S. Fourth Fleet."

"Are all your people out?"

"My staff moved out last night per my orders and arrived aboard the *Harry Truman*. We still have our two officers in the field. I'm the last one in station. I will re-establish contact as soon as I'm aboard a U.S. vessel."

"Copy that," Drescher said. "I'll inform the director. We'll be expecting your call."

"Drescher, I need the director to make a call for me," Marisa advised.

"What's up?"

"The plan is for everyone to get flown out to the *Truman,* but I need to stay on-site until we retrieve Burke and Stryker from the field. *Vicksburg* is the closest ship. I need the director to talk to the SecDef or someone else with some pull and get me out onto that ship."

"I'll mention it to her."

"*Grazie.* Talk to you soon. Caracas out." The line went dead.

Drescher turned to the bullpen and pointed at the array of monitors on the front wall. "I want the embassy in Caracas on that screen *now!*" Everyone in the room scrambled. The senior watch officer had never yelled like this before that any of them could remember.

Puerto Cabello, Venezuela

They parked the truck farther out this time, at least three miles from the CAVIM site. The hike to the hilltop would be far longer . . . Jon estimated it would be nightfall by the time they reached the summit and made it back to the truck, assuming the SEBIN didn't intercept them first. The humidity was no worse than a Virginia summer but Kyra was sure she'd be sweating heavily within the hour.

"That's all you brought?" Jon asked. The girl had holstered her Glock and no other weapon was in sight.

"I left my HK under a rock with the comms gear," she told him. "I was traveling light at the time. If you'd brought it and the rest of the gear back when you came down, we wouldn't have to do this right now."

"I was also traveling light," he told her.

Kyra's smartphone sounded in the truck's cab. "I'll get it," Jon announced. He jumped from the bed, threw open the passenger-side door, and disconnected the phone from its charging cable. The screen showed a single bar for reception. "Sherlock," he announced.

"Sherlock, this is Quiver. The station is about to be overrun and I'm bugging out. I'll contact you as soon as I reach the fleet."

For the first time, Kyra saw Jon reel, his mind scrambling to answer. "Copy that," he finally said.

"You and Arrow—" Jon heard the call drop. He stared at the screen in surprise. *No Signal.* He lowered the phone, then dropped it on the passenger seat. "We just lost the embassy," he said, quiet.

U.S. Embassy
Caracas, Venezuela

The line died.

Marisa looked at the smartphone screen in surprise: *No Signal.* She dug another phone out of her desk and it delivered the same message. *The cell towers are down,* she realized. The timing was too good to be coincidence . . . and that meant the mob coming over the wall was under Avila's control. Anyone they caught in the building would find themselves at the tender mercies of the SEBIN by nightfall.

"Time to be going," Marisa muttered under her breath. She ran for the hall.

The Oval Office
Washington, D.C.

"He let them go?" Rostow asked in disbelief. "They killed two U.S. sailors and he let them go?"

"Sent them back across the red line to port," Feldman confirmed. "After his chief engineer fixed their navigation system and the ship's medical officer treated sixteen wounded Venezuelan sailors. No fatalities."

Rostow cursed, crumpled the cable report the national security adviser had given him, and threw it across the Oval Office. The director of national intelligence held his peace. "Who's the captain of the *Vicksburg*?" the president asked.

Feldman had to consult a binder for that answer. "Dutch Riley. Good service record—"

"He doesn't make admiral as long as I'm president," Rostow ordered. "Taking the ship would've given us a card to play with the media—"

"With all due respect, Mr. President, you've got that anyway," Marshall pointed out. "There's visible damage to the *Vicksburg*'s hull. The chief of naval operations says the sailors killed in the incident will be arriving at Dover Air Force Base later this morning and you know the media will cover that. I think Captain Riley's decision to release the *Almirante Brión* will play well overseas, and especially with the countries that voted with you on the UN resolution. It makes President Avila look like the aggressor and your quarantine like a measured response."

Rostow grunted but chose not to rebut the DNI's observation.

The Oval Office door swung open and an aide hurried inside, clutching a piece of paper. Rostow pulled the report out of her hand and skimmed the text. He stared at the paper for a long time, long enough to make Feldman and the staffer uncomfortable. "Thank you," he said. "That will be all."

The staffer shuffled out a little slower than she had entered and closed the door behind. The president passed the report to Feldman. "CIA and State both say the Venezuelans are coming over the wall at the embassy."

"But everybody's going to get out," Feldman noted, not looking up from the paper. "That's good news. You won't have a hostage crisis to manage like Carter did. That cost him reelection as much as anything else," he observed, still reading the report. "This works in our favor as long as they only get the building."

"Don't you see it, Gerry?" Rostow asked. "This whole thing is coming apart. Avila's not going to negotiate. He's attacked one of our ships and he's trying to seize the embassy. He wants to throw us off until he can figure out what to do." The president stood up from the couch, walked to the Resolute desk, and pressed a button on his phone. "Get me Kathy Cooke at CIA," he said. The secretary in the reception room outside the Oval Office complied.

"Good morning, Mr. President," Cooke said.

"I just got your report on the embassy. What's new with the warhead?"

"We have no new information on the state of the warhead itself. However, the latest imagery at the facility suggests they might be getting ready to move it. I'll bring it to you—"

"Don't bother," Rostow said. "Just send the files to the Situation Room. What're you seeing?"

"A new convoy of five-ton cargo trucks are lined up at the CAVIM plant by the boneyard. There were no heavy vehicles on-site prior to their arrival a few hours ago," Cooke confirmed. "We can't say for sure—"

"If they move that warhead, can your people track it?" Rostow said, cutting the woman off.

"We can't guarantee it, no," Cooke replied. "Satellite coverage isn't perfect. We could get some drones in the air but the Venezuelans do have an air force. Without a tracking device on the warhead itself, there's always a chance we could lose it."

"That's not acceptable," Rostow said.

"It's the reality, sir," Cooke replied.

"How many troops are stationed at the CAVIM site?" Rostow asked Cooke.

"We don't have a precise number but our analysts believe it's somewhere around two hundred," she replied.

"Thanks, we'll let you know what we decide to do." Rostow pressed a button on the phone, disconnecting the call.

"We could send in a Special Forces team to recover it," Feldman suggested. "That invasion option is still on the table."

Rostow shook his head. "I don't want casualties," he said. "It's one thing for Avila's people to kill ours when they cross the quarantine line, it's another for us to invade their country, put boots on the ground, and then have them come out in body bags for the media to see. But we can't lose the thing. If Avila squirrels it away somewhere and then it goes off next year in

Baltimore or Denver or who-knows-where . . ." He trailed off, then shrugged. "If they're trying to move it, we have to take it out. Call the National Security Council. I want the SecDef and the Joint Chiefs in the Situation Room in thirty minutes."

U.S. Embassy
Caracas, Venezuela

The SH-60B Seahawk touched down on the grass as Marisa threw open the door to the rear courtyard. She sprinted across the asphalt onto the grass as the helicopter doors slid open and the last members of the embassy staff started to board, naval aviators pulling the civilians in. Marisa recognized the ambassador as the last man to climb onto the first aircraft. *Good for you, sir,* she thought.

She reached the second and the Marine sergeant who had ordered her out grabbed her hand and pulled her up. The helo began to lift off before he slid the door shut.

The Seahawk rose into the air, whipping the short grass underneath its blades until it cleared the embassy building, then leaned forward and began to move north. Marisa craned her head over the sergeant's shoulder and looked out the window, down at the complex. Civilians were racing through the main gate and over the fence by the hundreds. The guard shack by the entrance was burning, smoke rising into the air high enough for the Seahawk to pass through the dirty column of ash.

The glass doors to the front entrance were already smashed open and the mob was moving inside.

Puerto Cabello, Venezuela

"You didn't tell her what we're going to do," Kyra noted. She checked the rearview mirror. The highway behind was still empty.

"She'd say it was stupid. She'd be right."

"And yet here you are," Kyra said. "Besides, wasn't this your idea?"

"Do you remember Sherlock Holmes's old maxim that once you've eliminated the impossible, whatever remains, however improbable, must be the truth?" he asked.

"Yes."

"I have my own variation on that. Once you've eliminated the worst options, whatever remains, however stupid, must be the best option available," he told her.

"And people say you don't have a sense of humor."

CIA Director's Conference Room

Holland's link chart was a masterpiece ten years in the making. The graphics depicting Hossein Ahmadi's proliferation network had more than five hundred pieces scattered across it, with lines connecting people and companies, showing who had called whom, who had done business, where the money had flowed. The paper showing the Ahmadi network was eight feet long, three feet high, and getting wider by the year. It was a complex work of art so large that Holland's office had invested in an industrial-size large-format printer just so he could put it all on one page. It was as close to producing a Monet as any DI analyst ever got, and there was the curse of the job. So long as Ahmadi was free to do business, Holland could never finish the chart because the Iranian doctor was making new contacts and creating new front companies, forcing the young man to add more and more nodes to the array.

Holland was tired of it. Ten years was enough; he now had five more banks and a tangle of new lines added to the picture, and he renewed his vow that he was going to make Dr. Ahmadi retire from business. That decision was out of his hands, but he now had friends in high places who were paying attention.

"That's an impressive piece of work, Mr. Holland," Cooke said. "Twenty-five years from now, when they can declassify everything, somebody should frame it and hang it in one of the hallways."

"Thank you, ma'am," the analyst replied, letting some pride seep into his voice. "It would be pretty to look at if it wasn't showing something so ugly. But here's what I wanted you to see." He pointed at a series of linked nodes sitting near the right edge of the paper. "These are the front companies that hired the IRISL cargo ships that made the Venezuela trips. This"—he pointed to a bank in the center of the new nodes—"is the bank that secured the bonds for those companies for all of those trips. Treasury sent over the records and I was able to dig up some extra information from the Counterterrorism Center and the Information Operations Center. They've been helping track where Ahmadi's money goes and between the two, I've got his operation figured out."

Holland moved back toward the center of the chart and waved his hands over the graphics. "This is the core of his network. Ahmadi receives money from the government in Tehran through a series of banks and front companies, which he then funnels into a secondary series of front companies that do business in

Europe and Asia. That's where he buys the nuclear tech that he ships home to Tehran. The money has always been moved through at least three front companies before any purchase is made and the technology always passes through at least three more front companies before it gets back to Iran."

"That's all to evade sanctions," Cooke noted.

"Right," Holland agreed. "But here's the good part." He moved back to the new nodes on the far right end of the chart. "These front companies stand apart from his usual network. The rest of this"—he waved at the other parts of the picture—"is for buying nuclear technology and bringing it home. But this"—he pointed to the new nodes—"is for *selling* nuclear technology, as far as I can tell. None of those last five IRISL shipments were handled through his usual network."

"Meaning what?" Cooke asked.

Holland took a deep breath. He was about to leave the realm of pure fact for the land of analytic conclusions. "Whenever Ahmadi buys technology or moves money, he usually accounts for it with the mullahs through the central banks. But this operation in Venezuela is going through an outside bank he doesn't use for anything else." Holland traced a line from the new bank on the chart across the page to another node. "The Venezuelans have been paying Ahmadi through this bank here, and after the money comes back to him, he's been diverting funds to this bank in Switzerland."

The implications took a few seconds to settle in. "He's skimming funds," Cooke realized.

"I think so," Holland said. "I've been looking at this stuff for ten years. I always got the feeling that the mullahs have given him wide latitude in how to run the proliferation network . . . not wanting to burden themselves with all the messy details, as it were. But the money behind this operation is all running through a separate network that doesn't connect to anything linked up to the regular organization. I can't imagine that the mullahs would approve of this. If they find out that he's skimming funds and endangering their nuclear acquisition network, going home could be a very dangerous proposition for him."

The CIA director finally smiled. "Good work, young man. Get this all ready to take on the road. You're coming to the White House with me."

CAVIM Explosives Factory

The sun was far above the low hills in the distance by the time they approached the summit. They hadn't seen or heard a SEBIN patrol until they'd come within a mile of the base, and the Venezuelan jeeps were staying within a few hundred yards of the fence line. Jon and Kyra closed the last mile largely on their stomachs, pushing through the underbrush with their elbows and knees. Kyra watched her partner, tried to imitate his movements, and found herself impressed by how smoothly he moved.

"It doesn't look like they're running extra patrols," she said, almost whispering. "If anything, they've pulled them all closer in."

"The wider the radius out from a fixed point you want to patrol, the more people you need to cover the area," Jon explained. "We got through once. The riots are probably tying up the military, and if they don't have more people available to expand security here, it makes sense that they'd draw them closer in and sacrifice distance for coverage. Makes our job easier, if we're lucky."

Kyra's legs burned as they pushed up the back side of the hill. There were some tire tracks in the underbrush now. Some crazed SEBIN driver had tried to steer his vehicle to the top, slid out on the steep grade, then turned back down. If anyone had made it to the top, they'd finished the journey on foot, and her own tracking skills weren't good enough to find signs of that in the leaves and dirt. She scanned the hillside below, saw nothing, then paused to listen. She heard vehicles in the far distance, but no voices. "Almost there," she said quietly.

Kyra shifted the Glock in her hand and moved forward.

USS *Vicksburg*
11°22' North 67°49' West
75 miles north of the Venezuelan coast

Marisa first saw the *Vicksburg* when the Seahawk was still ten miles out. She'd had to take it on faith that Kathy Cooke would twist the SecDef's arm and her faith had been rewarded much sooner than expected. The trio of helos had all gone "feet wet" over the Atlantic, the pilots had confirmed which was carrying the chief of station, and the other two had peeled away from the third, headed for the *Truman* a hundred miles east. The unfortunate passengers aboard Marisa's Seahawk, a pair of senior Foreign Service secretaries and a Marine, had been surprised to learn they wouldn't be joining the ambassador and his party on the C-2A Greyhound that would fly him out. *Vicksburg* would ferry them over, just an hour or so late. The CIA chief of station had other business to conduct, the *Vicksburg* was the closest ship, and her needs trumped theirs so long as she had officers in hostile territory.

The Seahawk arced around the ship, tilted aft, as though the pilot wanted the passengers to see the damage to *Vicksburg*'s hull. Marisa stayed silent, but the other civilians couldn't hold their peace, curses and gasps erupting as they saw the hole in the ship's island. They were still a quarter mile out by the station chief's guess. Engineers were welding plates over the open wound, and she could see the small lights of their torches flashing and dropping sparks into the blue water.

The helo took its place over the aft end of the ship and Marisa looked down at a flight deck that was too small for the purpose. *And still moving,* she realized. *Vicksburg* wasn't a stationary target and the Seahawk pilot was matching the forward motion of the vessel as he descended. Marisa was sure that maneuver was far harder than he was making it look. The Seahawk was maybe sixty feet long, as best Marisa could judge, and the flight deck seemed smaller than that. She supposed the pilot could've lowered a cable and let the ship winch them down, but the Atlantic water was calm, visibility good, and the pilot didn't bother, putting the aircraft down on the center of crosshair painted on the deck and giving his passengers a landing as smooth as any they'd ever felt. They uttered silent prayers of gratitude and scurried from the helicopter with the help of sailors outside as soon as the side door opened. Marisa waited until the rest were gone, then crawled out, declining the proffered hand of the master chief standing below to help her.

"I need to speak with the captain," she yelled over the noise of the hangar doors sliding open.

"You're Mills?" Master Chief Amos LeJeune asked. "Come with me, ma'am."

Marisa had expected an escort to the *Vicksburg* bridge, but it made sense, she supposed, to have her conversation with Dutch Riley in a more private space. The J2 (intelligence) office was a Sensitive Compartmented Information Facility not unlike those at headquarters, probably not that different from the other offices aboard the *Vicksburg* except for the massive spin-dial lock on the heavy door. The SCIF was empty now except for the two of them, whether by some order Riley had given out of earshot Marisa didn't know.

The captain closed the door behind them and took his seat on the edge of one of the low desks bolted to the bulkheads. "Well, Miss Mills, you got me down here," Riley said. "What can I do for you?"

"I have two officers who were out in the field when the mob surrounded the embassy and they couldn't get back—"

"And you want me to execute a personnel recovery mission?" the captain interrupted.

"Something like that."

"I sympathize, but I just finished a shooting match with a Venezuelan warship that could've started a war," Riley told her. "I don't want to press my luck by violating Venezuela's sovereignty without direct orders."

"Captain, my people are in clear and present danger. They are in the woods somewhere, not ten miles from the coast—"

Riley held up his hand to cut her off. "I have no doubt that you're telling me the truth and that your people are in some serious trouble. You've got promises to keep but I've got orders to follow. If we can help your people, we will, but I'll need the green light from some higher-ups before I can violate Venezuelan airspace, and that's the end of the argument."

She felt her anger surge inside her, but fought it back. Cursing this man would accomplish nothing and she might well need his help later. She had no cards to play here and she was in no position to make enemies. "Captain, I need to contact Langley and then my officers."

"You can use anything in here, and I'll tell comms to render any assistance you might need," Riley said, waving toward the rest of the SCIF. "We'll get you set up with a rack and mess privileges for as long as you're here."

Marisa nodded blankly. She could hardly think. "I understand," she said.

"If you'll excuse me, I need to get back to the bridge."

"Of course." The captain let himself out of the security vault, the heavy door closing behind him with the sound of clanking metal. Marisa looked around, saw that she was alone in the intelligence center, then barely stifled a scream of frustration.

White House Situation Room

The members of the National Security Council looked around the table, counting heads. They weren't idiots. Fools did not reach these men's level and they weren't oblivious to the fact that some members of the council weren't sitting at the table—SecState, CIA director, all of the staffers. The only men around the table, they noted, were the ones directly involved in the movement of military forces and everyone else was out of the room, probably to minimize leaks, and that meant covert action was on the table. *Then shouldn't Kathy Cooke or Cyrus Marshall be here?* they would be wondering.

Time to stop that. Rostow didn't bother to thank them for coming. Subordinates didn't merit that particular courtesy. "Gentlemen, the best intelligence we have right now suggests that the Venezuelans are preparing to move that warhead," Rostow said, nodding at the screen. A staffer worked the touch-screen control from his seat at the desk and the monitor at the front of the room went live, a satellite video of the CAVIM site playing on the screen. Cargo trucks were lining up at the chemical factory loading dock. "If it goes missing, we might not find it again before it turns up somewhere we won't like."

"And you don't want 'the smoking gun to come in the form of a mushroom cloud'?" the SecDef asked.

Rostow frowned at the inference. He'd been a vocal critic of that particular argument when it had first been made more than a decade before. It rankled him how often he'd found himself having to sustain the policies of predecessors that he'd attacked during his election campaigns. "What I want is to either seize it or destroy it," the president replied, evading the question. "I want a plan on the table that we can execute immediately to make that happen."

The chairman of the Joint Chiefs reached under the table, opened a briefcase, and pulled out a binder. "We've had a CONPLAN worked out for similar contingencies ever since Chávez first started inviting Iranians into his country," he said. "It doesn't precisely address the current logistical situation but we can adapt it in short order. That said, Mr. President, we need you to answer a few questions."

You were ready for this coming in, Rostow realized. There'd been no looks of surprise, no confusion at all. They'd anticipated this and coordinated among themselves before they'd set foot in the West Wing. No, these men were not idiots. That's what military men do, he realized—prepare for contingencies and he was just another contingency to them. He kept the anger generated by that thought off his face. "Proceed," he ordered.

"Sir, depending on the operational window, seizing the CAVIM site is possible," the chairman answered. "The logistics aren't complicated and Venezuela is close enough to U.S. soil to let us place airlift assets over the target site without midair refueling on the inbound leg. We could certainly put enough troops on-site to make it happen with a high probability of success, but we need to know three things. First, do you want the operation to remain covert or do you want a public show of force? Second, what is your tolerance for casualties? Third, do you want the facility destroyed after the warhead is seized?"

Rostow rocked back in his chair. *Casualties.* That nuisance again. "I don't care if it remains covert. In fact, I think we should send a message to Iran and anyone else who's trying to develop their own nukes in our half of the world in violation of the Non-Proliferation Treaty. Obviously, I want casualties kept to a minimum." He shared looks with Feldman. The sight of coffins being unloaded at Dover Air Force Base was something he didn't want on CNN and the other news networks. "And do I want the facility destroyed? Yes. I don't want them trying this again."

"Very well," the chairman said, nodding. "Our analysts and Kathy Cooke's concur that the CAVIM site appears to have somewhere around two hundred armed personnel at present. Assuming those men are all armed, to assure a high probability of success and minimize the probable number of casualties, we'll need to move forces at least at a five-to-one ratio—"

"Five-to-one!" Feldman yelled. "That's a thousand men. You're talking about moving an entire brigade!"

"Sir, that would just be for the CAVIM site—"

"Wait . . . 'just the CAVIM site'?" Rostow repeated.

"Mr. President, you yourself pointed out at the UNSC that the Venezuelans have numerous other facilities involved in this enterprise. If you want to ensure that they can't try this again, then I assume you'll want those facilities destroyed as well. So we're talking about one or more brigades *per facility*. At least an entire division total, possibly more—"

"You'd be invading the entire country!" Feldman protested. "You'd have to take on the entire Venezuelan Army."

"Please don't think I'm speaking lightly when I say the Venezuelan military wouldn't be a problem if it came to that," the chairman observed. "Yes, we are talking about deploying entire combat brigades. The First and Second Brigade Combat Teams, Tenth Division, stationed at Fort Drum in New York specialize in mountain warfare and would be our choice for taking the CAVIM site. The First and Second BCTs, First Infantry Division, out of Fort Riley in Kansas—"

"Stop," Rostow ordered. "Just *stop*. This is overkill."

"No, sir, it's not," the SecDef countered. He took a deep breath. Guiding a president through military planning without appearing insubordinate was always a delicate affair. "Sir, what you're really asking for is the guaranteed elimination of an entire country's ability to proliferate weapons of mass destruction. That means an entire infrastructure has to be dismantled or destroyed with a high degree of confidence. And there are three levels at which you need to think that through. The first is tactical . . . how do you want these facilities seized and destroyed? Do you want us to round up the key personnel involved for detention and debriefing? We'll need to gather considerable intelligence on the ground to confirm that the entire infrastructure has been identified, targeted, and neutralized."

Neutralized, Rostow thought. *Such a clean word.*

"The second is operational . . . how do you want to move the forces into the theater needed to execute those tactics?" the SecDef continued. "The CONPLAN answers those tactical and operational questions. But if you want to deviate from it by deploying fewer forces, that will affect the probability of success we're prepared to offer and will likely result in higher casualties. The way to keep our men from getting killed or wounded in large numbers is to keep the fight short and overwhelm the enemy quickly. If the Venezuelans choose to make this a national fight and mobilize their full military capabilities, then we'll have to discuss logistics for reinforcing our brigades on the ground and possibly launching a counteroffensive that will buy us enough time to confirm the nuclear infrastructure has been destroyed."

Rostow turned and shared looks with Feldman, incredulous.

"You said there were three levels," Feldman pointed out. He was sure he didn't want to hear what the man was going to say.

"The third level is strategic, and that one's entirely

your call, not ours," the SecDef advised. "You can't mobilize an operation of this size without other countries noticing. We know the Iranians are involved in this, so how will they react? They could start car-bombing our bases in the Middle East or tell Hezbollah to start launching Katyusha rockets into Tel Aviv. So how will the Israelis react? There will be global blowback to this, which is why the SecState should be here." He nodded toward the empty chair. "And there's the issue of how all of this will affect our intelligence and counternarcotics operations. Will the Colombians support the operation? It would be helpful if we could stage out of their bases along the border—"

"Stop!" Rostow ordered again. He certainly didn't want the man saying that Kathy Cooke or the DNI should be in the room. The president rubbed his hands against his eyes, then ran his hands through his hair as his mind raced, trying to process the arguments the military officer was laying out. *This isn't going the way I hoped,* he told himself. *Why couldn't Avila just fold?* "I'm not prepared to invade an entire country," he finally admitted.

The chairman nodded sympathetically. "The other option would be air strikes," he offered. "That would eliminate any possibility of seizing the warhead, but we can pretty well guarantee destruction of the facilities that we know about. The question then would be whether our picture of the entire infrastructure is complete."

"Casualties?" Feldman asked.

"There's relatively little risk that the Venezuelans could shoot down a B-2, and the *Truman* can establish air superiority and clear a corridor if necessary. She's already had combat air patrols running in case the helicopters evac'ing the embassy staff needed cover."

"Then do it—" Rostow started.

"There is one potential issue with that course of action, sir," the SecDef said, interrupting.

"What?" Rostow asked through clenched teeth, failing to contain his exasperation.

"Ms. Cooke's people haven't been able to deliver the video they collected of the site, so we still don't have any solid intel on the interior of the factory where the nuke is being stored. It's supposed to be a chemical factory, but nobody knows whether that's true or whether the interior has been rebuilt. If the Iranians had a hand in it, they might have a hardened bunker underneath. That's what the Massive Ordnance Penetrator is for, but it was designed to take out hardened facilities underneath mountains," the SecDef advised. "You can use a MOP against that type of site because the mountain will collapse down and trap any nuclear material. But if this site doesn't have a hardened bunker, or if the bunker isn't very far down, the MOP could blow nuclear material up and out. It could turn into a giant dirty bomb."

"What about a MOAB?" the president asked.

"Same problem," the chairman told him. "Anything powerful enough to guarantee that the entire facility and the warhead get taken out runs the risk of spreading radioactive material all over the countryside."

Rostow nodded, leaned back in his chair, and pretended to think. "Better that than a nuclear device going off on U.S. soil and spreading fallout all over *our* countryside."

"I can't disagree with that, but our allies in that neighborhood won't be so understanding," the chairman counseled. "The SecState will have his own kind of cleanup to do."

"Our allies don't get to vote in our elections," Rostow said. He stared at his SecDef as he pushed himself away from the table, ready to leave. "Cut the orders."

CAVIM Explosives Factory

Elham leaned against the cargo truck, the hard metal pushing into his lower back. His men stood off to the north, out of the way of the SEBIN soldiers who were scurrying between the convoy and the chemical factory, carrying boxes stuffed with papers and bits of equipment the Iranian soldier couldn't identify. Carreño was standing near the main entrance, yelling at some subordinate, the Spanish flying from his mouth so quickly that Elham couldn't understand anything but the profanity. The SEBIN director was anxious, he saw. *No, not anxious . . . afraid,* Elham realized. *The wages of incompetence are fear,* he thought.

Cleaning out the CAVIM site was a feckless exercise. Even if they moved everything out, down to the last scrap, they wouldn't escape. The Americans knew there was a nuclear weapon here.

A memory roiled up in his mind. He had been sent to arrest a man once, a fellow Iranian suspected of taking money from the Israelis to betray his country and his God. The traitor had grabbed a woman and put a gun to her head, threatening to kill her unless he was allowed to leave. Elham had stared at the gunman and his hostage through the scope of his Steyr. The building was surrounded, no food or water would be sent in, the traitor would be allowed no sleep. *How long can you stay awake with a gun to her head? How long can you go without water before you surrender?*

And if you shoot her, then what? he had thought. The man would collapse from thirst or exhaustion before the woman died from lack of either and killing the hostage would erase all the leverage he had, as he learned when he had panicked and made good on his threat. Elham had killed him before the woman's corpse had hit the floorboards, a single shot to the head from a hundred yards. Taking the hostage had accomplished nothing. He had kept Elham and his men at a distance and earned a few minutes of life, nothing more. Killing the woman would have certainly earned him a death by hanging had they bothered to take him alive.

This was no different. The United States would not be held hostage by a brigand such as Avila and it couldn't be killed with a single warhead, only angered. The Americans would strangle this country until the device was found, every ship searched, every plane grounded for years if necessary and Avila's bid to capture American spies would not change that equation now. A few U.S. tourists were sitting in Venezuelan jails, but that would just earn more scorn and outrage from the UN. Threatening such innocents only made the Venezuelans the clear villains and earned them no leverage at all. And if Avila used the warhead? The United States would end his rule, and possibly his life, as surely as Elham had ended the traitor who had shot his hostage.

Neither would Iran escape, Elham was sure. The supreme leader could always cut off Ahmadi, claim he was acting on his own initiative, but even that would require admitting that Iran had, in fact, been pursuing nuclear weapons. Perhaps it was time finally for that, time to open up the facilities at Fordow and Parchin and Ramsar. That wasn't his decision to make but it was the only outcome he could see that left his homeland in a better place than it was before. It was also one that his own leaders would refuse to accept. They would dissemble and lie and the sanctions and isolation would go on and on. Eventually they would get their bomb and celebrate their certainty that the revolution was now secure amid the economic and diplomatic ruin that Iran would become. They would pay a very high price to gain a security that was really within their grasp now and that they didn't need nuclear weapons to reach.

Ironic, Elham realized. He hadn't considered before that violence might not always foster security . . . might diminish it, in fact. It was a strange thing for a soldier to admit, and one he was sure that Ahmadi and Carreño and all the rest never would. Deceit and violence were all they really understood when the trappings were stripped away.

The game was already finished. These men just didn't want to accept the fact.

You're in it too, Elham told himself. But there was nothing for him or his men to do here . . . carry some crates perhaps, but he would not bother. What he wanted was some way to change the game itself and there were no such options that he could see. So he stood by the truck, cradling the Steyr, and wondering when the Americans would tire of it all. He looked into the sky. The American satellites were there. Surely they saw what was happening and wouldn't stand for it.

When are you coming? he thought. Soon. They had to be coming very soon.

509th Aircraft Operations Group,
13th Bomb Squadron
Whiteman Air Force Base
Two miles south of Knob Noster, Missouri

As a general rule, the United States Air Force didn't give its aircraft individual names like the Navy did ships, but the B-2s were an exception. The *Spirit of Oklahoma* was nearly as old as the younger airman driving the hydraulic lifter that loaded the GBU-57A/B Massive Ordnance Penetrator (MOP) into the bomb rack. The ground crew weren't privy to the details of the bomber's mission orders, but none of them had to guess where she was going. The United States only had eight of the bombs and there was only one place on earth now where anyone felt 5,300 pounds of high explosive needed to drop uninvited out of the sky.

The crew chief checked the team's work, then sealed up the bomb-bay doors and started working his way around the bomber, methodically stepping through the preflight inspection. Time was short on this one, he'd been told, but he refused to cut a corner. There was no point flying all the way to Puerto Cabello if the *Spirit of Oklahoma* couldn't put the bomb on target when she arrived.

He finished just after the pilots, both captains, entered the hangar, suited up with helmets in hand. They did their own inspection, mirroring the crew chief's procedure as they checked the weapons specialists' work. Satisfied, they climbed the stepladder in the landing gear well, boarded the black wing and took their seats in the cockpit. The airmen rolled open the hangar door and the crew chief stepped out onto the tarmac, donning a headset, the communications cable uncoiling behind him as he walked.

Standing in front of the massive black bird, he called out to the pilots and confirmed their response. The three stepped through more of the preflight sequence together, tested the controls, and loaded the flight plan into the computer. The pilots finished the sequence and the crew chief walked to the side, coiling the communications cable in his hand as he went. He turned and gave the pilots the hand signal to proceed forward, marshaling the B-2 onto the tarmac.

The *Spirit of Oklahoma* rolled out of the hangar and taxied to the assigned runway. She was the only plane to fly this morning. Clearance from the tower for takeoff was immediate. The stealth bomber's engines cycled up, the pilots lowered the flaps, and the aircraft accelerated down the runway and lifted off into the dark gray Missouri sky. She turned south and glided quietly into the low clouds that quickly stole her from the crew chief's sight.

CAVIM Explosives Factory

The hike to the top had taken longer than Jon had predicted. The last few hills had been steeper than Kyra remembered, with rocks erupting from the underbrush, forcing them to take a more convoluted path to the top. Jon showed no sign of the strain, but her legs were on fire by the end and she was grateful when he called for a stop.

Kyra huddled behind the tree line, gun in hand, with Jon just behind her, searching the area with the Barrett's Leupold scope. They watched the clearing for almost a half hour before she finally judged that they were alone. Still, they moved around behind the trees until they reached the leeward side of the hill that overlooked the CAVIM plant. Men in the valley below were alternately running between buildings and trucks or standing around with guns, scanning the edge of the forest just beyond the fence, determined not to allow another incursion. Kyra smirked as she saw a line of them standing by the southern fence, watching the ordnance field.

Carreño is down there. She knew it as surely as she knew Jon was beside her. His operation had been compromised in the worst way he could have imagined. He wouldn't leave the cleanup to subordinates.

"There," Jon said, pointing at the valley. There was a line of five-ton cargo trucks by the chemical plant, engines idling, she judged by the exhaust rolling out of their stacks. "They're loading up. Looks like they're cleaning house," he said.

"You think Langley knows?"

"Probably."

"Maybe we should hold this position," Kyra suggested. "If they're cleaning out, we might see something worth a call."

"Any chance we can do that the easy way?" he asked.

Kyra pulled the smartphone from her cargo pants and checked the screen. "Still no signal," she muttered.

Without a word, Kyra pushed forward and ran from the trees toward the spot where she had built her blind. She kept low, her head down, her hands brushing against the low clover and weeds as she ran. She heard Jon moving behind her, surprisingly quiet, more than she could manage. It was thirty yards to the site.

The blind was demolished. A stab of regret shot through her, coming from someplace inside she couldn't identify. The little tent of brush and branches had been her protection, however feeble, for a night and she felt violated by its destruction.

No time for that, she thought, and pushed the feelings away. "The antenna is gone."

"I threw it in the woods after I pulled the cable," Jon said. "I'll look for it but I'll be surprised if it's still there."

Jon went for the tree line and Kyra began moving through the brush again. The flat rock was . . . *there.* She scrambled to it. The brush was still in place. Perhaps the soldiers hadn't been thorough in their search, or had come at night and hadn't been able to see well enough in the dark. She pulled the brush and netting away, then grabbed the flat rock under the lip and slid it to one side. It was all there, the HK where she had left it, the radio unmoved. "At least we have the transceiver," she said into her headset.

"Antenna's gone. We'll have to find another one," Jon replied.

"Yeah, they're just lying around all over the place." Kyra pulled the LST-5 radio out of the hole and set it on the rock, its cables falling over the edge into the dirt.

CIA Director's Office

"What can I do for you, Kathy?" the SecDef asked. She'd tracked him down in the Tank, the conference room in the National Military Command Center of the Pentagon. He couldn't recall ever having talked with the CIA director on the secure phone before. They'd shared some small talk at social functions since he'd assumed the office a few months earlier, but nothing official. She'd been professionally close to his predecessor, who'd retired at the end of President Stuart's term. Lance Showalter was now fly-fishing in Montana somewhere, maybe drafting his memoirs, and the current secretary of defense could only hope that his own tenure would end so well. Current events weren't promoting his faith in that particular future.

"I have two officers on the ground in Venezuela. They had to shelter in place out in the field when the embassy got surrounded. I need you to authorize a personnel recovery mission," the CIA director replied.

"The president has approved?"

"Not yet. He will."

The SecDef grunted in response. "We've got enough air- and sea-lift assets in theater to spare some units. Where are they?"

"We're not exactly sure at the moment, but somewhere around Puerto Cabello," Cooke admitted.

"Near the CAVIM plant?" The SecDef's voice took on a worried tone that sent a shiver down Cooke's spine.

"I don't know. At one point they were conducting surveillance in the hills around the facility."

"If they're anywhere close, you have to pull them back."

A dark feeling invaded Cooke's chest. "What's going on?" she asked.

"The White House hasn't told you?"

"I haven't heard anything—"

"Kathy, I don't know why POTUS didn't invite you to the meeting. He didn't invite Marshall either." The SecDef paused, and Cooke could hear him assembling his thoughts. "There's an air strike under way on the CAVIM site . . . B-2 bomber with a Massive Ordnance Penetrator. The president wants to kill the nuke before Avila moves it."

"How long?" she asked, trying to keep the panic out of her voice. She had no idea where Jon was, but the man's way with misfortune didn't give her much hope.

"I cut the orders and the plane took off from Whiteman two hours ago. It's twenty-five hundred miles to the target." The SecDef was thinking out loud now. "B-2's max cruising speed is a hair over six hundred miles an hour. It's like flying from D.C. to Vegas. So a little over two hours at most, depending on weather," he said, finishing the calculation. "I hope your people are nowhere near there, Kathy. There's no way I can authorize a personnel recovery mission anywhere inside that box until after the strike."

"I understand," Cooke said. "I'll call you back when we have a better idea where our people are."

"If they're still near Puerto Cabello, *Vicksburg* is the closest ship. I'll give Captain Riley a heads-up."

"Thank you."

CAVIM Explosives Factory

"Batteries are dead," Kyra said. She realized that she should have expected it. She'd left the unit powered on before she'd entered the base, needing it to be active to handle her radio communications during the incursion, and Jon hadn't known where it was to turn it off when he'd abandoned the hilltop. Without being connected to the small solar panel that charged them, the batteries had simply run out. Kyra pulled out the solar panel, set it on the rock, and aimed it toward the sun. "We're charging again."

"It'll take a few hours before it's charged enough to make a long distance call," Jon told her. He was staring down at the idling convoy through his rifle scope again.

"Before they roll out?" she asked.

"Doesn't matter without an antenna." Jon shrugged. "No way to know how close they are to leaving." He lowered the rifle and offered it to her. "Take a look."

Kyra took the Barrett from Jon's hands, noticing that he seemed relieved to let it go. She shouldered the Barrett and put her eye to the scope.

One of the trucks was backed up to the loading dock. A small forklift was nudging forward, a metal cylinder strapped onto its teeth, technicians surrounding the operation. "What is that?" Kyra asked.

"My guess is a nuclear transport container. That's probably what those pirates cracked open on the *Markarid*. Your buddy Carreño sent in that team of dockworkers you found to close it back up and they got cooked doing the job."

"Marvelous," Kyra muttered, deadpan. "Where's the warhead?"

Jon just shrugged.

Kyra shifted the rifle gently to the right. She could see into the open beds of the other trucks. Some had small stacks of boxes, files and papers, she thought. Others were loaded with larger metal crates, but none seemed the right size for a warhead.

CIA Director's Conference Room

"Any word?" Cooke asked as she came through the door.

"Not exactly," Drescher replied. "We know where

they are. We just can't talk to them." He pointed at the flat-panel display mounted on the front wall.

Cooke walked around the table and stood in front of the monitor. Her task force had kept the overhead imagery of the CAVIM site on the screen since the revelation that a nuclear weapon was inside. Drescher zoomed the picture out until the chemical factory was a small square in the upper left, then pointed. "Here." He panned the picture, switched to infrared, and zoomed it back in.

Cooke gasped. Two bodies were lying side by side on the hilltop, moving slightly, the smaller of the pair clearly aiming a weapon. "Why did they go back?" she asked, incredulous. *Run, Jon!* she wanted to scream at the television, make him hear her by force of will. Her sense of duty took hold. She could not lose her composure in front of the troops.

"Good question," Drescher replied. "Our best guess is that they left some gear on the hill and went back for it. If that's the case, we're not sure why we still can't contact them. Our other theory is that they learned about the Venezuelan bug-out and went to run surveillance. But we've got no way to know until they call us. The cellular network is down countrywide and they're not answering on the LST-5."

"We have to reach them," Cooke said, panic creeping into her voice.

Drescher heard it. "What's up?" he asked quietly.

Cooke looked sideways at her friend, leaned in close to him, and spoke, her voice as low as she could make it. "POTUS has ordered an air strike. They're going to put a MOP down on the site in less than two hours."

Drescher's eyes went wide, the first time she could

recall ever seeing the old curmudgeon surprised. He'd worked the Ops Center long enough to see it all. "I'll call the assistant director for military affairs. He'll plug us into the National Military Command Center," Drescher advised. He lowered his own voice a bit. "Ma'am, Jon and Kyra are a half-mile away and up a hillside on high ground—"

"You think that's far enough?" Cooke asked, doubtful.

"I don't know," Drescher replied.

"Any chance they'll hear the bomber coming and run for it?"

"What kind of bomber is making the run?" Drescher asked.

"A B-2."

"Then no," Drescher told her. "I went to an air show at Joint Base Andrews a few years back. A B-2 did a flyover from behind the crowd, just a few hundred feet off the ground. I was looking sideways at one of the helos on the tarmac and saw it coming out of the corner of my eye. But I never *heard* it coming until it was over us. Northrop Grumman did some kind of crazy acoustical engineering . . . you can't hear it if you're in front of it. I thought the beast was gliding in unpowered." He nodded at the screen. "The first time anyone there will know it's inbound is when the bomb goes off."

Cooke felt her legs starting to go weak. She sat on the edge of the table and clenched her fists.

"Clear the room," Drescher ordered the group. They didn't need to see this. "Report to the Ops Center. Whatever you're doing, stop, and figure out how to contact those officers on the hill. I want updates every ten minutes. Somebody get the ADCIA for military affairs to call over to DoD and get us a live feed to the bomber. You have two hours."

CAVIM Explosives Factory

"There it is," Jon said. The SEBIN soldiers had backed a new truck up to the loading dock and dropped the tailgate. The forklift was carrying a large metal crate and inching forward, like the driver was afraid he would go too fast and the crate would slide off the front if he braked. The worker bees were standing back and all other action around the area had stopped as everyone watched.

"No way for headquarters to see that," Kyra said. There was a roof over the loading dock that would prevent satellites from seeing the cargo.

She took the rifle from him and watched the scene. "They're terrified of the thing."

Jon grunted. He'd missed that detail. "They probably are. After seeing those roasted dockworkers, they probably think the nuke would do the same thing to them if they stood too close," Jon suggested. "How long before the radio's got a decent charge?"

Kyra looked over. "We're up to one percent on the battery."

CIA Director's Conference Room

The minutes were crawling and racing at the same time and Cooke couldn't keep her eyes from moving between the monitor and the digital clock on the far wall above it. "I should have pulled them out," she muttered. "Screw that, I should never have sent them."

"Based on the information you had at the time,

you made the right decisions," Drescher told her. He picked up the remote control to the monitor and adjusted the volume on the feed from the B-2.

"Feet dry," one of the pilots announced. The B-2 had just slipped across the northern coast.

"They're not going to make it, are they?" Cooke asked. *I'm sorry, Jon.* The tears were swimming in the corners of her eyes and she fought to keep them from streaming out, refusing to lift her hands.

Drescher just stared at her, then picked up the phone and dialed the task force downstairs. "This is Drescher. Give me some good news." Cooke looked at him, hopeful. His expression didn't change.

40,000 feet above the
CAVIM Explosives Factory

The CAVIM site was less than five minutes from the coast. The plane was automated to the point that it was practically a drone, so there was little for the pilots to do. The computers noted that the bomber had reached the appropriate coordinates and the bombbay doors rolled open, breaking up the aircraft's silhouette and degrading its stealth capabilities enough that the Venezuela air-defense radars finally were able to see it for the first time. It wasn't going to matter. The Massive Ordnance Penetrator slipped out of its cradle into the sky and the doors closed up again, having been open for less than five seconds. Its stealth profile restored, the B-2 disappeared from the Venezuelans' screens without warning and the plane banked left, beginning the turn that would put it back on the landing strip at Whiteman before nightfall.

The MOP had its own GPS guidance system.

Free of the plane, the bomb took stock of its location, calculated the optimal path to its target, and began shifting its tail fins, adjusting its trajectory as the high Venezuelan winds tried to push it away from its destination. It would have taken a hurricane to move it. The Massive Ordnance Penetrator weighed over fifteen tons.

CAVIM Explosives Factory

The last of the SEBIN soldiers clambered aboard the cargo trucks and closed the tailgate. Satisfied, Carreño walked to the waiting town car and climbed in, seating himself in the front passenger seat. Ahmadi and Elham were waiting inside.

"Everything is secure," he told the others. Carreño picked up the Motorola radio sitting on the dash. "Move the convoy out," he ordered. "Stop for nothing. I want to be in Caracas before dark."

"*Sí, señor,*" the lead driver replied. Carreño saw dark smoke spew from the trucks' exhaust stacks and the first of the five-ton transports began to roll forward.

"There they go," Kyra said. "I hope somebody up there is watching." She waved at the sky, then saw movement out of the corner of her eye. She looked up. "Jon?"

He saw her staring up and scanned the sky until he saw it.

GBU? It had to be. A Tomahawk cruise missile wouldn't be arcing down in a vertical line and the object was moving too slowly to be any kind of ballistic missile. That meant a bomber had deployed it within the last minute. Jon stared beyond the falling weapon but couldn't discern the plane that had loosed it. *Too high to make it out,* he thought. B-2 and B-52s both could reach fifty thousand feet, ten miles up, but he'd heard B-52s flying at altitude and now he'd heard nothing—a B-2, then.

The only question was what kind of ordnance the U.S. Air Force had just chosen to put on target. He'd seen smart bombs used in Iraq when his unit had called in air strikes on the occasional building filled with stubborn insurgents determined not to come outside. This one seemed larger than any Jon was familiar with, given the size and distance, and B-2s could carry anything in the U.S. arsenal, including nuclear weapons. He doubted it was one of those . . . hoped, really. They were done if it was nuclear.

It would hit in fifteen seconds or so by his estimate, and it was going to hit close. He wasn't surprised. There was only one target worth hitting. He stared at the weapon as it hurtled downward, seeming to come straight toward them.

Five seconds later, he finally figured out the weapon type. "Get down!" he yelled. Jon turned and heaved himself toward Kyra.

CIA Director's Conference Room

Drescher zoomed the picture out. The image of Jon and Kyra on the hilltop was overlaid in a separate box on the lower right. The entire convoy had moved out of the picture now.

Cooke stared at the monitor, hands over her face, her eyes fixed on the separate feed of Jon and Kyra. She saw one of the thermal figures lunge toward the other. *I'm sorry, Jon, I'm sorry, I'm—*

The image of the CAVIM building went completely white.

CAVIM Explosives Factory

The trip to the ground took a little over fifty seconds. The Massive Ordnance Penetrator ripped into the chemical factory's roof at terminal velocity.

As big as a large van, the MOP was designed to penetrate two hundred feet into hardened concrete bunkers. The CAVIM plant didn't offer nearly so much resistance and the bomb smashed through every floor in less than a tenth of a second, crushing more than one technician on its way to the subbasement. The falling weapon cratered through the building's foundation, then burrowed into the earth and traveled almost two hundred feet farther through the dirt and rock before its onboard computer decided it had gone far enough.

The MOP's payload detonated, fifty-three hundred pounds of high explosive igniting in a fraction of a second. The shock wave went supersonic, compressing everything in its path to the density of steel, and traveling back up through the solid earth around it.

The entire building came off the ground as the earth rose up underneath it, rippling outward in a circle like an earthquake driving upward and out from a fault line. The shock wave broke through and the building pancaked from bottom up, smashing it all to gravel, the walls disintegrating into particles small enough to vaporize in the fireball that followed an instant later. Smaller outbuildings around the plant disappeared, crushed between the writhing earth, the solid wall of air hardened by the shock wave, and the fireball that trailed behind. A mushroom cloud erupted out of the earth where the MOP had burrowed, sucking air and dirt into the sky higher than the foothills.

The cargo trucks were five hundred feet away from the point of impact, well inside the blast radius. The artificial earthquake reached the first cargo truck and lifted all five tons of it off the ground, flipping it end over end. The shock wave struck it faster than the speed of sound, stripping away the tires and metal sides, twisting the frame like rubber, and shattering the bones of the soldiers in the cargo bed before their brains could recognize that anything had happened at all. The second truck followed the first, slamming into what remained of its brother. All of the trucks took flight in a fraction of a second, the soldiers inside killed before the heat of the now-dying fireball ever touched them. The entire convoy came to rest hundreds of feet from where the shock wave had touched them, the trucks twisted and crumpled, lying on their sides.

Carreño's car was another three hundred feet ahead—just far enough to spare its passengers. The shock wave hit the vehicle, shattering the windows and driving the air at a few hundred miles an hour, sucking the oxygen from the occupants' lungs. The town car flipped over onto its side, end over end, until it came to rest on its right side, all four passengers unconscious and bleeding from their noses and ears.

Kyra saw the shock wave for a fraction of a second, barely enough time for her mind to register the sight before it reached her position. It was a perfect circle of distorted air expanding out as it vaporized everything it touched. It passed over the security shack she had penetrated, then the fence, which disappeared into shards smaller than nails. The new shrapnel flew into the woods and cut into the trees microseconds before the shock wave touched them, shredding the smaller ones into splinters and bending the larger ones over until their trunks finally exploded, sending them tumbling into the hillside.

Behind it, the ground rolled like an ocean wave, a perfect circle of moving earth expanding outward until the flash from the explosion forced Kyra to shut her eyes.

The shock wave was dying now, slowing down and losing force from the moment of its birth. It expanded into the trees, ripping branches loose into the air. Still it pushed out, spending its energy to rise up the slope. Kyra yelled as she felt it hit, like a giant fist punching her over the entire surface of her body, knocking Jon off her and sending him rolling through the high grass. Her cry was lost in the screaming air, the loudest sound she'd ever heard. She could feel her eardrums vibrate inside her head and without a thought her hands covered her ears, trying to save her hearing. The earth rumbled and the solid wave rolled underneath her, throwing her and Jon into the air.

CIA Director's Conference Room

Cooke stifled a cry of her own as she saw the MOP explode and the screen wash out. She turned away from the monitor, covering her face with her hands. Drescher said nothing, didn't move.

They're dead, she realized. *They must be dead.* It was the only thought she could keep in her head.

"Kathy," Drescher said after a short eternity. He'd

never called her by her first name. She looked up. The Ops Center watch officer was pointing at the monitor.

On the screen, in the separate window in the lower right, Cooke saw two thermal figures, bodies, lying prone on the ground, still.

Then they started to move and Cooke couldn't restrain a small cry of hope.

CAVIM Explosives Factory

"Jon?" Kyra couldn't hear her voice over the ringing in her ears. Her balance was shot. The world spun around her and she stumbled forward as she tried to rise, falling onto her hands and knees.

He was in the high grass behind her, twenty feet away, dragging himself to his feet. He made his way to her side, no small feat. He lifted her to her feet again and she fell against him, unable to keep her balance. He caught her, put her arm around his shoulders, and held her upright.

They turned and looked at the valley.

The CAVIM site was gone, erased from the ground, a mushroom cloud reaching into the sky to a height Kyra couldn't begin to guess. The chemical factory was a crater in the earth, the outbuildings vaporized, the security hub missing, with only a small corner of one charred foundation to mark its previous location. Smaller craters in the ordnance field marked where the shock wave and the fireball had detonated the unexploded ordnance that had littered the ground.

"There," she said, pointing, almost having to yell so he could hear her over the ringing in his ears. The convoy was scattered out beyond the crater, Carreño's town car another football field's length beyond them. The trucks were on their sides or backs, clearly wrecked beyond repair. "You think it survived?"

"I don't know," he admitted. "Trucks weren't vaporized . . . nuclear . . . nuclear transport caskets can take serious punishment." He was still trying to catch his breath. "If they put it in one of those . . . might be intact."

"Have to find out." Kyra pushed away from Jon and stumbled forward, her balance returning more slowly than she wanted. She searched through the grass and found the HK, still in working order. The Barrett was the heavier rifle and had traveled less distance in the same direction.

"Radio's intact," she heard Jon call out behind her. She turned his way. The LST-5 had just missed landing on a large rock after being thrown into the air, and Kyra realized for the first time how lucky she and Jon were not to have come down to earth that way. Either of them could have, maybe should have broken backs or bones.

She reached into her pocket and checked her smartphone. It was still in one piece, courtesy of the MIL-SPEC case holding it. Breathing was coming easier now. "We finish this. We make sure it's dead, then we get out of here."

Jon pointed at the mushroom cloud. "They can see that all the way to Puerto Cabello." Another pause, another deep breath. "The SEBIN will be coming. If you see anyone down there, run for the truck."

"I'll try. But if we get separated, take the truck and head for some town that's not on fire. Try to find a way to reach Mari or HQ."

"I'll be watching," he said.

Kyra began to make her way down the hillside, still unsteady on her feet.

Jon exhaled, then reached down and picked up the Barrett. It was heavy in his hands.

CIA Director's Conference Room

"What are they doing?" Cooke asked. One of the thermal figures on the screen—Kyra, she guessed, judging by the smaller size—was walking away from the other. Jon laid himself prone on the ground.

"Going down to check out the blast site?" Drescher guessed. He panned the satellite image away from the blast crater until he found the wrecked convoy trucks. "The nuke might've survived."

Don't get killed. Don't get caught. Bring home the intel. The words ran through her mind, a cruel reminder that she had put the two officers in harm's way. Now Kyra was trying to bring home the intel and Jon wasn't trying to stop her. *He must think the nuke survived too,* Cooke told herself.

"Get me the SecDef," she ordered. It took Drescher five minutes to comply with the order.

"I'm a little busy, Kathy," the SecDef replied.

"We think the nuke might have survived," she told him. "I assume you're watching the live feed?"

"We are."

"One of our officers is approaching the crash site from the northwest. I know both members of the team personally. She wouldn't be doing this if they didn't both think there was a chance the warhead is intact," she advised.

"If that's true, we might have to bomb the site again," the SecDef told her. "*Truman* can hit the site within the hour."

"The SEBIN will probably have people on-site

within a few minutes. If you do that, there will be casualties."

"There were already casualties," the SecDef replied. "I don't think that'll stop the president. But I'll see if we can get some boots on the ground instead . . . secure the perimeter and maybe retrieve any nuclear material. Not likely, so don't get your hopes up."

"I want those personnel retrieval assets ASAP."

"Has Rostow approved?"

"No. But if my people find out whether the bomb is dead, that'll tell you whether you have to hit the site again."

"Works for me," the SecDef conceded. "Okay, it's a go. I'll get permission later. But your people have to pull back to some other checkpoint. I'll order *Vicksburg* to launch as soon as that happens."

"I'll let you know," Cooke said. She hung up the phone. *They're coming, Jon.*

CAVIM Explosives Factory

Her balance was better, the ringing in her ears quieter now, and Kyra began to jog down the hill, then run as she felt more steady on her feet. She reached the bottom and sprinted as hard as she could to the edge of the site where the fence had once stood. There was no building to provide cover, but she supposed the same was true for any survivors, and she saw none. She moved forward, walking into the compound, the HK raised to her shoulder.

Charred earth crunched under her boots and she saw little fires everywhere, the surviving debris burning where it fell. The smoke was settling, creating a fog that limited her vision to a few dozen feet. She made her way past the broken foundation of the security hub and walked east, stepping over the blackened gravel that lay in clumps on the ground. A quarter mile to the north, she reached the edge of the crater where the chemical factory had stood. The bowl in the earth was at least thirty feet deep to the bottom and she couldn't judge the distance across . . . well over a hundred feet at least. She prayed that the fireball had eaten whatever chemicals had been stored inside the building, or that any surviving nuclear material was now a thousand feet above her head and getting blown out to sea.

I hope that reprocessing center was somewhere else.

Kyra made her way around the rim to the opposite side and raised the rifle to her shoulder.

She finally saw the convoy through the smoke. Kyra ran as quickly as she could without destroying her aim. She saw no motion, no movement, no survivors. She reached the first truck, which was resting on its back, tires missing and burning fluids spread around the crushed front. She moved around to the back, looked under the metal floor that had become the ceiling of the cargo bed. There were soldiers inside and she tried to suppress the urge to vomit that surged up from her stomach. This time she failed and she spewed her breakfast onto the ground.

Do the job, she ordered herself. Kyra forced her mouth closed and moved to the next truck.

This one had fared no better than the first. Its frame was twisted and the cab rested on its side at an oblique angle to the bed. Kyra raised her rifle again, her hands shaky, and she stepped around the front. She saw the driver inside through the shattered windshield. He was a bloody mass, his head resting on the passenger door.

The canvas cover over the back was shredded open. Inside were the crushed bodies of a dozen men, twisted at angles her mind refused to believe.

Of course it'll be in the last one, she thought. It made sense that it would be in the truck closest to Carreño's car.

Elham opened his eyes and still couldn't see. The blood from the gash on his head was running over his eyes and he reached up and wiped it away with his hand. Still blurry, he looked around.

The car was on its side, driver's side pointing to the sky. Ahmadi was beneath him, still belted in, unconscious. In the front, neither Carreño nor the driver was moving and he couldn't tell from this angle whether they were living or dead. The front windshield was entirely opaque, the glass spiderwebbed from a thousand fractures. The side windows were gone and the soldier felt a slight breeze run down into the cab, carrying the smell of smoke and dust with it.

Nothing felt broken, though most of his body felt bruised, so Elham reached down and unlocked the seat belt, grabbing the leather handle to stop himself from falling on Ahmadi. He climbed out of the shattered window, his body quietly protesting, and he pulled himself out and dropped to the ground. He smelled gasoline. The fuel tank was certainly ruptured. One bit of flaming debris falling from the sky could turn the car into a pyre with everyone inside.

He couldn't see the CAVIM site behind him for the smoke and dirt in the air. The convoy was a series of shattered wrecks. Fires were burning everywhere and all of the outbuildings were gone. He uttered a silent prayer that was as much a plea as an accusation leveled against Allah. His men had been in the back of one of the cargo trucks. His entire unit . . . *dead now, surely.* All good men who had deserved better than to die at the hands of some pilot whom they'd never had the chance to fight.

What did the Americans hit us with? he wondered. Not a nuclear weapon. They wouldn't have survived that. He'd heard about some of the larger thermobaric bombs the Americans had, the Mother Of All Bombs and such monsters as that. They'd used one of those, surely.

Then Elham saw movement. His eyes didn't want to focus, but he forced them, and he saw her . . . a woman in cargo pants and a T-shirt, with a rifle raised to her shoulder, moving behind the nearest five-ton cargo truck.

The truck that had carried the warhead.

Elham stumbled around to the back of the car. The trunk was crumpled and hanging partially open a few inches. The car's frame had bent, cracking the trunk's door loose. He grabbed it, pulled, and grunted as it moved a few inches. He pulled again, then looked.

The Steyr's case was there, still in one piece, but too large to pull through the narrow opening. Elham put his boot against the rear bumper, braced himself, then pulled on the trunk door again. It slid a few more inches in the dirt.

The scene at the last truck was little different from the others except that some of the bodies of the SEBIN soldiers had been thrown out of the vehicle onto the ground. She stepped around them, looking at the bodies. There were no survivors. The convoy had been too close to the point of impact.

The last truck was lying on its side. There were no bodies inside this one, to her relief. She stepped inside the back, her foot coming down on the canvas cover that had been the roof and was now the floor. She reached into her pants pocket, pulled out the Maglite, and turned it on.

The metal crate was four feet square, intact, but dented on all sides with holes punched through it in several places from debris or sharp corners of the truck bed as far as she could tell. Kyra pointed the light inside the largest gouge in the metal she could find and looked in.

The light played over a large green cone, still secured inside its thick metal box.

Kyra stared at the device. *How many kilotons?* she wondered. A hundred? Five hundred? A megaton or more? Fission or fusion? Uranium or plutonium core? What design?

It survived, she thought. That was what mattered.

The enemy still had a warhead.

The crate was far too large and too heavy for her to move by hand and the cargo truck was destroyed.

Then she heard the first sounds in the distance, the rumbling of vehicles. She checked her watch. It had been almost thirty minutes since the bombing. The SEBIN in Puerto Cabello had seen the mushroom cloud, maybe even heard the explosion. They had tried to call the factory and gotten no answer. Now they were coming. They would secure the warhead, load it onto another truck, drive it away, and the United States would never find it again until Avila or Ahmadi was ready to reveal it.

Can't let them just have it, she thought. She needed to buy time. Jon could hold the SEBIN off with the

Barrett for a while, but they'd eventually find him, flank him, and that would be that.

Kyra stared at the crate as she heard the truck getting closer. Then she reached into her pocket, pulled out her phone, and checked the battery charge . . . 72 percent. She set the HK down, reached into the crate, and wedged the phone inside behind some of the foam padding lining the edges, out of sight. She shined the light inside and looked for it. Satisfied that it wouldn't be easily spotted, she turned off the Maglite and put it back in her pocket, then grabbed the HK and backed out of the truck.

The bullet hit the truck's metal bumper, missing her head by six inches and Kyra heard the supersonic *crack* as it passed by her ear. She jerked away from the sound, her heart hammering in her ribs. She dove behind the truck again, rolled to a crouch, and raised the HK. There was no second shot. She looked up at the bumper.

The bullet had passed through it, tearing a hole and splaying the thin metal skin open like the peel of an orange. She stared at it, eyes wide, then swept the rifle over the space in front of her, every sense hyperactive, looking for the threat. Whatever caliber the weapon that had fired that shot, it was too large to be a sidearm or a carbine. It was big . . . *Sniper rifle? Like the Barrett.*

Elham muttered and slid the Steyr's bolt forward. It should've been an easy kill, the distance to the target less than a hundred meters, but the world was still spinning too much and he'd missed the shot. Now the target had taken cover and was aware that she was being observed. That always made the second shot harder. He chambered the second round and put his eye behind the scope again.

The smoke was covering the field of fire and Jon couldn't see much. The breeze was picking up and starting to blow some of the dark cloud away, creating holes in the smog, and he could see parts of the wrecked convoy.

He heard the deep, low snap of the rifle shot. *That wasn't an AK,* he knew. Someone in the valley had a bigger rifle than that. He held the scope on the wreckage, looking for a target. The wind shifted the smoke and he finally saw Kyra crouched behind the farthest truck. He swept the Barrett left and saw the dim outline of the town car another hundred yards away.

"C'mon," he muttered. He couldn't see a target.

Kyra stuck her head out just far enough to see, then pulled it back, and another rifle shot struck the cargo truck, hitting metal somewhere she couldn't identify. "What kind of moron shoots at a nuclear weapon?" she muttered.

Elham heard the approaching vehicles behind him. He didn't need to hit the target now, he just needed to pin her down until the SEBIN arrived. They would flank her and either flush her out for him to shoot, or they would shoot her themselves. Probably the latter. He didn't care now.

He saw the woman stick her head out for an instant and he rushed the shot. He knew it wouldn't hit her from the moment he jerked the trigger. But she would hear it and stay in place. Time was her enemy now, not his.

The wind finally pushed enough of the smoke aside just as Jon heard the second shot. He saw the man standing at the corner of the town car, a large rifle resting on the upended trunk—

—and the memory of al-Yusufiah came roaring back into his head. He saw the insurgent on the roof standing by the mortar, ready to drop a shell down the tube when Jon's own bullet had opened his chest to the sunlight behind. The emotions of the moment came back a second later, the shock and the shame that had taken so very long to suppress broke through, clenching in his gut. It had always been there, right at the edge of his thoughts and he'd fought it down every day.

And if he shot this man, the new memory would pile onto the old one and he would have two animals he would have to keep in the cage of his mind. He didn't know if he had the strength to do it.

And then he heard the low rumble of the other trucks in the distance. In another minute, Kyra would be outnumbered and the SEBIN would kill her.

Jon closed his eyes and sucked in a lungful of air, then let it go—

—and held his breath as he felt the wind on his face, blowing right to left, and he shifted the Barrett. He felt calm. Then he pulled on the trigger until the Barrett roared.

The .50-caliber round hit the town car and Elham felt the rush of air push against his chest as the slug punched through the side of the trunk, then the lid and the metal scratched his abdomen as it splayed outward. He fell backward, then scrambled forward, grabbing his Steyr and diving behind the car for cover.

He looked at the holes in the trunk and saw the downward angle between the two.

The sniper was back in the hills, hiding in an elevated position. The Iranian soldier had limited cover, only the car, while the American gunman, who had an entire forest, now had the range.

The odds had just shifted to the other side. Elham didn't even know where to shoot.

The front and rear windows of the cargo truck both had shattered and Kyra leaned around the warhead crate to look through. She saw the man fall backward, then grab his rifle and throw himself behind the town car. Jon had taken the shot from a half mile away and come within inches of hitting the target. *You missed your calling, Jon.*

Kyra heaved herself out of the truck bed, leaned around the corner, raised her HK, and emptied half her magazine at the town car just to let the sniper know she was closer to him than Jon. Then she turned and ran for the next wrecked truck in the convoy.

Jon saw Kyra make her move. *Good girl.* She ran out of his sight picture and he kept the scope on the man behind the town car. The sniper leaned out, trying to see his own target, and Jon pulled the trigger again. The bullet took a little less than a second to cover the distance before gouging the dirt by the car and the sniper pulled back. *Just stay down.*

Kyra threw herself behind the last truck and took a second to catch her breath. The vehicles were much closer now. She had less than a minute before the first SEBIN reinforcements would be on-site. The smoke wasn't as dense now as it had been on her first approach, but it was still heavy enough to obscure her view of the car.

She pushed herself back onto her feet and sprinted out into the open, running toward the crater. She reached the edge, made her way around it as fast as her tired legs would move, and then ran straight for the tree line.

Jon saw Kyra enter the woods. *Time to be going,* he thought. He jumped to his feet and slung the Barrett over his shoulder. He stuffed the LST-5 into his pack and then ran down the hill for what he prayed was the last time.

CIA Director's Conference Room

Cooke exhaled hard. "They made it out."

"They're in the woods but they're not out. That entire stretch of country is about to get overrun," Drescher replied. He unfolded a National Geospatial Intelligence Agency Evasion Chart on the table. "They're here," he said, putting his finger down northeast of Morón. "Everything in all four directions is a mess of hills covered by forest. That'll make a helo extraction problematic . . . but not impossible. But the countryside goes flat and empty east of Morón. If they can get that far a lot of the variables just go away, but they'd have to get through the town to make it happen. The military is probably going to lock that place down."

Cooke nodded. *They can make it.* Someone in the

Ops Center was panning the feed, keeping it on Kyra's thermal image as the woman ran through the forest. "Approved. Get the coordinates for an extraction site ready to deliver. And get the SecDef on the line."

"Yes, ma'am."

The hills north of the former
CAVIM Explosives Factory

Kyra stumbled and went down in the dirt. She pushed herself up and got her legs moving at full speed again. She had no idea where Jon was or how far it was to the truck. They'd left the truck three miles away. *Forty-five minutes if I don't stop.* She wasn't sure she could keep that up.

The SEBIN would kill her if they caught her now.

Kyra ignored the pain in her legs and her lungs, and she ran.

CIA Director's Conference Room

"What's the word, Kathy?" the SecDef asked. The encryption on the secure line created a slight hiss in between his words.

"My people were at the site but the MOP didn't get them. They're on the move. I need *Vicksburg* on standby to execute that personnel recovery mission."

"Yeah, we saw one of them recon the blast site. If she can confirm whether we got the nuke, she'll be my new best friend. I've cut the orders to *Vicksburg*. Captain Riley has a helo on standby. All he needs is the extraction site."

"My people have a nice spot all picked out, but we

don't have a way to contact our officers and give them the coordinates. If we make contact, we'll direct them to the location, but if not, your people might have to make this up as they go."

The former CAVIM Explosives Factory

"Get me out of here," Ahmadi ordered. His voice was shaking.

"Are you hurt?" Elham asked.

"Nothing serious, I think."

The troop transports rumbled in through the dust clouds, kicking up some dust of their own, and slid to a stop in the loose dirt. Soldiers began to disembark, jumping from the back, and discipline died as they saw the crater for the first time. Curses and prayers to God Almighty went up until Elham cut them off. "Get over here," he ordered, ignoring the fact that he had no authority over the locals. "We have casualties."

The soldiers slung their weapons and pushed the car back onto its tires, drawing groans from the occupants. Elham opened the doors and a medic moved in to check the men over. "Is the weapon intact?" Ahmadi asked weakly.

"I don't know," Elham said. "I haven't checked it. The truck that was carrying it is destroyed, but the transport crate is durable. There is a chance."

"Good. Inspect it, then have it loaded in another one of these trucks as soon as possible. We have to move it before the Americans try again," Ahmadi ordered, then began coughing hard. "I heard shooting?"

"The American spy, the woman, came down from

the hills to see their work. She reached the back of the weapon transport by the time I was able to get out of the car," Elham told him. "I tried to stop her, but the sniper was in the hills again and gave her cover. She fled on foot, that way." He pointed north.

"How long since she ran?" Carreño asked. His sense of time was sketchy.

"Four or five minutes. Not long," Elham said.

Carreño pulled himself out of the car and turned to the gawking soldiers, still staring at the burning crater. "Find them!"

USS *Vicksburg*
11°22' North 67°49' West
75 miles north of the Venezuelan coast

"Permission to come on the bridge," Marisa announced.

Riley frowned at the voice, turned, and recognized the speaker. "Granted," he said. The station chief stepped through the hatch and approached the captain, who was standing over the Electronic Chart Display. He offered her a piece of paper as she came near. Marisa took it and skimmed it over.

"Orders straight from the SecDef. You just got your helo, Miss Mills," Riley said. "We're at Ready Thirty right now. Pilots will be briefed on the mission in ten minutes if you want to be there."

"I want to go," Marisa told him.

"I figured you would. So did your director. The orders allow it, so get suited up. Just stay out of the crew's way."

It was only her dignity that kept Marisa from running off the bridge.

The former CAVIM Explosives Factory

Elham had seen other men frightened like Ahmadi was now. The Americans called it the "thousand-yard stare," the blank face of a man who had faced death for the first time and realized that he was no one special, that he could die today as easily as anyone else. Men like him were accustomed to the soft life with all the amenities they could want. Such men gave no thought to their own mortality. Now the Americans had come within meters of killing him and Ahmadi's mind was refusing to process the event.

Elham had no sympathy for the man at all. *The law of the harvest,* he thought. *You have always made men like me reap what you have sown. Now the Americans are making you reap your own works.*

"Señor!" he heard one of the SEBIN soldiers yell. Elham turned and saw the uniformed officer run up to Carreño. "As you ordered, we are setting up roadblocks on all the nearby highways, ten-kilometer radius. They will be in place in ten minutes."

"Ten minutes," Carreño repeated with disgust.

"How long since the woman fled?" Ahmadi asked. The fear in his voice had vanished now, replaced by fury.

Elham checked his watch. "Almost forty minutes."

The hills north of the former CAVIM Explosives Factory

Kyra dragged herself over the last ridge. Her legs had forced her to slow down almost ten minutes before and were finally starting to give out. She had heard no dogs, no soldiers behind her. Helicopters had overflown the forest at a low altitude, each one sending a new shot of adrenaline through her system, but there was no way they could see through the dense canopy overhead. But she couldn't push herself much farther and even the adrenaline wasn't enough to keep her going now.

She jumped down the leeward side of the ridge, letting gravity pull her through the dirt and loose leaves on the forest floor. The truck was at the bottom. She came to rest by the front bumper and let herself lie on her back for a minute, sucking air into her lungs.

The foliage she and Jon had put up to cover the vehicle had been removed and Kyra felt panic rise in her throat, thinking the SEBIN had found the truck. Then she saw Jon standing by the driver's-side door. She couldn't speak, her lungs still heaving too hard and fast.

"Good to see you too," he said, tossing her own words back at her. Jon reached down and helped Kyra to her feet. She leaned on him until she was able to crawl into the truck. Jon took his place in the driver's seat, fired up the engine, and the rear tires spewed dirt.

CIA Director's Conference Room

Cooke kept her eyes on the imagery feed and watched Kyra reach the truck and Jon help her in. They weren't even close to safe, but they were no longer on foot and hope began to rise in her heart.

"Cell network still down?" she asked.

"Yes," Drescher said. "I don't think Avila is going to do us any favors. The Pentagon is watching this too. They'll have to guide the helo in once our people stop moving."

The hills north of the former
CAVIM Explosives Factory

The roads through the hills were all unpaved, barely depressions in the underbrush. Jon kept the truck going as fast as he dared, but the trails were narrow and uneven.

"Think we can make it to Highway Three?" Kyra asked. "Head north and we could put some road between us and Morón."

"I'd bet money the SEBIN are throwing up roadblocks everywhere," he said.

"Jon, I left my smartphone with the warhead," Kyra told him.

He reeled at that bit of news. "So they can track it . . . smart."

"So where do we go now?"

"Someplace high," Jon said. "These PRC handhelds only have a four-mile range, and without the antenna, the LST-5 is only good for line of sight. So we need to find someplace high up where we can get power and splice an antenna."

"Where?"

"Good question," he said.

Avenida Falcón, southeast of the former
CAVIM Explosives Factory

Sargento Javier Oliveira leaned against the jeep and shifted his rifle so he could scratch his face. The humidity was making his neck itch and the asphalt under his boots and his green uniform were both soaking up the sunlight, making it impossible for him and the other five men in his unit to stay cool. He wouldn't have had patience for this duty even if it had been cool with an Atlantic breeze running past. The ocean was only a few kilometers to the north. A week ago the women had been coming out in numbers, but the riots had forced the beaches to close, leaving Oliveira and his unit to swelter in the barracks on base when they weren't out on the streets, trying to keep the rioters and looters from running free. The ones protesting Presidente Avila were bad enough. The ones support- ing the *presidente* were worse, thinking themselves agents of the law and free to do Oliveira's job for him and pummel anyone they thought was an enemy of the state.

Then the Americans had bombed that explosives factory to dust. Oliveira had seen the mushroom cloud from the base and for a few moments had thought the United States had used a nuclear weapon against his country. He'd crossed himself and started to say his final prayers, but he realized after a few seconds that there had been no flash of light and no electromag- netic pulse. Whatever bomb they'd dropped had been enormous, but it wasn't nuclear and Oliveira knew he would live.

Then the orders had come to establish roadblocks and detain any Caucasians who approached. Rumors had been spreading among the other troops for days that there were CIA spies hiding in the hills. Oliveira hadn't believed it until the bombing.

He gritted his teeth and spit. They wouldn't come by this station. There were no cars on the highway now, no doubt the result of the other roadblocks in both directions cutting off any traffic that would other- wise pass through. This intersection was the connec- tion where the Avenida Falcón met the single paved road that ran into the now-destroyed factory complex and any Americans surely wouldn't be coming down *that* street. Oliveira wasn't the smartest of soldiers but he understood maps and math. These hills were hundreds of miles square. The chances that they would pass by here—

Oliveira cocked his head as he heard the vehicle for the first time. It was a large engine, running fast, like someone had the accelerator mashed to the floor, and it was getting louder. He looked down the road and saw nothing, then checked behind him. Avenida Falcón was empty, the entrance road to the destroyed factory was empty. The other men scanned the roads and checked their rifles as they muttered to themselves. *Then where—?*

The truck screamed out of the woods, coming off some small trail through the trees that they hadn't been able to see from their station. Its tires hit the asphalt a hundred meters away and the driver cranked the wheel hard, turning south, and immediately accelerated in a straight line away from the roadblock. Two of the other men raised their rifles and fired a few rounds, but hit nothing.

Oliveira ran for the cab of his jeep and turned on the radio.

"Six men, two jeeps." Kyra turned her head back and looked at Jon. "The turnoff to Highway One is a half mile down on the left."

Jon shook his head. "There'll be more of those jeeps on the big roads." He looked left into the town. Black smoke was rising in columns from three points in the town. The riots had reached Morón.

"If we stop, we might not be able to get moving

again," Kyra warned. "Someone spots us when we're on foot and we're done."

"Maybe," Jon conceded. "But we won't last long out here on the roads. We can outrun some jeeps but we can't outrun their radios. They'll coordinate on us and drive us until we run out of gas or road." He turned left onto the first side street into Morón.

The former CAVIM Explosives Factory

The forklift had finally arrived but couldn't reach the warhead crate inside the wrecked cargo truck where it had settled. Elham had stood by watching as five soldiers managed to drag it out, with Carreño cursing their incompetence from start to finish. When it was finally in the open, the forklift driver got the metal tines underneath and the soldiers had strapped it on. Loading it onto one of the new trucks was going slowly.

"*Malditos!*" Carreño muttered under his breath. "We should have been gone twenty minutes ago. The Americans could put another bomb down on us any-time now."

You should have been in the truck when they hit us the first time, Elham thought.

A soldier came running up to Carreño, radio in hand. "Señor!"

"What is it?" he demanded.

"The Americans just ran a roadblock southeast of our position here. They were seen turning east into Morón on Highway One."

"I want that town cordoned off!" Carreño ordered. "Pull men off riot control if you need reinforcement. I don't care if the entire place burns. Do you under-stand me?"

"We've already alerted all of our units."

The soldiers locked the tailgate as the men inside finished strapping the warhead's transport crate to the truck's bed. "*¡Terminado!*" one of them yelled. *Finished.*

"We leave, *now*." Carreño looked up at the sky, afraid of what might appear overhead. "*¡Vámanos!*" he ordered. The soldiers clambered aboard the jeeps and trucks and the convoy finally started to move.

Morón, Venezuela

Jon sent the Toyota through the streets fast enough to alarm Kyra, but the neighborhood seemed empty, the occupants either out rioting in another part of Morón or hiding in their homes. Jon scanned the buildings, muttering to himself as he rejected one edifice after another. Kyra looked right as they hurtled through another intersection—

—the riot in the next street over filled the gap one block down, a few hundred people at least gathered in one of the town *centros,* with a line of soldiers trying to subdue them all. People were running in two directions, either toward the fight or away from it. Some civilians held signs aloft, uniformed men were swinging nightsticks, a man caught one in the head—

—and then the scene was cut off by the next row of buildings as Jon kept the truck moving. The road passed under a freeway, probably Highway 1, she thought, which cut the small town in half running east–west. A line of jeeps filled with soldiers rumbled by on the overpass.

"I think half the army is coming together here," Kyra said.

"There," Jon said finally after another thirty seconds. Kyra followed his finger and saw an apartment building, ten stories of nondescript concrete with terraces protruding at every floor on all sides.

"Your call," Kyra said. Jon accelerated, covered the last six blocks, and stopped the truck in a narrow alley across the street from the apartments he had chosen. Both analysts climbed out and went for the equipment in the back, then sprinted to the end of the narrow space.

The sign at the intersection to the left announced that the street was CALLE 10. Kyra checked the thoroughfare, in both directions. "Empty." She led off, rifle raised, and sprinted across the street to the nearest door, a dirty wooden entryway smeared with old graffiti. It was unlocked and they entered, closing it behind them.

The stairwell ended in a small shack on the rooftop, with a television antenna rising off the top. Kyra crouched down behind it, dropped her pack, and pulled out the LST-5 and the tool kit. "I'll get this going."

"You going to be able to splice into that thing?" he asked, nodding at the antenna.

"I think so, but it'll destroy the cable and be a crap connection," Kyra said. "How far do we need to broadcast to reach the blockade line?" she asked.

"No idea," Jon said. "The ships will be just outside the international boundary if we're lucky. If all we've got is line-of-sight, those mountains could be a problem."

"I need five minutes," she told him.

"I'll sweep the perimeter and find the approaches." Jon hefted the Barrett and jogged to the northern edge of the roof.

The radio declared that it had 10 percent power when she turned it on. She programmed it to the emergency frequency, checked the encryption, then took the phone handset. "Mayday, Mayday, Mayday. Arrowhead, Sherlock, GPS coords one zero point four eight two four minus six eight point two zero one six six . . ."

USS *Vicksburg*
11°22' North 67°49' West
75 miles north of the Venezuelan coast

Marisa got lost on the way to the communications room and made one wrong turn, which led to two more and a request for directions. She finally reached the right hatch more than a minute after she'd been summoned. Master Chief LeJeune stood inside, leaning over the shoulder of some junior officer whose rank Marisa didn't bother to identify. He waved her in. "Looks like your friends finally decided to call."

Marisa grabbed a headset before the communications specialist could ask another question. "Arrowhead, Quiver. Report your status."

"All present and accounted for, no casualties," Kyra replied. "We could use some good news." The signal was poor and static played with her voice.

"Good to hear you. Our friends here on the water have a green light to come get you and a 'green deck' for launch."

"You've got our coords. We're squatting on the roof of the tallest building we could find. You come into town and we'll pop smoke. I don't think you'll miss us."

"Copy that, Arrowhead. Hold tight and we'll be there soon—"

"Quiver," Kyra said, cutting her off. "I inspected the package before we had to bug out. The crate was damaged but the package was intact, repeat, it was intact. I hid my smartphone inside the crate. It's got GPS but the cellular network is down and we've only got a few hours before the battery runs dry."

LeJeune did the Navy proud with the profanities he quietly wove together at that piece of news. "I'll tell HQ and DoD. They've got AWACs, Prowlers, and half the drones under heaven right off the coast. One of them will find the signal," Marisa advised. "Hunker down. We're coming for you." She turned to the communications officer, made a slashing motion across her throat, and he ended the transmission. "Can you get a message to Langley for me?" she asked.

"Yes, ma'am."

Marisa dictated the message, then ripped off the headset and ran for the hatch.

Morón, Venezuela

"That's it, they're coming," Kyra said.

"So are the bad guys," Jon observed. He pointed back toward Highway 1. Kyra grabbed her HK and followed him to the edge of the roof.

The convoy had just turned onto Highway 1 when the radio chattered at them. "Two hostiles spotted on a rooftop, Calle Diez. All units converge."

"Driver! Take us there!" Carreño ordered. "I want to be there when we take the Americans into custody. Tell the cargo truck to keep going. We'll catch up to it shortly."

"Don't be an idiot," Ahmadi seethed. "The cargo is

more important than the Americans. We should stay with it."

"Are you afraid, señor?" Carreño asked. "There are only two of them. We'll have them in custody and we'll arrive in Caracas with the cargo and a pair of *estadounidense* spies captured on our soil. The Americans will have to back off then. We are about to win this game."

The driver turned the wheel and the jeep turned off Highway 1 into Morón.

CIA Director's Office

Drescher came through the door. "Message from Mills out on the *Vicksburg*," he said as he put the printout on Cooke's desk.

1. Communications established with Arrowhead and Sherlock. Team sheltered in Morón, situation untenable. *Vicksburg* commencing personnel recovery. COS Caracas will accompany.

2. Arrowhead reports that warhead survived MOP detonation, but was able to hide smartphone in transport crate. HQ will be able to track via GPS until batteries die if damaged crate doesn't block signal.

3. Regards.

"They're in Morón?" Cooke asked, shocked. "What are they thinking going into a populated area?"

"Might not have had a choice," Drescher said. "Imagery shows the locals have thrown up roadblocks everywhere. They might have been funneled in."

Cooke nodded, staring blankly at the page. "Call the White House," she said, handing the paper back to Drescher.

Over the Atlantic

Marisa was climbing out of her skin in the back of the Seahawk. The helicopter lifted off from the *Vicksburg*'s deck less than five minutes after Jon's call. The Seahawk hugged the Atlantic, moving almost 170 miles per hour and still not going fast enough. The crew was professional and she was trying to keep her composure. Staying calm had always been trouble for her when Jon was involved.

The door gunner double-checked his harness. Marisa stared at him, saw he was a young kid, nervous, probably his first time going into combat. She leaned over and laid a hand on the GAU-17/A minigun the young soldier was rechecking. "You know how to use that thing?" she yelled so he could hear her over the rotors.

The soldier grinned. Where did the CIA find women who looked this good and knew how to handle guns? "Hoo-yah, ma'am! Looking to give my girl a proper workout!" he answered.

Marisa smiled. Giving a young man a chance to show off for a woman always took their minds off what was really going on.

Over the Atlantic

"Sherlock, Quiver," Marisa said into her head mic. "Seahawk en route your position, ETA . . ." She looked to the airborne tactical officer sitting in the copilot seat. He held up both hands, all fingers extended, then one hand with two fingers up. "Twelve minutes."

"Copy that, Quiver," Kyra called back. "Sooner would be better. We have hostiles inbound."

"Can you hold?"

"We'll let you know in two minutes."

Morón, Venezuela

Jon put a new clip in the Barrett and loaded the first round, then set the bipod mount on the edge of the roof and put his head down and his eye to the Leupold scope.

The Venezuelan vehicles were still a half mile away, perhaps thirty seconds from his and Kyra's position judging by the number of cross streets and their rate of speed. The convoy had three jeeps, four men each, and a troop transport carrying probably three times that many in the back—that unit alone could over-whelm his position. The truck first, then.

Jon took a breath of air into his lungs, let it out slowly, then stopped his breathing lest the rise and fall of his chest throw off the aim.

He put the crosshairs on the grille of the large transport and raised them slightly to compensate for the bullet drop over the distance. Jon put his finger to the trigger and pulled back, taking up the slack. The trigger pulled easily, then resisted. He kept his pull smooth, more force behind it now. The exact moment of the shot was a surprise—

The world was moving in slow motion and the .50 round seemed to rumble out of the barrel, kicking up the dust on the roof in a small hurricane that it pulled along behind in a spinning vortex and filling his sight with a brown haze. The muzzle brake blew hot gases out to the sides in a small storm that whipped Kyra's face, forcing her to close her eyes and turn her head away.

The transport hit a small pothole a fraction of a second after the Barrett fired. The slug closed the distance while the truck's cab dipped down slightly, angling into the shallow ditch enough that the bullet passed above the grille. It struck the hood and tore a furrow into the metal until it punched through and hit the engine block. The two-inch round shattered the metal, throwing shrapnel into the piston assembly and shredding hoses, hot fluids spewing out in small gushers. Crushed and misshapen, the slug tumbled end over end until it hit an iron slab too thick to penetrate. The bullet angled up and punched its way back through the hood, then through the windshield. It hit the driver's right arm above the elbow, spraying blood, shattering the bone into a thousand splinters, and ripping out enough flesh and muscle to leave the lower arm hanging from the upper by only a few bits of skin. The driver screamed in shock and twisted the wheel with his good arm as he convulsed in terror. He would have been hard-pressed to keep the truck under control as the front bumper hit the low rise of the concrete sidewalk even had he not been thrashing in his seat.

The driver, delirious in his agony, hit the wheel, spinning the truck as he tried to avoid the concrete wall. The transport made a sharp turn and the men in the back yelled and cursed as they felt the machine roll at an unnatural angle under their feet. Its center of gravity too high for the turn, the truck rolled onto its left tires and the transport pitched over onto its side, throwing men out of the back. Half of the soldiers broke bones as they hit the ground, their bodies rolling along for a few dozen feet until they stopped, lying in crumpled heaps, bloody, several with compound fractures. Two more were crushed under the truck bed as it slid along the ground for almost twenty feet until it finally came to rest. The few men who were still able to move dragged themselves back to the toppled machine, its rear right wheels spinning on their axles.

Kyra let out a cry. "Nice!"

"I'll take it," Jon agreed. "How many in the jeeps?"

Kyra scanned the approaching fleet of vehicles. "I count twelve. Still too many for me to handle with this—" She patted her machine gun. "They'll put shooters in the other buildings and flank us, easy."

"Time?"

She checked her watch. "Helo is still ten minutes out. You want some smoke? It would give us some cover."

"Save it," Jon ordered. "It won't last long enough and it'll just keep me from seeing downrange. Don't want those boys moving up on us."

Carreño's jeep hit a deep pothole, throwing him toward the roof until his seat belt dug into his shoulder and lap. Ahmadi hadn't bothered to fasten his and struck the metal top, bending his neck. The man muttered an oath in his native tongue after gravity brought him back down to his seat.

Elham looked back to check his condition, but found his eyes drawn to the scene behind them. "We lost the truck," he said. The other two soldiers in the back twisted in their seats and looked. "Miserable driver—" one started to say . . .

Jon moved the rifle again. The closest jeep was maybe a third of a mile away now, twenty seconds from their position, maybe a bit more. He put crosshairs on the engine and went through the mental checklist that his father had burned into his memory, never to forget.

Breathe.

Relax.

Aim.

Slack.

Squeeze.

The Barrett rumbled again and the jeep's engine died a violent death, steam and fluids spewing from the grille. The vehicle rolled to a stop more than five hundred feet away. The men inside would need long minutes to cover the ground, but they would have entire side streets and no shortage of cover from Jon's rifle.

"Two to go," Kyra said.

Jon said nothing. She wasn't sure he'd even heard her. Her partner was staring downrange, his entire world defined by the image in his scope.

"Side street! Turn off—" Elham started to yell. Steam and hydraulics erupted, blinding him to the high-rise that was still more than seven hundred feet away. He heard the engine tear itself apart, sounds of grinding metal that seemed to be screaming and cursing at the men who had driven the vehicle to its death.

The jeep to their right swerved around them, its driver gunning the engine in a mad effort to close the distance. One of his passengers leaned outside the window to fire his rifle, at what target Elham couldn't imagine, but the fool didn't get off a single round before that vehicle's engine too erupted in smoke as black as the oil spilling out of it.

Elham twisted in his seat and saw the wrecked troop transport and a sister jeep both disabled, the former more than two hundred feet behind him. He looked forward again and judged the distance between the dead cargo truck and the roof of the apartment building—something over a half-kilometer, but not too far.

But why were they holding position here? Carreño had men coming from all directions. They would surround the building, establish firing positions, and keep the Americans from shooting off the roof's edge until a team could take the stairs—

This is their extraction point, he realized.

The American military would be here soon, maybe with helicopter gunships, and Elham did not want to get caught in narrow, walled streets when those machines came over the skyline.

Elham kicked open his door and ran for the back of the jeep. He could have huddled in the front seat, the destroyed engine between him and the Americans, but he could do no good there. The jeep doors themselves were useless as cover . . . any gun that could break an engine from that distance could punch a bullet through the doors. "Get out of the jeep!" he ordered the others. They scrambled to follow and tossed themselves onto the street behind the vehicle, Ahmadi almost crawling underneath it.

The last jeep crashed to a stop with black smoke rising out of the hood before the Barrett's echo died. The men scrambled out of the vehicle, afraid the engine was going to catch fire and the jeep burn with them inside. They hunkered down behind it, then came out running for the cover of Ahmadi's jeep while one of their company fired his rifle in Jon and Kyra's direction.

Neither analyst bothered to duck. The man was shooting from the hip and couldn't have hit them at half the distance handling his weapon like that. Jon put a round at his feet and the man twisted to run so suddenly that he fell on the asphalt. The Venezuelan dragged himself back up and ran after his comrades.

"You know, you haven't actually hit anybody with that thing," Kyra noted.

"Not trying to," Jon replied.

She checked her watch. "Nine minutes." *Four vehicles in less than a minute,* she thought. *We might live through this.*

Jon swept the field, looking for men trying to move up. A head stuck out, then pulled back behind one of the dead cars. Jon didn't waste a shot. The soldiers were staying put and none of them seemed confident enough of their skills to try a rifle shot at this distance with open sights.

"Eight minutes."

Jon saw movement behind the second jeep he'd taken out. The engine on that one had broken out in flames and he held the scope on the burning wreck. The soldiers were pulling something from the back.

Elham saw the soldiers pulling out a large crate. *Idiots.* He pointed violently at the intersection ten feet away. "Move up on the side streets," he yelled. But the men refused to listen. At least the fools would serve as a distraction. The Iranian threw open the cargo door to his own dead car and pulled out his rifle case. He dropped it on the ground, threw the locks, and raised the lid.

The Americans weren't the only ones who could hit a target at this range.

"You see that?" Kyra asked.

"Yeah, I've got it," Jon assured her. He lined up the crosshairs where the soldier seemed likely to stand.

The Venezuelan soldier stepped out from cover, the RPG-7 launcher on his shoulder. It would be a thousand-foot shot, well within the effective range of the weapon if he had the time to fire. Jon refused to give it to him. He pulled the Barrett trigger and the bullet tore a large chunk out of the concrete wall behind the man. He dropped the RPG and fled for cover.

Jon ejected the Barrett's empty clip and reached for his satchel to pull out another—

Elham locked the bipod on the Steyr and set it on the side of the jeep. The angle on the Americans' position was poor. The shooter was in an elevated position, giving him a low profile. Elham would get one shot at best and that would be hurried. His opponent would see him, line up, and Elham would have to get his shot off first.

He reached for a bullet tucked into his vest, this one an armor-piercing round. He slid the black-tipped slug into the ejection port and pushed the bolt forward. A regular round would probably have done the job, but he saw no point in being stingy. He pulled the cap off the Leupold Ultra M3A scope mounted on the rail above the Steyr barrel.

"Jon! One o'clock!"

He moved the rifle to the position Kyra had called

out and saw the soldier lining them up with a long-barreled rifle. *Sniper,* Jon thought. *That's no good.* "Back! Get back!" he yelled. He needed two more seconds to reload the Barrett and he didn't have them.

The Steyr's barrel spewed fire. The Iranian's .50 round hit the roof just below the edge where the American rifleman was crouched. The bullet blew through the concrete with a hideous crunching sound that Kyra had never heard before.

Elham swore. He'd never fired at an elevated angle so steep and had underestimated the drop rate of the bullet. He looked through the scope . . . he hadn't hit the Americans, of course, but they were out of firing position. He pulled back on the bolt, ejected the spent casing, and loaded another round.

Jon pushed the Barrett clip into the rifle and loaded the first round. "You got him?" he called to Kyra.

"Yeah, I saw where he's set up."

"You think you can get his attention with that thing?" He nodded at her HK.

"How far is it?"

"Seven hundred feet?" John guessed.

"At that range, getting his attention is about all I can do with this," she said. "She's not a long-range gun."

"Don't need you to hit him," Jon told her. "Wait until he shoots again, then put a few in the asphalt close enough to make him think about it."

One of the Americans turkey-peeked over the edge. Elham's shoulder took the hit as the Steyr sounded again, and the round punched into the lip of the roof for a second time. He waved the Venezuelans forward. A few refused, two others nodded and began to run.

Elham turned back, put his eye to the scope—one of the Americans, the woman, was firing in his direction. He heard metal rounds hit the jeep over the noise of Ahmadi yelling in fear, heard sharp pops as the slugs buried themselves in the frame, and he saw a few puffs of dust kick up from the building walls nearby, nothing too close. Seven hundred feet was a difficult shot under these conditions for anything other than a long-range gun with a good optic mounted on the rail. Still, given the range, the woman had done as well as her weapon would allow—

The jeep's rear tire blew out and the exploding rubber that decompressed less than five feet from Elham's head sounded for all the world like a mortar shell to his ears. His eyes shut involuntarily against the blast of dirty, stale air that struck his face, blinding him. On pure instinct, he grabbed the Steyr and rolled back to his right. Two degrees farther left and the American's shot would've ripped his brain out of his skull. *Praise Allah.* Still, the American had him targeted, while Elham's own sight picture had been destroyed. By the time he could line up again, the CIA officer would put the next round through his head.

"You shoulda blown his stinkin' head off," Kyra observed. Jon wasn't shooting to kill and she knew why. She prayed that shooting to scare would be enough.

"No thanks," he said. "Check the side streets and get ready to pop smoke," he ordered. Kyra ran to the north side of the roof and saw a dozen Venezuelan soldiers running up the street toward them. She knelt down, raised the HK, and pulled the trigger. Three rounds of fifteen hit the lead soldier, one in the hip, two in the legs, and he tumbled onto the street.

Jon heard her firing. "How we doing?" he yelled.

Kyra shook her head and ran for the roof's east end.

Over the Atlantic

Marisa covered the microphone with her hand. "How long?" she asked. The pilot held up three fingers.

"Arrowhead, Quiver. We are ETA three minutes. Can you hold?" Marisa asked, trying not to yell into her mic.

"Quiver, Arrowhead. LZ is not secure, repeat, not secure. We have a convoy of hostiles pinned down to the west, but there are more coming from the other three directions. Our position is about to be surrounded and we cannot retreat."

"Say again, you have a *convoy* pinned down?" Marisa asked.

"Roger that, Quiver."

Go Jon, go, Marisa thought. The pilot turned back to her and covered his mic with a glove. "How many on your team?" he called back.

"Two," Marisa replied. The pilot uttered a curse of approval and awe.

"Arrowhead, do you want us to clean up the LZ a bit before we set down? We've got some presents ready for your hosts."

"Negative, Quiver. Bad guys will be coming up inside the building by the time you show up—" Marisa heard the line go dead.

"Arrowhead? Arrowhead?!" *Hurry up!*

"Feet dry," the pilot announced. Marisa looked

down and saw the blue water of the Atlantic meet the sand of a Venezuelan beach.

Morón, Venezuela

Jon picked up the Barrett and moved away from the edge of the roof. There was no point in sniping now. He ran to the radio and checked the display as Kyra ran back and joined him by the stairwell entrance. "They're inside," he told her. "And I saw a few running into some other buildings. They get on those roofs and we aren't going to have any cover."

"Radio's dead," Kyra told him. "Out of power. Helo is two minutes out."

"You keep them from coming up the stairs," Jon ordered. "I'll cover the other rooftops if anyone comes out."

Kyra stepped inside the tiny shack, looked down over the railing, and heard boots on metal. The stairwell wrapped around in a circular fashion, leaving a hole in the center all the way to the bottom. She could see movement, bits of dark uniforms five stories down. She held the HK over the rails and sent the rest of her clip down the stairs. Men yelled and she heard the rhythm of heavy feet on the steps turn to a clatter of men diving for cover. Someone returned fire and Kyra jerked back as the bullets buried themselves in the shack's plaster ceiling. She swapped out the empty clip for a full one, racked the slide, then pointed her gun down again and let the soldier know she was still there.

Outside, Jon reached into his pack and pulled out two M18 smoke grenades, olive drab with bright red tops. "Kyra!" he yelled. She stuck her head out and he tossed one to her. He pulled the pin on the other, released the spoon, and tossed the device toward the center of the roof. Red smoke began to pour out in a thick cloud.

Inside, Kyra did the same and dropped the grenade down the stairwell's center hole. It fell four stories before finally hitting a railing, metal on metal, green smoke rolling out and shrouding the narrow climb in a dark fog within a few seconds. Kyra followed the grenade with more rounds from the HK.

"LZ in sight," the pilot said. Marisa looked ahead of the Seahawk and saw the red cloud growing on a building rooftop. On the street below, soldiers were moving through the streets toward the apartment complex.

The door gunner saw the dead trucks and jeeps littering one of the streets to the west. "Your people do good work, ma'am!" he yelled.

Marisa grinned back at the young man, sending a thrill up his spine.

"There!" Jon pointed north. Kyra followed his arm and saw the Seahawk boring straight for the building faster than she had thought a helo could go. She turned back to the stairs. The smoke had filled the entire stairwell now down to the floor, but the sound of the boots on the metal steps were closer, maybe three stories below. She fired the HK over the railing again until it ran dry, trying to buy a few more seconds, and the men below scattered again.

The Seahawk pilot pulled up the nose and dumped speed so fast that Marisa felt her stomach throw it-self against her ribs. The helo dipped, then swung sideways and came down on the roof, landing hard, the rotors blowing the smoke away in a whirlwind, the door gunner facing the stairwell entrance.

Kyra didn't wait for the order. She turned and ran for the helicopter, Jon behind her by two steps. She reached the door—

—and found Marisa's outstretched hand. The woman pulled her in onto the metal floor. Jon pulled himself aboard behind her, tossing the Barrett onto the floor.

Bullets struck the steel door behind the older woman . . . someone was firing up at the helicopter from the ground. "Go! Go! Go!" the door gunner yelled.

The pilot pulled back on the collective, then forward on the stick before the Seahawk was ten feet off the roof. The helicopter surged forward and began a turn back north—

"RPG!" the door gunner called out. Kyra looked out the open door as she fumbled with her seat harness and saw the contrail rising up from behind one of the trucks Jon had killed. The helo lurched hard as the pilot dove underneath the rocket-propelled grenade and it sailed over their heads, missing the metal bird by a dozen feet. The pilot pressed the stick forward hard, diving between a pair of higher buildings. The Seahawk was running a hundred miles an hour and accelerating when it cleared them.

"You okay?" Jon yelled at Kyra. The young woman nodded. He turned to Marisa. "It's about time—" He stopped midsentence.

Marisa was on her knees, blood staining her T-shirt in a spreading pool on her left side. "Jon—? I'm sorry . . ." She toppled forward into his arms.

He stared down at her in shock. "Get me a blowout bag! NOW!"

Elham lowered the Steyr and watched the American helicopter race off into the northern sky. He gotten off one shot at the moving Seahawk and hit it too high. "So much for catching your spies," he told Carreño.

The Venezuelan cursed in disgust. "Someone get me a jeep!"

White House Situation Room

"It survived?" Rostow practically yelled the question at his national security adviser.

"Yes, sir, it did," Cooke confirmed. "The MOP took out the entire CAVIM site, the convoy, and everyone inside the blast radius, but the nuke was in some kind of hardened transport crate already being moved out." She didn't point out that the MOP had almost taken out Jon and Kyra. She was sure that Rostow had never been worried about that. "One of our officers managed to get in close enough after detonation to confirm visually that the warhead survived."

The DNI's jaw dropped. "She was that close?" Marshall asked.

Cooke nodded. "She got inside the back of the cargo truck that was transporting it. She says the transport crate had been cracked open but there was no way to recover the warhead before reinforcements were going to arrive. Carreño's people have since loaded it into another truck and it's on the move."

"Great. Just great," Rostow groused. "We've lost it."

"No, sir, we haven't," Cooke said. "Our officer hid a phone inside the transport crate. Once she was able to tell us that, we started tracking it. The signal is intermittent and not terribly precise. We think the crate is interfering, but we do know that the warhead is on its way back to Caracas. But we'll lose the signal for good once the battery dies."

"How long?" Feldman asked. The national security adviser sounded desperate.

"Eight hours if we're very lucky," Cooke estimated. "Probably less."

"We've got to kill it," Rostow said. "Gerry, call the SecDef. I want another air strike—"

"Mr. President, I don't think we can target the warhead precisely enough for an air strike," Cooke told him. "It would be a very messy operation—"

"I don't care about the mess!" Rostow yelled. "I'm not going to tell the American people that we had a chance to take out a nuclear warhead in our hemisphere and *missed*!"

"Dan, wait a second," Feldman said, his voice surprisingly quiet to Cooke's ears. "She's probably right—"

"What, you're listening to her now?" Rostow demanded.

"Yeah, I am," Feldman said. "This whole thing has been a mess from the start and Kathy's the one who's been keeping this disaster from falling completely apart with duct tape and prayer. If she's got an idea of how to get out of this a little more gracefully than using an F-35 to turn a nuke into a dirty bomb in the middle of Caracas, I think we should hear her out."

Rostow looked at his adviser, then to the DNI, who nodded. "Fine," the president said, clearly not thinking so. "What do you suggest?"

"Sir, this is Marcus Holland," Cooke said, extending her hand toward the analyst. Holland had been sitting in the row of chairs along the Situation Room wall, desperately trying not to be noticed. "He's one of the analysts who's been working on our task force since this all began. I think you should take five minutes and listen to what he has to say."

The president glowered at the young man and Holland tried very hard not to shrink into his chair. "Well?"

USS *Vicksburg*
11°22' North 67°49' West
75 miles north of the Venezuelan coast

Vicksburg had turned to put the wind twenty degrees on the port bow, making the Seahawk pilot's life a little easier. He hovered the helicopter over the flight deck, the wind minimized to prevent the rotors from producing more lift, and he pushed down on the collective as fast as he dared. Kyra felt the helo's rubber tires touch down, the pilot killed the engine, and she saw a small group of sailors in coveralls and helmets shuffle out, bent over to keep their heads well below the spinning rotors. They secured the Seahawk, rolled open the doors, and the medical team ran out.

Marisa was stretched out on the helo's metal floor, Jon leaning over her, his bloody hand pressed against the bloody stain on her shirt. "Gunshot wound to the chest, upper right quadrant," he yelled as they climbed in and lifted her onto the stretcher. "We treated with Celox for bleeding. She developed a tension pneumothorax and we aspirated with a fourteen-gauge needle and applied a HALO chest seal . . ."

"You treated for shock?" one of the corpsmen yelled.

"Yes!" Jon replied.

The corpsmen lifted the stretcher board and started to run as fast as they could together, two men on either side of her.

Kyra jumped out of the Seahawk, her boots set down on metal and she closed her eyes, tried to suck in a deep breath of Atlantic air, and tasted jet fuel in the small hurricane whipped up by the rotor wash. Jon was running behind the medics and Kyra chased them down.

The corpsmen were yelling at the sailors in the passageways, who flattened themselves against the bulkheads to make room. Kyra lost track of the minutes it took to reach sick bay. Jon tried to follow but one of the corpsmen put a hand to his chest and backed him out. "Out here, sir."

"No, I—"

"In the passageway or in the brig, sir. Doesn't matter to me."

Jon stood still, saying nothing as the corpsman closed the hatch. Kyra looked at her partner but didn't speak until the metallic echo created by the metal door closing faded into silence. "Is she going to make it?" Kyra asked.

"Blood loss and tension pneumothorax are the primary causes of ninety-three percent of all battlefield deaths," he said, his voice flat. "I treated those. So it depends on what kind of damage the shot did inside her chest cavity." He stared at the closed hatch.

"Jon, if you want to stay here until—" Kyra started.

"Mills!" The CIA officers turned their heads to the master chief, who was making his way toward them.

"She was injured during the operation," Kyra yelled.

"Then who's your senior officer?"

"That would be me," Jon said. There was no emotion in his voice.

"You've got a message from Langley," LeJeune yelled back. "Looks like you might be getting back in the air pretty quick."

Palacio de Miraflores
Caracas, Venezuela

Avila had never tasted better rum. His predecessor gave him the bottle of Black 33 after choosing him for the presidency. With the Bolivarians counting the votes, the election had been a formality staged for the benefit of foreign observers. Avila had always intended to break open this particular bottle on his last day in office and share it with whomever he chose to follow him. Now that seemed more unlikely by the hour.

He looked past his desk at the far window. Light smoke was wafting up past the gates and for a minute he wondered whether the mushroom cloud from Morón hadn't reached Caracas. *Idiot,* he called himself. He had enough reasons to worry without making up stupidities like that. The mobs were clashing outside, held back only by each other and the army now. He'd given the order to open fire on the masses if they came over the fence to Miraflores, but he didn't know whether the soldiers outside would obey. Other men in his position had learned that military loyalty had its limits and Avila realized that he didn't know exactly what those limits were. He had never been a soldier, not like Comandante Chávez or Bolívar himself. Avila didn't know how these soldiers thought, not really, but he did know that every coup in his country's history had come from the army. He couldn't trust his protectors any more than he could trust the rioters outside. His only consolation was that the army wouldn't execute him on sight. If they turned, they would need him to make public statements to preserve order once the government fell. Avila *was* the government. His closer associates were just functionaries whose loyalty he was sure extended only so far as the benefits he could provide them. That had been a mistake, to surround himself with so many bootlickers. Dissent was not to be tolerated in the end, but letting his subordinates actually speak their minds on occasion might have earned him a bit of real loyalty to be tapped when he needed it.

Too late now for it. God was cruel that way sometimes, letting His favored children learn lessons only after those lessons would have been useful. Avila poured another shot and set the glass on the desk.

The door to the office opened and his secretary stepped inside. "Señor Presidente, there is a call for you—" the aide started.

"I'm not taking any calls!" Avila yelled.

"I think you should take this one, sir," the aide persisted.

Avila looked up at the functionary, surprised at the young man's insistence. He was unused to his subordinates countering anything he had to say. "And why is that?"

The aide looked terrified, whether of Avila's response or the caller's identity, the *presidente* couldn't tell. "It's the president of the United States."

Avila gaped at the man for a moment. His hand snaked out from under the desk, hesitated, then he touched the speaker button. "This is Presidente Diego Avila of the Bolivarian Republic of Venezuela," he announced.

"President Avila, this is President Daniel Rostow of

the United States of America," came the reply. Some unseen translator on the other end repeated the words in Spanish.

Pleasantries seemed pointless. "You have committed an act of war against my country, President Rostow—" Avila started.

"True," Rostow replied, which left the Venezuelan surprised. "But the *Almirante Brión* fired on the USS *Vicksburg* before that. And you violated the Nuclear Non-Proliferation Treaty and the Treaty for the Prohibition of Nuclear Weapons in Latin America and the Caribbean before that. So why don't we just forgo any little games of trying to prove who provoked who, shall we?"

"What do you want, Mr. President?" Avila replied, trying to control his tone. The alcohol was making it difficult not to slur his words.

"As you are aware, I ordered the destruction of the explosives factory at CAVIM. I am also prepared to order the destruction of the other sites involved in your proliferation program at Ciudad Bolívar, at Aragua, and Monagas. B-2 bombers carrying similar ordnance that you cannot detect with your air-defense network are already en route to those sites with orders to attack if I don't recall them in the next few hours." Avila hoped that was an outright lie but had no way of knowing. "We also know that the warhead you've been developing is en route to Caracas as we speak. I'm prepared to destroy it by any means necessary in the next few minutes if you don't agree to terms."

"You *estadounidenses* have dictated terms to South America long enough!" Avila yelled into the phone. "You will not give me orders like a dog sitting at your table—"

"Listen to me very carefully, sir." Rostow cut him off again. "There is no scenario in which you keep your nuclear facilities and that warhead. You are close enough to my country that the U.S. Navy can continue the blockade of your country indefinitely and I have the United Nations' blessing to do so. Your neighbors have sealed their borders. If this continues, I will seek sanctions against your economy. The only thing that will enter your ports will be food and medicine. Nothing, and I do mean *nothing,* will be allowed to come back out. We will strangle you. North Korea will look like an open freeway compared to how much cargo will be allowed to transit your country. Your own people are rioting against you. I doubt they'll love you more when your economy implodes and your country has a history of coups and revolutions. Do you really think that you're immune?"

Rostow stopped for a moment and let the threat sink in before continuing. "But you can avoid all of that. Agree to terms and none of that will happen. I won't try to topple your government. You could probably even blame this mess on your predecessors and I might be persuaded to say a few good words about how cooperative you've been in coming clean about the illegal programs that started before you came to office."

Avila took several deep breaths, then fell back in his chair, considering Rostow's words. He sipped at the rum, thinking, then shifted the phone, pressing it against his shoulder with his head as he took up the bottle and began to screw the cap back on. "And what are your terms?" he asked carefully.

"I have only three," Rostow told him. "First, you open up your nuclear sites to the International Atomic

Energy Agency for inspection and dismantling. Second, you deliver the warhead in the next three hours to a site that I will designate and give it up to a U.S. Special Forces team."

"And number three?"

Rostow told him.

Avila set the rum on the desk and pushed it away a few inches. "I do these things and you end your blockade immediately?"

"Your coasts will be cleared within twenty-four hours."

Avila frowned. "My friends will not like this."

"You'll still be in Miraflores to hear their complaints. Are we agreed?"

"*Sí.*"

"Thank you for your cooperation, Señor Presidente," Rostow said. "I look forward to an amicable resolution of this matter. And if you choose to deviate from this plan in the least degree, I promise you will regret it." The line went dead.

Avila hung up the phone, stared at the last dregs in his glass, and swallowed them. Perhaps Comandante Chávez was still pleading his case in heaven after all. He looked up. The secretary was still there, almost trying to hide behind the door. "Please bring me a radio. I need to talk to Señor Ahmadi."

White House Situation Room

Rostow cradled the phone. "That felt good," he said.

"Nice job," the DNI agreed. "Your voice had just the right tone of nasty."

"Cooke's idea plays to my strengths," Rostow said.

Maracay, Aragua, Venezuela
130 kilometers southwest of Caracas

"Is he with you?" Avila asked without preamble.

"*Sí,*" Carreño said.

"Where are you?!" Avila demanded.

Carreño shifted the radio handset away from his ear slightly to save his hearing. "We have just passed north of Maracay. We will be in Caracas in ninety minutes, maybe less if you can clear the roads."

"And you are with the cargo?"

"No," Carreño admitted. His driver had been killing the jeep trying to catch up with the convoy after the fiasco in Morón and still hadn't managed to close the distance. "The truck driver reports that his convoy is just east of La Victoria. I've told them not to stop and expect to rejoin them within the hour." He looked out of the passenger window at Maracay. The sun was setting behind the jeep and darkness had settled over the city enough that he could see fires burning in the *centros. They're rioting here too,* he realized. Was there any part of the country that this madness hadn't touched?

"Good. I want you to take the cargo and our friends directly to the airport," Avila said. "If they ask any questions, tell them that we will be flying them out of the country after they arrive."

Carreño rocked back in his seat at that news. *What are you playing at? Fly them where?* he thought. The Americans had established a no-fly zone, cutting off the north and east. The Colombians were denying overflight to the west, the Brazilians to the south. *Guyana?* he thought. "You're certain that's wise?" he asked carefully.

"You understand what we must do?"

"I'm not certain what options you are considering," Carreño said after a moment's thought. He pressed the handset against his ear to keep Avila's voice from leaking out. Ahmadi and Elham were in the backseat and he was sure he didn't want them to hear whatever the *presidente* was about to say. He wasn't certain how much Spanish they understood.

"I received a call from the American president. They know everything, Diego," Avila said. "They know where the warhead is now—"

"How?"

"I don't know, but they do. The security of this operation has been destroyed and we cannot allow a war with the United States. They would topple us and give the country back to the capitalists. It would destroy the Bolivarian revolution," Avila said.

"I can't disagree with that. We have always been playing a dangerous game," Carreño agreed.

"I had hoped that if you could catch the American spies that we could trade them for our survival. But now they're gone, we are left with two choices, and using the warhead would mean war. You understand this?"

Carreño had to force himself not to look to the backseat. "Yes."

"Good. You are with Señor Ahmadi?"

"*Sí.*"

"Let me talk to him," Avila ordered.

Ahmadi saw Carreño swivel in his seat and offer the handset. He frowned, took it, and held it to his ear. "What?"

"I'm very pleased to hear that you are unharmed, my friend," Avila said.

Anger erupted from inside him and Ahmadi made no attempt to contain it. "We were very nearly killed, my *friend*," he said, the sarcasm in his voice countering the title. "Our facility at Morón is *gone*—"

"I am aware," Avila replied, trying to calm him down. "Diego told me everything earlier. It is a great loss for both our countries, but that is a problem to be solved in the future. At this minute, we must deal with our immediate problems as they stand. Once we do that, we can find a new way forward. You and the cargo are the two most important assets that remain, so what matters now is your safety," Avila assured him. "We have your aircraft waiting for you at the airport with a full tank of fuel and I have arranged for a secure destination. I don't want to share its location on this line, but you will be safe. You have my word before God Himself."

Something is wrong, Ahmadi thought. "And you will meet us at the airport?" is what he finally said.

"I don't think that would be wise. Without question, the Americans are trying to track my movements. I wouldn't want to lead them to you and endanger your safety any further."

He won't come, Ahmadi thought. "Very well. Be well until I see you again. *Asr be kheyr.*" *Good night.*

He passed the phone back to Carreño. "They are setting us up, I think," he said to Elham in quiet Farsi. He was sure that the SEBIN director couldn't understand their native tongue.

"Why do you say that?" Elham replied, following the civilian's lead in the choice of language and keeping his own voice low.

"Avila has always been an obsequious twit but this is different. He has always flattered me to get what he wanted. Now he flatters me to get me to do what he wants. There is a difference," Ahmadi said.

You would know, Elham thought. *You understand flattery from both sides, don't you?* "What are you thinking?"

"I am thinking that we are pariahs now. These men want to give us up to the Americans for their own benefit."

We? You are the pariah. The Americans probably have no idea who I am. "It's possible," Elham conceded. "They lost all of their cards to play when the American spies escaped. Now we two and the warhead are their cards."

"What can we do?"

Now you listen to counsel? Elham wanted to scoff. *You plunge the world into chaos and then expect others to save you from your own stupidity.* Still, Ahmadi was an important man with secrets that could hurt their homeland if they ever came to light. The government might not be excited to have him come back at the moment, but neither could the soldier just let the Americans have him.

Elham considered the options, then he spoke. "You must start thinking like a soldier . . . think of strategy and tactics. We do nothing for now," he told Ahmadi. "We have no leverage as long as we are separated from the warhead. *That* is our only asset. The Venezuelans won't use it on their own soil and the Americans know it. We have no such inhibitions, so once we load it on the plane, what the Venezuelans think won't matter and the Americans will bargain directly with us. They will perceive us to be very dangerous people. So we do nothing until we reach the plane, and then we act."

"Very good, I agree," Ahmadi told him.

You would have agreed with anything, I told you, wouldn't you? Elham thought. Ahmadi was intelligent, devious in his own way, but he was not cunning. That failing was going to be the end of him, Elham was sure, and maybe sooner rather than later, depending on the next few hours.

USS *Vicksburg*
11°22' North 67°49' West
75 miles north of the Venezuelan coast

"This is stupid," Jon said, holding out the cable from Langley. Kyra had watched him as he'd read it through, which had taken him three tries. Her partner was distracted.

Kyra took the paper and read it. "They seriously think the Venezuelans are going to cooperate?" she asked.

"Kathy says we've got their word," Jon responded.

"Because we've been able to trust that so much for the last twenty years," Kyra scoffed. "This is not a good idea."

"It's that or the president starts bombing things again. And orders are orders," Jon said. "How long until we move out, Master Chief?"

"We're at Ready Fifteen, right now," Master Chief LeJeune responded. "Captain has already called for flight quarters and the pilots have a 'green deck' as soon as the Seahawk gets topped off."

"How's our station chief?" Kyra asked.

"She's in surgery," LeJeune responded. "Doc Winter is good but we're not exactly a full-service hospital, if you get me. She's critical. He's trying to keep her stabilized so we can evac her out to *Harry Truman* on the other Seahawk."

"Jon, I can take care of this if you want to stay with her," Kyra offered.

"No," he replied, anger in his voice. "We'll need to visit your armory," he said to the sailor. "A Barrett's no good at close range and we'll need something bigger than Glock 17s."

"I'll ask the captain, but I'm sure we can accommodate," LeJeune advised.

"Jon, go down there," Kyra said. "She needs you—"

"She's unconscious. There's nothing I can do for her," he said. "And we have our orders." He walked out, leaving Kyra staring at him as he went.

Simón Bolívar International Airport
Maiquetía, Venezuela

Carreño's driver turned the jeep onto the airport access road and pulled through the gates that led to the hangars beyond the landing strips. The convoy of cargo trucks pulled aside to park, one excepted, that continued on behind the SEBIN director's jeep.

It was full dark now, the moon hanging low in the sky just above the flat Atlantic horizon. Ahmadi saw no aircraft on the runways, which he supposed was the fault of the Americans and their no-fly zone. It was a perverse irony that it actually helped the Iranians now. No flights meant passengers and airport workers had no reason to be here, leaving the airport and the tarmacs empty.

"There." Carreño pointed at one of the hangars. A group of soldiers, at least a small company, stood in a formation in front of the metal building. "The building is secured, as promised."

Ahmadi grunted, felt Elham poke him gently in the ribs. He looked down. The soldier passed him a pistol in the dark, below the level where Carreño's driver could see the exchange in his rearview mirror. Ahmadi took the small gun and slipped it into his coat pocket.

The Venezuelan soldiers started to roll the hangar doors open. The interior lights were on and he could see a Boeing 727-200 parked inside. But the engines were silent, he realized, and the exterior lights unlit. He could see that from the tarmac more than a hundred yards away. The nav lights, the taxi lights, the strobes . . . all were dark.

Where's the pilot? Ahmadi thought, panicked. He should've been aboard. The SEBIN were supposed to be guarding the plane but he'd hoped the pilot would've had the good sense to get aboard—

They didn't bring the pilot, Ahmadi thought, angry. Or had the SEBIN detained him? The Iranian's mind was racing now and he couldn't slow it down. He tried to think about nothing, to calm his shaking hands. *Focus on the plane.* Elham was right. If they could make it to the plane—

But the SEBIN cordon stood between him and the Boeing . . . at least three dozen uniformed soldiers, every man armed with an assault rifle, any one with enough firepower to butcher him like a pig, to do to him what he'd told Elham to do to those Somali pirates.

Calm yourself! he thought. Avila wouldn't bring him to the airport for an execution. If the Venezuelan wanted him dead, he could have ordered the convoy to stop at any point. There had been a few dozen men in the trucks. They could have pulled him and Elham from the jeep, shot them both, and left them to rot in the woods at a million different places. No, to bring them to this point just to kill them made no sense. Avila wanted the Iranians off his country's soil, not dead, surely. But Avila was playing the game, trying to benefit himself. Ahmadi understood that, so he understood Avila, no? He knew what he would do in Avila's place and this possibility was frightening.

The armed soldiers finished opening the hangar door and Carreño's driver started to move the jeep forward again. The uniformed guards stared as they approached and Ahmadi was sure there was murder in their eyes. He curled his hand around his gun as the truck approached the line and he started to pull it out—

Elham put his hand on Ahmadi's and shoved it roughly back down. "Don't be stupid," he said in Farsi. "They outnumber us. Don't give them any excuse. I will talk to them, then join you inside."

The driver pulled the jeep into the hangar, turned right, and parked it under the far end of the Boeing's left wing.

Ahmadi sucked in a breath and quietly praised the God he rarely obeyed.

Someone had pulled the rolling stairs into place and opened the Boeing's door. Ahmadi reached the top and put his hand inside his pocket, getting a grip on the pistol as he put his foot down on the carpet. He turned the corner and looked into the cockpit. There was no pilot, no copilot, and Ahmadi cursed. He turned back—

Two men stood in first class. One was a sailor, U.S. Navy by the uniform. The other was grubby, dressed in cargo pants, tan boots, his clothes dirty and face unshaven and unwashed, with a handgun holstered in a thigh rig and an M4 carbine hanging from a shoulder sling.

"Hossein Ahmadi," the uniformed man said. The American man in grubby clothes translated the sailor's words into Farsi.

"I am he," Ahmadi replied in English, contemptuous. "Why are you on my plane?"

"Mr. Ahmadi, my name is Captain Albert Riley of the USS *Vicksburg*. On behalf of the president of the United States of America and acting with the authority of the UN Security Council, I am here to accept your surrender."

"My surrender?" Ahmadi said, almost sneering at the man. "You have no authority here. We are in Venezuela and this plane is Iranian territory—"

"I beg to differ, sir," Riley told him. "You have no diplomatic credentials and this plane is not a registered diplomatic aircraft."

"We are still in *Venezuela*," he argued.

"True enough," Jon said. "Presidente Avila and President Rostow have reached terms of agreement regarding your custody. Technically speaking, you're being arrested by members of the Venezuelan police, who are standing outside this aircraft, and being transferred to U.S. custody for transport to the USS *Harry Truman* until such time as we can arrange an extradition flight to the United States of America. We're just going to skip past the step where they arrest you and go straight to the part where you get transferred to our custody."

Carreño stood by the base of the stairs, listening as one of the SEBIN soldiers whispered in his ear. The director looked up at the plane door in amazement. "And we're to cooperate?" he asked. The soldier nodded. "Who is their representative?" he asked.

The soldier pointed behind his superior. Carreño turned—

—the woman who had beaten him within an inch of his life was standing within two meters of him. "You," he said bitterly.

"Yes, me," Kyra said in Spanish. "Keep your hands out of your pockets or I'll finish what you started."

"What I started—?"

"You remember the bridge over the Guaire?"

Carreño's mouth fell open. "That was you."

"That was me. How's the nose?"

"You won't touch me again," Carreño sneered. "You're not here for that now."

"Nobody said I couldn't take on a little side mission," she replied.

"Touch me and I'll have you shot."

"No, you won't. Gentlemen?" she yelled.

Several squads of U.S. Marines marched around the side of the hanger. Where they had been hiding in the dark, Carreño had no idea. "Let's not start anything ugly," the woman said.

An Iranian soldier approached. "You are the American in charge?" he asked in good English.

"Out here, yes," Kyra replied.

"My name is *Sargord* Heidar Elham of the Army of the Guardians of the Islamic Revolution."

"I'd be happy to call Presidente Avila," the Navy captain said. "He can explain—"

"Don't bother," Ahmadi growled. "I don't want to speak to that *kosskesh*—"

At that moment Elham passed through the plane's door, followed by Carreño and a woman dressed in cargo pants and a T-shirt, armed with her own pistol and M4.

Ahmadi turned his glare to his countryman. "You know what they're doing?"

"I've been told," Elham replied.

"Are you going to stand by and let them do this?"

"Yes," the soldier told him.

"What?" The blood drained from Ahmadi's face. "You said now was the time to act—"

"And I am acting. I kept you pacified until we reached the airport," Elham told him.

"You knew?!"

"I suspected," Elham said. "As I said, they lost all of their cards to play when the American spies escaped. But it was not entirely true that we were their only cards. The warhead is no card at all for them as long as it sits on their soil, which left *you* as their only card. I am nobody, a nonentity to the Americans, and that makes me of no worth at all. It also means that I have little to fear so long as they get you."

"You betray me!"

Elham exploded, grabbing Ahmadi by the shirt and slamming him against the bulkhead. Jon and Kyra raised their carbines, fingers on the triggers. Carreño jerked in surprise and the younger woman thrust her M4 at him, the end of the barrel not a meter from his face and the SEBIN director lost control of his bladder. Jon carefully raised a hand, put it on the young woman's gun, and gently lowered her weapon.

"You're a coward and a fool," Elham hissed at his superior. "I've dealt with you death merchants before. You never fight yourselves. You build weapons that men like me have to use, soaking ourselves in blood while you sit at home drinking and whoring. And you tell everyone how wonderful it would be if you could build and fire the ultimate weapons that would kill thousands upon thousands. Then you start mewling because someone dares to point a weapon at you."

"But we have the warhead! We can—"

"Look out the window, you idiot!" Elham ordered him. He released Ahmadi so the man could turn his head.

Ahmadi leaned over the seats and raised one of the window covers. Across the hangar, American Marines were unloading the warhead crate from the back of the cargo truck. Venezuelan and Iranian soldiers were standing around, making no move to stop them . . . were, in fact, holding their formation outside the hangar. *If they aren't stopping them, they're cooperating,* Ahmadi thought. "Who are they?" he asked.

"Those are U.S. Marines," Jon replied.

"It is over," Elham told him. "Now give me the pistol in your pocket."

Ahmadi gritted his teeth, hissing through them, and pulled the gun. The armed Americans shifted their rifles. He glared at them sideways, then thrust the pistol against Elham's chest. "I should kill you."

"That would be very difficult without a clip in the gun," Elham said.

"What—?" Ahmadi twisted the pistol and checked the grip—empty. "Why give it to me—?"

"I gave you what you wanted so that you would do

what I wanted, which was to sit down, do nothing, and be silent," Elham said. He pulled the gun from Ahmadi's hand. "And so you did."

"You are a traitor," Ahmadi said, his voice cold. He turned back to Jon and Riley. "I presume that you would grant me asylum in exchange for information—"

Faster than Jon's eyes could follow, Elham dropped the empty pistol while pulling a second Sig Sauer P-229 from the small of his back. He raised the gun to Ahmadi's head and pulled the trigger. The 9mm round punched through Ahmadi's skull and buried itself in the bulkhead, spewing blood and viscera in its wake.

Ahmadi crumpled to the floor, the carpet underneath turning dark red.

"Put it down!" Jon yelled, his carbine less than a foot from Elham's chest. Pulling the trigger would gut the soldier at that range.

Elham obeyed, kneeling and setting the pistol on the floor next to Ahmadi's shattered head, then stood and raised his hands where Jon could see them. "You have nothing more to fear from me," he told him. "Ahmadi was a fool, but I could not let you have him. He was a dead man from the moment he set foot on this plane."

Jon stared at the Iranian soldier, then waved him off the plane. "Surrender to the Marines on the tarmac." Elham nodded and walked out through the hatch.

Kyra stepped in behind him, then stopped and faced Carreño. "Your people shot me in the arm," she told him. "That night on the bridge."

"We all do our duty."

Kyra smashed his face with the butt of the M4,

dropping him to the floor by Ahmadi's corpse. Then she walked down the rolling stairs.

Jon stood on the tarmac and watched as the Marines finished securing the warhead in the CH-46E Sea Knight helo. Kyra moved in next to him, her carbine hanging loose from its harness. He looked up at the Boeing and watched the SEBIN soldiers lowering Carreño's prone form on a stretcher. "They weren't very happy when you cracked him in the head again."

"I wanted to shoot him in the arm," Kyra said. "It would've been fair."

"Maybe," Jon said.

"The president's not going to be happy about Ahmadi taking one in the head. We could've ripped Iran's entire nuclear program open with him in custody," Kyra said.

Jon nodded, exhaled, then finally asked the question he'd been wanting to avoid. "Have you contacted *Vicksburg*?"

"Just got off the radio with them," she said. "Jon . . . Marisa died. The doctor said that the shrapnel he pulled out of her chest looked like a fragment from a .50 round. The bullet must've hit the Seahawk and splintered. The piece that hit Marisa nicked one of the arteries leading to her heart and tore up her lung. She never woke up."

Jon just nodded slowly and said nothing. "The Venezuelan military doesn't have any .50 rifles in their inventory. Their snipers use Dragunov rifles . . . they shoot a 7.62-millimeter round. But the Iranians have Steyr rifles. Those shoot .50 millimeter rounds." He looked over at Elham, sitting next to Ahmadi's wrapped corpse in the Sea Knight, hands bound with zip ties.

"You think he did it," Kyra said, following the direction of his eyes.

"It doesn't change anything whether I'm right or wrong."

"Yes, Jon, it does," she said. "All the time."

DAY NINE

"What can I do for you, Cy?" Rostow asked. The Secret Service agent closed the door behind the director of national intelligence as he entered. The president stood behind the Resolute desk, shuffling papers and arranging them in a leather portfolio. "I've got a briefing in ten minutes in the Press Room."

"I understand, sir, I'll keep this short," Marshall told his superior. He took his place opposite the desk and stood stiff, almost a military stand of attention. "I'm here to ask you to refuse Kathy Cooke's resignation."

"Refuse it? I ordered it." Rostow glanced up at his chief intelligence adviser, an unhappy look. "And I'm going to announce it in the briefing. Denied."

"Then you'll be announcing mine as well," Marshall told him. "If you refuse, I'll direct my own public affairs officer to release a statement to the *Post* to that effect."

Rostow stopped moving papers, stared at Marshall, then sat down in his high-back Gunlocke chair. "What is this about, Cy?" he asked, his voice tinged with anger. "Cooke's retiring a hero. Her people recovered a nuclear warhead. She goes out on top, but she's going out."

"Mr. President, when I accepted this post, I was aware that you have no particular use for the intelligence community, which is fair enough. You aren't the first president to look down on our profession," Marshall started. "Over the last year, I've gotten to know Kathy Cooke. She's an honorable public servant and a fine leader who has acted in the best interests of this country and her people. Under her command, the CIA could be a tremendous asset to your administration. But you've only ever looked at her as a means of garnering political capital and you hate CIA for reasons I can't fathom. Once this event broke, I had hoped that we could perform in a way that would change your opinion, but instead, I have been deeply disturbed by the callous way you've treated her and her officers. I should have intervened on her behalf sooner, but once we learned there might be WMD in Venezuela, I felt it important to support the effort to find it and eliminate it even if I didn't approve of your decisions."

"Tread carefully," Rostow warned.

"I'm your principal intelligence adviser, sir," Marshall reminded him. "Or at least I'm supposed to be. In that capacity, I feel that I owe you my honest opinions. And in my opinion, you and your national security adviser demonstrated poor judgment through the crisis and are doing so again now in asking Kathy to resign—"

"How dare you!" Rostow cut him off.

"I dare because I'm a career military and intelligence officer and I will not serve under a man who is willing to sacrifice intelligence officers for his own political ends!" Marshall said, refusing the interruption, his own temper flaring. "I'm a flag-rank military officer, so I understand and appreciate ambition—"

"I thought military officers also understood insubordination," Rostow said, quietly furious.

"I understand it perfectly well. And I'm prepared to accept the consequences of my choices, sir," Marshall told him, undeterred. "But frankly, sir, you wanted your own Cuban Missile Crisis and you were perfectly willing to endanger American lives to get it. But worse than that, you didn't even expect Kathy's people to succeed. You were setting her up to fail so you would have an excuse to fire her. You were willing to endanger American lives just to force Kathy out of her office and save some political capital in the process. That I won't abide."

Rostow glared at Marshall. "She serves at the pleasure of the president."

"As do we all. But there is an inherent, unspoken trust among federal servants and soldiers that their president will treat them fairly, and that he certainly won't treat them like expendable assets for political ends. You violated that trust, as many of your predecessors have before you. I won't be a party to it and I will resign before I become part of that machine."

Rostow leaned back in his chair, studying the DNI with a cold look. Marshall held his gaze, then went on. "But honestly, I don't think you want that to happen. The problem with being part of a Cuban Missile Crisis is that historians will spend the next hundred years picking the event apart. With legacies come inspection. Journalists will question every decision that was made, every word that was said. They'll be asking to talk to each and every one of us until we're all dead. And I can't speak for Kathy, but my recollection of events and your behavior in particular will be shaped very heavily by the next decision you make."

The president laughed, disbelieving what he'd just heard. "That's a bluff. Everything that just happened is classified. I could order you not to talk and send you to jail if you did."

"You could, but the press has a way of finding out details even when nobody is talking," Marshall countered. "And you won't hold this office forever.

Everything will get declassified in twenty-five years, assuming one of your successors doesn't decide to release it all sooner. It might not happen for a decade or two, but it will happen, and maybe sooner than you think. And Kathy is only in her late forties. She'll outlive us both."

"Blackmail, Cy?"

"That's not my intention, but I suppose it depends on what your true priorities are, sir," Marshall informed him. "But there is a clean way out."

"And what is that?" Rostow asked.

"Promote her."

"Promote her?!" the president repeated, incredulous. "Please, Cy, you're wasting my time now."

"Did you know she was Navy before she came to CIA?"

"I read that somewhere," Rostow replied dismissively. "What does that have to do with anything?"

"In the Navy, it's accepted that the captain of a ship has more freedom to act than an admiral behind a desk." Marshall nodded. "The intelligence community is no different. The CIA director is more powerful than I am in a lot of ways and I think you know that. So here's my suggestion—I still don't have a deputy. You nominate her for the post, Congress will confirm her, probably unanimously. You'll get to install your own man as CIA director. She'll become the deputy DNI, she won't have an agency under her immediate command. She won't have as much power to act, but she gets to serve and retire on her own terms."

The president paused to think. "And I look good for promoting the first woman CIA director to a higher post?" Rostow commented, staring at the Seal of the United States on the Oval Office ceiling.

"I'm sure," Marshall said.

"Or I could fire you for coming in here and talking to me like this . . . replace you both."

"You could," Marshall conceded. "Though I'm sure the press would want to know why both the new director of national intelligence and the CIA director lost their jobs on the same day, especially after they helped the president of the United States score what will unquestionably be one of the biggest foreign-policy successes of his tenure."

Rostow considered the argument, the debate raging in his mind apparent to the man standing on the other side of the desk. "If I agree, I don't want to deal with her again. I don't want to see her in this office again."

"I can't promise that. The world might not cooperate. But I'll do my best to keep her separated from you."

Rostow nodded after a few moments, still unhappy. "I'll think about it," he said. "You can leave now."

"Thank you for your time, Mr. President." Marshall turned, walked to the door, and let himself out. Rostow stared at him until the door closed, then fought down the urge to throw his portfolio across the room.

CIA Director's Office
7th Floor, Old Headquarters Building
CIA Headquarters

There were almost no boxes, surprisingly little for her to pack away. A few of the curios on the walls had simply come with the office and never had been hers. Most of the other objects sitting on the shelves she had chosen to give up, all gifts from foreign dignitaries that were expensive enough that they had become government property the moment she'd accepted them. If congressmen couldn't take a bushel of apples from a constituent, they certainly weren't going to let an intelligence chief take a scimitar from a Saudi prince without making her pay for it. She could have bought them back for their market price, which in most cases would have been a sizable fraction of her salary, so she opted to let the Agency keep them. Now the museum staff had taken most of them away for storage, to languish in some wooden crates in a warehouse at the Farm or wherever the Directorate of Support kept such things. She'd never thought to ask. Eventually, some future curator would pull the best pieces and put them under glass down in the hallways for future masses to ignore as they walked past.

One object had never been put on the books. Kathy picked up the broken aircraft gauge. It was a piece of the heads-up display from that Chinese stealth plane that Jonathan had brought back the year before. He had guessed it was the altitude indicator. She pulled it out of the Plexiglass cube he had put it in, turned it over in her hands, then put the open box on the coffee table. That one was coming home.

Her cigar humidor sat on the table beside the cardboard storage box. Kathy hefted the small cherrywood box and opened it. Five tubes rested inside, still sealed, with words written on the sides in permanent ink. She set the box on her desk, the top still open, and picked up the cigar tube lying there—a gift from Drescher. The man was a Mormon and therefore didn't smoke, but he apparently had no moral objection to giving her a cigar. He knew she would never smoke this one, so perhaps in his mind there would be no harm done.

She just hoped the man's religious leaders hadn't seen him browsing through a cigar shop for the Cohiba. She scrounged for a Sharpie, found one, uncapped it, and scrawled *Caracas 2018* on the side of the tube. Kathy examined her handiwork, then dropped the tube into the humidor. *Six. Not bad for two years.* There had been others, lesser operations that might have merited the ritual, but she was a woman of high standards.

The packing done, there was almost nothing left but a few meetings and farewells. Tomorrow, around noon, she would deliver a farewell address to the workforce in the auditorium, which would be broadcast to the outbuildings over the internal television network. Then, at the end of the business day, Kathy would walk out of the building and a security escort would take her home. In two years or three the new CIA director would invite her back to attend the unveiling of her official portrait, which would hang down in the main-floor hallway. He would give her a warm if perfunctory introduction and she would say a few words about her two years holding the post. There would be polite applause, some happy and brief reunions, perhaps a luncheon on the seventh floor in Agency Dining Room 1, and then she would leave again, reminded in the most painful way possible of the adage that no one is indispensable. If and when she might ever be invited back after that, she had no idea.

Kathy put her cigar humidor into one of the packing boxes and finally saw Jon standing by the door. Her secretary saw him at the same moment and chose to excuse herself from the room for official reasons that Kathy was sure were entirely contrived.

"Hi," she said.

"Hi."

Kathy stood there, rooted to the spot, unsure what she could say. "I'm sorry," is what finally came out.

Jon shook his head slowly. "You have nothing to apologize for. You were right."

"Right? Every decision I made was wrong. The mission wasn't low risk—"

"You were right," he interrupted. "You were . . . you *are* the CIA director. You made a decision based on the best information you had. It was information I gave you, so I can hardly complain. Things went south. That wasn't your fault. But *this*—" He waved a hand around the office. "This is wrong."

"This was inevitable," Kathy told him. "Rostow never kept me on because he believed in me. He kept me on for—well, it doesn't matter why he kept me on. He was always going to replace me once there was no more political gain in keeping me around." Kathy watched him as he looked around the room. She doubted that either of them would ever see the inside of it again after tomorrow. "You never told me about you and Marisa," she chided him quietly.

"Nothing to tell."

"You two were serious," she observed.

"I was," Jonathan said. "Her, not so much."

"I don't think that's true," Kathy told him.

"She left."

"She regretted it. At least, Kyra thinks she did."

"It doesn't matter now."

"Yes, it does." Kathy walked over to him, reached up, put a hand on his cheek, and turned his face toward her. "You might not think so, but there are people who care about you. Even if they aren't very good at saying it . . . or always free to show it. I didn't know Marisa very well . . . I just met her once, when I assigned her to take over Caracas station. But something tells me that she really cared for you."

Jon nodded, not agreeing, but, maybe for the first time she'd ever seen, trying to understand her feelings. "I did come on official business," he told her. "You are still the director for another day."

"I suppose. What is it?"

Jon held out a briefing binder. Kathy sat on the couch and Jon took his seat beside her. She opened the book. The first page was a cutaway diagram of the Iranian nuclear warhead. "The Department of Energy reverse-engineered the warhead, with an assist from some of our people and a few other agencies. They sent over the blueprints this morning."

"And?"

"The Counterproliferation Center compared them to every nuclear weapon design that every known proliferator has peddled for the last thirty years. The layout doesn't match any of them. Those were all older designs, uranium fission with an implosion setup usually. Ahmadi's was a two-stage fusion-boosted design with a secondary. Polonium-beryllium trigger, tritium initiator, the whole smash. And it's got a plutonium core, so someone is reprocessing nuclear waste."

"Do you think the Iranians developed the design?"

"Not likely. This design is a serious jump from anything that's been for sale and the Iranian nuclear program has had Mossad's full attention for a long time now."

"Stolen? From the Russians or the Chinese?"

"The Iranian intelligence services are good, but I doubt they're *that* good," he replied.

She looked at him suspiciously. "You always have a theory."

"Not one that I can prove at the moment. I need more time to do some research."

"But what do you think?" she persisted. "Your guesses are usually pretty good. Another nuclear proliferator?"

"Not just a nuclear proliferator . . . a *weapons* technology proliferator," he corrected her. "That Chinese plane the *Lincoln* shot down last year was a better design than the Chinese should have been able to field at the time, even with technology they stole from us. The engines alone were more efficient than anything the PLA has ever managed to put into the air. And now someone helps the Iranians manufacture a nuclear warhead with a design far too complex for any first-time proliferator to develop on their own. I think you can count on one hand the number of countries with advanced warhead designs who also design and build jet engines."

It didn't take long for Kathy to run through the mental list. "Not many candidates, and most of them are friendlies. I don't like that at all."

"Neither do I. But someone is helping countries make generational leaps in technological advances, trying to get them up to par with us and our allies."

Kathy nodded, then flipped through the pages in the binder. "I'll call the DNI and arrange a meeting so you can brief him. He's a good man. He'll take it seriously." She closed the book and looked up at Jon, staring straight into his eyes. "I'm worried about you."

"I've already signed up to speak with a counselor in case there's any PTSD—"

"That's not what I meant," she corrected him, shaking her head. "Jon, the Red Cell isn't terribly popular around here . . . never has been. I always gave you cover, but now that I'll be gone? You and Kyra have scored some big wins lately that've left some office directors a little jealous. There will be a lot of people moving to close you down and I doubt Rostow's man will do anything to stop them. I don't know where you or Kyra will end up and I don't want to see you wasted."

"More than I've already wasted my career?"

Kathy winced a bit. "I always thought you could do more than you were doing," she admitted. "But if you're happy, I have no reason to complain."

"I don't know if 'happy' is the word, but I don't have to stay here," he told her. "There are other places I can work. Kyra's got nothing to prove by staying and I expect two Intelligence Stars will score her a decent job. She deserves a third for what she just did down south."

"So do you and I've filed the paperwork for it. But don't be surprised if Rostow's man kills it."

"I was never in this for the awards," he told her.

"I know," Kathy said. *That's one thing I've always loved about you.* "Jon, would you like to come to dinner?"

He sat back, surprised. "A date?"

"Yes," she said. "We've lost enough time and there's no reason to lose any more now. I'll be a private citizen, out of your chain of command. I think we should pick up where we left off . . . if you still want to."

"I would like that," he said. Jon finally smiled, not much, but enough.

Kathy leaned over and put her arms around him. He did the same to her and they held each other until the phone rang. "Sorry," Kathy said. "I am still the director for another day." She pulled away from him, stood, and walked to her desk. She hit the intercom button. "Yes?"

"Sorry to disturb you, ma'am," the secretary said. "Call for you. It's the director of national intelligence."

"Put him through," Kathy said. She turned back to Jon. "I guess I have to take this."

"I guess you do. I'll let myself out . . . but I do have one favor to ask."

CIA Headquarters
Langley, Virginia

The calligrapher fumbled with the keys, then finally managed to get the right piece of metal into the lock and he pulled the creaky drawer open. The tools were all there, just as he had left them six months before. *Too soon,* he thought. He wished that the pen case, the ink bottles, and the rest of his instruments were getting more time to gather a little dust. But the director had called him again this morning, before his computer had finished booting up and his coffee had cooled down, and like that his happy morning had come apart.

He lifted the tray out, carried it to the worktable, and set everything out in its place. The ink bottles each got a quick shake to make sure the contents hadn't congealed, and then he pulled out the Gillott number 303 nib, fitted it into the pen handle, and set it on the marble rest. The ink was French, powdered gold mixed with gum arabic according to a recipe that was a century old. The pen held the Gillott nib, which was used for only one task. It sat unused for months at a time, sometimes years, in a small locked cabinet. *The longer the better,* he thought. But the director had called him this morning and asked for his services, so the calligrapher had set aside his other job, extracted his tools, and waited for the Book.

The Book of Honor was large, twenty inches by thirty-two when open, and bound in a brown, pebbled Moroccan leather cover. There were two pages inside with deckled edges, both made at a French mill that had first opened, by pure coincidence, in 1492. The handmade Arches paper was the best on which he had ever practiced his craft. Inscribing letters using ancient techniques with fine ink on these excellent sheets should have been pure joy for him, but he couldn't take pleasure in it. By definition, he did this job at the worst of times and it was a lonely burden. The calligrapher was the only person who wrote in the Book and he used this pen and this ink only when he had to do so.

He idly wondered how many stars he would be asked to draw today. The suicide bombing at Khost in late 2009, almost a decade ago now, had forced the calligrapher's predecessor to inscribe seven stars in one day. Over a hundred stars had been added to the Book since 1947, better than one per year on average. Nearly a quarter of those had been added in the last two decades and the world wasn't becoming a safer place.

He prayed that the number today would be small. The left page of the Book had two columns, both full to the bottom with stars, years, and names. The right page also had two columns. The first was full. The second now had only a few inches of space left to spare. The Agency would need a new book soon.

But regardless of the number, the process for each was precise to the point of being mechanical. After using a pencil to sketch out the star, the year, and possibly the name, if that was allowed, he would dip his pen in the small black bottle far enough to cover the tip, then remove the excess on a rag. He would trace the star and fill it in, then remove the nib, clean it, and set it aside. Then he would fit the pen handle with a different nib, a Mitchell round-hand square, size three and a half, set it on a small marble rest, and uncap a second small inkwell, this one half filled with Japanese sumi ink as black as space itself. The ink would flow smoothly over the pencil lines he had laid down earlier. He would hold his hand by force of will. A single misplaced stroke would render the Book unfit for display. As he finished each entry, he would repeat the process for the next.

A quick turn of the pencil in the sharpener and everything was ready. The calligrapher double-checked his equipment and then sat back. Nothing to do but wait for the director to show up with the Book.

He didn't have to wait long. The door creaked open behind him after five minutes, maybe less. He wasn't watching the clock. The calligrapher closed his eyes for a quick second, then turned to face the senior officer. "Ma'am, I—"

He stopped short. *Who are you?* "Forgive me," he said after an awkward pause. "You're not the people who usually bring up the Book."

"No, I guess not," Jon said. Kyra stood next to him, holding the Book of Honor. "We asked to do it this time and Director Cooke agreed. I hope you don't mind."

You two must really be something. Cooke considered that duty to be almost a religious matter. To give it up to someone else . . . there was a story there and he wondered how much he could ask. "It's not my book, so it's not my place to mind." He extended his hand. "Charlie Stanton."

Kyra shifted the Book so she could hold it in her left hand while she reached out with her right. "Kyra Stryker. This is Jonathan Burke."

"A pleasure." Stanton looked at the pair. Burke was keeping a neutral face but Stryker looked fairly somber, which was unfortunate for such a pretty girl. The reason for it was obvious. "You can lay it down here."

"You want me to open it? Sorry, I'm not sure how you usually do this."

"That's okay." Stanton gave Kyra a reassuring smile. "A little care and respect is good enough, and we'll forgive anything else."

Kyra set the Book of Honor on the table and gently opened it, holding her breath while laying both sides flat. She was scared to death that she'd tear the pages and didn't relax until she could back away from the tome. "How did you get this job?"

"Learned from my mother," Stanton said as he sat down. He reached for the pencil. "I figured I could make a little money on the side doing wedding invitations, stuff like that. Then I did one for a group chief of mine after I started working here. He got promoted to the seventh floor, then the previous calligrapher retired and my old boss floated my name. I guess I was the only candidate. Not too many people know how to do this by hand anymore. That was all ten years ago. I promise, I never asked for it."

"I can't imagine why anyone would," Kyra said. "Do you enjoy it?"

"Worst job I ever had. But maybe the most important," Stanton admitted. "Are we doing the name or just the star?" He already knew the answer in his gut. He hadn't heard of any deaths, either on the cable news networks, in the *Post,* or through the rumor mill that was, by far, the most efficient system of the three. That meant a covert operation had gone wrong and there would be no names in the Book again, just the year and a star. Maybe more than one.

"Just the star," Jon confirmed. Cooke couldn't sign off on this one. Not until Avila was dead or rotting in a Venezuelan jail and maybe not even then, depending on who replaced him.

The star, singular. Just one, then. He looked up at Stryker. She was trying not to cry, and failing. "You knew him, didn't you?"

"We were there," Kyra said with a shaky nod.

"Who was he?"

"She," Jonathan corrected him. "Marisa Mills." Kyra's face broke out in a sad smile and tears finally started to roll.

"At least you two made it out," Stanton said. "At least I only have to draw one."

"There will always be more," Jon said.

"I wish you were wrong." Stanton reached down, picked up the ruler and the pencil, and leaned over the Book.

Acknowledgments

Any list of supporters must begin with my wife, Janna, whose willingness to be a single mother for months at a time makes writing a book possible; whose faith in my writing exceeds my own; and who keeps my head on straight. I love you.

As always, the professionals at Simon & Schuster—Lauren Spiegel, Miya Kumangai, Shida Carr, Norma Hoffman, and many others who work so hard to make every book the best it can be, and far better than I could make them by myself. I live in fear of the day that I have to work with a different team because this one has set a high bar that any other will be hard pressed to meet.

Jason Yarn and Ken Freimann, who help filter the ideas that are working from the ones that are failing. Brutal honesty can be bitter medicine but this patient appreciates the results of the unsparing diagnoses these gentlemen deliver.

The CIA Publications Review Board, which makes a potentially difficult process as painless as possible. Despite accusations to the contrary, I've never found them to be difficult or bent on unfair censorship.

Finally, Rachel Hanig-Grunspan, one of the great friends of my life. You accepted a hard decision that helped me but hurt you far more than I ever intended. I hope someday to find a way to make it up to you.

Turn the page
for a sneak peek at
Mark Henshaw's
thrilling novel

THE FALL OF MOSCOW STATION

PROLOGUE

"Operator." Alden Maines gripped the phone tight, his eyes closed, his teeth grinding hard together. This line was reserved for one purpose only and he had only one case officer on the street tonight. There were twenty people standing around him, all silent, watching him. They'd come the moment the phone had called for their deputy chief's attention.

"GRANITE . . . site MANGO." It was Kyra, he was sure, but her voice was slurred.

"GRANITE, report your status," the deputy chief of station ordered. There was no reply. He repeated the order and heard nothing but silence, the line still open. Maines cursed under his breath and cut the connection to stop the locals from tracing the call to either end.

"Abrams! Raguskus!" he called out. Two members of the circle jerked hearing their names. "Get down to the garage and fire up the van. Search and rescue—"

"Don't move, any of you!"

Maines looked over at the man who had countermanded his order, fury drawn on his face. Sam Rigdon, chief of Caracas Station, came into the room, wrestling his way through the line of bodies surrounding his deputy. "Was that Stryker? If she's in trouble, she can sit and wait it out. She probably screwed up the op and led the SEBIN right to Carreño. I'm not going to throw any more bodies at Chávez's people. She can get herself home. You keep your butt in that chair."

"No."

"Excuse me?" Rigdon replied, surprised.

"I said no," Maines told him again. He turned back to Raguskus and Abrams. "Go get the van ready," he ordered again.

"If anyone moves, I'll send 'em back to Langley—" Rigdon started to threaten.

"Then you'll send us all back!" Maines yelled. "You know that Stryker didn't lead anyone to Carreño! He used you to lead her to them! Everyone here but you knew that Carreño's a double, but you didn't want to believe it. But you were worried enough that we might be right that you decided not to go find out for yourself, so you fed Kyra to the lions instead. You're a coward, Sam. You've run this station into the ground, you've put everyone here at risk, and now the most junior officer we've got might be bleeding out in a safe house because you didn't have the stones to go out and man up to your own dumb mistakes. So we're done taking orders from you. You want us to follow you? Then get behind the wheel of the van and help us get Stryker home. Otherwise get out of the way."

"This is insubordination!" Rigdon yelled.

"I prefer the word 'mutiny,'" Maines told him. "Yeah, 'mutiny' works for me."

"You leave this room and I'll be on the phone with the director of national intelligence before you—"

Maines's fist drove itself deep into Rigdon's stomach, bending the station chief over and driving the air out of his lungs in a hard, gasping wheeze. The deputy pulled his fist back and pulled it upward, slamming into his superior's nose. Maines's knuckles made an audible crack as the bones fractured against Rigdon's skull. The station chief's head snapped up, the blood already flowing from both nostrils as he fell onto his back, the carpet doing little to cushion his hard landing.

"I'll dial the number for you," Maines told him, shaking his hand. "Feel free to tell him I did that, and let him know that if he tells me to stand down and abandon Stryker to the SEBIN, he'll be telling Congress why. And if you get in our way again before we bring Kyra out of the safe house, you'll end up in the infirmary before she does, you got me?"

Rigdon couldn't answer for the blood rolling down his face. "Anyone else on his side?" Maines asked.

"Screw 'im," someone from the back said. "We ought to trade him to Carreño for Kyra." Murmurs of assent and open curses erupted from the group.

"Thought not," Maines said. "Raguskus, call the infirmary and have some of the people standing by. Sounds like she's hurt. I don't know how bad, but she was unresponsive. Then get a trauma kit down to the van," Maines ordered. "Kain, you line us up some transportation out of the country. If she's seriously wounded, we won't be able to get her out on a commercial flight, so you'll have to get creative."

"I'll figure something out, boss," the woman said. She pushed her way past the two men behind her and ran for her desk.

"Good," Maines said. "Winegar, get a group together and start monitoring the local police bands and any of the SEBIN frequencies that NSA has cracked open. If they're getting anywhere near MANGO, I want to know about it . . . and we might need some help avoiding their people on the way in and back out again."

"Will do," a tall, older man replied. "Raguskus, Pitkin, you're with me." The group of four marched out of the room.

"Good . . . and if he"—Maines pointed at the bleeding senior officer on the floor—"if he tries to get up, someone feel free to drag him out to the street and out him to the first policeman you can find. They probably already know who he works for, just let 'em know that we don't want him anymore."

"Long as you don't care what shape he's in when they get him!" somebody called out.

"Doesn't matter to me. If we're getting charged with mutiny, let's make it a story they'll tell at the Farm for the next hundred years," Maines ordered. "We roll out of here in ten."

He was on foot now. The SEBIN cordon was enormous, at least twelve blocks square, which meant there were holes everywhere. The deputy station chief had worked his way inside easily enough, but Raguskus and Abrams were still probing for some way to get through in the van. The rain had picked up in the last hour, the drizzle turning into a drenching gush from the dark gray heavens and cutting visibility down to a half block in any direction.

The safe house was on the fourth floor of a high-rise apartment complex ahead. It was inside the SEBIN search radius from what Winegar had been able to discern from the radio calls, but Maines wondered if the Venezuelans were either patient or organized enough to search every domicile in the area. He doubted it. The real question was whether Kyra Stryker was in stable condition and could survive in place long enough for the security services to give up the search.

He looked at his watch. It had been an hour since

Kyra's emergency call. *This could all be moot*, Maines told himself.

A police car roared by him, siren screaming out, the tires spraying him with a heavy wall of water. He ignored the discomfort. Maines was soaked through already.

He turned north up the alleyway off the Avenida Urdaneta. The service entrance was ahead on his left, a few dozen feet. He pulled his spare key, unlocked the entry, and slipped inside. The rain resumed pounding on the metal door, like the angry fists of the locals trying to batter their way into the building.

Maines shook the water out of his hair, took a few steps ahead, and stopped, looking down. Spatters of blood made a dotted line across the dirty tile floor to the hallway. He cursed. The rain had erased whatever blood trail Kyra had left on her way to the building, but any idiot could follow the line inside.

He ran out into the hall, walking along the red trail himself, praying it didn't lead to the safe-house door. The lighting was dim, and the blood was hard to see on the grubby floor. That was cause for hope. He stepped around it, tracing the line to the stairs, then up and ending at the fourth floor. There was no question in his mind now.

Maines ran down the hallway, still looking down until the blood stopped in front of one of the apartments. The number matched the one in his memory and the station chief cursed again. He pulled his key, unlocked the door, and let himself inside.

"Stryker?" he called out. There was no answer. The lights were on and the red line led into the bedroom. Maines pushed the door open.

Stryker was on the bed, not moving. He ran over,

saw her eyes were closed. "Stryker!" he repeated. She didn't answer.

Her leather jacket was on the floor alongside one of her shirt sleeves, crumpled in a bloody red heap. A crude bandage was wrapped around her upper right arm. He checked the rest of her limp form for wounds and found none, then exhaled the deep breath he hadn't realized that he was holding. *Flesh wound*, he thought. She won't bleed out. He searched around, found the empty QuikClot package and morphine syringe in the bathroom. *Good girl*, he thought. Kyra had packed her own wound with the coagulant, then dosed herself to kill the pain. She'd probably ingested too much morphine, but she would survive that if it hadn't killed her by now. Her breathing was still regular, her pulse thready and fast, but not enough to scare him.

Could move her, he thought, *if Rags and Pitkin can get the van here.* The blood trail in the hall was still a problem . . . *or an opportunity*, he thought.

He dug through the trauma kit in the bathroom and extracted a ziplock bag and a pair of the latex gloves inside. He donned the gloves, then retrieved Stryker's blood-soaked sleeve from the floor and stuffed it into the plastic bag.

Maines ran back out into the hall, then down the stairs to the first floor. He pulled open the bag, pulled out the shirt, and began to squeeze the cloth gently onto the floor, extending the woman's blood trail away from the stairs. *Hate to do this to some poor sap, but better them than us*, he thought. He dripped the blood down the hallway another thirty feet, then curved the line to a random apartment door. The bloody sleeve went back into the bag along with the latex gloves. Maines stuffed the gory package into his coat pocket and sprinted back to the service entrance. A janitor's closet was nearby, locked, and he kicked the door in. A mop and bucket were sitting inside. He lifted the bucket into the utility sink, filled it a quarter up with water, and hauled it and the mop back to the stairs. It took him less than ten minutes to run the wet implement across the forty stairs to the fourth floor, erasing the bloody line that led to her door. Another thirty seconds cleaned up the tile leading to the safe house, and then he was inside again, the evidence of Kyra's run wiped away. The Venezuelans would still be able to find the trail on the stairwell using luminol and a UV light, but he prayed they wouldn't be so thorough once they found the second trail he'd created.

Maines touched his earpiece. "This is MALLET," he called out, the broadcast encrypted by the radio clipped onto his belt behind his waist. "I've located GRANITE, condition stable. Site MANGO is not secure, repeat, not secure. What's your status?"

"Still looking for a hole," Raguskus called back. "Bad guys are everywhere. We're parked five hundred meters from your position, engine cold, lights out at the moment."

"Hold your position," Maines ordered. "Will advise . . . wait." The sirens, which had been rising and fading since he'd dismounted from the van, had gotten close now. He moved to the window, split the blinds a hair, and looked down.

At least five cars, some unmarked, had stopped on the street. Men in tactical uniforms were spreading out along the sidewalk, some senior officer directing his subordinates down the side streets. "Hostiles at my position," he reported. "They'll be coming in the building."

"Any possibility of evac?" Pitkin asked.

"Negative," Maines replied. He looked back at Kyra. The woman was still unconscious on the bed. "I'd have to carry GRANITE out . . . no good cover for action on that one."

"Roger that," Pitkin answered.

Maines moved to the apartment door, leaned against it, listening for voices or footsteps. They were four stories up, and he doubted he would hear anything, but the stairwell was close.

Two minutes passed and he heard a yell, then other cries . . . heavy footsteps somewhere below, he couldn't tell how many, but he would've guessed a dozen men if he'd had to lay money on a number. Then yells again, cries of surprise, someone protesting in guttural Spanish. The SEBIN search team had found the blood trail and followed it to its obvious end. They'd found nothing, assumed the family living in whichever apartment Maines had set up had treated their wounded prey and helped her escape to some other site. They would spend a long night in an interrogation room. Maines truly hoped that the SEBIN would accept their story and let them go, but if not, it was not his problem.

"This is MALLET," he called out. "Hostiles have been diverted. Wait fifteen, then start her up and see if you can't find a hole. I think the cordon will start to break up."

"Roger that," Raguskus called back.

Maines parted the blinds again and watched the SEBIN lead a struggling couple out of the building into the street. The man and wife had no raincoats and they were soaked to the skin in seconds. Their hands were bound in front with zip ties. They protested their innocence and no one cared. The security team forced them into a waiting van, then boarded their own cars, and pulled out. The area was clear within ten minutes except for the onlookers and gawkers, still awed and amused by the spectacle.

"MALLET, this is PIGGYBACK, we have a hole," Pitkin called out. "Will be at the way point in two minutes."

"Roger that," Maines replied. He let the blinds fall closed, moved to the bed, and checked Kyra's pulse. The girl was still down, but her pulse was steadier now. He grabbed her leather jacket and lifted her in his arms, her head cradled against his shoulder.

He moved slowly, careful to avoid the doorframes, handrails, and walls as he maneuvered his unconscious charge through the apartment, the hallway, and down the stairs. Maines didn't bother to look around corners or down bends on the stairwell. If there were still SEBIN in his path, he would not be able to outrun them with Kyra in his arms. He encountered no one. The blood trail on the bottom floor was smeared now from the bootprints of a dozen soldiers who hadn't been interested in collecting evidence for a prosecution.

Maines reached the door to the service entrance and managed to open it. The rain outside hadn't slackened in the least. The van sat five feet beyond the door, engine idling. The double side door slid open and he lifted Kyra in, Raguskus reaching out to pull the unconscious woman inside. He didn't bother to close the building door behind him and Pitkin had the van in motion before Maines could slide the van door closed.

"What've we got?" Rags asked, opening the trauma kit.

"One gunshot wound to the right triceps. Looks

like she packed the wound, tied it off, and dosed herself with morphine without checking the syringe. Lost a significant amount of blood, but I don't know how much," Maines replied. Abrams nodded, checked Kyra's handiwork, and set to work fixing her shoddy bandage. "Any word on an exfil plan?"

"I talked to Kain five minutes ago. She's got a private cargo flight lined up out of Colombia. We'll have to drive her across the border, but I know a few back roads across that aren't patrolled by the locals. Chávez uses them to ship supplies to the FARC, so we'll have to watch out for guerrillas, but we can manage them. We'll meet up with one of our pilots at a small airstrip outside of Cúcuta. Flight runs to Panama, then to Florida, then to Dulles. It'll take her a couple of days to get home, and some of the puddle jumpers will be running pretty low to the ground and the Atlantic, so I hope she doesn't get airsick."

"From the looks of her, I don't think that's going to be a problem," Rags said. "It's a nasty wound, boss. She lost a chunk of muscle most of the way down to the bone. We'll have to keep her on morphine the whole way there. She'll need surgery when she gets back, and physical therapy after. I don't think she's going to remember much about the next few days. But she'll make it."

Maines nodded. "Good to hear. Question is what to do about that idiot back at the station."

"Nothing we can do," Pitkin replied, disgusted. "Director of national intelligence put him in there, nobody below him can pull Rigdon out. But I'd bet after this, none of us are going to be down here very long. Stryker just proved that our best asset is a double agent for Chávez. We're probably all burned now. We might as well not bother coming back once we cross the border."

"Roger that." Maines looked down at Kyra's face one last time, then leaned back against the van's metal bulkhead and closed his eyes, the tension starting to drain from his own body. *Seventh Floor idiots at Langley,* he raged to himself. *Not, not just there. At Liberty Crossing and the White House too. Making a* political donor *a station chief. They don't care about who they put in front of the guns. They just want to run their little wars and push their little armies around. We're all just cannon fodder . . . loyalty only running in one direction. Didn't used to be like that, and no way to fix it. No way at all.*

Maines opened his eyes and listened to the rain pounding on the thin metal walls of the van and the broken asphalt under the tires. "SEBIN knows all of us know, thanks to Rigdon. Might as well not bother coming back once we cross the border," he repeated, his voice quiet.

Fools. They're all a bunch of fools up there.

There were more borders in the world than the ones on the maps.

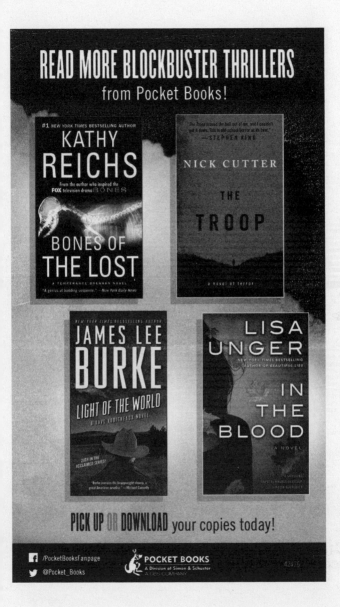